"I Should Have Been Here."

"You had business in town, Mr. Brandon," Jake Trexler said. "That judge's party. And you couldn't have done anything; you'd be dead now with the rest."

"I should have been here."

A stamping and jingling and the squeak of an ungreased axle marked the appearance of a high-sided farm cart at the edge of the irregular circle of light from the dwindling fire. Two men lifted one of the bundles on the ground and carried it gently to the cart. The cloth over the head slipped, and Brandon saw the blank face of his wife, Elise. The pine-knot torches and lanterns that lit the scene sent light shimmering over the face, lending it a seeming animation—a scowl of rage, a grimace of fear, a glint in the open eyes as if she were seeing him for the last time.

Brandon looked at the men holding the lanterns and torches, and a line from a wartime song came to him:

> *I have read His righteous sentence in the dim and flaring lamps . . .*

The sentence is death, Brandon thought. Not Elise's, not the others'. The Kenneallys. If there is any sense to anything, any justice, they have to die. Thank God the law will see to that. . . .

THE TRACKER #1

→ Mask of the Tracker ←

D.R. BENSEN

POCKET BOOKS
New York London Toronto Sydney Tokyo Singapore

This book is a work of fiction. Names, characters, places and incidents are either products of the author's imagination or are used fictitiously. Any resemblance to actual events or locales or persons, living or dead, is entirely coincidental.

An *Original* Publication of POCKET BOOKS

POCKET BOOKS, a division of Simon & Schuster Inc.
1230 Avenue of the Americas, New York, NY 10020

ISBN: 0-671-73834-8

First Pocket Books printing June 1992

10 9 8 7 6 5 4 3 2 1

Cover art by Bill Dodge

Printed in the U.S.A.

The law's the law," Cole Brandon said. "It's in the statutes and the court decisions, all there. Not the easiest thing to tickle out—that's why we're needed, and why we're paid—but you can always find out what it is if you go at it hard enough."

"The law's the will of society," Charley Todt said. He gestured around the richly paneled room, indicating the thirty or so men of varying age but consistently prosperous appearance who stood chatting. "And it's all of us—judges, lawyers, prosecutors—that see to it that that will's enforced. The law's what we do and what we say, and the statutes can go hang, Brandon. That's why it's a low thing to find some fiddling quibble of a precedent to get some thieving hound off and set him free to thieve again."

The room, the National Hotel's best small reception parlor, was thick enough with cigar smoke to suggest that there was a keg of leaf Havana smoldering in a corner. The fumes of sour mash whiskey and beer—this being St. Louis, with more Germans than many cities in Prussia—blended with it to produce an eye-watering fog. Brandon had come to Judge Wiede's retirement party purely as a professional obligation, but it hardly seemed worth it now, what with the stifling atmosphere and the conversation or discussion or argument with Charley Todt, inspired by drink to be as doggedly opinionated as he was in court.

"It was there, and no great shakes to find it out, Charley," Brandon said. "The point of law was clear, and there wasn't anything to do but dismiss." His client might well have been guilty, but sloppy arraignment and bad witnesses had blown the case apart. He visualized the peace he could be enjoying with Elise and her father and aunt out at Mound Farm, sitting on the porch and watching the crisp fall twilight. After deciding he needed a week off from running his mercantile empire, Berthold Ostermann had drafted his sister Gertrud and his daughter Elise Ostermann Brandon to accompany him to the family farm, situated a few hours out of town. Brandon would have been there this afternoon, having cleared the last of the week's work early, except for the Wiede party. Lunsford, Ahrens & Brandon could have gotten by with representation by Jim Lunsford and Jake Ahrens—surely two out of three partners showed enough respect.

"You're missing it, Brandon." Charley Todt poked Brandon's chest with a stubby finger, at the same time taking a gulp from the heavy tumbler he held, as if holding Brandon back from a sudden lunge as he drank. "Times like these, the depression, everybody's uneasy, still unsettled from the War, too. Men out of work, losing farms and homes, they're ready to make trouble. Society—the real society, the people who matter—they have to keep that trouble down. The law, you have to use it to keep order, make sure that crime's punished and seen to be punished. Keep society together, not find little ratholes to let the vermin loose."

Brandon saw that anything he might say to Charley Todt at this point about the sacred fabric of the law and the attorney's obligations as an officer of the court would sound like the pattest of law-school lectures, and would penetrate neither Charley's thick skull nor the protective bath of alcohol now insulating his wits from sense.

The lack of a reply did not affect Charley Todt's discourse. "You were in the Judge Advocate General's office during the War, Brandon, if I recollect. Useful, necessary, I don't deny that. But it ain't the same as being in the line. You enforce the law with the bayonet, enforce it with chain shot, you don't worry about precedents, Brandon. You get to see what matters. You punish criminals, you don't turn 'em loose."

Brandon had never been able to see that killing half a million soldiers and untallied civilians and filling the reservoirs of hate brim-full for a generation was a more suitable way of settling a political problem than the most complex, drawn-out, and quibbling legal processes imaginable. He supposed, though, that if he had spent four years shooting and being shot at he might have had a different viewpoint. He might even have turned into something like Charley Todt, which was reason enough to be grateful for having been spared that. Maybe Charley was trying on attitudes for a city or county prosecutor's job. Brandon thought he had heard that Nebel & Todt's practice was slipping a bit, fees still as high as ever, but fewer ready to pay them.

"Believe Walt wants me. Good talking to you, Charley," Brandon said. He evoked a social smile, nodded, and sidestepped out of Charley Todt's immediate range, then turned and walked toward Walt Ahrens. He was intercepted by one of the hotel's waiters serving the party. "Mr. Brandon, someone outside to see you."

Brandon nodded and made for the door, glad of the interruption. Maybe, once outside, he could just not bother to return, get on home to Walsh's Row, and get a good night's sleep before an early start for Mound Farm.

In the corridor, the gas lamps illuminated a tall man in a dark suit and plug hat. The man took off his hat and held it in front of him. "Mr. Brandon? Cole Brandon?"

"So I am. And?"

The man held his hat by its brim first in one hand, then the other. "I . . . Mr. Brandon, there is trouble at your wife's family place out west of town—there's—"

"At Mound Farm? What kind of trouble?"

"Bad trouble. Hard to say right now how bad. There's . . .

well, the plain fact is, your folks there, they're kind of hostages."

Brandon stared at the man—long-featured, nondescript hair cut short, hard-finish worsted brown suit and vest; he looked sane and sober enough—and knew with a sickening certainty that he was not spouting lunacies. "I've got to get out there," Brandon said.

The man nodded. "I'm on my way—I'm Jake Trexler, I'm a railroad detective—and I came here to tell you and bring you along if you wanted, which it seemed nineteen parts certain you would. There's a special train being made up at the station, with railroad police and some state militia, and we'll be on it. Should pull out in ten minutes or less, so we'll have to move to get over there. Tell you about it while we're on the way."

Brandon looked at the closed door of the reception parlor. It would be ludicrous to step back in and make his apologies for leaving Judge Wiede's party, and purely horrible to have to give his reasons. "Let's go."

"Tell it from the beginning," Brandon said. He and Trexler had the front of the head car to themselves; some city police officials and militia officers talked excitedly in the rear seats. Behind them, the passenger car and three boxcars held a mixed detachment of railroad police and state militiamen and over a dozen horses. The locomotive gave a belching blast of steam and the train shuddered as the driving wheels started the ordeal of their first turn. The points of light in the station drifted back slowly, then sped up. As Trexler talked, Brandon's gaze drifted to the window, where his reflection was superimposed on the night blackness outside, sometimes lit out of existence by the streetlamps and the warm squares of lit house windows.

"Hard to believe it," Trexler said, fishing his watch from his vest pocket and looking at it, "but the whole thing began not seven hours ago—just on noon, the way we hear it."

At seven minutes before noon that day, on the Chicago, Rock Island & Pacific line, in a wilderness stretch just a few miles north of St. Louis, an unusually large gang—ten to a dozen men—stopped a southbound train, killed the engineer and clerks in the express car, robbed the passengers, and blew open and emptied the express safe.

"Big haul in gold," Trexler said. "St. Louis banks needed it in case of a run." Brandon nodded. Since the collapse of Jay Cooke's banking empire a year before, the country had spiraled into a depression, and banks all over were at constant risk. It was onerous to keep large gold reserves on hand, but one failure to pay out on demand could start a reaction that would wipe out the whole city's banking system.

The gang would probably have melted into the tangled wooded hills and ravines of the region if two farmers had not run into them as they raced through a clearing. The shots the fleeing robbers snapped at the two missed but served to alert them that there was something serious going on—and one of the farmers had recognized the gangleader. "Gren Kenneally," Trexler said. "This fellow knew him from the War. Gren was in the guerrillas; rode with Quantrill some, on his own more. Don't know if the farmer was in the guerrillas himself or was one of them that got threatened or burned out by them; they didn't take telegraph time to send such details as that. But he recognized him all right and found the nerve to trail them whiles he sent his pal to the nearest town where they had some law and a telegraph office."

The messenger had aroused the town authorities to get on the trail of the robbers; word had just come through on the wire of the CRI&P robbery, and they came to the obvious—and correct—conclusion that there wouldn't be a major crime and Gren Kenneally in the same area without a direct connection between the two. A hastily gathered posse followed the farmer to the spot where he had left his friend, and it was able to follow his and the robbers' westering trails until they caught up with him and joined him in the chase.

They had what looked like the good luck to come out of a heavily wooded area to see the gang riding in a tight bunch across an open field with a stone farmhouse and outbuildings a little distance off.

Brandon could picture the scene vividly. He had stood looking at Mound Farm from the edge of the woods often enough, and he could see even now the twenty-foot-high hump of the Indian mound that gave the place its name, and the fortlike farmhouse that had been a French trading post eighty years before. The riders would be off to the right of the mound, darkly shadowed by the early afternoon sun in front of them, the tarnished gold of empty cornstalks, stirrup-high and ready to be cut and stacked in shocks.

"Seems they didn't stop to parley," Trexler said, "just opened up with whatever arms they had as soon's they saw them. Probably good policy with that kind, but they were too far off to do them any harm."

The gang, which had been idling along loosely strung out, unaware of pursuit, replied with a better-aimed fusillade, which drove the posse back in momentary confusion; then, in response to yelled commands that carried faintly to the posse, the outlaws formed into a curved line and rushed the farm buildings.

"I understand they were in the place and firing on the posse in about no time," Trexler said. The posse members had taken up positions around the front of the house but were reluctant to shoot until shot at, since the farm's residents were clearly inside, except for an unlucky hired man who lay ten feet outside the front door, evidently shot down just for being where he was when he was.

"That would be Tom Burke," Brandon said.

"Only one of your people known to be hurt so far," Trexler said. "Fact is, we don't know how many's there, or who they are. Can you—"

"Finish telling me what's happening—or what's happened—first," Brandon said.

"Standoff," Trexler said. "Posse on the outside, the Kenneally gang and whoever else on the inside. They yelled out to the gang to surrender, gang yelled back they wasn't about to, and they had hostages that'd be the first to die if there was a try at attacking the place. Posse people finally figured that it wasn't something they should be handling and sent someone back to town to wire St. Louis what was going on and asking what to do about it. And this"—he gestured back toward the conferring officials in the rear of the car and, presumably, the troops and horses behind them—"is what. Now, what people do you have out there?"

"My wife," Brandon said evenly.

"Oh, damn. Sorry to hear that."

"Her father." Trexler said nothing this time. He had the look of a man who was reserving comment until all the bad news was in.

"My wife's aunt, her father's sister. And the help. Tom Burke—no, he's not . . ." Brandon took a breath and continued. "There's the cook and housekeeper, and the boy who looks after the horses—only a kid, really . . ." With pretty poor chances of growing beyond being a kid, too, he thought.

"Seven in all," Trexler said.

"Six, there's—oh, the cook and housekeeper are the same woman; she does both jobs."

"Ah, *that's* where I went wrong," Trexler said, as if pleased to have something solved. He's not asking me their names, Brandon thought, and I'm not giving them. He doesn't want to see them as people with names and faces until this is all over. Until it is, he'd rather see them as the Wife, the In-Laws, the Cook-cum-Housekeeper, the Stable Boy. . . . So would I. I do *not* want to see Elise and Father Ostermann and Aunt Trudi and Annie Wysock and Billy Heggins in danger and scared and . . .

"Thing you want to keep in mind is," Trexler said, "these fellows are going to want to cut the best deal they can, trade your people for a getaway. If they . . . hurt them, then they lose that card. One thing about the Kenneallys, they do what they do for the profit of it mostly, not for the fun."

Brandon's mouth twitched in a brief facsimile of a smile. Trexler's words and tone were close to what he himself had often used to convince a client that the trial would work out better than it seemed at the moment. He hoped that there was more substance to what the railroad detective said than there usually was to his own attempts at encouragement.

What looked like a firelit ghost flickered by the window, a

man's head and shoulders and an indistinct shape around it—a lantern in a buggy lighting up the driver. Now there was unbroken darkness outside; they were away from towns and villages, going through the kind of wilderness that these—

"Kenneallys?" Brandon said. "You mentioned just this Gren Kenneally; did he have some kin with him in this?"

"Don't know," Trexler said. "But there's plenty of his kin in his trade, and it's the family's way of looking at things I was talking about."

Brandon had about as much interest in the history of the criminous Kenneally family as in the morning price of hogs in the Chicago market, but he was glad enough to listen to Trexler's exposition—it was some distraction from the dire speculations about what had happened—what could be happening now—at Mound Farm.

"First anybody heard of 'em was back in the '20s. Peter and Quint Kenneally, they were river pirates and thieves and what-have-you, part of the crowd at Natchez-under-the-Hill. Scattered with the rest of 'em when they got burned and shot out of there, kind of drifted down to the Ozarks, over in Arkansas, with their women and a kid or so. Set up in a strong place in the hills and settled into a steady line of work as reavers—like pirates still, but on land. Folks called 'em 'P and Q'—for Peter and Quint, you see—and when they said 'Mind your Ps and Qs' down that way, they were for sure serious about it. Banks, stages, stores, farms—they'd rob 'em and ride off to where they came from, and nobody felt much like following 'em in there."

In the late thirties, Quint Kenneally—Gren's father, Trexler noted—moved up across the Missouri line, first into secure quarters in the mountains, then down onto some farmland. "Maybe he was trying to turn respectable, hard to say," Trexler said, "but he got mixed up in the Mormon business in '38 and got a name for violence—most of the folks there were against the Mormons, too, but Quint went too far for them." Brandon had no recollection of the Mormon expulsion, which had happened a few years before he was born, but he knew that it had been an ugly moment in Missouri's history.

"Had his hand in lots of things after that, even got elected sheriff of his county once, some storekeeping, some freighting. Along with it, everyone knew he was into underhanded stuff—robberies, swindles, and what—but he was good at getting connections with important men in the county and around, and everybody saw pretty quick that he couldn't be touched in the ordinary way, so it was best to knuckle under and do business with him as best you could. His boy Gren got to be something of the same sort of fellow, only wilder than the old man."

When the War came, Missouri was divided in allegiance, and nowhere more bitterly than in the countryside. St. Louis's cosmopolitan and mercantile outlook aligned the city—and the state government—with the Union, but the largely southern-derived rural reaches had important elements of Confederate sympathy, inflamed by the years of strife with the militant Free Soilers of Kansas, some of whom regarded slave-state Missourians as subhuman and fair game for justified murder. Guerrilla bands formed almost at the outset of the war and began harassing Federal troops and terrorizing possibly Unionist farmers with equal enthusiasm—the farmers, being more lightly armed and in smaller groups, got more attention.

"Nobody knew where Quint Kenneally stood," Trexler said. "Seems to have seen how the wind was trending, sold up what he had that was worth anything, and was gone away before First Bull Run, down again into the Ozarks. Gren, though, he went with the guerrillas, rode some with Quantrill, like I said before—was one of those in the Lawrence massacre over in Kansas—then went off on his own. Some folks said he was a hero, some that he was a plain monster—any road, there was a lot of killing and burning done, but that's nothing special for the time. There's men that's merchants and judges now that did things eight years ago that any jury away from here'd have them hanging for, but what the folks figure is, you can't mend what's past, and what's done in war can best die with the war so everyone can get on with the farming and the trading."

But Gren Kenneally, like a lot of Missouri guerrillas, wasn't able to let the passions of wartime—or at least the opportunity it presented for excitement, savagery, and plunder—die. Like the James brothers, only on a smaller scale, he had refused amnesty and turned to outlawry.

"Holes up in some deep holler in the hills, comes out when he feels the need for some cash or some fun. Law people—I don't mean lawyers like you, Mr. Brandon, but the police, the railroad detectives, the Pinkertons, and so on—know he keeps in touch with the main family, sometimes goes down to work with them on their jobs. I don't know that much about him, for he hasn't been my business, kept away from the railroads. Until now. Now he is my business."

And mine—no, Elise's and the others', Brandon thought. He'll be mine, one way or another, after we get to Mound Farm.

"Over the next rise, I think," Brandon said. "Hard to be sure in the dark." "Dark" was not a totally accurate term; the troopers riding ahead of Brandon, Trexler, and the commanders of the mixed force carried lanterns that lit the road ahead enough to allow the horses to move briskly along; the tiny island of light emphasized the overarching blackness of the moonless night, strengthening it by competing with and dimming all but the brightest stars.

Brandon shifted uneasily in the saddle, trying to find a more comfortable seat. This was no time to be worrying about a sore backside, but for a man unused to riding, the five miles from the railroad, taken at a brisk, jarring pace, had been progressively more uncomfortable. Elise rides—one reason she likes being at Mound Farm. If I rode, maybe I'd have been—maybe I'd be with her more. Maybe I'll make some time to ride with her. . . .

He noticed that he could see the advance guard of troopers more clearly than the light from their lanterns allowed—it was as if they were riding into a faint dawn ahead—but the brightening sky was to the west, and the sun was on the other side of the earth.

When they topped the low crest, Brandon saw the low hulk of the ancient mound, deep shadow on one side, glowing like a huge dying ember on the other; glints of red danced across the field of emptied cornhusks—reflections of the flames that whirled above the roof of the stone house and wrapped the stable behind it.

Without any gesture or word of command, the whole body of riders spurred their horses down the slope toward the burning buildings and the knots of men that scurried around them. Brandon's soreness was forgotten as he urged his horse out ahead of the rest. As he neared the farmhouse, the heat of its flames washed over him.

"Oh, God, Mr. Brandon!" Brandon recognized the man who cried out as a storekeeper from the next town, presumably one of the posse slapped together to chase the train robbers, chase them right to this place of fire and—he smelled it now—the stench of blood and death. The outcry and the broken note in the man's voice told the story. Brandon felt as if he had been turned to stone and clamped to the saddle; then Trexler slid to the ground and reached up to help him down. Brandon came awkwardly to life again and made his legs and body fold and unfold in the right sequence to get him down to earth, as if it were something he had never experienced.

The flames were dying now, and steam rose as men poured buckets of water passed hand to hand from the yard pump onto the smoldering house. Brandon stood watching, not aware of feeling anything or of thinking anything: a man watching a burning house, like someone in a steel engraving in the illustrated papers—very detailed but not real, neither the house nor the man.

"Mr. Brandon." He came back to himself and was flooded with the fear and horror that being himself meant now. Trexler was standing in front of him, his face shimmering in the glow of the fire. "It's . . . bad. It's . . . all of them."

Brandon nodded. "About an hour ago," Trexler said. "Must've been when we weren't far from where the train stopped; it looked as though things'd settled down for the night. Posse figured the gang might try to get away under cover of darkness, but the way it was, that wasn't the worst that could happen."

"No," Brandon said, looking at the house. The roof was gone now, and flickering light came through the glassless windows in the thick stone wall. Half a dozen men were bent over some cloth-wrapped bundles he could see indistinctly on the ground well away from the house.

"Then they opened fire, the gang, that is, on where they figured the posse was, lots of 'em shooting rapid fire. Hit a few horses, probably mostly by accident, but it kept the men from moving in on the house. There was some yelling and screaming from inside, but nobody could tell who or what it was about, and some of it was Rebel yells, like the gang had gone fighting crazy. Then there was an almighty puff of fire, looked like something'd set a store of coal oil off—"

"They kept it for the lamps," Brandon said. "My wife always made sure there was enough; didn't want the lamps to run out."

Trexler nodded. "Anyhow, both the house and stables was burning right away, and the posse rushed the house. But there was more firing, right out of the burning house, and this time some of them was hit, since they was out in the light where they could be seen. And that must've been when the gang rode off, out toward the back—there was the noise from the fire, and the horses screaming in the stables, and shooting still going on. Nobody knows when they went, and when they realized the gang was gone, they saw they had to do what they could to save the house and maybe the people, so they did that instead of following." He paused for a moment and looked tired and old. "But . . ." He gestured toward the still bundles on the ground.

"Were they . . ." Brandon gestured toward the dying fire of the house.

"No. Shot. Don't know yet if 'twas by the gang or whether they got caught in fire from the posse, or both. They tell me there wasn't . . . they didn't hear . . . what I mean, it don't seem like they suffered long," Trexler said.

"I should have been here," Brandon said.

"You had business in town," Trexler said. "That judge's party. And you couldn't have done anything; you'd be dead now with the rest."

"I should have been here."

A stamping and jingling and the squeak of an ungreased axle marked the appearance of a high-sided farm cart at the edge of the irregular circle of light from the dwindling fire. As if it were a regular, practiced thing with them, the men near the long bundles on the ground stepped away into two lines facing each other, making an avenue to the cart. Brandon and Trexler stepped into the line nearest them.

Two men lifted one of the bundles and carried it gently to the cart. The cloth over the head slipped, and Brandon saw the blank face of his wife, Elise. The pine-knot torches and lanterns that lit the scene sent light shimmering over the face, lending it a seeming animation—a scowl of rage, a grimace of fear, glint in the open eyes as if she were seeing him for a last time.

Her body was lifted onto the cart bed, and the next member of the procession of the dead was borne toward it; Brandon could not identify this one and was glad. He looked at the men holding the lanterns and torches, and a line from a wartime song came to him:

I have read His righteous sentence in the dim and flaring lamps . . .

The sentence is death, Brandon thought. Not Elise's, not the others'. The Kenneallys. If there is any sense to anything, any justice, they have to die. Thank God for the law that will see to that.

2

You want justice," Warner said. "You want to be sure that the savages who slaughtered your family pay for it with their lives, don't you?"

"Yes," Brandon said.

The detective leaned forward and slapped his hand firmly on his desk. "And you had better get it clear right now that there isn't any way you can have that."

Brandon looked at him blankly, waiting to find out what he meant.

"Justice is all of them dead and howling in hell," Warner said. "Only way you could have that is finding some bounty hunters who'd track them down, kill them and bring you their ears as proof. And the only place you'll find those bounty hunters is in the dime novels. The Nationwide Detective Agency can't give its clients justice. We'd best be clear on that."

Brandon looked past the detective and out the windows of the second-floor office. The low warehouses across the street hid most of the river from sight, but he could see the wooded bluffs of the southern Illinois shore. Above it the featureless sky was a wash of bright gray, like a dust-filmed window lit from behind. The pale light filled the high-ceilinged room of the detective's office, picking out details with clarity but leaching the life and color out of everything. It was as though he were looking at—were part of—a fading photograph.

"Oh," he said after a moment, realizing that some response was expected of him. "Well, yes. I can see that."

"Now," Warner went on, "with that out of the way, we can discuss what Nationwide *can* do for you. We can't get you justice, we can't get you vengeance. But we can make a damned good try at tracking the men who were involved, putting them into the hands of the police, and securing enough evidence to have them tried and convicted. Are you clear that's what you want?"

"Of course," Brandon said; once again, he was aware of having waited longer than was necessary before his reply. He was still stunned from the horrors of the night before last, but he was also suddenly less certain of what he wanted. "I'm . . . the law, it's my work, I have to live by it. What happened out at Mound Farm, that's what happens when there's no law. . . ."

"I'm glad you see that," Warner said. "Most men with your kind of grievance, they just want to see somebody killed for it, and not too worried about if it's done right or even if it's the right man. So—"

"You have to trust the law," Brandon said. "Otherwise there's nothing."

"That's right, Mr. Brandon. So anything this agency can do for you, it's toward helping the police and the legal process—that's understood, is it?"

"Understood," Brandon said. The pale light from the window gave Warner's smooth-shaven face the hard, dull finish of a skull. Brandon remembered his own face from the shaving mirror that morning and supposed he looked even worse. The light had been dim there, and he hadn't been able to see his eyes, just two shadowed sockets under the forehead.

"I'm not offering you any guarantees," Warner said, "not on results, anyhow. But Nationwide has a network of informants all over western Missouri, Kansas, Arkansas, and Texas—not regular operatives but people we can pass the word to, people who have connections on the far side of the law and a way of hearing things. That's where we have the edge on the Pinkertons: They're first-rate professional detective agents, but they rely just about completely on their staff, and they don't want to get their hands dirty panning for information in muddy waters."

Warner paused and looked appraisingly at Brandon. "Our way of doing things is the best for this kind of job, no doubt about it. But it's also more expensive than the Pinkertons' methods. When we want information, we have to be prepared to pay for it, and to pay the people something to be where they're going to pick that information up. And when there's people like the Kenneallys in it, that have influence where you mightn't think and that're dangerous as a bachelor rattler, our people are going to need some extra encouragement. So . . ."

Brandon gave an impatient chop of his hand in the air. "Don't worry. There's plenty of money for that. Plenty." A partner's share in the growing income of Lunsford, Ahrens & Brandon, Attorneys-at-Law, and Elise's one-fifth share, inherited from her mother, of the Ostermann enterprises. (Whether she had inherited anything from her father was questionable, since who had died first could not be determined; Brandon had decided to waive any claim and let Berthold Ostermann's assets remain with his blood family.) Yes, one way or another, there would be enough money to track down his family's murderers. Of course, if they hadn't been killed, he wouldn't have had enough money to hunt the men who wouldn't have killed them. . . . Bizarrely, he was also the owner of the place where they had died; Elise had loved the place, and her father had deeded it to her on their marriage. Something would have to be done about that some day.

Brandon's and the detective's hands performed their intricate ballet of passing papers, dipping pens, and scratching figures and signatures onto agreement forms, blotting wet ink, fingering greenbacks from a billfold, fanning them to count. . . .

"Now, I'll be on the wire about this right away," Warner said. "Have my own key in the back room here and a connection to the Western Union wire. The first word'll be a thousand miles from here before you're a block away. So we'll be started—but, as I said, I can't guarantee results, and whatever they are, they'll likely take quite some time."

Brandon studied the man facing him with detached interest. Middling, that seemed to be the word for him. Middling height, middling build—you wouldn't say a tall man or short, thin man or stout; middling. Dark hair cut on the short side, clean-shaven, face a touch dark, light-brown eyes. Strong nose, prominent cheekbones, thin lips, grimly compressed, gave the appearance of individuality, yet it seemed to him that the face would be a hard one to recognize or remember. It seemed to have no definite nationality—you could say "That fellow's French" or Polish or Dutch or even Turkish, and nobody would say "You're a liar."

Brandon had known the face all his life, but he was hard put to see what was familiar about it now; it would have been difficult to swear on the stand that he knew this man.

A plump, short figure moved behind the man—recognizable, even unmistakable, to a generation of St. Louisians as Breitmann the tailor—and slid a cylinder of black cloth onto the left arm.

Brandon felt it slip smoothly into place as Breitmann tucked and pinned the sleeve, his motions aped by his mirrored image. "The finest goods, Mr. Brandon," Breitmann said. "Last you for a—" He stopped abruptly. Long wearing was not necessarily an important quality in a suit of this sort. "Don't worry, Mr. Brandon, it'll be ready in time for the funeral."

Only a quarter-century since it opened, and it's filling up, Brandon thought. Why not? Good location, great view, easy enough to get in: Just die.

From the green expanse of Bellefontaine Cemetery, already well punctuated with gravestones and monuments, he could see the sweep of the river and the bluffs on the far side and, downstream toward the heart of the city, the vast arches of the new mile-long bridge. Contrary to the usage of popular novelists, the skies were not weeping for the three now receiving their final formal prayers from the minister at the triple gravesite; the sky was a hard, bright electric blue. Trees on the Illinois shore flamed with the first touches of autumn, and though the air was cool and crisp, the sun bit through the black wool of Breitmann's hurried but meticulous fashioning.

It was a day for beginnings, not endings. From the prayers, the minister seemed to think so, too, but Brandon had little inclination to assume that Elise was now enjoying celestial concerts or would at the Last Day be reconstituted as she had been four days before. Whatever there was of her now was the kernel of memory left in Brandon's brain.

And in Krista's, of course. He looked across to where Elise's sister stood with a clutch of Ostermanns he had never gotten clearly sorted out in his mind during the three years of his marriage to Elise. Cousins and such, an August—pronounced *Ow-gooste* if you wanted to avoid an indignant correction—a Hans, a Berthe, and so on—or *und so weiter.* With no sons, Berthold Ostermann had brought up Krista to the business, and now, with shocking suddenness, it would be hers to run.

Shutting out the minister's words, he studied Krista's face. A year younger than Elise, she had something of her sister's features, though mixed with a kind of dark strength that contrasted with Elise's blond fragility. He wondered if the Elise she remembered was the same person he had known and loved.

Brandon had been profoundly dreading the moment of his last act of participation in the ceremony; but holding the clod of turf, dropping it onto the casket lid, and hearing the hollow thud, like a summoning knock, seemed to happen to someone else, someone he was observing dispassionately from a distance.

"Cole." He was aware that it was some moments later, and that he was some distance from the graves, and that he had no idea how he had gotten there; Krista was walking beside him. "I hope it's all right, that Elise is with Father and Aunt Trudi, not . . ."

"Brandons don't go for family plots," he said. "My parents are up in St. Joseph, where I grew up. Elise was an Ostermann twenty-five years before she was a Brandon, so she belongs here."

"There's . . . when you . . . I mean, there's space next to Elise for . . ."

"I thank you," Brandon said. Nice to have my resting place settled—but I won't be resting for a while yet. There is some business to see to.

Warner's estimate of "quite some time" turned out to be unduly pessimistic. Two days later Trexler appeared at Brandon's brick townhouse in Walsh's Row in midmorning and was shown to his study.

"Mr. Brandon, great news! They've got one!"

"The—"

"Yes, one of the Kenneally gang—not Gren Kenneally himself but one of them that rode with him and did the . . . was at Mound Farm. All tied up proper and on his way to St. Louis in a boxcar with the barrel of a shotgun in his mouth in case he feels like trying to escape."

Brandon felt a jolt of warmth like the impact of high-proof bourbon at the image of the killer helpless in the grip of his enemies, under threat of instant death, at the thought that if he survived, it would only be for a humiliating trial, a brief, terror-filled confinement, and forced participation in the elaborate ritual of execution. The picture and the thought were more vivid and real than the drift of papers on his desk, though it was sorting out those papers and determining where they would go and what would be written on them that would assure Nationwide's payment for the outlaw's capture. If, of course, the agency were responsible.

"Was it the Nationwide that—"

"Right," Trexler said. "They came through smarter than I'd hoped for—I can claim I did you a good turn, steering you to Warner, and I'm glad it seems to be working right. One of their people out in Pike County knew some of the fellows that'd been riding with Gren Kenneally this last while and kept his eyes out for such as soon as he had the word on the wire from Warner. And by George, didn't one of those he knew come riding through a day or so later! The Nationwide man didn't let on he knew he was wanted—in fact, didn't know that he was, just that one time he'd been in with Gren—so talked to him friendly-like over a drink or so for a time."

Listening, Brandon poured himself two fingers of bourbon from the crystal decanter that stood like a lighthouse in the sea of papers on the desk. "And he told him about the train robbery and the . . ."

"Not in so many words," Trexler said, shaking his head at Brandon's "have-one?" gesture with the decanter. "But he was moving careful-like upriver, aiming to cut over west, where he said he had some business to settle over some work he'd done. Was plainly anxious not to be seen or knowed, and even though he figured the Nationwide man for one of his own kind, looked like he was thinking of making sure he wouldn't be able to discuss his whereabouts with anybody. Didn't try it, which was maybe a mistake, though the Nationwide man was ready for a play like that and might have finished it off there and then."

"But we wouldn't have known if he was one of the robbers or not," Brandon said.

"And the Nationwide wouldn't have got the capture bonus you agreed to," Trexler said. "Their man in Pike knew very well that the Nationwide don't pay for winning a gunfight. He figured there was enough probability to hold this fellow—name of Casmire, as it happens—and also knew that the constable in his town was at least medium honest and no special friend to the Kenneallys, so he tipped him off and talked reward some, and next thing, the fellow was arrested and on his way here. Warner let the railroad know about it, as they have an interest"—for the first time since Trexler had told him of the robbery, Brandon remembered the two postal clerks and the engineer who had been the robbers' first victims—"and they told me, and I came on here to tell you about it first thing. You've got a right to first word, God knows."

"Thanks. What now?"

"The farmer who tracked the gang had the best view of them, and he's on his way here. If he identifies the man, then there'll be a fast indictment and trial—I don't see any way that he's not going to swing."

"So that'll be one of them taken," Brandon said slowly. "The first."

Trexler fished his watch out of its pocket and looked at it. "That farmer should be at the jail about now, telling if they've got the right man. Want to come down and have a look at him?"

Brandon shook his head. "I don't want to know him. Time enough to look at him at the trial."

"Not much to it," Warner said. "The one witness is all the prosecution has, but he'll be enough."

Brandon, on the spectators' bench next to the detective, grimaced in agreement. Trexler, on Brandon's other side, asked, "Who's defending Casmire?"

"Name's Todt," Warner said.

"Charley Todt, of Nebel & Todt?" Brandon asked. Warner nodded. "Court must have appointed him counsel," Brandon said. "Don't see that this fellow could afford their fees—he'd have had to be carrying a lot of cash on him, and I doubt he was. Interesting to see what Charley'll do when there's no money in it; not much, I'd think. Must have let his guard down to let himself be lumbered with something like this." Remembering their conversation at Judge Wiede's retirement party, Brandon doubted that Charley Todt would do much more than go through the motions on behalf of his client; with a criminal-loathing lawyer to defend him, Casmire hardly needed a prosecutor. It looked as though he wouldn't be getting much of a fair trial, but Brandon found himself not at all displeased at the prospect.

The men on either side of Brandon darted quick, interested glances at him, and Brandon realized that this was probably the first time since the night of death at Mound Farm that he had volunteered a comment that had almost the quality of normal conversation. Perhaps it was the comfortable familiarity of being in a courtroom once again, even under these circumstances, and identifying himself more as a member of the bar than as an interested party—a bloodless, abstract term to describe the haunted survivor of a murderous horror, but suitable to the surroundings.

Brandon settled back on the bench to observe the trial. "Enjoy" wouldn't be the right word, he told himself, but there was some satisfaction in being back in a world he knew.

An hour later that world seemed to have exploded like an overstressed boiler on a riverboat, leaving things distorted, shattered, and fogged with confusion. He watched as Charley Todt's suave cross-examination of Jonathan Gans, the farmer who had encountered and shadowed the fleeing robbers, turned harsh.

"You recognized Mr. Casmire in this group of men?"

"I did."

"At what distance?"

"Ah . . . mebbe four rods."

"Fifty feet or more. As far as out through that window and into the street. And it was early afternoon? Bright sun, high in the sky?"

"It was."

"And the men you saw were wearing hats?"

"They was."

"So their faces were largely or completely obfuscated?"

Gans looked blankly at Todt. "How?"

Todt sighed impatiently. "The word means 'shadowed'—do you understand that?"

"Ah, yes, I guess."

"So this shadowed face you saw at this distance—you say you recognized it as that of a man you had met nine years before—in the brief interval before he and the men he was with fired on you and your companion, that you knew him as a member of a guerrilla organization, that you had known him so well that without a scintilla of a doubt you knew him again in the instant of a fortuitous encounter?"

Gans paused before answering. It was clear to Brandon that the farmer was trying to work his way through "scintilla" and "fortuitous," but the effect was of uncertain recollection. It was also clear that Charley Todt was doing a better job than an unpaid assignment as counsel called for.

"'Course I knew him," Gans said. "Was with them that burned my farm in '64. Him and Gren Kenneally both, and some of the others that was in that bunch I run into last month."

The prosecutor stirred uneasily, but didn't seem able to find a reason to object to the line of questioning—though he knew as well as Brandon that bringing in the still-sharp matter of wartime guerrilla action would be likely to divide any jury: half willing to hang any ex-guerrilla on general principles, the other half anxious to turn him loose on other but equally general principles.

"Did you know him as James Casmire?"

"Never had a name for him; just a face."

Todt snapped the next question without allowing an instant of silence: "Did the man you remember have a beard in 1864? Did he?" he added as Gans paused to think, filling the void with jabs like a pugilist hammering a retreating opponent: "Bearded? Clean-shaven? One or the other—you'll surely remember, Mr. Grant—"

"That's Gans," the farmer said, seemingly glad to have found something he could be firm about.

"Good that you remember your own name, sir; you don't seem to be clear on much else."

"Objection!" the prosecutor called. *Finally,* Brandon fumed inwardly.

"Sustained," the judge said. "Mr. Todt, you have some latitude on cross-examination, sure enough, but try to keep it somewhere in the temperate zone." The mild tone and lawyerly pun told Brandon that the judge wasn't too displeased at Todt's carving-knife approach.

"You couldn't forget those piercing blue eyes, eh?" Todt said.

"Ah . . ." Gans looked at the defendant, who had just bowed his head to stare at the table in front of him, concealing his eyes.

"Were they blue, sir? Brown? Pink? Were they the same color ten years ago as they are now?"

"Well of course they was!"

"And what color was that?"

"I . . ." Gans squirmed in distress. "You don't reckernize a man by the color of his eyes, that ain't—"

"By what, then? Hair color? What is the defendant's—no, sir, don't look at him, look at me and tell me! Height? How tall is he? What about the scar on his face—what side is it on?"

Charley Todt at his best had a mesmerizing force to his delivery, but in Brandon's experience, Charley Todt reserved his best for high-paying clients. Something was going very wrong here. Gans was gaping at his cross-examiner like a pole-axed ox; and the prosecutor, seeing what was being done to his only witness, was rapidly taking on a similar expression.

"Is there a scar at all? Can you tell me, sir? Ah . . ." Todt stepped back, and the force and fire seemed to drain out of him. "That's really not fair now, is it, Mr. Gans? Throwing all those questions at you, fast like that, not giving you time to think. Why don't I leave it to you—that's the reasonable thing. Just you look here at me, not over at the defendant, and describe him for me. What he looks like, never mind whether you're talking about ten years ago or now, that doesn't matter, just . . . a description. So we could look at that man and say, yes, that's him, that's the one Jonathan Gans told us about, I'd know him anywhere."

Gans looked at Todt helplessly. "I ain't . . . I don't know how to . . ." He seemed to stiffen himself to wait for Todt's slashing attack.

"Can't describe him," Todt said sadly. "Eyes, scars, beard or not . . . no one thing to mark him as the man you think you saw . . . at fifty, sixty feet for an instant, with bullets flying past you and the shadow of his hat brim like a black mask. And, by God, you had the sand to follow him and the rest, Mr. Gans! I'll tell you, I wouldn't have had the nerve, and not many here would, either. But following him, Mr. Gans, that's one thing, and seeing him sharp and clear, that's another."

Brandon, feeling a growing dread at what was happening, could not suppress a trickle of admiration for Todt's tricky handling of the witness. Almost any lawyer—he himself, probably, included—would by now be making points with the judge and jury about the unreliability of the witness's identification: "Are you asking the jury to believe" and so on. But Charley Todt was taking the riskier route, staying with the witness all the way. Somebody was getting his money's worth—and it still didn't seem in the cards that Casmire had that kind of money.

"You saw a man," Todt said, so softly that Gans had to lean forward to hear him. "You saw a man riding with another man you knew, and it seemed to you that the first man was a man you had seen once years ago. Now you say that this man is that man, though you can't say what makes you see him as that. Well, well, that's what you say, Mr. Gans, and it's not for me to say that you lie."

Todt looked at the defendant. "I am that man's lawyer, and I am bound to defend him, but I have to say that he isn't much. He wouldn't have been arrested if he hadn't been known as a crook of some kind—maybe not the kind you say you think he is, but a crook all the same. So probably, no matter if you do stick to your story, it won't be any huge injustice—likely he deserves punishment, so it doesn't much matter how he comes by it."

Todt smiled at the witness. "So . . . I've done about all I'm going to, Mr. Gans. Up to you now. You're under oath, so all you have to do is swear, on your soul and on your sacred honor, that this is the man you saw riding with those fiends, that this is the man who burned you out ten long years ago. . . . Swear then, Mr. Gans, that you're so certain that the fires of eternity and the terrible punishments for perjury have no terrors for you. Mr. Gans, we await you. Swear."

Gans's mouth worked as if it had dried out completely.

After a minute, he said, "I . . . thought—it seemed so like . . ."

"Thought," Todt said softly. "Seemed. Mr. Gans, if you are rock-certain, bone-certain, then you must swear, even if it is hard. And if you are not rock-certain, bone-certain . . . why then, you can't swear, and there's an end to it. Swear, Mr. Gans, if you can."

The courtroom was silent. "Mr. Gans," the judge said after a moment, "will you confirm your identification of the defendant?"

Gans shook his head.

"No further questions," Todt said.

The prosecution's redirect examination did nothing to restore the witness's confidence nor, apparently, the jury's belief in the worth of his identification of Casmire as a member of the train-robbery gang.

Brandon found himself almost doubting it as well—but the defense's production of a couple of merchants from Bonne Terre, well over fifty miles from the locale of the robbery, who had been doing some business with Casmire at the time of the robbery, resolved the doubts. He knew the breed, the smooth men with a veneer of respectability, who had criminal connections and obligations and, when the time was right, could be produced to provide an unassailable alibi. They were pretty much single-shot weapons—rarely usable more than once, and certainly not at all frequently—so deploying a brace of them here was a signal that somebody with some heft had taken an interest in saving Casmire's neck.

The course of the remainder of the trial was as chaotic and futile as the scampering of a beheaded chicken—there was still some activity, but the thing was dead. Gans, recalled for more questioning after the merchants' smoothly presented testimony—rehearsed enough to smooth out the marks of rehearsal, Brandon was sure—was totally demoralized and was unwilling to be sure about anything. That Casmire "could've been" the man he saw with Gren Kenneally was as far as he would go.

The only question was whether Charley Todt would want

to run the case through the jury for a virtually certain acquittal, which would give him the exercise of an all-stops-out closing argument that would probably be the talk of the St. Louis bar for some time; or would he ask the judge for a directed verdict, which would wrap everything up fast.

"Your Honor," Todt said, "now that this good man"—he made a graceful gesture toward Gans, who sat stupefied in the front row of benches—"has realized that he cannot identify the accused as the man he saw—not even probably, let alone certainly—and unimpeachable witnesses have testified that he could not have been anywhere near the location of these unspeakable crimes, I submit that there is no case to answer, and request that the court direct a verdict of not guilty."

The prosecutor, with the scowl of a man sucking on a lemon but unwilling to spit it out, signified with a bitter mumble that the state had no objection. The judge, as aware as Brandon that what was going on had only a tangential relationship to justice, and also that the legal process left him no choice, spoke the words that discharged Casmire from custody.

"Shit," Trexler said.

"Took a peck or so of greenbacks to pay for all that—lawyer and witnesses, I'd say," Warner said.

"Charley Todt gets top dollar." Demons, phantoms, and monsters howled and writhed and sobbed behind Brandon's eyes; the blood-smeared faces of his dead sneered at him; but he spoke evenly. He rose and walked with his two companions out of the courtroom and into the rotunda gallery under the vast dome of the courthouse. The massive painted figures in the murals looked like groups of insane people doing insane things, and that was fitting enough, considering what had just happened.

"Worth it, this time, anyhow." Warner's voice echoed in the domed space. "He's the right man, you know. Gans didn't make any mistake; I talked to him and I know. Just that that damn lawyer took him apart stitch by stitch till all the stuffing came out."

"That's what we do," Brandon said. He looked back and

saw Todt accepting the congratulations of a couple of colleagues near the entrance to the courtroom. He moved away from Trexler and Warner and walked toward Charley Todt. Casmire was standing off to one side, with the two merchants who had provided his alibi. He glanced toward Brandon, who realized that he had no notion whatever of who the man was approaching his lawyer, or what he had done to that man.

"Charley." Todt stiffened, then turned to look at him.

"My sympathies, Brandon. Couldn't have been easy for you, with your . . . involvement, and I'm sorry to have had to seem to act against what you would want. But there was no case, d'you see, so the man had to go free. You and I, we know that—the rule of law, that's what we live by, isn't it?"

"You did a fine job, Charley," Brandon said. "Smoothest I remember to have seen. Have to congratulate you."

Todt looked at him dubiously, clearly uncertain if the congratulation was meant to be accepted.

"You gave it your best," Brandon said heartily.

"Well, thank—"

"And that doesn't come cheap, Charley. Who paid for it? For them, too?" Brandon jerked his head toward the witnesses, now alone as Casmire drifted toward Todt. Waiting to be told what to do next, I expect, Brandon thought.

Todt chose to misunderstand the slur on the merchants' integrity and veracity. "The gentlemen paid their own train fares here, Brandon. As for the matter of my emolument, the amount and the principal client are confidential matters, and I'll trust you know better than to try to pursue that line further."

The gibbering rabble of the unavenged dead surged in his head, yet he saw himself, as if viewed from somewhere near the ceiling, talking and gesturing to Charley Todt like a marionette moved by manipulation, not a self-powered human. But now the strings seemed to fray and snap, and the puppet jerkily moved into its own mad motion.

"A damn *secret,* is it?" Brandon said thickly. "You will by God tell me who paid you to free a murderer, you crooks' whore! I'll have it out of you no matter if it's hid in your gut—rip it out of your bowels if I have to!" His voice rose to a howl as he reached for Todt's throat.

Out of control as he was, Brandon was still partly viewing the whole scene from that curious distance, noting now that Casmire, alarmed, was moving toward his assailed lawyer; an armed bailiff was moving in on him even more swiftly, raising a hand to pull him away from Todt.

Smoothly as a ballet dancer making an intricate step seem effortless, Brandon dropped one hand from Todt's throat, snaked the revolver from the bailiff's holster, thrust it over Todt's shoulder to point at the startled Casmire, and pulled the trigger rapidly three times.

To Brandon's heightened senses, the noise of each shot was as loud and reverberating as the report of a cannon and seemed to take long enough so that he could see the horror and shock send ripples over Todt's face as each explosion slammed his eardrum and fouled the air with the reek and fog of gunsmoke.

Through the haze, he saw Casmire's face, shocked eyes, and gaping mouth making three *O*s, and beyond, a shattered window and a starred hole in the wall paneling. *Missed every goddamn shot, fool!* Then hands wrenched at him, tearing the weapon from his grasp; something hard hit him on the head, and darkness swooped in on him; his vision contracted into a quickly shrinking bubble, with Casmire's astonished face at its center, until it shrank to nothing and winked out.

3

Warner couldn't find out," Trexler said. "And if he couldn't get that sort of information pretty quick, it ain't probable he'll get it ever—anyhow, not in time to satisfy you."

Brandon stared at the heavy tumbler cradled in his hands on the bar. The gaslight glinted blue-white on the glass of whiskey.

"Mr. Todt's not inclined to be forthcoming," Trexler went on, "and no wonder. He's still got a ringing in his ears after a week, and a good bit of hair scorched off of his sideburns. Anybody asking around even for the time of day, acting for you, Mr. Brandon, is not going to get far around them law offices. Nor anywhere else in St. Louis, I don't doubt. The cops and the judge took it into account, what happened to your family, and didn't want to make it a jailing matter for you; and I guess Mr. Todt figured it'd make him look foolish and mean-spirited to press charges or let Casmire, so you're away and clear for that. But I would say you've used all the credit you've got by now, and you can't look for no favors from much of anybody around here."

"We know anyhow," Brandon said.

"Know who really paid for Todt and the witnesses, yeah,"

Trexler said. "Whoever it was that handed over the cash and gave the instructions doesn't matter; it's got to go back to one of the Kenneallys. Not Gren, for he doesn't have the strings out to fellows like those merchants, to haul on when they're needed. That'll be Quint, most likely, though it could be Peter. No way to prove it—or anything else, though—and no way to find 'em. They could be back deep in the Ozarks, or they could be further west. One notion is they're shifting headquarters out to the Neutral Zone over to Texas and the Indian Territory, some away from where they're known, looking to improve the shining hour out on the frontier. Maybe Casmire's gone to join 'em—out and away right after the trial, and nobody's seen him since that's mentioned it."

"Go west, young man, like Horace Greeley says," Brandon said. He studied his and the detective's reflections in the bar mirror. Two nondescript men having a meaningless conversation. Since his explosion into violence in the courthouse rotunda, Brandon had been feeling detached from his emotions and his very self, particularly from the certainty of his trust in the law. Not only had he seen justice blatantly perverted, he had set about looking for that justice in a totally lawless way, which meant that his basic code was a sham.

"That's what I'm doing," the detective said. "Going west. Company's sending me out to look into some stuff that's going on on the Northern Pacific, out past Salt Lake City. Grifters and strong-arm men working the construction crews, hurting 'em bad enough so that the work's falling off. Catching a train out tonight, in about half an hour."

As if on cue, a locomotive approaching the station a couple of blocks away gave a hooting whistle at a level crossing; and like a distorted echo, a late-docking ship shrilled a different note from just off the granite wharf that sprawled for two miles along the city's riverfront.

"Oh." Something clenched in Brandon's stomach, a reflex of protest, or perhaps fear. Trexler was not a friend, but they had shared some terrible moments, and that was a bond he had with no one else. With anybody but Trexler, he seemed to be talking through a sheet of muslin, seeing and hearing almost normally, but definitely separated from the other. Sometimes, if he drank just enough—not too little, not too much—the veiling sheet would vanish, or at least he would not be aware of it.

"Mr. Brandon," Trexler said. Brandon turned to look at him. "I'll tell you, I'm not sorry to be away from this. What I'm going to, it's your normal kind of crookery, theft and assault and malicious mischief, a hothead killing or so. Nothing like . . . that was as bad as anything I saw during the War, and the same kind of lunatic savageness. Kind of crime I'm used to dealing with, it makes sense even if it's bad. This didn't."

Trexler lifted his glass and looked somberly at it, then took another sip. "Warner tells me you're having him keep at looking for some more of the gang. I guess you can't do anything else, and God knows the railroad'll be happy if he turns in some of them. But . . ." He looked intently at Brandon. ". . . find 'em or not, there'll be an end to that some time, and you'll have other things to get on with. Might be a good idea to be paying attention to those now."

He fished his watch from his vest and looked at it. "Best be on my way." He nodded to Brandon, then turned and walked to the bar door and out into the gaslight-washed street.

At the sound of the front-door knocker, Brandon looked up from the papers he was studying.

His housekeeper opened the study door and said, "Miss Ostermann to see you." Before she had finished, there was Krista, as always enough like Elise to make his heart turn over.

"Thank you, Mrs. Logan." The housekeeper turned and left the room. Krista moved to him and embraced him briefly.

"First time I've seen you since the funeral," Brandon said. Her dress might have been the same as the one she'd worn on that day, a little over a month before; maybe not—it had a more everyday, less ceremonial look. All the same, it was black; all of Krista's clothes for the next five months would be. Then it was half-mourning, he remembered his mother telling him once, with a deep color like purple allowed.

"I wonder you can see me now," Krista said, gesturing at the maroon drapes over the study windows that left the gas chandelier overhead and the lamp on the table to light the room. "Wouldn't you like some fresh air in here?"

"Fresh November fog and coal smoke isn't my idea of healthy. Right now I feel best closed in here. Everything outside, it's all kind of strange to me, fog even when there isn't fog. I don't like it."

Krista sighed. She unpinned her hat, set it on the table, and sat in the morocco chair facing Brandon. "Have you decided what you wish to do with Elise's share?" When Brandon said nothing, she went on with a touch of sharpness: "Elise's interest in Father's firms that you've inherited—there are some decisions to be made, and since you're now a one-fifth shareholder, you will want a voice in them. Someone has to take Father's place, for one. I sent a note 'round to you last week—didn't you get it?"

"Oh . . . yes," Brandon said. "Sorry, of course I did. I just . . . was a bit abstracted for a moment. Now, yes, I've been looking over Elise's papers here." He gestured at the stack of documents on the desk. "It all seems in order."

Krista looked at him intently, as if his face were hard to see in the lamplit room. "You haven't come to any decisions about the companies, about what you want done? Or at least what opinions you'd like to give?"

"Ah . . . I've . . ."

"Of course!" Krista said brightly. "I was forgetting that you are a professional man, Cole. In matters of law, of course you know your way around. But yes, you never did take much interest in trade. Elise didn't either, so it's not to be wondered at." Elise, Brandon acknowledged inwardly, had lacked interest in quite a lot besides business. She was lovely, lovable, and loving, which was a lot to say about somebody, but almost all there was to be said about Elise. Krista, her shadow-twin, was as lovely, but with a sharp, driving intelligence and candid curiosity about almost everything she experienced. Whether she was loving, or would let herself be lovable, was something Brandon didn't know.

"If you are agreeable to it, Cole," Krista said, "I can look after your interests with our firm. When it was Elise's, Father and I did that anyhow, and she was happy not to be bothered. With everything else on your mind, you may not want to be, either. That way you can receive the income but not have to get involved in decisions."

"I . . . it doesn't seem right, me getting part of your family business this way," Brandon said.

"It's terribly wrong," Krista said. "Not that you're to have it, dear Cole, but *how*. The wrong is poor Elise and Father and . . . and the rest being . . ." Her voice broke and her face twisted; Brandon came out of his feeling of near-subservience and acceptance of her sureness to see her as a doubly heartbroken young woman.

Krista took a deep breath, and her face fell into its previous composure. "As a man of the law," she said, "you know that that's how it goes. The survivors inherit. We must mourn, but we must also accept what those who loved us chose to leave to us, and be grateful that they wanted to give us that. Then we must move on with our lives and be thankful for them."

"How do you move on," Brandon said, "when the animals who murdered your family are alive and laughing? When the law can't find them or can't keep them? What am I supposed to *do?*"

"Something. Whatever is possible. But not *nothing*, not ever nothing." Krista leaned over the desk and tapped the pile of papers into neatness. "It's agreed, then? I'll take these, speak for you, vote your shares? I'm more than willing for you to do it if you prefer, but . . ."

Brandon shook his head. "Best you do it, Krista. You'd be better at it than I would, for sure. Not that that's saying much—right now I feel as though about anybody would be better at about anything than me."

Brandon was taken a shade aback to see that Krista

appeared to be considering whether what he had said was in fact true. "Actually, Cole," she said after a longer pause than he liked, "I believe you could do anything, or be anything, you put your mind to. What you *will* do, that's another matter."

Thanksgiving, Christmas, New Year's Day, Twelfth Night, Valentine's Day—the public holidays and those that had been private celebrations for him and Elise—loomed on Brandon's personal horizon, sped toward him, and then were past in an instant, leaving him numbed. He felt that it would be a mistake to insert himself into the warm embrace of the Ostermann circle; and whatever it was he needed, family comforts didn't seem part of it.

Laborious effort at the firm's office helped him to restore his dedication to the law. There was a kind of solace in working through a case, seeing that the seemingly confusing aspects of it worked out in a final, complex order, and then seeing that order prevail in court. Jim Lunsford, the senior partner, said he'd never seen such careful, elegant work; it was like surgery or fine embroidery.

To Brandon, it was more like building or bricklaying: Course by course, he re-erected the structure that had been the temple of his belief since law school, and the walls grew reassuringly higher with each case he prepared.

Only there didn't seem to be anybody living inside them.

"Mr. Brandon," Warner said, "it's not my custom to try to get a client to dispense with our services, and I suppose the main office would make it hot for me if they thought I was. But I'm bound to tell you two things."

Brandon looked past the detective at the gray blanket that filled the window over its view of the roofs of the city, black in the waning February light, and the masts and stacks poking over the riverfront warehouses.

"First, we've been on this over two months and, aside from Casmire, haven't come up with anything solid. There are always rumors, and we've followed them up. In my opinion, Mr. Brandon, there's no point to this any more.

Some of those fellows may turn up some day, somewhere, and be caught, but it isn't likely to be through anything we're able to do. I have to say that at this point you're not getting value for your money. We're doing the work, but what we can do isn't worth much to you."

Warner paused and looked soberly at Brandon. "Next, Mr. Brandon, it really isn't any of my business, but it seems to me that you've done all that can be done about the terrible thing that happened, and it's a pity it didn't work out as you—and we—hoped. But going on with it isn't sensible. I really hope you can see your way to ending this now."

"Why not?" Brandon said. The reports from the agency had become a feature of his life, but he realized that he had not expected them to show anything for a long time, or even hoped that they would. Warner was right, all that was in the past.

"Good. I'll prepare the final bill and get it to you. Something else that doesn't really bear on the assignment, but it might interest you," Warner went on. "Casmire didn't get far after his acquittal. I just lately learned that he went on a drunk, wound up on a boat to New Orleans, got shanghaied, and is now an unwilling seaman someplace in the Gulf or the South Atlantic."

"Let us hope for a hungry sea monster," Brandon said.

The late winter and early spring of 1875 flickered by Brandon with the speed of images in a zoetrope. Work at Lunsford, Ahrens & Brandon went well; Krista reported profits without problems from his share of the Ostermann businesses; the weather was better some days, worse others. March, going out not so much like a lion as like a wet polecat, stirred an impatience in him. Whatever he was doing, it was no good. He was sure of the validity and worth of the law once more, but he had no emotional conviction that it meant anything, or that anything he did meant anything. He was acutely aware of the chorus of steam whistles from boats and trains that underlay the city's noise, of the throaty rumble of locomotive and steamboat engines, of the click of train wheels and the slapping chunk of the four-story-high wheels of the riverboats.

"Away." The word hung in his consciousness, coming to him at any hour of the day or night. What it meant, he wasn't sure, but it seemed to him that he should be some place, any place, other than where he was.

Once that became clear, he moved quickly. Lunsford and Ahrens were dismayed that their energetic and devoted partner was taking an indefinite leave of absence, but they agreed that he could do with the recuperative effects of an extended tour.

"We'll miss you, Cole," Jake Ahrens said, "but I have to say that new scenes may be the best thing to help you get over your loss." For a moment Brandon did not understand what he was talking about; then he realized that in abandoning his hope for justice and vengeance on the Kenneallys he had also let his mourning for Elise slip into the past. But it would do no harm to let his partners think of him as traveling to mend a shattered heart. That way they would be expecting him back some day, and it did not seem to Brandon that he would be returning. Whatever it was that had made up Cole Brandon had had the life drained from it; and somewhere, in another country or on a strange sea, it would quietly crumble and dissolve.

A breath of flower-scented air wafted into the room with Krista; or perhaps it was her perfume. Her dress was purple and gray, the half-mourning colors allowed after six months.

"It is right that you travel, Cole," she said. "If you cannot go somewhere in your life, then changing places may be a help." As always bone-honest, Brandon thought, but not hurtful about it except insofar as the truth hurts. Elise had tact, drayloads of tact, and who's to say which is better?

"Will you go to Germany? I was only a little girl when we left, but I remember how beautiful the Rhineland was."

"Haven't decided," Brandon said. "Get going and keep going, decide at each fork in the road which way to go next."

Krista nodded. "A true wanderer, that may be the best thing for you to be now. If you are meant to return here, you will." She paused and looked at him with evident effort and an unaccustomed shyness. "If you do . . . it might be that there will be a new life for you to take up, if you choose to."

Brandon masked his astonishment as he looked at her. What she had said was guarded enough to spare her shame but all the same unmistakable. And it meshed well enough with some part of his own feelings, or at least had once. Krista had always been a pleasure to be near, and he had had moments when he realized that if Krista had not been away at boarding school when he met Elise, he might well have courted the younger sister rather than the older. Right now he had to turn the offer aside without the hurt of outright rejection.

"If I'm meant to return, it'll be because this is where I want to live my life," he said carefully. "And yes, I would want it to be a new one."

Krista nodded; she had made her point, and had expected no more than that it should be registered. "Now, you will need money for this journey," she said. "That is what I came here to talk of. It is my thought that you will not want everyone in St. Louis to know where you are at all times. If you send to your bank here for funds when you need them, you know as well as I do that where they are sent will be common knowledge, and you will have St. Louis ladies calling upon you in London or Locarno, demanding that you show them the local attractions."

Her suggestion was that Brandon set up an account in a Boston or Philadelphia bank, into which his Ostermann income would be paid regularly. Brandon had not considered this problem, but he agreed that even an indefinite traveler needed a definite source of funds. Chicago seemed a better idea than an East Coast city, and Krista undertook to handle the arrangements.

After she left, Brandon smiled ruefully. Krista had shown an unexpected side, all right. If he stayed in St. Louis, he would be in for a more interesting time than he would have thought. . . . But no, "away" was the word still.

When he heard the front-door knocker, he thought it might be Krista returning, and he wondered what he might have to say to her. But the housekeeper showed in his law firm's office boy, who held an envelope in his extended hand. "From Mr. Lunsford, Mr. Brandon."

Brandon slid his thumb under the flap and broke the wax seal, then drew out the folded sheet of paper.

Dear Brandon,

A matter has come up with which I hope you will be able to aid the firm before you embark on your travels. We have been asked to supply counsel *gratis* to an indigent defendant in a criminal misdemeanor case, and believe that it is something suitable for you to undertake. Should you agree to do so, please repair to the Gratiot Street police station and request the particulars in the case of one Ned Norland, which the authorities are prepared to provide; they will also arrange for you to interview the said Norland. . . .

Brandon felt a trickle of amusement. Gentlemen, Brandon's escaping, but here's a last little task to lumber him with, and he can hardly complain, can he? He'll find everything there is in the law for this Norland, and if it doesn't go, there's no paying client hurt . . . and none of *us* has to waste time over it.

"My compliments to Mr. Lunsford, and I'm on my way," Brandon said.

Brandon strode along the street with a curious sense of excitement and anticipation, breathing in the freshness of the spring air. Flower scents drifted from a few private gardens and street plantings, perceptible in these brief weeks when the air was not laden with the reek of winter's coal and wood smoke or with the aggressive aroma of horse dung acted on by the summer sun.

Insubstantial clouds sailed across a pale, bright sky. Looking toward the river, he could see above the line of roofs the brightness of sail tops and riverboat flags snapping in the breeze. Carts and carriages trundled by him; people walked briskly along the streets and walks; it was strange to be surrounded by so much activity and purpose, strange and contagious. The city seemed to him almost like a fair-ground, set for a play or pageant, where something exciting was poised to happen.

Even the police station, which might have been built to radiate dourness and menace, its humped dome squatting toward its rear, glowed as the late-morning sun soaked into its stones, seeming more like scenery than a sober public building. His client, the silvery—if somewhat grease-tarnished—hair and beard that wreathed his lined face gleaming in the shaft of light through the high barred window of his cell, seemed like a mystic hermit, self-secluded to refine the fabric of his soul of all mortal coarseness.

The worn old man looked meekly at Brandon with faded blue eyes when the reason for his presence was explained. "Mr. Norland," Brandon said gently, "I'm going to do my best to get this settled for you." He took a quick look at the papers the police clerk had handed him. "The main thing, of course, is to cooperate with the police in finding the men who did the damage in the saloon and injured the four complainants. Your part in that must have been slight, and—"

"Wagh!" the old man screeched with an intensity that prickled the hairs on the back of Brandon's neck. "Others be damned! The day this child cain't redecorate a barroom er rearrange some toe-rags' arms and laigs without no help, why, that's the day he'll lift his own hair and hand it over t' the Injuns his own self, so it is! Three nostrils and holes bored for more, Ned Norland has, and belches thunder and sneezes lightnin', ain't never been curried below the knees! Wagh!"

Brandon's strategy of beginning Norland's defense with an offer of cooperation and a handsome apology evaporated somewhere about the middle of the second sentence of the old man's exuberant tirade. This was going to be a riper case than the firm had thought. Even—the thought came to him with the difficulty of rusted machinery groaning into motion—something he might enjoy.

4

"I expect I should've knowed how it was, when Astor got out of the fur trade in '34," Norland said, "but it always seemed to me as though the good prices'd come back fer prime pelts, so I stayed at the trappin'."

He paused for a pull at his lager, and Brandon took a shallow breath of the kind that lawyers learn to make in order not to sigh or snort impatiently at a dilatory client. After bailing the old man out of jail, they had come to this waterfront dive chosen by Norland for their forensic conference; and Norland had promptly embarked on what he considered "necessary background," which seemed to be everything that had happened to him since he'd struck out across the Missouri as a youth and become a fur trapper and occasional guide. Fascinating stuff, to be sure, with Indian fights, trackless wastes, harrowing ordeals, and even a whale sighting off the California coast when he'd been one of the first to find a way through the mountains—but it had taken an even hour to deal with the first half-dozen years. With forty more to cover before getting to the events of the night before that had occasioned their professional relationship, it looked like being nightfall by the time they reached that point.

"This is truly interesting, Mr. Norland," Brandon said. "But we may not need all the details for your case." He sipped at his own beer, finding it cooling in the early afternoon warmth, but, to his relief, only mildly pleasant—not the urgent filling of a need that any kind of booze had been only yesterday. Whether it was finally admitting to himself how it was and had to be with Krista, or the simple fact of taking an interest in the doings of someone other than himself and Kenneally's gang, that problem seemed to be in the past. With luck, it would stay there.

"Wagh! This child's tongue do get to waggin' as it was hinged at the middle, so it do," Norland said cheerfully. "Anyhow, the furs was done, so I went out on a few Santa Fee tradin' trips, guided some bunches o' Mormons crost th' desert, done some scoutin' for th' Army, minded a station on the Pony Express, went to buffler huntin' and then to pickin' up and sellin' the bones us buffler hunters left behind whenas we took the hides, done some commissary huntin' for the railroads, then come on back to St. Louis, which I'm now here."

Brandon blinked. Norland had picked up narrative speed from four years an hour to about three and a half per second, and the effect was a trifle disorienting.

"Come in last night on a packet from Westport Landin', as that's at the end of the KP line, which they give me a pass on it for work I done for 'em. Got a look from the gangplank at how ol' St. Louis'd changed since as I was last here, decided I wanted my cup pressed down, full measure and runnin' over beforesoever as I went to cut some trail there. R'ared back like any grizzly, snuffed the air, and followed my nose to a place about as close like this one as you c'n git. Which is why I brung you here, so's you c'n get the feel of what happened."

"Hanratty's," Brandon said, with a glance at the papers detailing Norland's arrest-worthy conduct.

"And this is Hamlin's, so you see," Norland said, employing a logic Brandon did not feel qualified to examine. The little he knew of these places suggested that Hanratty's would indeed be like this: a long counter facing a wall on which were nailed unpainted pine shelves holding rows of bottles; three tables and half a dozen chairs set around the sawdust-covered floor; a dust-filmed front window allowing a faded view of the street. The ceiling was high for a building of this type—perhaps nine feet; if Hanratty's resemblance went that far, Brandon wondered how Norland, or one of the confederates mentioned in the police report, had managed to damage it.

"You were at Hanratty's, then," Brandon said, "which is pretty much like this—ceiling this high, too, by the way?"

"High as a grizzly standin' on top of another grizzly," Norland said, which Brandon worked out to be about ten feet. "Now, I ain't been here since the Whigs was in, but I knowed this wasn't a place where a child steps up to the bar and says, 'I got over a thousand in my poke, paper, dust, coins, and nuggets, the fruits of a lifetime on the plains, in the mighty Rockies, learnin' the ways of the noble red man er the pitiless savage—take yer pick—guidin' the boys in blue acrost the deserts, and now I'd admire if everyone drank up on me.'"

Norland sucked down another two inches of beer.

"Fact, I don't know there's any place a man that's not got buffler chips fer brains'd act so. But what I meant, I seen it was a place whereas a child treads light and stays ready to jump sideaways. So I has a drink or some, quiet-like, and lookin' around at the rivermen and wharfmen that's the main crowd. And it come about that some of them fellers asked me to jine them in a game of chanst that they was amusin' thesselfs with, which I done that."

Brandon supplied the conclusion, as Norland seemed to have regained his fondness for needless elaboration: "And they cheated you out of your money, and a fight got going that did all the damage."

"Wagh! This child ain't about to let a passel of city rats snide him, nor he ain't!" Norland said indignantly. "Fact, I fattened my poke some handsome off them fellers, so's you can warrant the game was straight, their end of it anyhow."

Brandon's professional instincts were outraged. "Then you're not indigent, and you haven't got any right to free legal counsel! And you let *me* bail you out!"

"You offered," Norland said. "As fer the indignation, I ain't mad at nobody, and on the gratis lawyerin', they ast me at the *juzgado* if as I could afford to pay a lawyer, and I says no, so they sends me you. If I says yes, they sends me somebody and I'm already owin' him some pinches of dust before I gets a chance to size him up. This child can pay what's due, don't you worry, and now we've talked some, I'm feelin' some trustful in you, so I'm inclined to hire you."

Brandon framed a stinging reply, then let it go. The crazy old mountain man had imposed impudently on the legal system and on Cole Brandon, Esq., but if he hadn't, the said Cole Brandon wouldn't be getting his teeth into a case that might actually be interesting, not a legal exercise. He was getting a sense that the legalities would be the least important part of the case, too.

"So you've got money, that's good. We can probably ease things some if you can pay for the actual damage. So what did happen? How did the trouble start?"

"The fellers at the table started to hooraw me some, lookin' on me as some kind of figger of fun," Norland said. Brandon looked at the wrinkled, gamy buckskin, fringed with long dangling thongs, the tangled beard that hung from a face that might have been buckskin also, and declined to comment. "They said as how I had been amongst the Injuns for so long that I had likely had carnal congressin' with some o' th' women, and they pitied me fer havin' sank so low."

"And you resented that?" Brandon asked. "Being accused of, ah, familiarity with Indian women?"

Norland stared at him. "Hell, no! If you don't start sweetheartin' mountain sheep er b'ar, Injun women is what there is, out in them parts, and thank the Lord fer it! No, sir, it was the low-ratin' of the squaw that sparked this child's tinder. I been to fancy houses in San Francisco, and I played my part like a man with the *señoritas* after more'n a couple *bailes* in Santa Fee, but there ain't nothin' as lovin' and inventive as the right Injun woman. They are fer sartin the best there is between the two oceans at makin' a man know what his parts is fer."

"I see," Brandon said. Whatever he had been expecting, this was not it.

"So natcherly," Norland continued, "I tried to set them fellers straight, tolt 'em some of the things as a considerate Injun lady will do fer you, and bet 'em that their wives wouldn't come within a day's portage of such, and they got kind of touchy about me bringin' their wives into it, and I tolt 'em that their wives prob'ly wasn't makin' a tenth part of the use of what the Almighty give 'em to work with, and tried to give these fellers a few tips on what to get 'em to do, and they got upsot and jumped me. One feller that had jist got engaged to a gal that he had a pictur of in a locket was about cryin' with rage." Norland looked with pleased reminiscence at his glass.

Brandon forced himself to press on with his inquiry. "So the fight started . . . we may want to be careful about getting into the circumstances . . . and who jumped in to help you? They got away before the police came, apparently, and—"

Norland's eyebrows rose into the thatch of greasy hair that hung over his forehead, like grizzled rats dodging into the eaves of a house. "Help? What help's that? I tolt you in the jail, the time this child needs *help* in a little barroom shivaree, I expect the Mississippi'll run north and buffler'll lay aigs."

"Mr. Norland," Brandon said sharply, "the bar's fixtures were close to completely destroyed, there's not a stick of furniture intact, the streetside window's broken, and there's eight men with injuries ranging from a mangled ear to a broken arm and a possible skull fracture."

"Wagh!" Norland crowed. "That's the feller I th'owed up. Was on the table, see, doin' one of them Mex dances like when he grub for me, and I leans over, cotches him under the arms, and gives him a flyin' lift. Went up like a balloon, so he did, an' 'is head went halfway through the ceiling. Thought he might stick up there, and he did for a touch, but then he fell. 'Spect that's how he broke the arm."

"But the others . . ." Brandon paused. "You really did all

that damage yourself? Fought eight men and marked all of them and didn't take any hurt yourself?"

"A dozen Piegans at one and the same time has hankered after this child's hair," Norland said, "an' them armed to the earbones and lookin' to s'prise me. Was in a mild and peaceable frame of mind, so I was, so let six of 'em git away home." He hoisted one buckskin-clad leg onto the table and fingered the untidy thongs that dangled from its seams. Brandon saw that some of them were not strips of leather but rather small patches of leather at the end of four-inch hanks of coarse, dark hair. "Ah. Here's two of the ones as didn't git back t' the lodge." He fingered a pair of the hairy decorations. "Left the others with the Blackfeet as a play-party present one time, they're allus pleased to see a Piegan scalp even if 'twasn't them as lifted it."

Brandon studied the old man. He was beginning to believe that this weird bit of frontier wreckage might in fact "belch thunder and sneeze lightnin'." And that he was probably telling the truth about having devastated Hanratty's single-handed. If so, there was a highly interesting defense tactic possible. He recalled the old dictum that if the facts aren't on your side, talk up the law, and if the law isn't on your side, go with the facts. Here was the third situation, law and facts both against you, so . . .

"The defendant is prepared to plead guilty, Your Honor," Brandon said. As instructed, Norland sat at his counsel's table, hunched over and looking even frailer than he had in jail in the slightly too-large gray wool suit Brandon had forced him both to buy and to wear; his newly washed hair and beard shone like a white cloud around his face. He looked as if, had the windows been opened, a spring breeze from outside would have slid him from his chair. A number of men, most of them burly and most showing cuts and bruises around lavishly applied bandages, sat in the area reserved for witnesses, and glowered at Norland.

"Prepared," Judge Lamar said heavily. "That means he's not actually pleading yet, Mr. Brandon?"

"As Your Honor has kindly agreed to hear this case without a jury for the sake of expedition, I hope that a little informality may be possible, if it will also speed up the proceedings," Brandon said smoothly. "The plea requires some small clarification."

"No objection," the police prosecutor said at the judge's interrogatory nod. "If he'll give us the name of his confederates, we'll even consider reducing the charges if the complainants agree. Maybe dropping them," he added, looking at the wraith folded into the chair at Brandon's table.

"Is your client prepared to do this, Mr. Brandon?" the judge asked.

"Ah, no, Your Honor. In fact, he can't," Brandon added hastily as Lamar's eyebrows rose in menace. "There were no confederates. Mr. Norland acted totally alone, not in concert with any persons whatsoever."

"That ain't so!" one of the most heavily bandaged men called. "They was at least . . . I seen . . ." He turned to the man next to him, whose arm was bound to his side with several turns of linen. "Now, who done that to you?"

The arm fracture looked sheepishly at Norland. "Snapped it over his knee like ary stick."

"Your Honor," Brandon cut in, "we have witnesses not involved in this unfortunate misunderstanding who are prepared to testify that there were no other parties involved save the defendant and these complaining witnesses—plus, I understand, one or two who are unable to be present."

"Sam's shamed to be seen with most of his ear chawed off!" one of the men called. Brandon glared angrily at Norland, thankful that only from his angle of sight could it be observed that the old man was toying with what looked like, but was almost certainly not, a slice of dried apple.

"As I said, Your Honor, my client is prepared to plead guilty. Not only that, but to make reparations for the damage and injury he has caused—as far as that is possible," Brandon added, feeling that Sam's ear had gone beyond any reparable state. "Nor will he ask to avoid any penalty the court cares to exact. He is truly contrite, and indeed wishes nothing more than to make a clean breast of the entire matter, to allow himself the healing boon of public confession."

As he had thought might happen, a ripple of awareness and unease passed across the complaining witnesses, beginning with a sour-looking man in a checked suit, whom he took for Hanratty, the grogshop's proprietor.

"Amends!" Brandon said grandly. "That is what occupies my client's mind at this moment, Your Honor. Remorse gnaws at him." *Like a mountain man chewing his enemy's ear?* a subversive voice in his mind whispered, but he refused to break stride. "And he would expose his shame to the world. He has arranged to pay for half a page's advertising space in the *Post-Dispatch,* in which he will recount the whole sordid affair—how he let the demons of insensate rage drive him to inflict . . ."

He let the sentence die as the presumed Hanratty darted forward for an urgent conference with the prosecutor; the other complaining witnesses stirred in their seats, looking more uncomfortable than their wounds, visible and bandage-concealed, would account for.

The prosecutor looked at Brandon with an expression that nicely combined loathing and respect. "Your Honor," he said sourly, "the complaining witnesses are prepared to withdraw charges if the defendant will pay the costs of property damage and medical treatment. They feel that defendant's contrition and advanced years would make prosecution unjust."

"I see," Judge Lamar said. "You will pay, sir?" he said to Norland.

"Ned Norland's poke stands ready to stake Ned Norland's fun, that's how it is," the old man said. "Which I'll throw in enough for a round of drinks for them fellers to boot, so's they c'n toast Ned Norland's health."

"I see." The judge looked with banked balefulness at Norland, then at Brandon. "As there is now essentially no case, I'll dismiss what's left of it." He rapped on the bench with his gavel, then motioned Brandon toward him.

"You coerced your way out of that, Brandon," the judge

muttered. "Those men would be the laughingstock of St. Louis if it got around that they'd been whipped by one old man—even if he isn't the valetudinarian you're trying to pass him off as! Your tactic was nothing more or less than blackmail."

"You could say that, Your Honor," Brandon said.

The judge gave a wintry smile. "You've always brought a remarkable rectitude and scrupulousness into court, Counselor. Interesting to see that you're learning trial practice."

Norland insisted on paying Brandon the agreed-on fee in person rather than handing it over to the firm's clerk at the office, and they met for that purpose at the waterfront the morning after the trial. After Brandon stowed the gold pieces in his pocket, they strolled the wharf that extended a mile and a half along the Mississippi. Norland was impressed—though not especially favorably—with the changes since he had last seen St. Louis. "Didn't see it proper, comin' in at night, but, Lord! what a doin's there is here, for fair. Steamboats twicet as big as ever I see wherever as you look, and every kind of packet and bateau a-crowdin' up to the edge—an' the wharf's done turned to rock, so it has, peterfried like a forest I done seen out in the desert in Arizony."

"Solid granite all the way," Brandon said. "Most up-to-date waterfront along the river, we think." The spectacle was exhilarating even for someone used to it: the forest of masts, tall stacks, and cargo cranes; shouting longshoremen loading and unloading freight; the rumble and clatter of carts moving goods to and from the wharf area; the puff and shriek of donkey engines shoving freight cars along spur lines that ran across Front Street to the riverfront. Out in the river, a steamboat shrilled its intention to head in for a landing, while small sailing craft caught the light airs and scudded on purposeful tacks. The vast five-arched bridge served as a backdrop to the scene.

"When I started, hadn't much choice about where to go from here or how," Norland said. "Downriver t' New Orleans er up to Independence t' light out for the Rockies er the Santa Fee Trail. Now it's like one of them bills o' fare you git in a fancy restaurant, half as high as a man, with a couple dozen dishes t' choose from—you c'n go anywheres and anyhow. Makes it harder t' know what to do, some ways."

"And where are you going now?" Brandon asked. "Seen enough of the new St. Louis?"

"Enough and more," Norland said. "Time I knowed it, 'twas a live place, trappers in from the mountains with bales of pelts and the cash they got fer 'em, out t' have theirselfs a time and no nonsense about bringin' th' law in over a few scratches. I seen times at the Rocky Mountain House when there was more breakage and gougin' and blood spilt whiles as the boys was *dancin'* than in that foofaraw t'other night. I am studyin' to git on one of them steamboats and go downriver some, call on what kin o' mine there might be left over t' Crockett County in Tennessee."

The old man looked at the skyline with disfavor. "Place like this, they is just too much of it—goes on wherever as you look. My notion, a town is a place t' come to for pervisions and some hoorawin', and all's a child needs is enough fer that. All the rest—them trains and factories and offices and fancy stores t' sell stuff folks need t' live in a place that has factories and fancy stores—why, that idee just don't shine, so it don't. I b'lieve I will git on over t' Bellfountain Symmetry, say so long t' Manuel Lisa, that's buried thar, and git on. Manuel was a he'p to me whenas I was a kit, and I misdoubt he's gittin' many visitors these times."

Brandon had heard the old man's fragmentary story, but not until his mention of the legendary Lisa, one of those who had presided over the transformation of a frontier hamlet into a trading metropolis, had he had the full sense of how much of the past Norland's life encompassed—and what a short time that past in fact was. He himself had come to a St. Louis recognizably on the way to becoming what it was now, but in Lisa's, and the young Norland's, day, it had been the kind of town Norland considered normal, an outpost in the wilderness. The modern pageant of industry, commerce, and transport Brandon saw seemed for a moment insubstantial, a painted backdrop masking the true face of the land. "It'll be nice for you, seeing your folks," he said.

Norland spat into the river. "Not such a much, but it seems like the next thing to do. Was never one to map out whereas I was goin' fer the next hand-count o' years er so—what I always done was git quiet and let it come to me whar the next turnin' was, let the tale git tolt the way she's meant to. The Injuns know that, a man gits his medicine sign when he comes to be growed, and that's his guide from then on—he don't git in the way of what the sign tells him he's s'posed to be doin'. They don't b'lieve a man c'n figure out whereat he's goin' to be all that far ahead, 's if he was a train that could git switched onto the line fer Salt Lake City and know he'd be goin' there through Kansas City, Omaha, and Cheyenne, 'cause that's where the track runs."

A resonant wail from the train station a few streets away trailed off into the slow beat of a locomotive starting on its journey—bound for Salt Lake City maybe, but it could be almost anyplace. The metal networks of tracks and telegraph wires had shrunk the country until every part of it could be reached in a few days or communicated with instantly. Brandon had a sharp vision of the prairies and mountains that had been Norland's home, vast spaces to be traversed at the limited pace of man or animal.

"I am goin' to see my kin 'cause it's somethin' I'm meant to do before I go under, and I'm gettin' no sign pointin' me any which way in pertickler, so now's as good a time as any. Don't know how many of 'em there might be left back yonder, for this child's been gone a sight of years. Cut out whenas I was sixteen, and that's forty-some years agone. Wouldn't think it to look at me, but I tallied up to sixty-three last year."

"Don't look it, no," Brandon said, truthfully enough. Taking into account the mountain man's leathery, seamed face and (after the pretrial shampoo) white hair, Brandon would in fact have put him at either a youthful eighty or a severely used seventy. Only the piercing blue eyes and the lithe stride, curiously delicate, with one foot set down directly ahead of the other, toe first—and, of course, the cheerful carnage at Hanratty's—contradicted the impression.

"I'm doing some traveling myself," Brandon said. "New York for a start, Philadelphia maybe, then away someplace else. London, Paris, who knows?"

"Hum," Norland said. "Them places, they're like St. Louis, only more of it, ain't they?"

"Pretty much."

Norland shook his head. "Wagh! Not for this child! Where I been, you work, you hunt, maybe you starve some er git froze er snakebit er rubbed out some way else, er you don't, you go where you go, you see what you see, you got yer friends and you got yer enemies, and that's what there is. Cities, what I seen and hearn, there's bushelsful of miseries ain't ever even been spoke of out there, and armies of folks thinkin' they know how to do everything and make what they want to happen, happen." He sniffed the warm air. "And with all them horses fer the drays and carriages and wagons and whatall, it's worse'n a stable. Like livin' in a dungheap."

Brandon's city-trained nose had automatically filtered out the springtime reek of horse droppings, but, focusing freshly on it, he had to admit that it was truly rank—and worsened by the mingling of coal smoke and wood smoke, hot oil from laboring machinery, sweat-soaked clothing of passing laborers, rotting food from the gutters, a muddily corrupt whiff from the riverbank, and a sharp undertone from the brewery a few streets away. A shift in the breeze brought the rich stench of green hides to them, and Brandon wondered that not only he but the other hundred thousand St. Louisans, including the most determinedly refined ladies lived and moved unnoticing in a cloud of foulness. New York and Philadelphia, probably even London and Paris, would be worse.

"I'm traveling for my health," he said, wondering why he felt the need to justify his trip, then becoming aware of a leaden dismay at the prospect of carrying out his plans, and then making the further plans the next stage would call for. This was mixed with a queer sense of excitement as Norland looked at him fixedly, resembling a supernaturally reanimated mummy pondering the fate of the mortal confronting it.

"Naw, you ain't," Norland said. "Tolt yerself that, 'cause you need to pull yer boot out of a boghole that's suckin' you down. You been listenin' to me spillin' out my talk these couple days, plentiful as boudin comin' out of a buffler belly, but this child's eyes and ears don't close up whenas his mouth is open, and I been hearin' what you ain't been sayin' and seein' what you don't think you been showin'. The blue devils is perched on you and whisperin' things you cain't stand to hear, and you figure you'll shake 'em off on the cars to New York. But you won't. Whyever you got 'em, they'll fatten up in a place like that, and they'll talk louder and you'll feel 'em start to scritch and pull at you."

"That's nonsense," Brandon forced himself to say.

Norland ignored the clear lie and said, "Now, firstest thing as we need to do is git all this horseshit and the rest of the city stink blowed away from you."

"What in the nine circles of hell are you talking about?" Brandon said.

"You done me a good turn, gittin' me out of jail," Norland said. "Now I'll do you the same, fer you're in a worse jail than any the law runs. My kin in Crockett County can wait a while more fer their wanderin' boy. The next bend in the trail's comin' clear to my sight, and you'll be takin' it with me."

5

One horse's ass looking at another horse's ass, Brandon thought sourly as, two days later, he hunched against the drizzle, looking ahead at Norland's mount picking its way up the mountain track. What possessed you, Counselor, to allow yourself to let some withered old weasel cozen you into a damn *camping* trip? You could be riding the cars to Chicago or wherever, and you'd be a damned sight dryer than this.

He couldn't remember now why Norland's urging had seemed persuasive, but, on the evidence, it had been. The old man had talked of letting the open air of the mountains blow away the "blue devils" that thrived in the city, and some aberrant element in Brandon had jumped at the idea. Within a day the half-formed arrangements for the trip east had been changed and Brandon and Norland were rattling south on the Iron Mountain line. At the terminus, Pilot Knob, they outfitted themselves as Norland directed, buying a couple of serviceable horses and the minimum of equipment and food needed for a few days. Norland had been particular about getting sturdy oilcloth slickers, and Brandon was grateful at least for that when the light rain started shortly after they began climbing into the St. François Mountains.

"Put in some time here on my way from Tennessee 'fore I went to St. Louis, back in '28 or when," Norland said. "Went out and catched some beaver to git in practice and put together some cash for a stake. Not a patch on the Rockies, but wild enough then to give a man a taste of what it's like out thar, and likely one place that ain't changed much these forty-what years."

The misted landscape Brandon now saw had not, he supposed, changed much in ten thousand years. The track Norland led them along, navigating by no indications Brandon could detect, wound among budding hickory and oak trees, which were supplanted by pines as the trail angled upward. The horses plodded amid new vegetation Brandon did not know, and some kind of fern brushed wetly against his leg from time to time. Queerly shaped hills like giant potatoes or standing elephants loomed through the moist air.

The track dipped and snaked along the edge of a stream between two steep bluffs, and the gray morning deepened to a near twilight. Norland's horse moved ahead into a darker slot where the bluffs came almost together, and Brandon doggedly followed.

"Wagh! There's suthin' a man's eye could feast on till it fattens up, so it is," Norland said proudly, as if he had personally produced the change from the dismal atmosphere and gloomy vista of an hour before. Brandon looked out across the tumbled range of mountains. They were clad with deep-toned evergreens and the shimmering brightness of the emerging leaves on the hardwoods, enriched and emphasized by the midafternoon sunlight. He was willing to allow Norland to take credit if he wanted it. The westering sun to their left gave the effect of having driven the rain clouds offstage, where their tattered remnants continued to retreat eastward. A clear sky, pure blue but without the intensity that would come with summer, arched over them and down to their eye level at the horizon. They stood as high as any mountaintop that lay before them.

Brandon felt both exposed to the immensity of the wild landscape—in which no sign of habitation or other trace of human presence could be seen—and exhilarated by the sense that every quarter of the compass presented the possibility of unexpected opportunity or danger. And all less than a hundred miles from St. Louis! For the first time, Norland's stories had a setting he could make a stab at visualizing, even though the St. François range must be puny compared to the Rockies.

Norland pointed ahead to where the trees, mostly evergreens this high up, clustered at the far edge of the rocky clearing. "We has seen the sights, now it's time to find a place to fort up for the night, and—" He stiffened, peered at the nearest group of trees, slid the short rifle from where it was strapped to his saddlebags, and fired offhand without bringing the weapon to his shoulder. Brandon's eye picked up a flick of downward motion ending with an audible thump on the pine-needled carpet under the trees—"c'lect suthin' fer the pot."

Norland guided his horse to the trees, dismounted to collect the grouse—its head removed by his shot—and remounted, in a sequence as casual and practiced as that of a customer collecting the day's dinner at the butcher shop.

"These greens'll give a man a cleanout like you wouldn't believe," Norland said, waving a handful of vegetation he had pulled up. "Blood and bowels both. A man that's been forted up all winter like as a b'ar, why, it takes suthin' to get all his parts and attributes workin' ag'in so as they should. Yer Injuns wouldn't be so lightsome and frisky when the snow melts, ready to take yer hair er roast you alive fer fun, withouten these yarbs, and it makes sense to l'arn from 'em."

"These go into the pot, too?" Brandon asked. The plucked and disjointed bird was stewing in an iron kettle over the fire with an assortment of pungent plants Norland had gathered, and the smells coming from it seemed appetizing enough.

"Naw, them's food and seasonin', these is medicine," Norland said. Hunkered on the ground, studying the array of herbs on a rock in front of him, lit by the flickering glow of the cookfire, he seemed to Brandon like an ancient wizard studying the ingredients of his potions. "Sometimes you find ginseng around here, but I ain't this time. A good 'sang root, why, that'll make a old man young, and a young 'un do his part like two men. And nettles, they's worth pickin' whenas you find 'em—sting yer skin like fury, so you can imagine what they'll do fer yer insides—bile 'em up and drink the water."

It was no part of Brandon's intention to treat the forest as a grocery or a pharmacy, and he paid only perfunctory attention to Norland's display of his vegetative trophies and his expounding of their properties: This one was a remedy for snakebite and fever; that one expelled chills and damp; another altered the state of mind divertingly or alarmingly. "Injuns chew it so as the sperrits'll talk to them; that's when they git their medicine that tells 'em their totem and gives 'em their growed-up name. Never figured if 'twas that the medicine was changeable or some Injuns had better luck than others, but one'll come back callin' hissef Brave Eagle or Counts Many Coup, and another gits stuck with Dog Walks Sideways or such."

The greens Norland tossed in the pot flavored the stewed fowl deliciously, and Brandon relished his share, following it with "trail coffee" of ferocious strength, which the old man had prepared by letting a handful of ground coffee boil in the smaller of their pots until he judged it had matured.

The powerful brew kept Brandon alert for a while, countering the effects of the meal and the day's exertion, and he listened to Norland's comments as he lounged on his bedroll. "Wagh! That'll be a painter out thar," he said after a harsh coughing sound came to them out of the night. Brandon put away the image of a traveling artist afflicted with a severe cold that sprang to his mind; "panther," or mountain lion, had to be what Norland meant.

At a softer sound, Norland said, "Roostin' dove, likely. Some places I been, out among the tribes, chances it'd be a hand-blowin' woman, and the feller as reckernized the sound'd be in fer some prime huntin'."

Brandon pondered this. "The Indians use women to signal where game is?"

Norland chuckled. "Indeedy they do, and sweeter game than any buffler hump, I can tell you. Injuns is powerful respectable people, d'you see, and they don't hold with cotillions and church socials and promiscuous gallivantin's like as them, but they knows that men and women has their needs, so they got customs for that. So whenas a lady that ain't yet husbanded takes a shine to some feller, she lets him know she's got a kind of a call she can make by blowin' in her hand, like as this." He cupped one hand to his mouth and produced a piercing, mournful sound of surprising strength.

"Now, the feller she tells this to, natcherly he listens hard and remembers hard, for the chanst is that some night soon that there same call will come a-driftin' through the camp, and he'll reckernize that it ain't no dove er owl or whatso. And he'll say to any as might be nigh him that he b'lieves he'll step outside and see if the dog star has riz yet, and it might could take him some time to make sure of it. And he'll move away from camp and foller the sound, which it'll keep slippin' away ahead of him through the night, sometimes close, sometimes faroff." The old man sighed reminiscently. "Branches'll ritch out fer him and whop him in the eyes, but he don't care fer that, no, he don't. He tracks that woman's call through the woods, and then he finds her, and then it's sure-Sam wuth all the fuss. Wagh!" The exclamation had the reverent quality of an amen.

Brandon took another gulp of the bitter, powerful coffee and savored its warmth against the night chill rising from the ground. "You were, uh, called on yourself?"

"Was I not!" Norland said. "A young feller, a stranger that they hadn't knowed all their life, totin' all sorts of new songs and foolishnesses they hadn't heard of, plus which I'd had some groundin' in how ladies gets treated, about which them folks had no more notion than the babe unborn, natcherly my dance card got filled prompt. Why, there was women gettin' sore hands from blowin' into them, not to say sore in other places, too, fer reasons a gentleman don't care to talk of."

In the dwindling cookfire, a branch snapped and sent a drift of sparks upward, briefly brightening Norland's face. "But that come to a end when I married."

"Your wife didn't allow it?" Brandon asked.

"None of 'em'd stand fer it," Norland said sadly. "Said as if I went out after a hand-blower, they'd lift her hair and stuff it in the hole whereas my privates used to be. You never know when a Injun woman is funnin', but it don't pay to take chances like that 'un. But they seen that fair was fair, so they took it as their duty to make sure I wouldn't have time ner inclination to go woods-walkin', and if four women gang up and make it their business to see that a man wants to stay around the hearth and home and enjoy their persons, that man is by damn goin' to stay and he is goin' to enjoy, till there ain't hardly nothin' left of him but hide, hoofs, and tallow."

No wonder the old coot looks twenty years older than he is, Brandon thought. Mummified by fornification, something the Egyptians never thought of, I'll bet.

Wrapped in his bedroll and insulated a little from the night-chilled ground by a layer of luxuriantly needled pine branches, Brandon looked up at the window of night sky framed by the trees at the edge of the clearing. The stars were sharper and brighter than he remembered having seen—there was always some haze over the city, from the breweries and factories, steamboats and train engines. Even out at Mound Farm, the few times it had occurred to him to look at the stars, there had been river mist or stove smoke faintly hazing the sky, and always some points or washes of light to adulterate the dominion of the stars.

Here there was no light, now that the fire was out, no haze—probably even less air for the starlight to pass through, since he was a thousand or so feet higher than the city or, in fact, than any place he had ever been before. The stars were impersonal, almost fierce in their intensity. He used up his entire store of astronomical knowledge in locating the Big and Little Dippers and the North Star, and was struck by the notion that Norland would have had to learn to read the stars like a railroad map in order to find his way across the prairie and through the mountains. Could I do that? he wondered, and then wondered why he wondered. One thing a lawyer and businessman doesn't need to know is how to navigate the wilderness.

The fog was so thick that Brandon saw the protruding tree root only as the toe of his left boot vanished under it; then it caught him across the ankle like a blow from a club, and the momentum of his stride pitched him forward into a tangle of brush that held him for a heartbeat, then parted to fling him down a rocky slope.

Arms crossed in front of his head protected his face and took the force of the rocks that seemed to spring out and hammer or slash at him as he slid and rolled downward. His sprawling body slammed into a tree and bent around it like a horseshoe, squeezing the last breath out of him in a jabbering grunt.

Brandon pulled himself away from the tree and lay as comfortably as he could on the uneven ground. His left foot throbbed somewhat more noticeably than the rest of him, and he moved his toes gingerly inside the boot. They seemed to work all right, without any stabbing pains, so there were probably no bones broken. He extended the experiment to the entire foot, rotating it as much as the boot allowed. No problem there, either, so he didn't have a sprained ankle to worry about.

The only problem he faced was that he was completely lost in a fog denser than any he had ever seen, even on the Mississippi. It was not so thick that he could not see his hand in front of his face, as the saying went; but if it got at all far from his face—say at the end of an extended arm—it was a little blurred by the mist, and anything significantly farther away might as well not exist. He suspected that it was a low cloud rather than a fog.

He had awakened at what he supposed to be dawn, though there was no indication of the sun. He seemed to be inside an amorphously shaped room with a pale light radiating from its walls and ceiling so diffusely that nothing cast a definite shadow. He could just see to the edge of the clearing and could make out the blanket-wrapped mound that was Norland on the ground a few feet away from him. A dark mass across the clearing shifted, and he heard a faint whinny: their tethered horses waiting for whatever this day, if that was what it was, would bring.

The half-pot of coffee he had drunk the night before was demanding exit with increasing urgency, and he slid out of his blankets and stood. Sleeping fully dressed was hell on clothes, and some garment edges and folds had made creases in his body he could feel, but he appreciated not having to dig around for something to put on against the dank morning air. He moved to the edge of the clearing, stepped past a couple of trees, and found what seemed to be a suitable place for his needs. He rebuttoned his trousers and walked back to the clearing. After about twenty steps, he realized that he should be right about in the center of the clearing, standing on the ashes of last night's fire; but he was surrounded by trees that he didn't recall having seen before.

He turned about and tried to walk back to where he had stopped but could find no trace that he had been there. He walked more rapidly in what seemed to him must be the right direction, as it wasn't one he had taken before. A branch raked his face, just missing his eyes, and he recalled Norland's tale of being lured through the entangling forest by a Siren's soft call. Maybe it would work the other way. He cleared his throat and called out, "Norland!"

The fog around him seemed to soak up the sound. He called louder, then louder again, a full-throated cry that slurred the syllables of the name into a single urgent shout. He could almost sense the waves of sound slowing as they encountered the fog, finally stopping like a train drifting into the bumpers at the end of a spur.

Brandon was in the center of an egg-shaped chamber of luminous gray that moved with him as he walked, then scrambled over the tangled forest floor. Branches and vines and tree trunks reached into the room, then withdrew as he moved past them. At one moment he was sure he should stay where he was until the fog lifted and he could see to find his way back to Norland and the clearing; at another he was sure that if he moved quickly enough and changed directions often enough, he would be bound to find his way back.

The fall down the slope after he tripped on the tree root shocked him out of the frenzy that had come over him, and he rested for a moment, considering his situation. By now he was probably far from the clearing and thoroughly lost. If he went steadily down, he would find his way to a river that led out of the mountains and eventually to the Mississippi, though he would certainly encounter civilization before then. Without a horse and unused to the woods, this would take days at least, and he would stand a good chance of injury or an unpropitious encounter with a bear or a "painter" or a copperhead.

He could, instead, follow the slope of the land upward until he found what seemed to be its highest point. The camp was on a ridge, so that, once the high point was found, he had an even chance of picking the right direction to look for it. That presented better odds than the first choice, but still not very good ones.

"Without the facts, Counselor, you don't have a case," Brandon said aloud into the muffling mist. "No basis for decision. Ergo, await more facts. Let time produce said facts, and we will weigh them and decide on our plea. Stay absolutely here until the fog lifts and I can see my way back, the way I should have done as soon as I saw I wasn't where I thought. Come one, come all, this rock shall fly/From its firm base as soon as I." The unbidden quotation made him aware that he was feeling distinctly light-headed, a natural result of what seemed like quite a long time of frantic exertion on an empty stomach.

He looked around in the limited area of vision allowed him by the fog for something edible—berries, for preference, though he had a general recollection that they didn't appear in the grocer's until early summer, so presumably didn't grow in the wilds as early as this.

Under a tree he saw something that looked like a spring onion, and he thought he recognized it as one of the plants that Norland had put in the pot last night. He pulled it from the ground, brushed the soil off the white, bulbous end, and chewed it tentatively. It had a mildly onion flavor, with a touch of grass, and sent satisfying signals to his appetite. He followed it with several more, then looked around for something to add variety to his breakfast salad.

A leafy plant growing in a damp spot near a tree also seemed familiar; he remembered the tiny purple flowers with yellow centers that Norland had pointed out. Thinking it had been one of the spice herbs, he plucked a few leaves. He chewed these, finding them undistinguished in taste, and swallowed the masticated pulp. The fresh head of a dandelion caught his eye, and he recalled Norland's encomiums for this useful plant: the medical properties and culinary virtue of the leaves, and the ability of the root to serve as an edible tuber or, roasted and ground, as a remarkably bad substitute for coffee.

He levered the whole plant out of the ground, digging around it with a stick, and cleaned off the root, which looked like a starved turnip, as best he could. He broke off a piece and chewed it fine; it was bitter, but his complaining stomach received it and ordered more.

With something—if by no means enough—inside him, Brandon felt more at ease, and he leaned against a tree to rest and await what the day would bring. To his surprise, his eyes closed almost immediately, and he drifted into sleep.

When he opened his eyes it was with a sudden sharp snap, as if a curtain had been pulled from in front of a picture painted in minute detail and the whole of it was imprinted on his vision at once. Shadows of trees, sharp at the base, at the top fuzzed with new leaves, lay across the ground, and between the trees, the structure of their bark displayed in minute detail by the probing sun, he saw a vivid blue sky that seemed to pulse with its own life.

The scent of the woods, of plants and creatures that had lived and died there, was sharp in his nostrils, and it seemed to him that he could hear the forest's inhabitants moving through it, the trees gesturing quietly in the light breeze.

He saw, neatly positioned between the vee of his outstretched boots, a fat coil of glistening patterned rope perhaps five feet away from him. A wide, wedge-shaped head rested on the coil, jewel eyes looking at him, red cavern of mouth widening to show curved white needles.

I will get a forked stick and catch it right behind the head and hold it down and kill it, Brandon said with complete certainty, though he was not sure if he spoke aloud. He rose to his feet to look for the right kind of stick, and the snake uncoiled and undulated away into the brush, buzzing derisively with its rattles.

In a cold killing rage, Brandon followed. If he caught up with it before finding the right kind of forked stick, then he would do the job barehanded or with a rock.

The snake led him to the edge of a cliff, then slid out of sight into a crevice in the rockwall next to the cliff. Brandon grabbed but caught only a dried rattle, which pulled off easily.

He looked over the edge of the cliff and down to a grassy area about ten feet below. A fawn, so young that it was still unsteady on its legs, was investigating the new grass and flowers. Brandon's breath caught in his throat as he watched. From behind a bush a streak of yellow flowed, bowling over the fawn; with a gobbling growl, the cougar ripped out its throat and began tearing at the carcass.

Brandon gave a yell of horror and rage and recklessly dropped over the cliff, landed hard, rebounded, and dove for the predator. The cougar snarled, backed away from its kill, and retreated into the woods. Brandon saw that the view from this place took in an immense expanse, and he was sure he would be able to find the clearing he had left that morning; but following the cougar was the thing he had to do.

He entered the woods again, acutely aware that the animal might have climbed a tree and was waiting to ambush him; but he saw fragments of its yellow coat appearing and disappearing among the trees ahead. When he lost sight of it, its rank scent clinging to brush and grass guided him.

A sudden whirring of many wings behind him chilled him with a sudden horror as he envisaged a flotilla of huge moths pursuing him; but what flew over him was a flock of small birds, vivid red and green, curve-beaked like tiny parrots. Brandon had an uneasy intimation of unreality, but he dismissed it as he followed the cougar's trail.

He came suddenly face to face with it, as it turned and crouched to spring at him—then it snarled with rage and fled away between the trees and was lost to his sight. Brandon turned slowly to see what had frightened it.

The bear, standing upright and looking down on him, was half again his height. A wave of body heat and a smell of sweat, musk, and rot washed over Brandon. *It'll kill me or I'll kill it, maybe both,* Brandon said. Beyond the bear he could see the curiously vibrant sky and the crests of hills and mountains stretching away under the sun, but the bear was the only thing that concerned him now. Brandon blinked, and what stood before him was the ten-foot-tall stump of an ancient tree, as wide around as a barrel. Had the bear been a trick of his vision? Then its reek came to him again, and he whirled. It was on all fours now, but still seemingly almost as tall as he, eyes red sparks in the huge, shaggy head, mouth lolling open and the bright tongue sliding out.

The bear bunched its muscles and charged; Brandon slipped to one side and drove a sharpened stick he found he was holding hard at the back of its neck. The bear howled, aimed a swipe at his chest with a wide, clawed paw, and vanished into the trees. Brandon saw with detached interest that the blow had stripped away cloth and flesh, leaving white bone to shine through at his chest before the tide of blood covered it. Curious that it didn't hurt, but it surely would soon.

He set out to track the fleeing bear and followed the trail upward and to an opening in the trees. From there he could see the ridge curving around to the west, the tree cover broken by rocky open spaces. From one of these, about half a mile off, smoke rose, and he could see with microscopic clarity two horses and a crouching human figure. As he watched, the man rose and pointed upward what looked like a stick. A brief light winked at its end, and a cloud of smoke puffed above it; two or three seconds later, a flat cracking sound reached Brandon.

Norland and the camp, and not all that far away. The bear was headed in that direction, so if he kept after it, he would soon enough get to the camp and get his gun and kill the bear.

Even as it formed in his mind, the thought began to break up and fade. He was not surprised, looking down, to see his jacket still whole, if somewhat slit and battered by the rocks, and no evidence of injury to his chest. He shook his head and took a deep breath and started to make his way along the ridge. The sky was still now, and a familiar pale blue, not the garish electric hue he had seen earlier.

"Don't need t' tell you that plant wasn't no pot yarb ner blood tonic neither, I guess," Norland said. "Them purple flowers is unmistakable. Tolt you yestiddy them's one of the yarbs the Injuns use to git theirselfs their medicine visions; lets 'em see what their tale's to be."

"Powerful stuff," Brandon said, sipping the coffee that was Norland's approximation of the Universal Antidote. "I really believed what I saw was real—most of the time, anyhow. But one of the hallucinations was a flock of miniature parrots, looked like flying Christmas trees, and I kind of suspected then that I maybe wasn't in my right mind."

"Huh," Norland said. "That'd be the one thing you *did* see. Not so many of 'em as forty year ago, but there's still a sight of them little parakeets a-flyin' through the forest here. There's b'ar and painter and sarpints, too, but the ones you seen didn't ack like the real thing, and you can bet all yer plunder that ef a b'ar like that 'n had clawn you acrost the chest, you'd be showin' of yer ribs still."

Brandon looked at the black surface of his coffee and the dim, distorted reflection of his face in it. Those hallucinations didn't come out of nowhere. Whatever poison I gave myself, *I* imagined those beasts, and *I* felt what I felt, that I had to chase and kill them. Easy enough to see where that came from . . .

"Now," Norland said, "what come to you through that yarb, that was powerful medicine, wagh! It might could be that you should be a-studyin' out of what it means, and what it's a sign fer you to be a-doin' of."

"If I were an Indian," Brandon said, "it'd be a sign that I'm meant to find the men that killed my wife and the others and kill them. If I were an Indian, I'd also be being chewed up, killed, and swindled by the whites. I will trade the prophetic visions for a spot somewhere toward the top of the ladder, I think."

"So, so," Norland said. "Civ'lization's a wondrous thing, so it is. Teaches you to let all the old bad things go an' move ahead into the New Jerusalem, whereat the lion lies down upon the lamb and all. A great thing, not to have to count coup for your dead; considerable savin' in time and trouble."

With some effort, Brandon managed not to resent the satirically sugary note of the old man's voice. After all, whatever the tone, what he said was no more than the truth.

He looked at the clumps of hair and hide woven into the seams of Norland's leggings. That's the satisfaction you get out of hunting down your enemies: carrion mementos. However weak the law is, it's more lasting than that, and it's what's woven into my life—law and reason, not revenge, shame, sorrow.

And I don't need to escape, either. That poison bottled up inside me, maybe that's what's been making everything so flat, stale, and unprofitable. Now that boil's lanced, maybe I can get back to the life I know, get back to the office—Tommy Walt'll be glad enough of it, God knows!—even see if there's something to come with Krista.

The elation he felt at dropping the load of frozen apathy

he had carried for more than half a year dimmed a little when he saw the next step he would have to take. Mound Farm would have to be set in order—probably to sell, since it would never again be a place for summer living or family outings, even if he should, like Job, acquire another family. It would be possible to put the whole matter in the hands of an agent, never go near the place again. But then it would always have a horrible power over him, would be a place too dreadful to be faced. He would have to go there, revisit the scene of carnage, then let it fall into his past with the rest.

He had to do it, and he would be nearer whole when it was done. *But oh, God, I'll dread doing it alone. Okay, that's why I have to do it fast. First thing after I get back to St. Louis . . .*

"Been thinkin', Brandon," Norland said. "B'lieve we've seen these mountains enough fer this go. You ain't goin' t' git a more powerful entertainment out of 'em than what you got today, and it may be that you could take the rest of this 'scursion a mite less strenuous. These horses, they'll fotch as good a price in St. Louis as in Pilot Knob, and it's only a couple days' easy ride there from here, so I'm proposin' we git on down out of the mountains first thing termorrer and then mosey on to St. Louis, admirin' the countryside and a-purchasin' of cooked meals and night's lodgin's whenas we fancy."

"I concur in your decision, Brother Norland," Brandon said lightly, "and I'm prepared to write a supporting opinion. Don't believe a superior court'll reverse it."

Norland's points were good ones. But the convincer for Brandon was that Mound Farm lay only half an hour's ride off the main road back to St. Louis. He would be able to make the visit he had to sooner than he had expected—and he would have the support of a companion. Even if a pretty odd one.

"Nobody's been there since I had the stock sold off in the fall," Brandon said, "and I never did anything about having the fire damage cleared up. Maybe we can sleep in a barn or such, though another night outside won't harm us, especially one like this." A three-quarter moon not far above the tree-rimmed horizon dimmed the stars and picked out the shapes of trees and fences, and the occasional distant, sleeping farmhouse in faded tones of black, gray, and silver. It looked like the recognizable but transformed and muted image on the glass plate of a photographic negative.

The night was warm, and both men wore their jackets open as they rode side by side down the road the moonlight misrepresented as a white ribbon. Everything was different from that October night Brandon had last traveled this road, and riding this last stretch before the rise overlooking Mound Farm had not haunted him as he had thought it might.

Norland said, "I done some trappin' oncet, over t' the Sweetwater, and when I was leavin', I seen by a split rock there that 'twas a place whereat some Piegans ambushed me and some other fellers, years gone, and took the other fellers' hair, and put some arrers inter me, which that was as close as this child has yit come to bein' rubbed out, as the Injuns say. But when I was thar ag'in, it wasn't but a place, same as any other. Was a sight of beaver thar, but nothin' elst."

When Brandon had explained his reasons for detouring to Mound Farm on their return trip, Norland had made no secret of his opinion that the idea was not a good one, but had raised no objection to accompanying Brandon if he were set on it. Brandon supposed this random fragment of reminiscence was an oblique comment on the pointlessness of the side trip—with any luck, the final one.

The road tilted upward for a hundred-some yards, then leveled at the top of the rise. The fields of Mound Farm, furred with a carpet of weeds, stretched before them to a jumble of forms at the edge of their vision, the moonlight's tactful concealment of the ruins of the farmhouse and outbuildings.

"Wagh!" Instead of an expressive bark, Norland's signature exclamation came in a soft exhalation. He reached over and tugged on Brandon's reins, bringing his mount to a halt.

"What?" Brandon said.

"Lastest buildin' on th' left, outside edge of it," Norland said in a quiet mutter. "Suthin' movin'."

Brandon stared into the deceiving semidark and thought he detected some shifting in the blackness.

"Might could be a deer er some varmint," Norland said, "but if I puts a horse in thar, it fits that shadder better 'n anything elst."

"And deer don't look around buildings with a lantern," Brandon said. A point of light had sprung briefly into being in the central block of darkness that was the farmhouse, then winked out.

"That they don't." Norland looked calculatingly at the moon, now almost down. "Be full dark in a while, but I misdoubt we'd want ter wait fer that—that feller might be gone by then. We're lit up like opry singers here, so let's ease over t' that field and that line o' trees at the edge and move on down t' the house that way."

Brandon looked questioningly at Norland's dim shape. The shadowy movement and the light indicated the presence of an intruder; of that he was satisfied. The next thing was to consider what to do about it, but Norland seemed to be moving into action without letting thought enter into the decision. Yet reflection probably wouldn't come up with any better course. Who was prowling the ruins of Mound Farm and why were questions that would have to be answered, and he and Norland were the only ones around to extract those answers. "The trees'll take us to a fence at the other side of the house from the stable," he said. "We can hitch the horses there and do the rest of the way on foot."

It took them ten minutes of careful riding to pick their way along the woodlot, keeping to overgrown ground to avoid the chance ring of a horseshoe on stone; then they were at the fence corner, with the misshapen outline of the roofless house black against the sky, in which the stars were reasserting themselves as the light of the just-set moon faded. A faint yellow rectangle broke the mass of the farmhouse, lanternlight washing over an interior wall.

Brandon eased himself to the ground and dropped his

horse's reins over the corner post. Norland appeared next to him and touched his shoulder. Brandon looked around, and Norland gestured briefly with the rifle he held. Brandon nodded and slipped his own weapon from where it was lashed to his saddlebags. The lawyer in him questioned the need for arming two men to investigate a possibly innocuous prowler, but the night and the situation seemed to have their own logic, and it was more pressing: You don't go anywhere without being ready to deal with anything that might be waiting for you. If the last tenants of Mound Farm had been armed, the outcome might have been different.

Norland moved toward the house. Brandon followed, imitating the trapper's crouched walk and twisted course that took advantage of the random cover the farmyard provided—the pumphouse, a handcart, a few empty crates—to conceal their movement as much as possible from any watcher. Brandon's war service had been office-bound, but it seemed curiously natural and familiar to him to be on what was essentially a night combat patrol—natural, familiar, and curiously exciting as well.

Norland waited for Brandon in the shadow of the cart and drew him close. "Door," he said, not whispering the word but letting it coast on an outgoing breath.

Brandon, knowing from experience that a whisper could reach the farthest point in a courtroom—too often the ear of a judge who was not meant to hear the comment—replied in the same manner. "Back. Around left. Porch at front door—boards could creak."

Norland's shadow shrank into the night as he moved away. Brandon followed, testing the ground with each foot before setting it down firmly. Now was not the time to trip on something or kick a clattering metallic object.

An oblong of light picked out a field of debris and charred wood at the back of the house. The back door, leading to the kitchen, was either wide open or had perished in the fire; and from the size of the long axis of the oblong, Brandon calculated that the intruder must have hung his lantern from a ceiling beam that had survived the burning of the roof, probably from one of the hooks the largest cooking pots had been suspended from. A shadow briefly rippled the light. The line of the edge of the open doorway sprouted a knoblike growth, then was straight again as Norland retreated from his quick look inside and moved back to where Brandon waited.

"One feller," he breathed. "Ritchin' and rootin' around the farplace, looks like. He don't move er ack like somebody that's got company nearby." Brandon first took this for nonsense, then realized that it wasn't: In subtle ways, you behaved differently when you believed you were alone from the way you did when you knew there was someone near, even in another room. That would be the kind of thing someone living Norland's life would have to learn quickly if he was going to keep his scalp. "So I'll go in and quieten him whiles as you cover me."

Brandon and Norland moved to the edge of the doorway and each eased an eye to take in the interior. The kitchen had not been fully burned out, like most of the rest of the house, and a table and a couple of chairs stood amid the charred rubbish, and a lantern hung, as Brandon had figured, from a hook in the still-intact ceiling beam.

A crouched figure moved away from the fireplace that had served as the baking and roasting oven and bent to lift the lid of the woodbox next to the iron stove. This move turned the intruder's back to the doorway, and Norland dove silently across the room with the lethal grace of a weasel, seemed to flow up the man's back, and bore him to the floor with a thump that raised dust from every surface. His victim gave the beginning of a yell and the start of a convulsive threshing of his arms and legs, but both stopped as Norland gave a precise hand-edge chop to the back of his neck.

Brandon stepped into the room, pointing his rifle at the limp, sprawled form Norland was arising from, though it seemed a needless precaution. The roughly dressed man facedown on the floor seemed paralyzed, if not dead. Brandon considered that the crowd at Hanratty's had been luckier than they knew; evidently Norland had only been toying with them. Now that they had dealt with the prowler so successfully, Brandon felt a sudden unease. If this were a neighboring farmer looking in for some innocent reason, or any number of other blameless people who now seemed to have a possible existence, he and Norland would have some awkward questions to answer.

"We can invite this child t' explain hisself in a few minutes," Norland said. "That rabbit punch puts you out deep but short, onless it kills you outright. Takes some practice to git it down pat, but I does it right—*most* of the time. Lessee whatso he looks like in his beauty sleep." He grabbed the unconscious man's shoulders and wrenched them over. The lower body followed partway, leaving a hip pointing awkwardly at the ceiling and booted feet tangled with each other; the head flopped around, bringing the blank face into the dim light of the lantern.

"No beauty, though," Norland said, "so the sleep ain't done him much good. Got the featurin's of a triple-dyed bummer, anything from a horse thief to a back-shooter, I'd say."

"Not in the eyes of the State of Missouri," Brandon said harshly. "Been duly tried and acquitted, and discharged without a stain on his character. That's the one I told you about, the one they caught and had to let go when he got lied out of it. Casmire."

6

I seen the place was deserted and I needed summeres to sleep, so I come in here," Casmire said. "Din't mean no harm." He flexed his shoulders, but the rope that lashed him to the chairback held him firmly; his legs were tightly bound to the chair's.

"You didn't have no call to jump me," he went on, giving Norland and Brandon a pained look. "Not as if there was anything here worth fightin' over," he added, with completely unconvincing firmness. "Mebbe a few kickshaws as didn't burn with the rest of the place, but if'n you come across such, take 'em and welcome. I am on my way through here, just like you are, and we don't have any cause to frument no quarrels atwixt us. I appreciate you want to act cautious in comin' to a new place, and I hold no grudge fer what's done, but it'd be good sense to cut me loose of these ropes and bunk in fer the night. If you fellers has a mind to use the house, I don't mind the stables or the barn."

Norland chuckled with a mad glee that even Brandon found chilling. He realized that Casmire had not recognized him in the dim light and took him and Norland for hardcases like himself.

"Or," Casmire said huskily when Norland's horrid cackle

had died away, "I could get on my way west right now. Dead of night's a good time to travel; horse don't tire so fast. Be gone soon's you untie me," he finished, speaking with a forced hopefulness.

"Goin' west, be ye?" Norland shrilled. "T' steal a year's pelts from honest trappers, I'll warrant! This child's had the hair off'n two hand-counts o' varmints like such, and yours is next, so I swears and affirms!" The lanternlight, faint though it was, flashed impressively off the wide six-inch blade of the knife he flourished close to Casmire's face. Casmire could not see, as Brandon did, the quick contraction of Norland's right eye.

Brandon picked up the cue. "Don't talk crazy, Seth," he said. "This fellow's no fur pirate, just a traveler looking for a place to lay his head for the night."

"That's right," Casmire said eagerly. "Heading over to Dysart, in Kansas; got a chance of a good job there."

"I know that kind o' good job," Norland said. "Garrotin' honest trappers and hunters fer their pokes! Comin' at 'em from behind and twistin' a rope around their necks like as *this."*

"Nonononono," Casmire said, twisting as much as his bonds would allow in his attempts to evade Norland's demonstration of the garroter's craft. "Straight work. Cows and that."

"Stop that, Seth," Brandon said. "We got no quarrel with honest cowmen." Norland stepped back from behind Casmire's chair and grinned wickedly at Brandon.

"Nor you ain't," Casmire said. "I am pushing to get on out there soon, account I was s'posed to be there a couple weeks already, but I was on a ship as had to be refitted some and was late makin' port. Just hope I ain't missed the chance. Be some good pickings, place like that."

"You have friends out there, looking out to help you?" Brandon said. It may have been that the false amiability of the tone struck a chord in Casmire's memory, or that the play of light brought Brandon's features into an alignment that he remembered from the St. Louis courtroom.

"Oh, Jesus!" he said. "You're, uh . . ." He stared around,

experiencing the singular awkwardness of failing to remember the name of the man who had tried to kill him for participating in the massacre of his family. "This is your . . ."

"Cole Brandon," Brandon said coldly. "And since you know that, know that this is my farm, you've been here before, no matter what those lying storekeepers told the court. You were with Gren Kenneally."

"No!" Casmire said desperately; then, after a moment's thought showed him the futility of denial: "Well, yeah. But I didn't—that was Gren and some of the others; me and the rest, we just wanted to get away. It was Gren figured that the fire and the . . . that that would delay us gettin' chased, give the lawmen too much to handle all at once. That weren't no part of what I got into it for."

"Jist train robbery and murder," Norland said.

"Well . . . it ain't the same thing, you know? A man may be in the robbin' line and do what that calls for, but there ain't no call to burn houses or hurt folks that ain't involved." Brandon remembered the farmer's testimony at the trial that Casmire had ridden with Gren Kenneally's guerrillas during the war, with the main mission of burning houses and hurting people who weren't involved. He might or might not have participated in the slaughter of Elise and the others, but he was cut out for it, and his protestations were a futile sham.

"What are you gonna do with me?" Casmire asked.

"Take you to the nearest lockup." Both Norland and Casmire looked at Brandon with surprise, mixed in one with disgust, in the other with relief. "He's the law's to deal with from here on," he felt compelled to explain to Norland. "His presence here is grounds to reopen the case, and there's plenty he was never charged with last time, so double jeopardy isn't a problem. Main thing, if he's nailed for it, the police and the railroad detectives should be able to sweat information about how to get after the Kenneallys out of him."

"Hey, I ain't gonna tell any more—tell you anything like that!" Casmire said vehemently. "I don't know nothin' about where Gren Kenneally is anyways, and I wouldn't rat on the other fellers, no matter what the police does."

"Then you and me can have us a chat whiles we ride t' the *calabozo,"* Norland said unctuously. "I will tell you some interestin' facks about what the Piegan women does to a feller that has information they wants and ain't forthcomin' about it, and then I will tell you what the Nez Percé women does, and you c'n decide which you druther have tried on you. Then we c'n go back and c'nsider what yer duty to yer feller polecats really is."

Brandon noted two points from Casmire's protest: The retracted "any more" showed that he had let something drop about the gang's whereabouts; and "the other fellers" seemed to set Gren Kenneally apart from the group Casmire would not betray. And there was something a good deal more immediate.

"What were you looking for? Not shelter, that won't wash—we saw you hunting for something in here. What was it?"

Casmire sat mute.

"Heydee," Norland said. "B'lieve our trussed turkey yere cherishes th' notion of givin' us th' slip and comin' back here betimes t' pick up his pretties. How vain is the delusions of the infidel and sinner, like the preacher says."

"What would someone like this be after?" Brandon said.

"Not no lockets with a edifyin' sentiment wrote inside, er a favorite old pipe," Norland said, affecting deep thought. "Why, by thunder, cash! Legal tender fer debts public and privates—that's the only thing as'd prompt a feller like this t' break and enter."

"Agreed," Brandon said. "And, since it came from the train, what would that cash be in?"

"A bag." The rapid exchange had the quality of a grim game. "Canvas likely, maybe leather. How big?"

Brandon sketched with his hands a shape with the volume of about three loaves of bread. "About so."

"Big enough t' fit . . ." Norland looked around the kitchen, at the disarranged fireplace and its debris-masked brick facing.

Brandon pushed some rubble away from the brick and pulled open a dusty iron door set into it. "Here. Nicely preserved in the bread oven." He hefted a substantial canvas bag, secured at the top with a hasp and padlock.

The sight seemed to instill in Casmire a sudden frenzy, and he rocked the chair as he strained against his bonds. "Damn, damn, damn," he muttered.

"You left this in there t' see if it'd rise like sourdough bread er suthin'?" Norland asked. "Come back t' see if 'twas done yit?"

Casmire glared at them. "Wasn't me put it there," he said bitterly. "Gren done it. Didn't get to see just where he stuck it, or I'd'a been outta here before you fellows showed up."

According to Casmire, as the arrangements were being made for the gang's breakout after dark, the outlaw leader was alone in the kitchen with the loot from the train, dividing it into portions for each man to carry on their flight. Casmire, going about his assignment—splashing coal oil around to assure a quick conflagration when the place was torched, Brandon supposed—passed by the kitchen window and saw his chief at work. As Casmire watched, Kenneally looked around and swiftly slid one of the larger bags of coin and currency off the table, then moved out of Casmire's field of vision for a moment before returning to his seat at the table and the task of dividing the depleted loot with pedantic fairness.

"Clear to me he figgered it wouldn't be missed in the sharin' out, and he could double back when things was quiet and scoop it up," Casmire said.

"You didn't tell the others they were being cheated?" Brandon asked.

"Not the time for it, and not the man," Casmire said. "We had to break out soon and ride for our lives, and cheatin' or not, Gren was the onliest one could see us through. Also, the man that wants to complain about Gren Kenneally's doin's to his face had best see that Gren is lashed to a keg of gunpowder with a short fuse and a lit match ready before he tries it. Say 'You done such and so wrong, Gren,' then light the fuse and run for it, and jist *maybe* he won't find his way out of it and eat your tripes for breakfast. I wouldn't bet above thirty cents on yer chances, though."

He looked glumly at the open oven door. "I was close to sure Gren'd have been by to git this by now, but I guess I was lucky. Some ways," he added, after a pause for reflection. "Maybe what I heard's true—he hit out for California, stayin' there till it come time for the shareout. And when that's done, he'll drift on back here to get the extry."

"This shareout," Brandon said. "It's to be in this Dysart place you're headed for, and soon." Even though Warner was months off the case, he would be glad to have it reopened if there was a chance of taking some of the gang members in the act of sharing the loot.

"What? Oh, thass rich," Casmire said. "You thought—no, no, I have give up on expecting anything from that job, which it'd be bad luck to touch such money. Cowpunching, thass what I'm bound for Dysart to do, upon my soul and true honor."

He looked wistfully at the money bag, seeming to forget that he had condemned all the loot from the train as ill-omened, then brightened slightly. "Now, you fellows has the gelt, fair enough. But I know you has it, see, and while it ain't in my nature to confide in the law, I don't know as I wouldn't let somethin' slip when they was questionin' me. So how about you let me go, with maybe a double eagle or so for provisions, and split the takin's atween you without nobody the wiser?"

Brandon looked at him blankly. "That goes back where you stole it from—to the railroad."

Casmire's face sagged with dismay. The bloodthirsty old lunatic had been bad enough, but Brandon's intentions for the money went beyond the border of everyday madness, coming close to undermining the principles of the universe, as Casmire understood it.

"We better git a move on, then," Norland said. "If the jail's in that last town we passed through, we got a hour's ride thar, and later it gits, harder it'll be to find someone inter'sted in lodgin' this 'un in th' lockup." He knelt in front of Casmire and picked with his knifepoint at the knot securing the rope that bound the captive's legs.

As they fell away, Casmire straightened both legs with devastating swiftness, both boot toes catching Norland under the chin and flinging him backward. The ropes around his upper body whirled away in a loose tangled spiral as his arms rose from his sides like the flexing of a vulture's wings.

Pebbles of fragmented thoughts tumbled in the current of Brandon's mind: *Twisting in chair . . . at sea months, knows knots . . . KNIFE!*

Casmire lunged from the chair, snatched Norland's knife from the floor and brought it up in a long sweep meant to slice Brandon open from navel to breastbone. With a sureness that would have surprised him if he had been operating on a rational level, Brandon sidestepped, picked up his carbine from the table, and, like Norland shooting the grouse that first night in the mountains, fired without consciously taking aim.

Casmire's rush had taken him just past Brandon, and he had checked himself and begun to turn, bringing the knife around in another deadly sweep, when the slug took him just above the jaw. The sharp slam of the shot, painfully loud in the room, more than the blue spot that sprang up on his face, seemed to shove Casmire back against the wall, sprawling against it, then sliding down, as the knife clattered on the floor.

Brandon looked at the dead man staring blindly at the ceiling. He felt the carbine, the metal of the trigger and guard warm from his hands, and the barrel, hot from the passage of the exploding gas and bullet. He smelled the acrid tang of gunpowder and, he thought, the unpleasantly rich scent of fresh blood, though it was probably too soon for it to reach him from where red was pooling under Casmire's head.

He took a deep breath and felt the rush of air over teeth and tongue. The awareness of a strange tension around his cheeks and eyes made him realize that he was smiling broadly, openmouthed, down upon the man he had killed.

Norland twisted and sat upright, looking at Brandon. "You meant it to go by the law's way," he said, "but that 'un wouldn't have it so. You got one of 'em, and you c'd lift his hair, if that was yer inklingnation. So . . . that ends it fer you?"

The hours of delirium on the mountain came vividly back to Brandon, and he saw himself once again pursuing the predators, the snake, the murderous cougar, the nightmare-huge bear. Norland had said it was big medicine, and so it was. . . . The hallucinations of the animals he had tracked seemed to merge with the motionless figure on the floor, and neither the reality nor the illusion roused either fear or pity, only a deep spark of purpose.

"That begins it," he said.

7

The spade hit something that gave a metallic clink rather than the dull knock of the stones it had so far encountered. Brandon reached down and felt at the face of the spade, picked up the irregular object his fingers found, and slipped it into his pocket. Though the stars were bright now that the moon was well down, their light was not strong enough to show any detail, and whatever it was he had found would have to wait for inspection.

He could easily make out Norland, digging into the turf top of the Indian mound three feet away from him, but saw less clearly the wrapped bundle stretched out a little distance away. The grass caught what light there was and glimmered palely; a scatter of dark rectangles on it showed where they had laid the chunks of turf they had cut from the surface of the mound before digging Casmire's grave into it.

The idea had been Brandon's, and Norland had received it with surprised respect. The mound was high enough and the place deserted enough so that there was no chance that anyone would see the top before the advancing growth of spring and summer had effaced any traces of disturbance. Deep digging and the sacrifice of their heavy rubberized slickers for use as a nearly air-tight shroud should be adequate to prevent Casmire's remains attracting and being made a display of by carrion feeders.

Only for a moment had the thought been entertained of taking Casmire's body—rather than the living and interrogatable man—to the authorities. "You blame this feller fer massacreein' yer family, you shot off a pistol load at him in open court, and now you bring 'im in dead from yer farm, and with a load of stole money to boot," Norland summarized. "Was I a sheriff er chief of police, I don't know as I'd arrest you right off, but I 'spect I'd come to it after as I'd studied on it some. There is too much that don't set right with law-thinkin' fellers into it."

"You're right," Brandon said, abandoning quite casually the course that would take him in the directions he had followed all his life. The law, his life in St. Louis, the fabric of his past, seemed moment by moment more insubstantial. It seemed to him that he had just been born, or was on the way to being born, in this lamplit room in the company of a wizened antique of a wild man and a fresh corpse. Now that Casmire was dead, he felt nothing against him. For what he had been and for what he had done, Casmire had to be made dead, and so he was. There were more of them that had been and done what Casmire had been and done, and they had to be made dead, too. It was stunningly simple compared to the spidery mazes of the law and the quaking paths through the quicksands of love. Casmire and the Kenneally gang had taken away whatever made Cole Brandon able to live Cole Brandon's life, and what they had left of Cole Brandon would track them and kill them. It made a perfect equation, one of repeating subtraction.

"Any idee who's in thar with 'im?" Norland asked as he and Brandon knelt, easing the turf squares into place and tapping them to as near a seamless join as they could, working by touch alone.

"Old-time Indian chiefs, probably," Brandon said. "We never let anybody dig here, not that many wanted to. Lots of other mounds around here, and all they find is old graves when they dig into them. There's some that claim the mounds were built by people from Egypt or Phoenicia, that came here in Bible times, or by a race we never heard of—they didn't think the Indians were capable of it."

"Injuns can do what they've a mind to," Norland said. He rose to his feet and tamped a turf into place more firmly with his boot. "Run sixty miles in a day, live off the land—if it's desert er if it's snow mountains—whup the U.S. cavalry when the notion takes 'em. Don't see as shovelin' up some heaps o' dirt'd be beyant their powers. Best argument agin it'd be they got too much sense. Whichever, it comes in handy t' have yer own buryin' ground ready and set out fer handy use in case of sudden need, which is what we got."

Back in the kitchen, Norland inspected the spot where Casmire had fallen and kicked some ashes and dust over the dark-brown irregular stain that had caked onto the floorboards. "Visitors ain't likely, but why take a chanst on alarmin' any there might be?"

They sat down, and Brandon relished the easing of a multitude of stressed muscles. Digging, even in soft earth, for the better part of an hour, with an awkwardness caused by the enforced darkness, was an activity his city-gaited body wasn't used to, even after the days in the saddle on this trip—which, he suddenly recalled with grim humor, had been planned as a vacation, to give him a new perspective on life. It had certainly done that, and it was abundantly true that the old cares and concerns no longer bothered him.

The one visible reminder of Casmire was the padlocked canvas bag on the table, and they looked at it in silence for some time.

"Givin' that back t' the railroad persents some of th' same problems as givin' Casmire's carcass to th' law," Norland said finally. "You got to explain how you come by it and where. If you tell 'em here, they'll be out fer a look around, and likely find whatas you wouldn't want 'em to. And if you says you seen it floatin' amongst th' bulrushes in the river, they ain't likely to credit that tale much."

Brandon thought for a minute. He stretched out his hand and said, "Knife."

Norland squinted at him, then reached down, drew the wide-bladed knife from its sheath, and passed it to Brandon.

Brandon jabbed it into the tough canvas, made a long slit in it—just as Casmire had almost made in him, came the fleeting thought—and the contents spilled out in a tumbled heap, paper-wrapped rolls of coins, taped bundles of greenbacks, a few small, fat leather pouches. Norland poked one of these. "Ain't seen such in some while—gold dust. Some banks'll still take that in fer a customer, weigh it, and credit the account, but it's a seldom thing nowadays. This stuff"—he flicked a clawlike nail across a bundle of greenbacks—"is what's the fashion now, and it jist don't seem like true money."

Brandon made a rapid estimated count, hefting the rolls of gold and silver coins and riffling through the bills, a skill he had developed in his early days with the firm—it was very useful to have at least an approximate check on sums of money being transferred to or from a client, to assure that the final verified accounting was not too inventive. "If it was all 'true money,' it wouldn't come near fitting in this bag," he said. "I guess it at about eight thousand dollars, bills and coin together, and if it was all gold coin, it'd be thirty-some pounds—fifty and up if a lot of it was silver."

Norland whistled. "That's a haul and a half, fer sure." So it was, Brandon thought. Gren Kenneally took a damned long chance holding out that much: five years' good wages for a skilled craftsman, one year's profits for a mercantile magnate . . . and ample financing for a long-lasting hunting expedition.

Not since he had negotiated the intricate leasing and property exchange for Ostermann's warehousing facilities, wharfage, and a private spur line that nobody had thought possible had Brandon's mind assessed the factors in a complex situation so rapidly and surely. To do what he had to do, he had to drop out of sight, and under such circumstances that not too many people would start wondering where he was. There was money in the Chicago account Krista had set up, but getting at it would be something to do carefully, not in a rush. Taking a substantial sum out of his St. Louis account would raise just the kind of questions he didn't want to raise. Be a good idea to leave Jim Lunsford with power of attorney to act for him; then people wouldn't feel the inconvenience of his being away and wonder overmuch where "away" was. With the story of a trip to someplace unspecified already put about, his absence would present no problems, aside from financing his travels.

He looked up at Norland. "You're right: There are too many problems about getting it back to the railroad. It's a dead issue now, anyhow—the losses have been taken and made up or not, and it's done with. Whether you want to call it treasure trove or fair capture, it's ours. Half yours, half mine."

Norland shook his head. "I got a sufficiency, and more'd only weight me down. But, lookin' at it, so d'you. . . . I b'lieve as I can read yer sign yere, Brandon. If you're to cut loose to lift the hair off'n Kenneally and his pack, you got to move light, and not trailin' questions, so you leaves yer pelts and yer traps back at the camp and tells the fellers to keep an eye on 'em, and so long's they got the use of 'em, they ain't goin' t' be worryin' overmuch about whenas your return's t' transpirate." Brandon admired Norland's neat summary of the diversionary uses of fiduciary responsibility. "Which then you'll need pervisions and weeponry and what to buy 'em with, which is how you intends to employ theseyer funds. That's an enterprise gits this child's vote, so th' split's all yours, none mine. Wagh!"

Brandon knew better than to protest, and he nodded his thanks. The heaped money caught the yellowing lantern-light, but his imagination tinged it with red. There was blood on it, some six months old, some fresh today. There would be more.

He slouched in the chair, staring at the money, aware that Norland had risen and was wandering about the rubbish-cluttered kitchen, stooping now and then to inspect something and dropping it. It seemed to be the old mountain man's nature to know what there was to know about any place in which he found himself. Brandon's hands were jammed deep in his trouser pockets, and he now felt an unfamiliar cold, hard object in one of them. He fished it out and set it on the table—the bit of metal the spade had hit while he was digging Casmire's grave.

It was a dirt-encrusted oblong about an inch and a half across, something like a thick coin, made of what looked like rusted metal—maybe iron. He scraped some of the dirt from it with Norland's knife, and the blade dug into shiny red metal: tarnished copper, then, not rusted iron. With all the dirt off, he could make out a design on one side that seemed to represent a snake, curved around to swallow its own tail. On the other was an incised picture of some four-legged animal with a pointed snout and bushy tail: a wolf, at a guess.

He held it up to show to Norland, who was returning to the table. "Injun lucky piece er charm," Norland said. "Give us a look." He took it from Brandon's hand and looked at it closely, tracing the sinuous pattern of the snake, then turning it over. He looked from the wolflike figure to Brandon, then back. "Snake that don't let go . . . wolf that hunts till it gits whatas it's after . . . Wagh! Them's a couple critters in the same line of work as you be now, Brandon. Now, when you c'nsider as how some old-timey Injun put it into that mound back before the Flood er when, and it's been thar until as you turnt it up jist now, why, that's strong medicine. It's meant fer you, and you keep it by you, Cole Brandon, an' don't scorn to let it guide you whenas there ain't no other sign."

"Guide me? How?" Brandon asked, amused, taking back the coin and sliding it into his pocket.

"Whenas you need it, you'll know," Ned Norland said. "Now here's another fal-lal I jist picked up from the floor in the other room. Reckernize it?"

He held up what appeared to be a thick-stemmed dried flower. A closer look showed Brandon that it was a twig, the end of which had been artfully shaved and curled to imitate a mass of petals.

"No. Never seen anything like that before." Norland nodded. He had not had to ask directly, nor Brandon answer directly, if any among his murdered family and help had amused themselves with this sort of whittling, but the answer was there.

"Not fresh by a long ways, so not Casmire," Norland said. "Without you been entertainin' wanderin' flower whittlers unawares over the winter, we got to take it that this posy is th' pastime of one of the Kenneally bunch whenas there ain't no robbin' and what to see to." He tossed the wooden flower to Brandon. "Do well to keep that by you, too. Any luck, you c'n use it fer a grave marker fer one of 'em."

It was close to noon when they reached the outskirts of St. Louis the next day, at the southern end of the waterfront. They halted their horses and looked ahead. To the right was the forest of masts, sails, and stacks clustered around the docks; to the left the offices, factories, theaters, public buildings, and houses of the sprawling city.

Norland gestured toward the river. "Me fer Crockett County and th' warm welcome of lovin' fambly. And you?"

Brandon shrugged. "Wind up my affairs, then head off west. Casmire near as anything told us he expected to meet the others in Kansas—Dysart—to split the loot. I don't count on that, as it's been six months and he's been away from where he'd get news, but I'll get on to Kansas and sniff around. Not much but better than nothing."

"May see you ag'in, may not," Norland said. "Luck with what you got to do."

"Thanks," Brandon said. He touched his hat brim and turned his horse toward the church steeple that marked the street his house stood on. It wasn't much of a farewell, though the best he could come up with, to a man who had probably changed his life more than any other. Except Gren Kenneally.

Dear Krista:

As you know, I have been planning an extended course of traveling for some time, and I have taken the sudden decision to embark upon it today. I feel that an unobtrusive parting is best, so I am leaving without formal farewells, for which this letter must substitute. I look forward to my eventual return to St. Louis, if that is to be.

In my absence, the duration of which I cannot now estimate, the arrangements you kindly suggested for the payments of the income from Elise's share of the Ostermann interests to the Chicago bank should continue until further notice.

In closing, dear Krista, let me assure you of my continued regard and of my hopes that in the fullness of time we may resume our familial and friendly connections.

Very sincerely yours,
Cole Brandon

Brandon carefully slid the letter into the copying book and closed it gently. He opened the book and retrieved the letter, checking that the mirror-image was preserved on the thin sheet of blotting paper. It was a cumbersome way of keeping records of correspondence but an advance over having to have a fair copy made by hand of every letter and document.

The letter was fish-cold, no doubt about it, but it was a business document as much as a social one, and would probably be read by eyes other than Krista's. She would know that, and would read between the lines for whatever meaning was hidden there. Brandon himself was unsure what that might be, but aware that he was making an attempt at leaving a doorway open—to be entered "in the fullness of time" or not, as it would turn out.

Like Krista's, the other letters he had written to those who would deal with his affairs made no mention of where he would be or for how long. There would be a stir in the office when the sealed, addressed envelopes were found on his desk in the morning—he had told no one of his return to St. Louis and had come down to the deserted office well after dark—but not enough of one to arouse any interest in looking into his whereabouts. There would be enough to do in arranging to carry out his instructions.

Brandon looked at his watch. The fast packet for Leavenworth was leaving at eleven, and it was ten now; plenty of time to make it, but he should be getting ready to walk to the wharf. Rather than taking the train up to the Kansas Pacific, which he had selected as the most likely line to try in picking up the elusive scent he sought, he had chosen to make the first leg of the journey by river. He was known to too many train crewmen from trips to Chicago, and even if he were not sought after, a chance mention that Attorney Brandon had been seen heading north and west on the cars would conflict with his carefully vague mention of a trip east.

From the stern of the packet laboring its way upriver, Brandon looked back at the patches of gaslight glow in the city—mostly around the waterfront, as crews loaded and unloaded cargo far into the night, and the saloons and cribs spilled light into the streets, and, inland a few blocks, the fairylike glow of the lanterns strung over an outdoor beer garden, from which he could hear the faint sounds of a band.

A vertical shadow slid slowly across the scene, blocking it inexorably from Brandon's vision, and he saw that the boat was passing close inshore under the massive concrete abutment of the new bridge. When the last of the city lights were hidden, he turned and looked forward, into the featureless night that stretched ahead.

8

The second day of Kansas looked to be even less interesting than the first, which Brandon would not have thought possible. The afternoon before, heading west from Leavenworth, there had been a variety of towns and comparatively dense settlement, some woods and hills. But now what slid by the car windows was mainly grasslands, hour after hour, unrolling like a giant diorama painted by an artist determined to go on and on depicting prairie until he got it right.

Brandon would have preferred that the train had kept on through the night rather than stopping to afford the passengers the hospitality of a trackside inn; dozing upright in the car seat would have been at least as comfortable as trying to sleep on the cornhusk-stuffed sack the inn had claimed to be a mattress, and he would have been a hundred miles and some nearer his destination by now. If the timetable held, they would get to Dysart by midafternoon.

He could gauge the depth of his boredom with the trip by the fact that he was wishing that the news butcher—the youth who prowled the train selling newspapers, books, candy, food, and a remarkable array of useless sundries with a persistent enthusiasm—would make another appearance. The kid, who looked to be about seventeen, was almost unbearably cheerful and a first-class pest, but his extravagant extolling of the virtues of whatever he had on offer from the tray he carried through the cars at least broke the monotony.

The train slowed and whistled. Brandon opened the window—the wind was drifting the locomotive's cinder-laden smoke to the other side of the train—and looked out at another sunbaked farm town sliding into view. He considered getting out to stretch his legs on the station platform as some of the other passengers were already doing but decided against it. He wasn't particularly comfortable in the seat, but he was used to it by now.

He saw that the young news butcher, for once without the tray supported by a strap around his neck, was making use of the opportunity for an off-train promenade on the station platform. Maybe he relished the feel of solid ground under his feet after hours of walking through the jolting cars. Or perhaps, Brandon thought, he wanted a moment of leisure to check his finances, as he was now bringing out a slender sheaf of bills and fanning them as if to count them.

That this was an imprudent course was demonstrated when a man in dirty overalls who had been leaning against the station wall when the train came in ran at the news butcher, hit him behind the ear with a clubbed fist, snatched the bills, and ran down the platform, leaving his victim reeling and clutching his head.

Brandon leaned halfway out the window, braced his feet under the seat and, as the thief passed beneath him, reached down and grabbed his head with both hands locked under the chin. The man's feet continued running, off the platform and into the air; then he slid out of Brandon's grasp, his body slammed onto the platform, and the bills scattered from his hand.

The news butcher ran to retrieve his money, scooped it up, then darted for the car steps as the train jerked into motion again. The luckless thief stared glassily at the sky and the moving car.

* * *

"I should've known better," the news butcher said. "With the hard times, there's fellows laid off work all over, plus the ones that never did work, and you can get hit on the head or garrotted just about any place out here if you look like you've anything worth taking. That was almighty quick thinking and quick acting, and I thank you for it, Mr. . . . ?

"Brooks," Brandon said. "Charles Brooks." He had not given much thought to an alias, but this would do well enough for the moment. He felt a touch of chilly dizziness; his old life was gone, and now so was his old name.

"I personally am Rush Dailey, and it's my pleasure to offer you this nearly cold bottle of lemonade as a token of my appreciation, Mr. Brooks." He pulled the bottle cap off with a heavy piece of looped wire and handed the drink over to Brandon.

"The job must keep you hopping," Brandon said.

"It does indeed," Rush Dailey said. "There's times I get tired as a horse, humping this stuff up and down the trains, though I know the passengers depend on me and that's a gratification. But I don't plan to be doing this forever, no sir. Out here, anything can happen, and I expect it won't be any too long before I hear opportunity knocking, and you can bet Rush Dailey won't be slow at getting the door open. There will be something come along, and I'll know it for what it is and I'll go for it, and my passengers'll have to get on as best they can without me. Strive and succeed, that's Rush Dailey's motto."

With a nod to Brandon, he resumed his commercial patrol of the train. Brandon recalled that on one pass, Rush Dailey's tray had been laden with a paperbacked selection of the works of Horatio Alger, Jr.; evidently he'd been sampling his own wares.

Brandon checked his watch. No more than an hour now to Dysart. Once there, he could begin looking for what had been drawing Casmire there; there would finally be some substance to this hunt, not just shadow. Dysart would be the start.

* * *

"Dead and waitin' for the undertaker to lay it to rest proper, that's Dysart," the lounger on the station platform said. "Most of the relatives and mourners has left or are leavin', such as me. Don't know as anybody's got off the train for anything but a leg-stretch while they're takin' on water and wood for the last week or so."

Brandon leaned against the clapboards of the station wall and looked at what could be seen of Dysart. There was almost no activity on the dirt street that ran beside the tracks or in front of the buildings that lined it. These all seemed to be covered with a faint pall of dust in the harsh sunshine, as if a light cheesecloth screen had been lowered in front of them. The effect of a stage set waiting to be taken down was added to by some obvious gaps in the frontage, holes left by buildings that had never been constructed or had already been demolished.

Some way to the east he could see what was, at this distance, a huddle of twigs; these, when the train had passed them as it slowed for the Dysart stop, had been an elaborate set of pens and runways ending in a platform at the side of a spur running from the main line. It had seemed to him that the hoof-churned earth and the lumps and spatters of dung in the pens were not very old, but there were no cattle in sight and somehow a sense that there weren't going to be, ever again.

"Happens to any cowtown," the idler said. "Farmers raise a stink and the politicians sniff votes in it, and the quarantine line gets moved west some more, and the trail herds start comin' in to the railroad further out, and the town dries up and blows away if it's been relyin' on the cattle trade. Which Dysart done that, so R.I.P. Dysart. A couple herds overwintered 'cause they got in late last year and couldn't get any kind of price; they shipped out a week or so ago and that was the last of Dysart. Biggest doings of the day now is to come on down here and see folks not getting off the train, like I'm doing."

Brandon recalled that tick fever supposedly transmitted by Texas cattle had been a sore point with Kansas farmers for the last seven or eight years, and that every year or so the state legislature drew new lines past which the trail herds could not go. He surveyed the moribund town again. Casmire would have been headed for an active cattle town, not this shell, so the change in Dysart's status would have been as much a surprise to him as to Brandon, if his travel plans had not been drastically altered. The difference was that Casmire would probably have had a good idea about where to go next.

"Inskip's the next place," the man said in unintended answer to the unspoken question. "Eighty miles and some on, just past the quarantine line. Town now; a couple months ago it was a few shacks for buffalo hunters and a trading post. But as soon's the line was set, the rush was on, and they threw up pens for the cattle and quarters for the herd drivers, and saloons and whoreshacks and suchlike civilizings. Soon enough you won't be able to tell it from the way Dysart was last year, right down to the Bright Kentucky Hotel, and soon enough after that the quarantine line'll move again and Inskip'll lay there bleaching like a dog turd, no different from Dysart now. I'm studying out whether to move on or to stay here, where it's already the way it's going to be there, and save the time."

Brandon made his way toward the head car, where the conductor, some leg-stretching passengers, and a few enterprising escapees from Dysart were grouped. Buying a one-way fare to Inskip from the conductor seemed the obvious next step in following up Casmire's intentions.

Two of the passengers who got on at Dysart found their way to the seat facing Brandon's, which had been empty since Leavenworth. They were a floridly handsome man of perhaps fifty and a dark-haired, foxy-faced woman in her twenties. Brandon could not decide if she were pretty, but she was certainly striking.

"Edmund Chambers, sir," the man said, giving a bow from where he sat. He gestured toward the woman next to him, who nodded. "My daughter, Elaine Chambers."

"Miss Chambers, Mr. Chambers," Brandon said. "I am Charles Brooks."

"You will wonder what we are doing here, I expect," Edmund Chambers said. When Brandon looked at him uncomprehendingly, he sighed and said, "No, I guess you won't. You don't recognize us by face or name, I see."

"I am not much of a theatergoer," Brandon said, making what seemed to be the only reasonable interpretation of Chambers's comment.

"But perspicacious all the same," Edmund Chambers said cheerfully, "since you unhesitatingly and correctly assert us to be devotees of Thespis. As to your inquiry about why we are traversing these wastes, virtually trackless but for those we are jolting along, thereby hangs a compelling tale."

Compelling or not, it was clear that Brandon was about to hear it, and it would certainly be preferable to watching more grass go by. Disentangling it from Chambers's elaborate presentation, Brandon gathered that he and his daughter had been comfortably ensconced in a touring repertory company for some years, then tired of the bickering and jealousies of the group and struck out on their own. "If there is stagecraft, if there is magic, my dear Brooks, then the panoply of the full cast, the ingenuity of the props, the pictorial appeal of the sets, none of these are needed. Many a fine drama can be reworked to suit the talents of two performers, much as an orchestral composition can be arranged for piano and violin."

Edmund and Elaine Chambers had toured farm towns, cowtowns, mining towns, and lumber towns over much of the West, with fair success. "Actually," Edmund Chambers said, "what they really appreciate is that we'll perform anywhere, and we're the only entertainment they'll see for months at a time. We're good—I maintain that fervently, of course—but I have to say that we'd probably be as welcome in many places even if we weren't. And the rewards for us are more than pecuniary."

"Bringing pleasure to deprived lives?" Brandon said.

"Not especially," Edmund Chambers said. "What I meant was, out here there's an incredible range of characters, all sorts of conditions—noble, vile, extravagant, cloddish—a vast gallery of types and individuals. Wherever we go, we observe, we absorb, we assimilate traits and quirks of personality and bring them to our interpretations of the roles we play. There is a reading of Hamlet I give that is affected beyond all belief by my observations of a faro bank operator in Santa Fe." Brandon could imagine that it would be.

"You know," Edmund Chambers said thoughtfully, "I don't know why people look on us actors as different. We try to be, of course, but all the same, it seems to me more and more that about everything people do is acting. The soldier isn't brave, the sage isn't wise, not on their own—they have to tell themselves they're brave or wise or whatever; they have to act it. And if they believe it, if they make the mask fit skintight, why, then it becomes the truth, the true face."

And what's my face becoming? Brandon wondered. He was grateful when Elaine Chambers changed the subject. "What we do that's really the go is improvising. We'll ask for a notion from the audience, and they'll give us one and we'll do a scene about it on the spot, inventing as we go along. That gets them every time."

Edmund Chambers was in the midst of an intricate anecdote about the improvisatory abilities of the English actor Macready when Rush Dailey stopped in the aisle next to them.

"Heydee," he said, this time carrying a tray containing combs, bootlaces, and grease-paper-wrapped candies of a violently sinister pink shade. "There is fell doings afoot in the car ahead."

As he had gathered from Rush Dailey's comments that the car ahead was mainly passengered by gamblers, sharpers, pimps, and their stock—on their way to add to Inskip's liveliness, he now realized—Brandon was not surprised. "What kind and how fell?"

"An unsuspecting traveler is about to be fleeced by a three-card-monte man," Rush Dailey said.

"He must be pretty unsuspecting if he's taken in by that

one," Edmund Chambers said. "Never been played as anything but a cheat game since it came up from Mexico."

"That is the hook of it," Rush Dailey said. "The jasper that's doing it is done up as an honest old farmer coming back from a trip east, and he's explaining how he got took by sharpers, and in the explaining he'll show how he can't work the cards the way the sharpers did, and he'll work his man up to a big bet, and to everyone's surprise he'll win it. This is a fellow called California Sam, and that is how he's known to work. So maybe, Mr. Brooks, you would want to put a stop to it?"

"Why?" Brandon said.

"For the general good and promotion of honesty?" Rush Dailey suggested. Brandon thought a moment and realized that these considerations had not weighed on him for quite some time, nor did they now. "No. And why aren't you the one to put a spoke in his wheel?"

"A news butcher has got to be a friend and provider to all," Rush Dailey said. "A butch that takes sides with one passenger against another and creates hard feelings, that butch ain't going to prosper, and the conductor is likely to throw him off the train in the middle of nowheres on general principles. But where you're concerned, this fellow that's up for shearing is a cattle buyer on the way to Inskip, which I understand is your new destination. If you got business there—which I ain't inquiring into, but it could be so—why, doing a service to a man that's well-connected in the principal trade of the place, that couldn't do no harm whatever, now could it? Doing a service to them that can help you along, why, there's nothing to beat it for getting ahead. You stop a runaway team that's imperiling the golden-haired daughter of a millionaire, and you're a made man." Evidently the Horatio Alger contagion had made deep inroads into him.

All the same, there was something to what he said. A cattle buyer would be one of the most informed men regarding the doings in a cowtown, and a grateful cattle buyer would be pretty free with that information. Information was Brandon's main need. "Suppose I do decide to help out the general good—how do you suggest I do it? Charge up and say 'This man is a cheat'? That kind of setup, I believe I'd be best carrying a gun, which I'm not."

"I couldn't hope to advise a man of resourcefulness like yourself," Rush Dailey said.

"Improvisation," Elaine Chambers said, "that's the thing. We'll go in and improvise him right out of there."

"All three of us?" Brandon said.

"I see this as a duo, Mr. Brooks," Edmund Chambers said. "It's the kind of thing that Elaine excels at—I myself tend to overact at close quarters. You and she should be able to bring it off if you'll follow her lead. I may suggest that if it's necessary to intimidate him at some point, you might ask him about the outstanding warrant from Natchez."

"You know this California Sam?" Brandon asked.

"No, but anybody of that age and persuasion is bound to have a warrant out for him in Natchez. Or at least to think that there's good reason for one to be."

Brandon and Elaine Chambers quickly roughed out a scenario that Brandon felt he could handle capably, and the two of them rose and walked to the front of the car and through the door.

Passing through the vestibules separating the two cars brought them to what seemed to Brandon like a different world. The car they had left had been quiet, about as clean as something propelled by burning wood through a country substantially composed of dust could be, and sunk in the torpor of long-distance travel. The one they entered was noisy, full of movement, pungent with the odors of perfume, liquor, tobacco, and sweat, and luridly aglow with the light of the westering sun filtered through shifting clouds of cigar smoke.

"Putting it politely, purgatory on wheels," Elaine Chambers murmured.

The scene was reminiscent of some of the more sensational covers of *The Police Gazette,* with the seats on either side of the aisle occupied by men ranging from overalled toughs who could be cowhands or garrotters—anything calling for muscle and recklessness—to broadcloth-clad fellows with tall hats who almost had to be gamblers or pimps or both, and by women of substantially one type and one mode of dress: colorful, cheap, and cut to expose unexpected areas of the body. "The Cyprian Sisterhood" or "soiled doves," the *Gazette* would call them, and, Brandon thought he could see through the eddying smoke, one of them in the front corner seat was in the process of getting further soiled. Another dove, Brandon was pleased to see, was poring over a dime novel; Rush Dailey had been able to find customers even here.

He and Elaine Chambers stood at the rear of the car, taking in the prospect, and quickly spotting the situation they were here to deal with: About halfway down the car on the left, a generously bewhiskered old man with a broad-brimmed straw hat sat facing a portly, somewhat younger man in a checked suit, and holding up three cards in one hand. The only off-key note in the car was the presence, in the seat next to which they stood, of a plainly dressed woman in a neat and not at all gaudy traveling suit; she was looking out the window and seemed completely detached from the rowdy universe of the rest of the car. Maybe a schoolteacher destined for Inskip and the probably thankless task of instilling learning in heads stuffed with tales of cattle drives, outlaw bands, and Indians. Her lap and the seat beside her were covered with books and other items that Brandon recognized as having come from Rush Dailey's stock.

Brandon and Elaine Chambers moved through the smoke of the swaying car to where the presumed sharper and his victim sat. Several men crowded interestedly around the two, watching the first act of the drama, which, Brandon saw, had just begun.

The ancient rustic was pointing at a sternly lettered sign posted on the car wall above the windows:

> WARNING: Beware of Three-Card Monte Throwers and Confidence Men Who May Be Operating on This Train

"That there selfsame sign was onto the steam cars whenas I went to Chicago, and I read it clear as isinglass," the old man chuckled. "Took it to heart, declined any and all games of chanst, until something come up I *couldn't* lose at—and that's how I dropped two and a half hundred dollars of what I got for my hogs. I was mad at first, then kind of tickled, for it was an almighty lesson to me that I wasn't such a smart article as I'd figured, and that's a lesson that's always worth some money to learn. Now, this game, it was played with three cards like these"—he flourished those he held—"the American Eagle onto one of 'em and the thirteen stars of the first states onto the other two. Now, the thing was to turn the cards over and move 'em about, then the other man had to pick which was the eagle, and if he done that he won and if he didn't, he didn't. Now, I thought I could spot which the eagle was, no matter how the fellow moved the cards about, and afore I knowed it, I was two hundred fifty dollars down and a lot the wiser."

As he spoke, he had been moving the cards on a folded newspaper on his lap to illustrate his discourse. When he finished, he held his hands up from the facedown cards and looked quizzically at the man facing him. The portly man reached for one card and turned it over, displaying the eagle.

"Well, of course I ain't the dab hand at foofarawing the cards that the cheats are," the old man said. "So if we'd had a bet on that, I'd of lost. But I b'lieve I can do a little better than that, if we was to have a wager of two bits or so on the matter to sharpen the interest."

The rest of the scenario was clear enough to Brandon: old Whiskers loses, fumes, raises the stakes, loses more, then gets apoplectic and offers to wager all he has on him, gets offensive about it; victim is reluctant, then notices a crease in the winning eagle card and goes ahead, matches the bet, and loses when the crease magically appears on a losing card. He considered that it was time to commence the improvisation. He looked at Elaine Chambers, who gave a brief nod.

She edged past an onlooker, clasped her hands, and gave a shrill wail, then called, "Father!"

The old man, who had taken the impact of her wail in his right ear, twitched convulsively, glared at her, and opened his mouth to speak.

"Not again . . . we'll lose everything this time!" Elaine Chambers said brokenly, dabbing at her eyes with her handkerchief.

"What is this?" the portly man said.

"My uncle here," Brandon said, pointing at the old man, "has lost most of what he had to cardsharps, and my poor cousin is nearly out of her mind with grief and fear that he'll dissipate the rest of her patrimony in the same manner. It's not his fault, poor fellow—a weakness he can't control." The old man's eyes bulged and his mouth opened and shut in a distinctly fishlike manner; he was the very picture of guilty amazement, lending convincing corroboration to Brandon's invention. "I don't for a moment," Brandon said, letting the flinty tone of his voice contradict his words, "suggest that your play is underhanded, but I believe you will prefer not to continue at it." Elaine Chambers's sobs sounded over the rattling of the train.

The portly man flushed and said, "Damn your insinuations, sir, and damn this game—oh, damn it, excuse me, ma'am," he muttered as the sobs took on a note of outrage. "I mean, of course I won't play under these circumstances, and . . ." He seemed to run out of comments, and rose from the seat, glared at the old man, at Brandon and at Elaine Chambers, then strode down the aisle in search of another place.

Brandon and Elaine Chambers retreated down the aisle and into the vestibule between the cars. As they passed the quietly dressed woman in the last seat, she gave them an appraising glance.

In the vestibule, Brandon said to Elaine Chambers, "That was great, thanks. Now you go on back. I suspect I'll have a little solo improvising next."

A moment after she left, the car door opened and the old man entered the vestibule from the front car. Brandon had been expecting fury or at least indignant bluster, but the old cardsharp apparently read Brandon's hand as a winning one and merely said, "So?"

Brandon drew on his recollections of Trexler's laconic, confident manner: "Off at the next stop, Sam. And when you ride the Kansas Pacific again, it's as a passenger only."

The old man gave him a shrewd glance. "Can't quite see that you can make that stick, son."

"Some folks in Natchez might have something to say about that," Brandon said.

The cardsharp's shoulders slumped. "They haven't forgotten about that, huh? No choice, I guess . . . Listen, you don't have any special feelings about what happens on the Atchison, Topeka, and Santa Fe, do you?"

"Not the least," Brandon said.

The next stop was in ten minutes, and Brandon, looking out the window, saw California Sam trudging down the platform as the train pulled out. He was alone as he did this, as Edmund and Elaine Chambers had moved to another seat in order to go over their lines for their proposed performance in Inskip, which had turned out to be where they proposed to debark.

"It's *The Taming of the Shrew* in under an hour," Edmund Chambers told him. "Myself as Petruchio, Elaine as the lively Kate. A real rouser, if I do say so. Be sure to come and see us."

Shortly after the train started up again, the portly man Brandon had detached from California Sam's toils appeared in the car and came to sit beside Brandon.

"One thing that old scoundrel said was true enough," said the cattle buyer, who gave his name as Perkins, "learning you're not as smart as you think is a worthwhile lesson, and I'm glad I got it free of charge, thanks to you. I like to believe I wouldn't have fallen for his game all the way, but I certainly had him figured for the genuine goods until that train butch put me wise after he'd left. Told me you'd been stung that way yourself once, so you make it your business to spike such games when you run into them."

Brandon answered with a short nod. Rush Dailey had figured out a better story than that Brandon's action had been motivated by a boy's unsupported report of a complicated bit of villainy that, come to think of it, he had no business knowing about. Whatever, here was a chance to get some information about what to expect in Inskip, maybe something that would suggest where to start looking for Gren Kenneally or one of those who had ridden with him—somebody, anyhow, that Casmire would have been coming out here to meet.

Perkins confirmed that Inskip was the new railhead for most of the herds coming up from Texas and that the first of them for this year were just arriving. "Prices are up a little from what they were last fall, but some of the fellows're going to be pretty sore at how far down they are from this time last year. Depression's settled in for sure, and the times'll be leaner for a while. With less money around, there'll be harder grabbing for what there is, and those men and women in the car ahead are schoolchildren compared to some of what's going to be there—shootings and throat-cuttings for amusement, holdups and garrotting as recognized trades. The railroad paid off the construction crews after they got to the state line and made sure of their land grants, so there's a lot of men around with no work and the habit of violence, as goes with the tracklaying life. You add in cowboys looking to let off steam after a month or what on the trail, and don't you just have a mix that'll blow the boilers right out!"

As he gave Brandon some examples of the extravagant, often dangerous, rowdiness of the cowtowns he had plied his trade in, Perkins seemed to relish the recollection of his experiences. Brandon supposed it made a change from inspecting stockyards and slaughterhouses or preparing budgets or whatever else Perkins did during the rest of the year back in Chicago. Come to that, what had brought Cole Brandon out here was a far cry from what he'd been used to, whether as a practicing lawyer or, for half a year, anesthetized survivor. Once across the Mississippi, the old ways and old rules didn't hold. Listening to Perkins's stories of low life and fast death in the cowtowns, it seemed to Brandon that the obsession that drove him, his determination to hunt down Gren Kenneally and the rest, was less lunatic than it had sometimes seemed to him. In this setting, in fact, it made good sense.

And from what Perkins said about what to expect of Inskip, it looked to be the place Casmire would have moved on to once it turned out that Dysart no longer held anything to interest men of the Gren Kenneally stripe.

"Be glad to stand you to a drink or so once we're in Inskip," Perkins said. "By tomorrow I'll know which saloon the buyers and cattlemen meet and dicker in, and I'll set up offices there, so to speak." He sighed. "Now there's one thing I'll miss about Dysart—the Bright Kentucky. One of the finest hotels away from a big city I ever saw: comfortable, good food, and a barroom so elegant that any deal you struck there looked like a winner for both parties. Even hardcases minded their manners there, for nobody, given to murders and maimings though he might be, wanted to chance being barred from the Bright Kentucky."

Perkins rose to his feet and stepped into the aisle. "Wanted to thank you, enjoyed talking to you, hope to see you, going back now. Can't all the games in that car be crooked, and I've a mind to get my dispositions and attitudes set for Inskip before we get there. So long." He tipped his hat and strode to the front of the car and through the door to the vestibule.

"Razor, worshrag, and shaving soap in its own cardboard mug, just the thing for freshing up in the worshroom at the rear of the car," Rush Dailey said, resting his tray, now laden with the items he had named, on the aisle-side armrest of Brandon's seat.

Brandon looked at the folded straight razors, the oily steel of the blades gleaming in the late sunlight. "About as far as you can get from selling life insurance, I'd say," he observed. "One jolt going over a switch while you're shaving and your throat's cut."

Rush Dailey shook his head. "Cheap stuff, don't take an edge sharper'n a hotcake, couldn't hurt yourself if you tried."

"Not much good for shaving, then," Brandon said.

"Can't expect Sheffield steel off'n a train butch's tray, now can you?" Rush Dailey said reasonably. "Now, you and that Mr. Perkins, you got along famously, I could see that, and I shouldn't wonder if he'll take you into his business or remember you in his will, considering the service you done him. It's wonderful how things happen out here."

Brandon looked across the sunset-reddened grasslands. Against the pale sky to the northwest, he saw a dark bulk, block-shaped, with curious projections from the top. As the train drew nearer, it resolved itself into a building, perhaps three stories high; Brandon thought he could make out a portico along one side. It seemed an improbably substantial—even elegant—edifice to find in the middle of the prairie, away from any vestige of a town.

As it had several times during the trip, the train jerked to a stop to allow the trainmen to hit the wheels with mallets for reasons never made clear, and Brandon hoped for a clearer look at the strange building, now nearly opposite his window and perhaps a quarter-mile away. For a second it seemed to Brandon that the train began to move backward; then he saw that the high grass by the trackside was not moving. But the building was, gliding with glacial slowness toward the west. He looked harder and made out some indistinct forms just showing above the top of the grass out in front of the building. He was able to resolve the bizarre mystery into something more nearly mundane: a building being towed across the prairie by a team of several pair of oxen. On further thought, the explanation wasn't much less odd than the initial impression. He was struck by the ludicrous fancy of a large family of emigrants choosing to travel west in their own home, gaining comfort and security from bandits and Indian attack in exchange for loss of speed.

"Now, that's a sight," Rush Dailey said, materializing out of the shadows that were beginning to fill the car and looking past Brandon at the building still inching away from them. "Expect it'll be a long time till I can afford to stay there."

"Why would you want to?" Brandon asked.

"That's a fine place, well knowed. And," Rush Dailey said, "well worth the effort of transporting, lock, stock, and lobby acrost the seas of grass from its past renown in Dysart to new glories in Inskip—the Bright Kentucky Hotel."

Giving some, but not much, credit for accuracy to the printed timetable, Brandon had expected that the train would get to Inskip around nine o'clock, only a few hours late. But more stops for wheel-tapping, a loose rail that the section crew had missed, taking on water, and allowing a small but complacently slow-moving herd of buffalo to pass extended the journey substantially, and it was well past midnight when the conductor bawled, *"Eeeenheep!* Pasners freenheep! Lloff freeenheep!" Brandon had talked to the man several times during the journey and knew for a fact that he was capable of clear articulation, particularly when it came to explaining the penalty charged for purchasing a new leg of the trip while on the train. East or west, it seemed to be the rule that announcements of vital information—such as where you were—be made loudly and indistinctly.

Brandon stepped down the car stairs and into what for a moment seemed like broad daylight. A row of gas lamps in white globes lined the street paralleling the tracks, and on a storefront across it, a huge arc light bathed the area around the station in a harsh white glare that bled the color out of what it illuminated. Brandon was among the few debarking from his car, but, as he descended the steps to the Inskip station platform, he could see that the head car was almost emptying out, with the gamblers, sports, roughs, and fancy ladies spilling onto the platform and rapidly moving off into the streets. He saw the Chamberses, carrying a large trunk between them, walking to the end of the platform and out of sight. The neatly dressed woman he had seen incongruously seated at the rear of the front car when he and Elaine had performed their improvisation for California Sam's benefit disappeared in the other direction, carrying a valise.

Rush Dailey, festooned with drawstring sacks, boxes, and a voluminous carpetbag, tottered toward him.

"Not going on west?" Brandon asked.

Rush Dailey shook his head. "Sold most everything there's a call for, so I'd best stock up here. Or look into other things as may occur. You picked a place to stay, seeing as the Bright Kentucky hasn't made port yet? 'Cause I've had word of a nice quiet place that does a clean bed and hot meals that you might want to try."

From a saloon down the block, muffled shouting, the rapid cracks of three gunshots, and a howling noise that might or might not have been laughter, suggested that a quiet boardinghouse could be a rare and worthwhile oasis in Inskip. "Sounds good. Where is it and are you going there?"

"Green frame house three blocks down and one over, Cottonwood Street, sign out front offering room and board from a Mrs. Elster, and I've fixed it up with the stationmaster to bunk out in the baggage room so's I can keep an eye on my traps and leftover stock. Believe I'll sleep sound tonight, I'm tired as a horse."

Brandon, carrying his valise along the echoing plankwalk that bordered the bleached night streets, past the raucous saloons that every other building seemed to contain, realized that he was dead tired, too. But every scream, laugh, curse, and outcry he heard convinced him further that Inskip was the sort of place the sort of man he was after would have to come to, sooner or later. This was where the hunt would truly begin.

9

Brandon opened the front door of the boardinghouse and stepped onto the porch, surprisingly wakeful after only a few hours' sleep. It would be an hour until breakfast; he might as well get a sense of what Inskip was like. The air was cool in the shadow of the houses scattered along the short street, but the sun bit at him as he crossed the spaces between them; not a hard bite, but a gentle nip of heat, a reminder that it would be doing what it could to barbecue anyone within reach come noon. There were no cottonwood trees on Cottonwood Street, just unpainted houses of varying states of competence and care in their construction—Mrs. Elster's was the most solid and the only one that looked as if anyone living in it could expect to be comfortable—and several partly assembled buildings surrounded by piles of raw lumber. Even at this early hour, two men were at work on one such would-be edifice, one tossing two-by-fours to the other, who hammered each rapidly into place on the ramshackle but growing frame.

Brandon came out onto Main Street, which stretched along the north side of the railroad tracks, and squinted down its length. Commercial buildings—stores of all kinds, a law office ("Land Deeds and Transactions Our Specialty"), a sign maker, barber ("Baths 25¢"), printer and newspaper —lined it randomly, some butted up against each other in groups of two to five, others standing alone; spaces from ten to forty feet separated the lone or grouped houses from each other. One large lot had a low boxlike shape of heavy timbers neatly assembled; Brandon guessed it to be the foundation for the approaching Bright Kentucky Hotel. A plankwalk in fairly good repair—it could not be much more than a few months old, given Inskip's recent origins—but stuccoed in many places with deposits of dried mud, ran along in front of the buildings and vacant lots; most of the stores had hitching posts and mounting blocks in front of them.

Farther down the street an odd-looking construction caught his eye, and he walked toward it—passing, he noted, Elm and Spruce Streets, both devoid, like Cottonwood, of trees. When he reached it, he saw a log-cabinlike structure about ten feet high and perhaps fifteen across on each side; a close-up look showed the "logs" to be railroad ties laid on their sides and alternatingly lapped at the corners, creating walls at least six or eight inches thick. A solid-looking door closed with a three-inch-wide flat iron bar pivoted across its front was the only apparent exit or entrance. It stood alone, but gilt lettering on the nearest building's front window proclaimed the presence of the city marshal's office, suggesting that the fortresslike small building was the local jail.

A strangled shout that probably would have been a curse if he had been able to hear it clearly drifted from across the railroad tracks and the buildings on Main's southern counterpart, Front Street. The bright lights Brandon had seen illuminating the street a few hours before were out now, but the level of activity had only declined, not vanished; there were walkers in the street, also staggerers and stumblers and, folded over a hitching post, one intermittent vomiter; music and voices, with sudden peaks of conviviality or anger, drifted from the four saloons that seemed to be open in the central two blocks. In the daylight he saw that most of them had a jaunty brightness that most buildings he'd seen from the train hadn't, the brightness of raw lumber the sun and rain hadn't had time to turn dust-brown.

Brandon stepped across the tracks and onto the Front Street plankwalk. The dark block of the jailhouse squatted forebodingly across the way, but Brandon doubted that the sight exercised much effect on the south-side-of-the-tracks population.

The door of a saloon he was passing opened, exhaling a blast of stale air, the wheezing of a concertina—trying to decide between "Camptown Races" and "Arkansas Traveler," apparently—and a hilariously incoherent man and woman. The woman's high heels clattered irregularly on the plankwalk as she and her companion lurched past Brandon. They seemed to be keeping upright mainly by leaning against each other and by some intricate bracing with their hands—unless they were trying to pick each other's pockets or conduct some amatory explorations that were at the least misdemeanors in the criminal codes Brandon was acquainted with.

They disappeared down an alley between two buildings. Brandon wondered if they would manage to do to, or with, each other whatever it was they had in mind before the liquor they had consumed claimed them, and if they would remember it afterward.

The slap of a flung-open door, a flurry of bootsteps, yells of expostulation and argument, and a howled obscenity swung Brandon around to face the source of the noise. Against the bright disk of the sun, still not much above the horizon, two agitated silhouettes capered and gesticulated.

"Sumbitch, you palmed a ace, I seen you!"

"I never, you bastard, and it was kings and twos took the pot nohow!"

"Call me bastard, you sumbitch? Sumbitch!"

Hot light winked from the middle of the shadow-play, accompanied by a sharp crack Brandon felt in his gut, and a thinning cloud of smoke spread above the contenders.

Neither figure fell, but one dodged, then grew larger and more distinct as it pelted toward Brandon. He got an impression of an angry, sun-reddened, unshaven face under a dusty, domed hat, and of a dirty but immense revolver carelessly held; then the runner stopped, turned, and fired in the direction he had come from. The sharp smell of burned gunpowder stung Brandon's nostrils.

The whole spectacle seemed unreal to him, and not very plausible, until the farther figure fired twice more and Brandon saw a six-inch splinter appear in the plankwalk a few inches from his shoe. He noticed that the previous denizens of the street had retired totally from the area or were contorting themselves to get behind whatever shelter the street afforded. One long step sideways took him into a space between two buildings, and he continued on his way.

He heard a rapid tattoo of four or five more shots, and a shout of rage or pain, then nothing. Maybe they'd used up their ammunition or worn out their quarrel. Maybe not, and the ending had been more decisive than that. Whichever, there was nothing about it that Brandon saw as his business.

There was mostly open space behind the Front Street buildings, though a straggle of shacks made a south-trending line a little to the west of where he stood, pointing toward a low bluff with a few trees poking up from it. Beyond it would be a river, he supposed; there'd have to be a good source of water for the cattle that would be awaiting shipment here.

Bare sunbaked earth gave way to low grass as the ground sloped up to the top of the bluff. Brandon paused there next to a low, stunted tree whose distorted branches testified to the molding force of the prairie wind and looked to the south.

The bluff was no more than twenty feet above the placid surface of the river—at this point about a hundred feet across—but that was enough height to allow him to see for what he supposed must be forty miles or more. A sea of tall grass glinted in the low sun and undulated under the wind. Hazy patches of orange and purple seemed to float on the grass—wild flowers, probably. A light, sharp scent, like mown hay but greatly weaker, drifted to him.

His first impression—that the plain to the south was table-flat—altered as he studied it. It was broken up with low hills and draws, arranged so as to provide a mile-wide stretch of land that seemed to stretch out of sight toward Texas like a giant winding road. This would be where the trail herds would come up any time now, herds that were already on their way from their home ranges.

To his left, the river curved southward, and north of it he could see the line of telegraph poles that marked the railroad tracks and, about half a mile off, the gleam of new wood in the maze of pens where the incoming cattle would be held after the trail drives.

When the herds started arriving, there would be the kind of action that Casmire had presumably been intending to find in Dysart—maybe action of the kind that would draw Gren Kenneally. This was a time for waiting and patience. He itched to move, to hunt; but there was no trail now to follow. If his instinct were right, here, somehow, was where he would pick up the scent he sought and begin to track those whose death was called for.

Under the immense vault of the sky, bleached pale in the east by the spreading glare of the sun, the deepening blue at the western horizon giving the last clue of departing night, the prairie stretched away limitlessly. Texas and Indian Territory to the south, Colorado to the west, there was where the trail would likely lead when he picked it up. Or it could be beyond, to Arizona, Wyoming, Utah . . . somewhere under this immense sky, the men he had marked for his prey were starting the day. He had no idea how or when it would come about, but within him, deeper and surer than any grief or rage, was the cold certainty that for each of those men the day was fast coming when the sun would rise and they would not be seeing it, or anything.

"Well, it's not home cooking," Jameson said, "but there's plenty of it." He speared a slice of ham and slid it onto his plate and added a generous load of fried potatoes from a deep dish in the center of the table.

The food seemed to Brandon as good as in most restaurants and rather better than in most homes, but Jameson seemed to be inclined to look for trivial flaws in anything he spoke of. Brandon guessed it to be a habit prompted by his trade, which he had proclaimed to be that of general household and farmstead supplier, conducted in a two lot-wide emporium on Main Street. Finding fault with the goods you were buying could work to cheapen the price some; but of course those faults would shrink or disappear when it came to selling the goods. Like conducting both prosecution and defense for the same client, it called for considerable flexibility.

Jameson, stocky, balding, radiating simple satisfaction in being Jameson, had been content to announce and discuss his business without inquiring into that of the other two guests at the breakfast table, Brandon and the no-nonsense woman he had noticed at the rear of the "purgatory on wheels" coach the day before. She had identified herself as Jess Marvell and Brandon had kept the name of Charles Brooks, under which he had taken the room. She was dressed in what might have been the same outfit she'd been wearing on the train, except that it wasn't rumpled or soot-marked, and ate with a healthy appreciation of the food, homelike or not.

"Ma Elster serves up good doings," Jameson said, "but it's a shame that the best food in an up-and-coming place like Inskip's is a boardinghouse. After you've done some shopping for the home or farm, you want a place to have a nice light meal or a nice heavy one, and there just isn't such here. Once the herds start coming in, there'll be people with money needing places to stay and have some respectable enjoyment, and they won't find 'em."

The facilities for unrespectable enjoyment, at least, were well and truly in place, Brandon thought, and staffed to overflowing, even allowing for what, on the morning's evidence, might be a high casualty rate.

"What we need," Jameson said, "is a first-rate hotel, like that one over in Dysart. What's it's name?"

"The Bright Kentucky," Jess Marvell said.

"That's something like it, I think," Jameson said. "Now, a place like that, it'd do some good for a town, and it's time that someone was seeing to it. Of course, if there's high-class people staying there, the riffraff'll be sniffing around to hooraw or rob them, so there's more police needed, and taxes raised to pay for them, though it's hard to break even as it is."

Having found enough negative elements in his own recommendation to satisfy him, Jameson gulped the last of his coffee, blotted his lips, rose, nodded, and stepped from the room. The sound of the front door opening and closing came a moment later, and Jameson was on his way to a day of extolling the merchandise he had, the day or the week before, tried to persuade the seller was close to worthless.

Brandon and Jess Marvell relaxed visibly at the merchant's departure and sipped their coffee, feeling no need to break the silence for some moments. Then Jess Marvell looked at Brandon and spoke. "You were on the train yesterday, saw the Bright Kentucky being towed, isn't that right?"

"It is," Brandon said.

"And you didn't mention to that man that the very hotel he was talking about was on its way here?"

"No," Brandon said. "He seemed mainly interested in informing us of his feelings and opinions. Facts didn't seem to be called for."

"Also, if you'd mentioned it, he'd have explained some more why it was a good thing and a bad thing and how remarkable it was to be able to tow a whole hotel across the prairie and why it probably wouldn't work in the end," Jess Marvell said. "And then I might have had to empty the coffeepot over his head." At Brandon's look of inquiry, she went on: "I'm the manager of the Bright Kentucky. Assistant manager in Dysart, but Mr. Tutt went back east, so I'm top man when it opens up again in Inskip."

Brandon did some rapid mental algebra, factoring in Jess Marvell's profession, her location in the car yesterday, her lapful of Rush Dailey's wares, and her knowledge that he had observed the hotel in tow and been informed of its identity. "A lot of that sporting crowd stays at the Bright Kentucky, I guess," he said. "So it wouldn't do for them to see one of the management interfering in something shady going on, so long as it wasn't on hotel premises—hotel people have to be neutral, like Switzerland, I expect. But you can't stand to see a good customer like that Perkins taken badly. So you pass a quiet word to the news butcher, he passes a quiet word to me, and the matter's taken care of without you getting your paws singed."

Jess Marvell smiled at him over the top of her coffee cup. "You've seen more of the town than I have, Mr. Brooks. If you have the time, would you care to escort me on a tour?"

When Jess Marvell took his arm as they descended the boardinghouse's front stoop, something inside Brandon twitched, more of a reminder than a pain. The last time a woman had taken his arm was at the funeral, when he had escorted Krista, and he was very aware of the faint heat and scent radiating from Jess Marvell as well as the light pressure of her fingers on the crook of his arm.

Two more men had joined the crew at work on the house on Cottonwood Street, and it seemed to Brandon that there was more of it in place than when he had passed it earlier. "Expect they're working to get this town built up fast so there'll be some use got out of it before the cattle trade moves on and it dries up. I saw Inskip yesterday from the train—how long did it last?"

"Two years, start to finish," Jess Marvell said. "They got the Bright Kentucky built about halfway through the first trail season, so we had a year and a half to make it pay and get it a reputation. That was the hardest work I've ever done in my life, but it was worth it. Now I know what I can do, and I came to see just *dozens* of things that there's need for and nobody seeing to them yet. I won't want for what to turn my hand to, for certain sure." She looked down the commercial frontage of Main Street, onto which they had just turned, with a bright and appraising eye.

The sun had moved southward in its ascent, and the facades of the raffish establishments across the tracks on Front Street were in shadow, and those of the stores and shops on Main had the benefit of a cheerful wash of sunshine that brightened what paint there was—mostly on the signs—and glinted on the gold lettering and curlicues that adorned Jameson's front windows.

The Front Street frequenters, the riffraff Jameson had complained of, seemed finally to have called it a day, Brandon noticed, or at least be taking a breather. Nobody was walking, staggering, shooting, or vomiting in the street, and the only person visible was a man sleeping in a very awkward posture next to an alley entrance. Or possibly not sleeping. Did places like this have regular hours for collecting those who had failed to survive the day's fun?

Sunlit Main Street was lightly peopled, with a better-dressed and more purposeful set of people than those Brandon had seen on Front a couple of hours before: early shoppers, a lumber-laden dray, a couple of men stepping into the barber shop; even the dusty-overalled men lounging against a water barrel gave the impression of loafing during the course of a job, not of never having had one. A tide of cool air carried a heavy sweetish-musty smell to them out of a just-opened door. In the storefront window a massive head half Jess Marvell's height, ringlet-maned, bearded, and topped with wickedly sharp curved horns, stared at them irritably. Jess Marvell looked past it with interest at the white-aproned butcher sawing at massive cuts of meat, and Brandon wondered if the Bright Kentucky would be featuring buffalo chops and steaks on its menu.

They resumed their walk, and Jess Marvell said, "That was something, how you worked it out about that cardsharp and how and why I brought you into it."

"It's what the facts added up to," Brandon said.

"Being able to see through things that way, that must be a real help to you in your business," Jess Marvell said.

"Any business'll go better if you can figure out what's going on, true enough," Brandon said lightly.

No question had actually been answered, and no answer had actually been refused. Jess Marvell gave a faint smile, and they continued down the Main Street plankwalk.

They were almost at the end of the heavily built-up part of Main Street, marked by the boxlike jail; beyond it only scattered buildings abutted the street, and some aligned planks laid on the bare ground indicated the intention of extending the plankwalk. In front of the town marshal's office next to the jail, a tall man in a tall hat sat like a folded ruler in a chair set against the building; the star on his vest marked him as the marshal, and the shotgun leaning against the wall next to him showed that he liked to keep the tools of the job handy.

The marshal rose as they approached him and stepped toward them. They stopped to see what he wanted of them, but he moved past them with a single surveying glance. Brandon looked after him and was surprised to see that the marshal's back was not the only one visible; in fact, almost everyone on Main Street was facing, and moving, away from him and Jess Marvell.

"Morning eastbound train's due in in a few minutes," Jess Marvell said, and Brandon saw that people were beginning to gather near the platform and shed that constituted Inskip's railroad station. "Until the trail herds start coming, trains are about the high point of the day, places like this. Certainly how it was in Dysart."

"Be a pity to miss the excitement," Brandon said, and they joined the drift toward the station.

None of the ten or so passengers who descended from the train was carrying luggage, so it could be presumed that they were out for a leg-stretch and not intending to debark at Inskip. They were substantially outnumbered by their audience, who seemed content to look at them with placid interest, much like cows contemplating countryside walkers.

One exception was the marshal, who surveyed the leg-stretchers keenly from under the broad brim of his hat, then moved on to do the same for the express clerks unloading some sacks from the express car just behind the tender. Another was a short, porcupine-whiskered man, who approached a passenger at the far end of the platform from Brandon and Jess Marvell and produced from the sack he was carrying what appeared at a distance to be a giant rat, which he offered for the passenger's inspection.

"Sir?" Brandon's attention was diverted from this odd transaction by a touch on his shoulder. "Train's stopping for twenty or what minutes," a tired-looking man said. "Can you tell me where I can get a fair imitation of breakfast in that kind of time?"

"Sorry," Brandon said. "I don't know the place; haven't been here a day yet."

The passenger turned to Jess Marvell. "Ma'am, could you—"

She shook her head. "I'm a stranger here, too."

The passenger looked at a bystander a few feet away, well within earshot. "Sir, can—"

"Sorry, can't help you."

The passenger sighed dispiritedly. "Nobody here seems to be *from* here."

"Oh, I am," the townsman assured him. "Been here since the early days, back in March. Why I can't help you, there ain't what you're after here. There's a restaurant, but it don't open till noontime—*if* the cook ain't too drunk or the canned goods didn't not come in. Some of the saloons has free lunch, but they don't set it out till towards sundown, that being lunchtime or breakfast for the folks they cater to."

The passenger looked mournfully back at the train. "Then I got to throw myself on the mercy of the news butcher. In another hour or so I expect I'll work up enough hunger so them sandwiches will look tasty. On the other hand, they'll be an hour or so staler. I kind of wish I had some bad troubles in my life. This would take my mind off of 'em."

"Nothin' better than a lively, gamesome, an' faithful pet to deevert the thoughts from cares an' sorrows, an' promote innocent mirth." The bristle-bearded man with the sack had, unnoticed by Brandon, moved down the platform and was standing next to them. He held up a squirming, gray-brown animal which, Brandon now saw, was not a rat, though it had an inquiring rodent face: The body was longer and leaner, the legs shorter, and the tail thicker.

"The prairie dog!" the whiskery man said. "Builds hisself mighty cities out on the plain, sets up his own guvmint and armies, runs his nation peaceable an' safe. Clever as a clerk an' artful an' winnin' in his ways, that's yer prairie dog. Also clean an' tidy in his habits an' given to barkin' at unexpected things, savin' the expense of keepin' a watchdog. Bring this rarity of the plains back east an' yer social success'll be assured as folks drop inter yer parlor night after night to watch the little fellow's pretty ways." The animal he held looked at his audience with irritable boredom and chittered at them, displaying large front teeth that Brandon estimated would reduce a set of parlor furniture to matchsticks in a few weeks.

"How much?" the passenger asked.

"Three dollars," the prairie-dog seller said. "Er a breedin' pair fer five so's you c'n profit by the natural increase—beggin' yer pardon fer the indelicacy, ma'am," he added, waving the prairie dog apologetically at Jess Marvell.

"If you'll dress out a brace of 'em," the passenger said, "I believe I could deal with the fireman to grill 'em on the firebox."

Brandon and Jess Marvell moved down the platform, not waiting to hear if the pet merchant was prepared to expand into butchery. The expressmen had finished their offloading and now lounged around the open door of the express car. The tall marshal was talking to a man who listened while locking the express-office door and climbing onto the driver's seat of a light wagon pulled by a pair of mules. "See you tomorrow, Marshal," the man said as the mules drew him slowly away.

The marshal's face was deeply shadowed by his hat brim as they passed him, but Brandon sensed his intense gaze and the probable assessment: no danger, but don't bank on it. He seemed quiet, even peaceable, but managed to convey the assurance that he was prepared to use his rifle or revolver to deal with any imbalances of the law that came up. And with as much efficiency and emotion as a teacher erasing an incorrect sum from the blackboard. Judging by how things seemed to operate across the tracks, Brandon guessed that the marshal was willing to let the predators do what they would with each other, so long as they didn't make the fatal mistake of preying on the taxpaying townsmen.

"You didn't tell those fellows your hotel was making its way here through the tall grass," Brandon said.

Jess Marvell shrugged. "I'm not making a secret of it, but I'm not spreading it around. If it gets talked to death before it gets here, then it'll be old news and everybody'll be disappointed when it turns out to be only a really great hotel with a really great manager. And anyway, the Bright Kentucky never catered to the train-meal crowd. That's a specialty on its own, getting people fed good meals and back onto the train in a quarter-hour or so, and not knowing how many'll need to be fed or what they fancy. Small wonder it hardly ever gets done right."

"But," Brandon said, looking at her closely, "it *could* be done right?"

"Anything can be done right," Jess Marvell said flatly.

Brandon felt the ghost of a smile twitch his mouth. Sidestepping implied questions about plans, and business was apparently not an exclusively male prerogative out here.

They had turned off Main onto the street next over from Cottonwood and were passing the side yard of the livery stable. It seemed to Brandon that there was something familiar about the back view of the person inspecting a long flatbed farm wagon that stood under the roof of an open shed. "Isn't that that news butcher kid from the train, what's his name?" Brandon asked Jess Marvell.

She shook her head, saying, "Name's Rush Dailey, I believe—didn't see him," but she didn't look back to see who Brandon had been talking about.

Interesting, Brandon thought. Each of us trying to figure the other out, because we know damn well that the other's keeping something significant hidden. Somewhere along here we're going to be in for some interesting cross-examination or maybe pretrial disclosure, I'd guess, but damned if I know why I should be interested or she should.

"The first herd isn't due in till next week," Perkins said glumly. "And that means there's damn little for me to do here. I wouldn't mind whiling away the time in this place" —he gestured around the barroom of the Bull's Foot on Front Street, which he had told Brandon was likely to be the unofficial office of the cattle trade in Inskip—"but there's things I better see to in Wichita before then, so it's back onto the train tomorrow morning for me."

He took a pull at his drink. "Now, about grass," he said, "grass is the key in the cattle business. Look at it one way, cattle are nothing but grass on the hoof. Now, there is your blue grama grass and your hairy grama . . ."

I am getting information, just like Rush Dailey said I would, Brandon thought, but not, I would say, anything that's going to get me nearer a Kenneally.

After what seemed like a longer time than it probably was, Perkins ran out of information, or the immediate need to impart it, and took his departure. Brandon looked along the bar of the Bull's Foot, which ran about thirty feet to the rear of the long, narrow room, lit by the dusty window facing the street and two smoky coal-oil lamps in the shadowy recesses. There was only a scattering of patrons, most of whom looked as if they had fallen asleep while sitting up. Cigar smoke and the smells of beer, spirits, and men a long way from their last bath hung in the air.

A man in a long coat and a tall hat sat alone at a table, his chair tilted back against the wall. He looked as torpid as a lizard sunning on a rock, but Brandon sensed that he was as aware of every movement around him as if he had been glancing nervously in all directions. There was a scatter of cards on the table, and Brandon recalled that during Perkins's discourse other men had joined Tall Hat at the table, and a few hands of something, probably poker, had been played. Casting back, it seemed to him that the game had ended suddenly, not with any argument, but quite abruptly. Had he been less numbed by the amount of information on grass being showered on him, he would have paid interested attention to what had been going on.

A mixture of sound—loud talk, a kind of complaining yammering, a shout or so—came from outside. The tall-hatted man picked up his empty glass, moved unhurriedly to a place at the bar about seven feet closer to the street than Brandon, and had his renewed drink to his lips when the street door slammed open.

A man stamped into the saloon, homing in on the tall hat. His own was a wide-brimmed, flat-crowned straw item, battered and spiked with broken ends of straw. Canvas trousers tucked into boots, and an aroma compounded of fresh and decaying vegetable and animal matter completed the picture of a farmer. The only unusual addition was a wide belt supporting a large holstered pistol.

The man at the bar turned lazily to face him, letting the front of his jacket slide open to reveal the handle of a pistol protruding from a burnished leather holster at his belt. Brandon thought that it would be an excellent idea to be elsewhere, but the room to the rear of where he stood was bare of effective shelter. The bartender had managed to disappear from his post in front of Tall Hat and reincorporate at the street end of the bar, taking a strong interest in something on the floor that seemed to merit close direct observation. Brandon shifted his weight so that it was balanced between his feet; he'd be ready to move wherever and whenever it seemed advisable.

"Doyle!" the farmer said.

The tall-hatted man looked at him expressionlessly.

"That game, it wasn't straight." The farmer's voice was unsteady; Brandon estimated the cause as an even blend of anger and fear.

"That might well be so," Doyle said.

The farmer gaped at him. "What the hell you mean? You're—"

"I know how I played," Doyle said, "and I played straight. You and your pals, I didn't see you cheating, but if you say you did, I'm not arguing the point."

The farmer's face darkened and the hand poised near the pistol at his side clenched into a fist, then opened tensely into a hovering claw. Brandon bent his knees slightly, estimating that a fast move might be indicated quite soon.

"You cardsharping son-of-a-bitch," the farmer said shrilly, "go for your gun!"

Doyle grinned, or rather let his lips drift open, showing slightly parted rows of teeth. It was like a dog's grin, or an ape's that Brandon had seen in a menagerie: mirthless, inhuman. He seemed to relax against the bar, leaning back on it, sliding his hands along the edge until his arms were fully extended and his hands as far as they could be from the pistol in his vest. His hat was tilted forward, shadowing the upper part of his face, but the fall of sunlight on the polished surface of the bar and on the glassware reflected upward, illuminating the facial shadows, and Brandon could see his eyes very clearly.

The farmer's hand bobbed over the gun, and his body seemed to twitch with indecision. "You robbed me!" he said, and Brandon relaxed an infinitesimal fraction. The faint whine that had crept into the man's voice reduced the chances of sudden gunplay by at least half, he guessed. Once that note came into the voice of a stubborn witness, in his experience, the game was all but over, and it was only a matter of time till the truth spilled out. The man who complains has ceded dominance to the one he's complaining to.

"You came to me to take my money," Doyle said. "Wouldn't play poker if you didn't think you could do that. Turned out you couldn't." He gave a mocking drum roll with the fingers of his splayed hands.

"Robbing honest folks," the farmer muttered. "Taking money they can't afford . . ."

"Twenty," Doyle said.

"What?"

"There's money on the table over there. My winnings—money I robbed you of, if you want to put it that way. Go over there, take one double eagle out of the heap, and get gone. That way you get to walk out of here, and you're twenty dollars richer than when you came in. You won't get a better offer today."

"Damn it," the farmer said, "I don't need . . ." His voice trailed off as Doyle continued to stare at him.

"Twen-ty," Doyle said again, with a precision and slowness that set the hair on Brandon's neck prickling. A talking automaton in some Poe story might talk like that, but the two syllables did not seem to have come from a human vocal apparatus.

The farmer took a step backward, his hand jerking as it tried to decide whether to resume a normal hanging position or keep up the pretense of being ready to draw the pistol. "It ain't enough," he said, without any force.

"Twenty."

The farmer turned and shuffled toward the table. Doyle's right arm flexed and a compact pistol appeared suddenly from his sleeve, nested in the palm of his hand, forefinger curled on the trigger, barrel pointing squarely at the farmer's back. Brandon tensed, but Doyle threw him a grin that held a touch of genuine amusement and slid the pistol into his jacket pocket.

The farmer, unaware that his feigned murder had provided his nemesis with a moment of flinty fun, picked up a coin from the table, turned and glared at Doyle, and walked dispiritedly out of the bar.

Brandon finished his drink and left a moment or so later. As he strolled along the clattering plankwalk, he considered what he had seen, looking at Doyle's eyes as he faced the farmer's lethal rage. There was no anger, no fear, no menace . . . no interest. Nothing. Maybe that was what had made the farmer back down, not the fear that he would lose a shootout, but a dim awareness that there was nothing inside Doyle to kill.

"*Pel*monico's," Edmund Chambers said thoughtfully, reading the heading of the smearily printed bill of fare. He looked at the waiter standing next to the table at which he, Elaine Chambers, and Brandon were seated. "You wanted to be sure nobody would mistakenly assume you are connected with the nationally famous Delmonico's, of New York City?"

"We would be happy as hogs for such," the waiter said, "the which is why we firstly called it *Del*monico's, so as to leave no reason not to make that there selfsame mistake and improve trade out of sight. But Mr. Jack Kestrel, that has eaten in the New York *Del*monico's, along with some prime places in Kansas City and Topeka, et here not much after opening day and told us misbranding was a hanging offense back in Texas, and if we kept on with the *Del* style to the name, he would import Texas law here and exact the penalty, beginning with the owner, then the cook, and work on down to the chore girl and me. He was joking, but the owner considered it'd be fun to go along with the joke." The waiter slid a defeated-looking towel over the table, with the chief effect of sending two dead flies onto Brandon's lap and then the floor. "Mr. Jack Kestrel has what they call a infectious sense of humor," he said. "If he says something in fun, other folks act on it immediate, then they might go away and study out what the joke was. That way, if they'd been mistook and it *wasn't* a joke, they'd still be alive anyways. So we are *Pel*monico's, and happy to serve you, gents and lady."

Their meals, when they came, were better than the railroad-station bystander's comments had suggested—nothing special, but not outright dreadful.

"Did you find a hall to hire for your show?" Brandon asked as they ate.

Edmund Chambers shook his head. "Nothing suitable built here yet. Sometimes you can work in a saloon, but most of the audience we'd want wouldn't go there. But we've set it up with the livery stable to use their yard, which isn't too much unlike the stage in Elizabethan times anyway. Got some handbills being done at the printer's right now, and we'll see what kind of interest we can drum up during the course of the afternoon. Curtain goes up, if we had one, at eight-thirty. Coming?"

"Of course," Brandon said. "Since I've seen Miss Chambers work so well impromptu, I'd admire to see a rehearsed performance. Got any idea how much of a crowd you'll draw?"

"Not really," Elaine Chambers said. "But the most possible, I expect. That boy from the train, the news butcher, he undertook to pass the bills out all over and talk the performance up, in exchange for being allowed to sell his things in the audience. In fact, it was him that came to us with the idea of using the livery-stable yard."

Brandon chewed on a piece of meat that had a reasonable probability of being chicken, and considered the fact that Rush Dailey had certainly approached the actors after he'd been looking over the stables for purposes of his own—purposes Jess Marvell had made a point of not noticing, or talking about. There was some kind of connection building up between those two, and Brandon sensed that threads of it were reaching out toward him.

10

The rich reek of coal oil from a dozen lanterns set on posts around the long flatbed wagon in the livery yard hung in the early evening air; the lanterns gleamed against the streaks of light remaining in the sky to the west.

Brandon stood in the considerable throng that bore witness to Rush Dailey's efforts at handbilling the town. By midafternoon the bills had been in every shop window on Main Street and tacked onto the walls of the often windowless establishments on Front, and Brandon, drifting with apparent aimlessness from saloon to saloon to see what information or impressions might surface, had seen him several times urging the attractions of the show on the patrons. As a result, the audience had a larger element of the sort that the merchant Jameson disliked than the Chamberses were probably figuring on.

Rush Dailey was moving among the crowd with his tray, hawking his wares while the audience awaited the announced hour of the performance. As he came near, Brandon observed that he was selling playing cards, paper-wrapped candy, and combs.

"Well, it wouldn't make sense to sell books here," Rush Dailey said when Brandon commented on his stock. "And

I'm out of the bottled soda water, which *would* go pretty well, and it would be tempting Providence to try the harmonicas here. This is about what I have that's safe to sell, and I got to say, it don't really matter. Seems that folks' minds are set to buy something when they're in a crowd like this, and it don't make much difference what it is. Right, sir, one comb ten cents, one deck of cards twenty, with our special bargain of two bits for both items purchased together, thank you," he said, handing over the goods to a roughly dressed man standing next to Brandon, to whom, from appearances, a comb might well have been an exotic novelty.

Brandon did not need to scan the crowd to see that the tall, and tall-hatted, marshal was not present. He had noticed during the course of the afternoon that the lawman's natural height and high-hat crown made his whereabouts evident at all times. That, and something slow and studied in his demeanor—and the massive rifle he carried casually—seemed to make the saloon patrons turn thoughtful when trouble seemed about to develop. And reflect that whatever they had in mind would probably not be worth it.

A flurry of clapping, shrill whistling, and stamping on the hardened earth of the stable yard greeted Edmund Chambers's entrance, which consisted of a lithe bound from the shadows of the stable to the wagon bed. He had—wisely, in Brandon's estimation—not tried for the full effect of Shakespearean costume, confining himself to tight dark trousers tucked into low boots and a bright-colored brocade vest over a loose-sleeved white shirt. He turned and lifted Elaine Chambers to the *ad hoc* stage, and the volume of the varied applause increased. Ease of movement rather than historical accuracy seemed to have determined her costume, which, in other than a dramatic setting, might have been taken for nightwear, and summer nightwear at that. Brandon noticed that the women in the crowd were not clapping as fervently as they had been.

Edmund Chambers bowed deeply, straightened, and raised both arms, quelling the applause. "Our thanks, good people of Inskip," he said, in a voice that surprised Brandon with its resonance and carrying power, "for your welcome, which we will hope to deserve. As our handbills warn you, we cannot offer the full version of Shakespeare's immortal comedy, nor would we wish you to stand in this yard for the hours that would require. Just as the fragrant, flavorful wine is distilled into brandy—all the power in a fraction of the space—so we have distilled this classic play into a dramatic dialogue of the two principal characters."

He stepped away from Elaine Chambers and gestured broadly at her. "Partake, good gentlefolk, of this refreshing brew, the essence of *The Taming of the Shrew.* Now here in Padua, a town not great, lived a rich merchant and his daughter, Kate. . . ."

As Elaine Chambers clawed and hissed at the air, embodying Kate's shrewishness, Brandon felt the power of the illusion sift over him: This middle-aged man and plain young woman posturing on a lanternlit wagon bed for a crowd of yokels *were* the brash Petruchio, the spitfire Kate. As Edmund Chambers had said, the thing was to fit the mask skintight, and the audience would have to believe.

Twenty minutes into the show, the power of belief was acting excessively on the man standing near Brandon who had bought Rush Dailey's cards-and-comb bargain package; evidently he was highly suggestible. "That feller is treatin' the lady *low,"* he rumbled to a companion. Petruchio had just dodged a blow from Kate and assisted her into a pratfall that shook the wagon.

"She ain't a lady, she's a actress," the man's associate said.

"Watch what yer sayin'," the comb buyer said dangerously.

"I mean, she's playin' a part, see, and so is he—they ain't really hittin' and wrastlin' and cursin' each other." Kate gave a piercing shriek and Petruchio a gloating laugh.

"Ain't they, by God!" the protestor said. "Bastard's gone too far this time, needs a lesson in how t' treat a lady." He jostled against Brandon as he hauled a revolver from his coat pocket and brought it up to point at Edmund Chambers.

At the sharp click of his left hand fanning back the hammer to cock the pistol, the crowd, as if long practiced in the maneuver, suddenly created a space of several feet around him, except for Brandon, who had not moved.

Without conscious thought, Brandon stepped behind the man, grabbed the man's gun hand with both his own, and levered it upward, prying at the fingers to break the man's grip. The pistol fired into the sky, the recoil knocking it out of the shooter's loosened grasp; Brandon caught it in his left hand, drew it back, then slammed it into the base of the man's skull.

The man slumped into the beginnings of collapse; Brandon caught him around the chest, shoved him at his astonished friend, and said loudly, "Quick work, Deputy. You just get this fellow down to the jail and let him sleep it off, eh?"

"I ain't no deputy. In fact, there ain't no deputy atall," the man complained to Brandon, fortunately speaking low enough not to carry far.

"Just get him out of here before they take a notion to lynch him," Brandon snarled. "Clear a path for the deputy, please," he called. "Nobody's hurt, just somebody a little the worse for drink, let's get on with the show."

In the uncertain light, nobody could be quite sure of just what had happened, he thought, and with any luck he wouldn't have attracted any unwelcome notoriety.

As the Chamberses, who had stopped in midscene during the brief excitement, resumed their identities of Petruchio and Kate, Brandon saw that Rush Dailey was looking not at the stage but at him, with unmistakable intentness.

A brief tour of Front Street after the well-applauded end of the Chamberses' performance convinced Brandon that his part in the disturbance at the show had not been much noticed. He returned to Mrs. Elster's boardinghouse satisfied that the unobtrusive anonymity he was depending on for gathering information was essentially undisturbed.

The table lamp in the front room was lit, though not fully turned up, and by its light Brandon saw Jess Marvell and

Rush Dailey sitting on the sofa, facing him as he came through the door.

"Evening," he said. Apparently the notion that had come to him at lunchtime about the connection being established between the two of them had been right. And he had a strong feeling that they were about to let him know how this was supposed to affect Charles Brooks.

"Will you sit with us awhile, Mr. Brooks?" Jess Marvell said. "I understand you had an interesting time at the play."

Brandon sat in a rocker across from the sofa. "A very spirited show, yes. Condensed Shakespeare, pretty potent."

"With offstage fireworks," Jess Marvell said.

"I believe there was some—"

"Rush saw just how it was, Mr. Brooks. Said you moved like lightning, had the man unconscious and hustled out before most people realized that there'd been a shot fired."

"Good of him to say so," Brandon said, wishing very strongly that Rush Dailey had said nothing at all; but that was too much to expect. The best he could hope for was that he had confined his reporting to Jess Marvell. And now, in fact, might be the time to find out why he would be reporting to Jess Marvell at all.

"You two are old friends?" he said.

Jess Marvell shook her head. "We got to talking on the train yesterday. Rush hadn't met a woman in business before, to talk to, and I have to say I hadn't met a news butcher, or anybody, quite like Rush. So we found we had a lot to talk about, and mostly it turned on our work and what we liked and didn't like about it and what could be better about it. And Rush decided Inskip might have more for him than the trains do, so he got off here to see about that."

Jess Marvell fell silent, and she appeared to be waiting for Brandon to be as forthcoming about his affairs as she had just been. When he was not, the silence stretched out until it snapped Rush Dailey's tolerance for inaction. "Miss Marvell and me, we worked it out," he blurted. "We *know.* We think. We think we know, I mean."

Jess Marvell looked at him with faint wonder and said, "What Rush means, Mr. Brooks, though you wouldn't know it, is that we've been wondering about you since the train: what your work is, what you're here for. It isn't any of our business, of course, but a person can't help wondering about things like that. And we believe we've hit on it. But don't worry, we don't mean to expose you."

Be interesting indeed, Miss Marvell, if you've divined the fact that I'm here to do murder. Necessary, and a thousand times justified, but premeditated murder in the first degree in any jurisdiction. Aloud, Brandon said nothing, he just looked at Jess Marvell and Rush Dailey with placid interest.

"You're a detective," Jess Marvell said. "A Pinkerton or so. You're after somebody—some robber or swindler or something like that—and you've followed him out here."

"Detective," Brandon said, turning the notion over in his mind. "What made you deduce that?"

"I seen it from the first, near," Rush Dailey said. "Way you spotted the bad stuff in those insurance policies, and how you handled California Sam—why, them things had 'detective' wrote all over them."

"And the way you think, how you work things out, that's not how most people's minds work," Jess Marvell said. "That's how detectives have to be, to outwit the crooks."

"And ever so spry and quick, too," Rush Dailey added. "The way you had that fellow with the pistol out and away in a winking, slick as a horse, that's detective work for sure."

"And you don't propose to queer my game," Brandon said mildly. "That's nice." This was going somewhere, he supposed, and it could do no harm to see down what corkscrew paths the two young people's ratiocination had led them.

"Better than that," Rush Dailey said. "We will be your eyes and ears. We will listen and look and tell you what as we see and hear."

"You've seen how Rush gets all over and notices things, Mr. Brooks," Jess Marvell said. Brandon, still wishing that Rush had done less noticing at the play, had to agree. "And as for me, you wouldn't believe the amount of information that comes over a hotel desk. And there's something else, but we'll get to that in a minute."

"Some time after we've thrashed out why you would want to set up as spies for an itinerant detective, if you should happen to be right about that," Brandon said. "I would think the hotel business would be enough of an occupation for you at least, Miss Marvell."

"Well, it isn't," Jess Marvell said. "I mean, I am good at it, and it's interesting, but it's a hired-hand job, even if it's called manager. Like I was saying this morning, there are things I can see to do, and I can do them, and I can be my own boss doing them. If I have the money to start up."

"Me and Miss Marvell, we been talking," Rush Dailey said, "and right here in Inskip, a place that'll have good meals ready when the trains stop, why, that place'll be a gold mine. And I seen that the livery stable had that big old wagon for hire, the one that the stage folks did their tableaux on tonight—"

"—and that you could get up meals on a cookstove someplace and put them in warming dishes, and have them hot at the platform when the train came in—"

"—and line up twenty places along one side, plates and knives and forks and wipe cloths, elegant as Pelmonico's and four times as fast—"

"—passengers fed and happy and back on the train in twelve minutes if we had to, but if we had something like that to offer, we could work it out with the railroad to stop for half an hour so they'd have time to eat comfortably. But I don't have money saved up, and Rush here doesn't either, so we will be your agents and find out what you need to know, and you will pay us a fee that'll get us set up."

It is a wonder, Brandon thought, that two people that are only a touch crazy in their own way can get together and come up with something that's more than twice as crazy as both of them put together. And the craziest thing is, the way things are out here, towns blooming and dying like petunias, it could work. Doesn't appear that the fool-killer's been able to raise the train fare out here, or the place'd be depopulated.

To his dismay, not only their commercial plans but the offer they had made him was making more and more sense.

Information's what I'm here to get, and I'm not getting so much as a sniff right now. Two more noses snuffling around, and noses that have a good reason to be stuck in lots of different places—yes, that could turn up some Kenneally scent, so it could. And they're nine parts right about me, anyhow: I'm doing what a detective would be doing, right up to the place where I'm supposed to place them under arrest; that's where the resemblance ends. No handcuffs, no file of evidence, just . . . His hand traced the bulk of the pistol in his jacket pocket. Counselor, you've been dealt a hand you didn't expect, but why not play it? Dealer doesn't seem to be ready for another one yet.

"It's remarkable how you worked it out," he said. "You're quite right, I can use some informants here, and you're also right that it's worth paying for."

What he told them of his quarry was true as far as it went—robbers of a train in Missouri, wanted for murder—but his account did not include the deaths of the Brandon family or the name Kenneally. The first had no relevance to any investigation by Detective Charles Brooks, of an as yet unspecified agency; and the second might dampen the enthusiasm of his investigators if they knew the clan's far-spread reputation, or endanger them if they did not. If they turned up anything to do with a reunion of train robbers, that would be as strong a lead to follow as he could ask for.

"Now, as for the pay," Jess Marvell said, "you don't know what we find out for you will be worth, and we don't know how much time we'll have to put into it, so it's hard to set a figure. I say the best is, let's see what we come up with and what it takes to do that, and we'll settle on a price." This seemed to Brandon to be unusually soft bargaining, until she added, "To come out of the hundred dollars you give us up front."

Brandon blinked. "It'd have to be pretty good information to be worth that."

Jess Marvell shrugged. "If it isn't, then what's left over is your investment in a sure-fire business. Might allow you to retire from the detective work."

Brandon considered a moment, then agreed, and he paid over the five double eagles to Jess Marvell. She looked at the nickel-sized gold coins in her palm with an expression of reverent delight, then slipped them into her handbag. "Thanks, Mr. Brooks. It'll be worth it, you'll see." She looked at him. "One thing . . ."

"Yes?"

"What are you supposed to be?"

Brandon looked at her, puzzled.

"Your disguise," Rush Dailey said. "You detectives, you don't go around saying 'I'm a detective,' for you'd never catch up with the crooks then, and it wouldn't be much better if you went around without ever saying what it was you did." As that was precisely what Brandon had been doing—and as he had, he now realized, given no thought to any kind of false identity—he was taken aback. Mistake to get so taken up with what you're doing, Counselor, that you don't pay attention to how it has to be done. . . .

"So what," Rush Dailey went on, "is your disguise? It's a deep one, I guess, for me and Miss Marvell, we haven't worked out what it's meant to be yet. But it'd be best for us to know, so as we can mention it to any that ask us."

Brandon reached back to Edmund Chambers's comments on using observation to create a role and act it, and the unwelcome spate of detail Perkins had fogged him with on the train and at the Bull's Foot, and said, as firmly as if it had been his long-laid plan, "Cattle buyer." Since Perkins would be leaving on the morning train, there wouldn't be any overknowledgeable people around to penetrate the story, and it would be some days, apparently, before there would be any cattle coming into Inskip to put it to the test.

He left them in the front room and mounted the stairs to his bedroom, with a growing sense that something might actually come out of this outlandish proposal. After all, Counselor, a lawyer turned manhunter pretending to be a detective masquerading as a cattle buyer—that ought to get something moving!

* * *

"Maybe I'll see you when I get back next week," Perkins said as he swung aboard the eastbound train. "What I've got to do in Wichita won't take all that long, and I'll be here again when the first herds get in."

"Maybe," Brandon said.

The engine screamed, snorted, grumbled, and began to inch its way forward. Perkins scrambled into the passenger car, calling back, "Expect I'll have enough sense not to get into a monte game this time, eh?"

Brandon wasn't sure. Trying a monte game under any circumstances was a loser's move, and a man who could do it once couldn't be counted safe from trying anything dumb. If the fool-killer really couldn't cross the Missouri, Perkins could be taking a chance going back to his territory.

As the last car of the train slid by and a scattering of cinders sifted onto Brandon's hat and shoulders, the tall marshal stepped up beside him.

"Seeing a colleague off?" the marshal said. His voice was the bearlike grumble you might look for in a wrestler awakened from hibernation; Brandon had expected something higher pitched from the long, lean frame—rather the way Lincoln had sounded the one time Brandon had heard him.

"Colleague," Brandon repeated, not making it a question, in case that would prove awkward.

"Cattle buyer like yourself, that Perkins, I understand. Going back to Wichita till the trail herds start coming in. But you're figuring it makes more sense to be on the ground all along, looks like."

Cattle buyer like yourself . . . what the hell's that about? Brandon wondered. If I threw myself into the part as hard as Edmund Chambers ever dreamed on, and made up like fury to book, I misdoubt folks would say that there goes Charlie Brooks, the nonpareil of cattle buyers, buy your cow as soon as spit at you. So how . . .

"That young fellow off the train told me what you did at the playacting last night," the marshal said. "Smooth work, but I expect you have to hold your own with the badmen, kind of job you're in. Till I talked with him, didn't know how lively it gets sometimes."

"Goes with the job," Brandon said. Rush Dailey didn't seem to lose any time at whatever he undertook.

"Way you did," the marshal said, "just what had to be done, no more, no less—that's something like Jack Kestrel would have handled it."

"Well now, Jack Kestrel, I don't know that I'd class myself with Jack Kestrel," Brandon said. Beyond the Pelmonico's waiter's exaggerated account of him—if it was exaggerated—he had no notion whatever of Jack Kestrel, but he sensed that a cattle buyer of any Kansas experience would be likely to know a lot about him. He wished Perkins had been more forthcoming about Kestrel and less about feed-lot management and grass strains.

The marshal's hat brim flapped as he snapped his head back for a boom of laughter. "God, no! If you was of his persuasions and tendencies, I'd have to figure out fast if I should take your guns, shoot you, or pin my badge on you. One Kestrel's sudden enough for me, a pair'd overload the plate. I don't look for him here until summer end, pretty near—had to overwinter his herd at Dysart, just got shut of it a while back, and so the drive won't be here until the season's pretty well along. But the thing you done last night, like I say, that was smooth enough for Kestrel."

His gaze shifted past Brandon and he stiffened. "Interesting," he said softly. Brandon turned and saw the shack that housed the express office at the far end of the platform. As it had been the day before, a wagon and its mule team stood outside, but they had company today, a compact, competent-looking horse standing stolidly with its head down, as if hoping that the dusty earth might sprout grass if stared at intently enough.

"Could be a customer picking up a shipment," the marshal said. "But he'd likely have hitched his horse to the rail, not just dropped the reins like that. Can't see anything through the window . . . believe a closer look might be an idea."

He stepped past Brandon and moved down the platform, holding the heavy rifle waist-high. Brandon was not sure why he followed—he hadn't been asked to, or told not to, but he felt compelled to see what was going on.

There was a flurry of motion Brandon could not interpret at the window, and the marshal muttered, "Yeah," and eased the rifle upward a bit. The express-office door flew open and banged against the building wall. A man, moving too fast for Brandon to focus on, carrying two white sacks in one hand and a pistol in the other, burst through the doorway, snapped off a shot in their direction, and crouched for a leap onto the back of the waiting horse.

The report of the marshal's gun seemed artillery-loud to Brandon, and the explosion of dust and pebbles under the horse's nose was more like the burst of a cannon shell than the impact of a bullet on dirt. The horse screamed and stood almost straight up on its hind feet, then plunged forward and galloped down Front Street. The leaping man sprawled in the dust for a fractional instant, then tossed the bags into the wagon, sprang to the driver's seat, plucked the whip from its socket, and lashed the mules while urging them to a running start with a shrill, gobbling whoop.

The marshal walked slowly down the platform as the man in the wagon continued to hit and yell at the mules, which continued to ignore him. When the marshal was within a few yards, he dropped the whip and said, "Aw, hell."

The marshal motioned with his rifle. "Down. Leave the sacks. Agent'll take 'em back in. If you've left him able to."

"Just tied an' gagged," the failed bandit reassured him. "No harm done to anybody, Marshal."

The marshal looked at Brandon and nodded toward the express-office doorway. Brandon went in, released the indignant clerk from his bonds, and accompanied him outside, where the marshal used the rope to secure his prisoner's hands.

The clerk remained in his office to restore it to order and to cradle protectively the two sacks of coin that had nearly been diverted from their intended recipient, the bank, and the marshal marched his prisoner to the blocklike jail. The gunfire had drawn the attention of townsfolk on both sides of the tracks, but all kept a discreet distance from the action, and Brandon was alone in accompanying the two principals.

When the prisoner had been locked in, the marshal returned to his chair outside his office and resumed his calm survey of Main and Front Streets.

Brandon had been wondering about something. "That fellow shot at us, he could have escaped with the money. Seems to me it would have been simplest to shoot him direct, instead of spooking his horse."

The marshal patted the rifle. "This is a buffalo gun, fifty caliber. Hit a man just about anyplace with it, even the foot, and he's a goner; the shock stops him like a clock. Now, along with my wages, I get paid by the arrest, two dollars and a half for misdemeanors and breaches of the peace, five dollars for serious stuff. Nothing for killing someone."

He seemed to contemplate the economics of life and death for a moment, then went on: "Also, shooting from the hip like that, you can be surer of hitting your target if it's the whole planet, not one man."

Brandon's purposeful idling around Inskip brought him no new information, though it did give him a chance to practice his role as a cattle buyer with the habitués of the Bull's Foot and deliver firm opinions on topics of which he knew nothing but what he had absorbed from Perkins's loquacity, though that turned out to be enough.

In midmorning he saw Rush Dailey in the livery-stable yard, applying a coat of paint to the long wagon and talking to a straggle of loungers. Whether he was gathering information or extolling the rolling restaurant service he and Jess Marvell proposed to provide, Brandon could not tell. In early afternoon he saw Rush Dailey moving along Front Street with his merchandise tray, going from one saloon to another.

The afternoon was oppressively hot, and he wondered if the river might provide a cooler atmosphere. As he walked south from Front Street toward the river bluff, he saw, behind one of the buildings, Jess Marvell talking to a couple of women on the back stoop; waiter girls from one of the saloons, he supposed. Whenever the Bright Kentucky got here, it would need staff, and a waiter girl who didn't want to keep on with the job until it ended in whoring, as it would, might be glad of the chance to change occupations.

The air by the river was still and hot, providing no relief. Brandon walked out to the still-empty cattle pens and visualized them as they would be in a week or so, filled with restless, bawling creatures that had made an epic journey from their home ranges, survived privation and peril, and were about to enjoy the luxury of a train ride to a sledgehammer between the eyes and a knife across the throat. There was money in killing them; that was why they would die. There was no money in killing the express bandit; that was why he lived. I've killed, and I mean to kill, but not for money. Maybe some day I'll think about whether that's better or worse; anyhow, it's what I am going to do. Be funny if those kids come up with something that helps me do that.

"There was a barn-burning, and the matter of some fowls misappropriated, and a dog-fight that wasn't run honest, and other such spoken of freely and openly," Rush Dailey said. "Plus some serious personal disagreements, some of them mortal, and of course the express-office business this morning, that you was in on. All that kind of thing, the fellows in the saloons, you couldn't hardly keep 'em from telling about and embroidering on. But nothing about train robbing. My opinion, if these fellows knew anything about that kind of thing, they'd be blabbing it out, they're that gossipy-minded."

Mrs. Elster's parlor was the coolest place Brandon had found in Inskip that day, and he felt less on edge as he listened, late in the afternoon, to his new agents' reports of their first day's inquiries.

"Some of the ladies I talked to have men friends that make a trade out of being on the far side of the law," Jess

Marvell said, "and they touched on things like cardsharping and swindling and grudge killings and acid throwing and counterfeiting—and some things I don't believe I'll mention here, that I'd hardly heard of before—but train robbing, no, here or Missouri."

"But we've only just started," Rush Dailey said. "There's lots more places to look at and people to listen to here, and Miss Marvell and me, we're going to do that. We have got the lunch wagon just about fixed up, and Miss Marvell has compacted with Mrs. Elster to do meals in her kitchen here, so's they can be run down to the station while they're hot. We'll be in business tomorrow or the next day, and folks'll come to us and talk over whatever's on their minds while they're eating."

"And once the hotel's open," Jess Marvell said, "there'll be a place where everybody comes, the Main Street people and the Front Streeters, just to see what it's like—and whatever there is to hear, it'll be heard. That's the way it worked in Dysart. So it's not important that Rush and I didn't hear anything useful today; it's not to be expected that we would."

"We detectives learn to be patient," Brandon said.

From outside the house there came a single distant shout, then a flurry of calls and a chorus of enthusiastic barking. Brandon looked out the parlor window, past the house diagonally across Cottonwood Street to the prairie beyond. Near the edge of the vast carpet of tall grass, perhaps a quarter-mile from the town, a three-story building, gleaming white in the rays of the descending sun, moved slowly toward them. Now Brandon could see the horned heads and dun backs of the oxen pulling the hotel and man standing on the front porch guiding them with a complex network of reins. Hats and shoulders bobbed in the grass, moving from the rear of the moving building to the front and back, shifting the huge logs on which the building rolled to provide a continuous moving surface. The first people from the town to spy the oncoming building were streaming out to greet it.

Jess Marvell and Rush Dailey moved to the window and

watched the Bright Kentucky Hotel grow infinitely slowly but inexorably larger.

The house movers and carpenters worked through most of the night, and by late morning the Bright Kentucky was settled on its frame foundation on the formerly vacant lot on Main Street, its wide porch making a shadowed recess in the line of buildings.

Brandon saw a flicker of motion as Jess Marvell moved past a front window, doubtless readying the place for when the furniture-laden freight team following the hotel would arrive.

He had put in a couple of hours drifting into and out of the Main Street stores, and had submitted to a haircut he didn't need for the sake of something to do as well as in the hope of absorbing some information he could use. He could appreciate how drinking, gambling, whoring, and killing came to be popular activities in places like this; there didn't seem to be all that much other activity on offer.

Whatever Jess Marvell might say about the hotel as a gathering place for the loose-mouthed element, he doubted it would be productive of what he needed, and the same went for Rush Dailey's meal wagon. True enough that patience was a prime requisite for detectives—and for less law-abiding manhunters—but patiently staking out an empty hunting ground was foolish. The one slim lead he had had was to Dysart, not Inskip, and following it to Inskip diluted its dubious certainty even further.

He found that he was considering where to go next, not if he would go. Nothing he had heard suggested that there was, or would be, anything for him in Inskip. But there was nothing to send him elsewhere, either.

He slowed his pace in front of the hotel, then stopped and went up the steps, across the porch, and through the wide front door. Jess Marvell was sweeping the floor of the lobby, and looked up as he came in. "It's going to be a mortal lot of work to get it ready," she said, "but it'll be truly grand when it is. I want to get out of here and be my own boss when I can, but the hotel business is in my blood, I think. If that lunch wagon goes well, I'll have to study out if there's a way to get some hoteling into it. You care to see the premises? I'd be glad to set this broom down for a while."

The wide staircase to the second floor did not seem to have been strained or loosened by the journey from Dysart, and the doorways and floor-ceiling lines on the second floor appeared straight and true.

"Bedrooms aren't very large, but they're airy and comfortable," Jess Marvell said, opening the door to the one nearest the head of the stairs. "Darn! No matter how you clean, there's always some trash left behind." She kicked a drift of small rubbish in a corner of the bare room, scattering it.

Brandon stooped like a diving hawk and snatched something from the floor in a hand as curved and tense as a talon; he had performed the action before he was aware that he was about to do so, and only realized why when he looked at what he held. He seemed to be looking down on the room from a great distance, seeing the dust motes floating in the sunlight that made bright flattened rectangles on the floor, and two tiny figures in the center of the floor.

"Who had this room last, in Dysart?" he asked. Jess Marvell looked at him uneasily, and he realized that his tone had been eerily calm, almost whispered—a startling contrast to the swoop and snatch of his retrieval of the debris from the floor.

"One of the cattlemen, up to sell a herd that had to winter over. He was here, oh, ten days, two weeks ago. Sam Canty's foreman from down in Texas. Jack Kestrel."

Brandon looked at what he held in his hand: a peeled stick, four inches long, intricately sliced and curled at the top in a convincing imitation of a flower—twin of the one in his valise, that he had picked up in the ruined house at Mound Farm.

11

"Well, it is the southbound coach when it leaves *here,"* the stage-line clerk said, "but after about four bitty farm towns, the line cuts over east to Boudin, where it crosses the cattle trail, then goes on over into Arkansas, terminusing at Fort Smith."

"Can I get a coach down into Texas at this Boudin place?" Brandon asked.

The clerk shook his head. "Have to go all the way through the Nations for that, and the company don't feel inclined to run coaches past a couple hundred miles of Indians. Bad enough the route dips down into the Neutral Zone for a stretch, as our law nor Indian don't run there, but we haven't had any trouble to speak of. Best you get a horse and gear at Boudin and head south on your own. By now the trail herds'll be coming up, so there'll be company along the way, even though it's going in the other direction."

Wondering at the back of his mind what kind of trouble the clerk thought wasn't worth speaking of, Brandon said, "You're pretty sure I can pick up a horse and supplies at Boudin?"

"Mister," the clerk said, "one way or another, I expect

you can find most things you'd want in Boudin. And lots else."

Brandon paid for his ticket, studied the timetable on the wall—which promised that he would be carried toward his destination somewhat faster than an energetic man might walk, the journey commencing in about an hour if the coach arrived on time—and stepped out of the stage office. The long flatbed wagon was no longer in the yard, and, looking down Main Street, he saw it next to the railroad-station platform, with some sort of superstructure giving it the appearance of an ungainly riverboat equipped with wheels. Two figures bustling around it were identifiable even at the distance of a couple of blocks as Rush Dailey and Jess Marvell, readying their mobile lunch counter for whoever might descend from the afternoon eastbound train.

Brandon considered strolling over there to use up some of the time before the stagecoach came in but decided against it. He had finished his business with Jess Marvell and Rush Dailey, and he had no inclination for good-byes, particularly with Jess Marvell after their last encounter an hour or so before. . . . It struck him that it had been a long time since he had parted with anyone he expected to see again. Though, if he chose to, he might well be hearing from his two self-appointed detective agents according to the plans Rush Dailey had laid out for him.

"A retainer, if you're familiar with the term," Rush Dailey said.

"It's not unknown to me," Brandon said dryly. The morning sun and the continuing noise of construction on the house down the street filtered through Mrs. Elster's front-parlor curtains, and a counterpoint of crockery and silverware clattering came from the kitchen, where Jess Marvell was overseeing the first batch of meals the lunch wagon was to dispense.

"For it, Miss Marvell and me, we keep ferreting out information and writing up what we find. And when you're in a place long enough to get mail, you let us know and we'll send the reports on to you."

Brandon wasn't sure whether he accepted this plan out of genuine belief in its usefulness, admiration for the pair's determined enterprise, or a desire to keep their curiosity working on his behalf rather than on the enigma he might present to them if he failed to keep up his character as a detective. With three good motives, anyhow, it seemed like the thing to do.

"Oh, it'll be amazing what we find out, I expect," Rush Dailey said. "What with the lunch wagon and the drummers and such at the Bright Kentucky, for they're a wonderful crowd for gossip, talkative as a horse; we'll know everything there is to be knowed, and winnow out the chaff and bind it up all neat for you."

"Without the chaff, what did you find out about this Jack Kestrel?" Brandon said. Immediately after finding the wood flower yesterday, he had quizzed Jess Marvell about Kestrel and set Rush Dailey to turning up whatever else he could. He had told them, without going into particulars, that such a flower had been found at the scene of the crime he was investigating and that its discovery in the room Kestrel had used was a lead that had to be followed up.

Jess Marvell had given him the basic information that Kestrel had served as trail boss for a herd sent up the trail toward the end of the previous season by Sam Canty, a rancher in Bascom, Texas, near the Elm Fork of the Red River. Low prices had obliged Canty to winter the herd over at Dysart and sell in spring, when the first beef of the year would fetch a premium. Kestrel had seen the cattle settled in, then vanished, returning a few weeks back to handle the sale of the herd before going back to the ranch. As far as Jess recollected, he was the last tenant of the room before the Bright Kentucky closed operations in Dysart.

"About the only handle I got on Mr. Jack Kestrel," Rush Dailey said thoughtfully, "is that there ain't a handle to him. Fellows I got to talking to me about him, each of 'em seen a different Mr. Jack Kestrel, seems like. Listen to one, he's mortal mean as a rattler; listen to another, he's a hard-working cowman, mild-mannered as any heath hen; another yet, he's a flaming sword of righteousness, driving out the evildoers and contumacious."

Kestrel, it appeared, was known—or reliably rumored—to have killed three or seven or twelve men in reasonably acceptable circumstances; had served as chief of police in one of the rail-line cowtowns that had flourished further eastward in previous years and cleaned the place up by methods still being debated; had gambled, sometimes as a pastime, sometimes as a trade, in many places; had brought the Canty herd up to Dysart with a minimum of losses and trouble and imposed an unusually effective discipline on his crew, who had failed to commit the standard outrages the town had come to expect; and had perhaps sharpened his cattle-trade skills by some profitable rustling.

"What one and all agrees on is that he's a dab hand with a gun," Rush Dailey said. "If he's not a gunfighter, as some claim, it ain't in dispute that he can gunfight whenas he has to or wants to. Nothing in all that to say he's the kind of man that would rob a train, or on the other hand that he ain't."

"I don't know what it says about him," Jess Marvell said, entering the parlor in time to hear the end of Rush Dailey's report, "but he doesn't . . . he isn't an active ladies' man, so to say. I mean, at the hotel, he didn't make that kind of trouble with guests he shouldn't have had, d'you see, and some of the women I talked to about chambermaiding and such at the Bright Kentucky, that moved on here from Dysart, they said he didn't visit . . . anybody they knew."

She put it matter-of-factly and in circumspect language, but Brandon was vividly conscious that she was talking about whoring and whorehouses—even though saying they didn't figure in Jack Kestrel's makeup, so *not* talking about them, in a way—and he had a sudden sense of complicity with her, as if she were showing him an album of brightly colored detailed engravings of the activities Kestrel didn't indulge in. In an almost hallucinatory flash, he saw that some of the figures in the engravings bore a singular resemblance to himself and to Jess Marvell.

He forced the image from his mind. As well he was leaving town in an hour or so, if his mind was going to start slipping its brake like that. *Downhill run on a steep slope, and a smashed wagon at the bottom, that's where you're headed, Counselor.*

Since Elise's murder, Brandon had not been troubled by the need, or any particular want, for a woman. He had registered female attractiveness—lately, of Elaine Chambers and Jess Marvell—in an abstract, uninvolved way, as a feature of the landscape of his experience, but had felt no impulse to do anything about it. During the months of his personal limbo, and during the week since the killing of Casmire had given him new life and a new goal, desire had had nothing to do with what Cole Brandon had become and was becoming. The lightning-bolt instant of awareness he had just experienced disturbed him, and he sensed dangers he had not taken into consideration. The journey south was coming when it was needed, apparently.

"If we find out anything useful to you," Jess Marvell said, "we'll send it on to you at this Bascom place, though the mail will take a time to get there. You may not want to be using your own name by then, so we'll send it to . . . oh, say, Colin Binn—easy for you to remember the same initials . . . and you can say you're a friend of his and pick it up at the post office."

Brandon agreed and went upstairs to pack. In his room, he turned his mind to Jack Kestrel. The conflicting images Rush Dailey had collected, and the comments of the restaurant waiter and the marshal refused to come together coherently. He recalled the dead-eyed gambler, Doyle, who had faced down the gun-bearing farmer in the Bull's Foot the day before yesterday—this Kestrel would be something like that, maybe. If so, he'd be a good candidate for the role of the murderer Brandon was seeking. The emptiness he had seen in the gambler's eyes marked someone who saw no important difference between life and death, his own or another's. *Of course, Counselor,* his personal prosecutor said, *that's the track you're on now, isn't it?* His private defense attorney objected: *Not the same at all—I'm seeing that justice is done.*

Of course.

Brandon looked down the street at the distant lunch wagon, wondering if it might not after all be a good idea to stroll over and take his leave of Jess Marvell and Rush Dailey; but a distant noise resolved itself into a rumbling and squealing of undergreased wheels and axles and the clopping of a couple of dozen hoofs on the hard-packed dirt of the road. The southbound coach rattled and swayed down the street toward the livery stable, the driver making no effort to spur the team to a last-minute dash for an impressive arrival.

Brandon leaned against a fence rail while the driver and the express messenger who rode beside him worked with the stable hands to unharness the team and put in fresh horses. Two passengers, a young man and woman, alighted and walked in the yard, bending and stretching in a way that did not speak well for the comfort of the trip so far. Brandon guessed them to be brother and sister from their shared style of blond good looks and generous—not plump but, say, corn-fed—build.

The door of the stage office flapped open, and Brandon was surprised to see the gambler, Doyle, emerge, escorted by the marshal. The marshal's high-crowned sombrero and the gambler's tall plug hat, each impressive enough seen on its own, now conveyed the impression of a headwear display.

The marshal's hat, or his office, seemed to have prevailed, as Doyle was clearly leaving against his will, though keeping a calm face about it. "'Course you ain't done nothing illegal," the marshal said cordially. "Normal business doings, friendly games of chance, disputes settled by the calming word, no complaints. You want to keep it that way, I want to keep it that way, and that's why you're leaving. You don't do anything the law can get you for, most times, but it comes about that them that has dealings with you *do.* Fellows like you, you're kind of a lightning rod for lawbreaking—it goes on all around you. A man's shot after being in one of your games, and a couple of boozed-up farmers been talking lynching, which could lead to me having to arrest 'em or shoot 'em, which the town council don't take kindly to me shooting taxpayers."

Doyle said nothing as he lit a thin cigar, creating a pungent, slightly spicy reek. The marshal took an unoffered cigar from the gambler's case before he could return it to his pocket, lit it, and puffed out a cloud of smoke. "Besides," he said, "this ain't any sort of a place for you yet, not until the trail herds start coming in. Boudin, now, there's your true and spiritual home. I'm doing you a favor."

"You could be," Doyle said with a thin smile. Brandon saw that he was looking past the marshal to the young couple, now shaking their arms as if to restore circulation or loosen cramped muscles.

By the middle of the next morning Doyle seemed to have taken some pains in seeing that the marshal's favor would be a worthwhile one. The afternoon previously, wedged on the narrow, back-facing seat next to Brandon, he had contrived to present himself to the young couple facing them—brother and sister, Brandon had been right on that point, Henry and Lucy Gans from Pennsylvania, in transit between a visit to a farming uncle up near Nebraska and one to Lucy's fiancé, a deputy U.S. marshal at the district court in Fort Smith—as a colorful, gentlemanly seeker of adventure on the frontier, properly reticent about his abilities and achievements but all the same managing to be persuaded to set out several fascinating incidents. Brandon maintained his identity as Charles Brooks, cattle buyer, but nobody appeared to care.

Doyle exercised considerable craft in his presentation, but with no life, none of the zest California Sam had brought to his work. Doyle's voice was animated, but Brandon, sitting next to him, could see that the shadowed eyes under the tall hat were as dead as they had been in the confrontation at the Bull's Foot.

For a while, Brandon thought that Doyle was staving off boredom, then that he was preparing the ground for a profitable poker game with Henry; but the aim of his strategy seemed pretty clear by the time they halted for the night for a change of horses, an abominable meal, and a night's sleep on sacks filled with cornhusks in tiny cubicles. The proprietor of the unconvincing claimant to the title of inn appeared to believe that stage passengers were to be stored rather than entertained, and the weariness and bone-ache produced by hours of riding in the coach to some extent justified him: Brandon was asleep deeply and quickly and so, as far as he could tell, were the others. Henry and Lucy were sharing a room, so Doyle, even if he had the stamina for it, could not make the move Brandon had come to see he intended. But he was sure it would be coming.

The next stage in the campaign was evident in the morning, when the passengers resumed their places in the coach. Brandon was, as before, next to Doyle and facing Lucy Gans. But beside her this time was the express messenger, ousted from his post beside the driver.

"Henry's so set up," she said. "It's quite a thing, for a stage driver to ask a passenger to sit up next to him. For all it's bumpier and you get the wind and the dust in your face and the sun bakes you, men set store by it. I expect it's the honor of it, for that's what men make themselves uncomfortable for the most, from what I've seen."

"That kind of favor from the driver means that the lad's recognized as being the type of fellow who belongs out here," Doyle said smoothly. "A tribute any young man would value."

Brandon considered that it was more of a tribute to the bills he had observed passing from Doyle to the driver, for reasons he had not understood till now, just after their disgraceful breakfast. Doyle would have until midafternoon, when they were due in Boudin, to make his best impression on Lucy Gans; though, with Henry back down from his lofty perch to escort her again, Brandon did not see what practical use the gambler might make of any achievements of that sort.

Doyle did the Othello role to the hilt, recounting daring

and improbable adventures and his modest but effective parts in them; and Lucy Gans made a convincing Desdemona, producing a counterpoint chorus of sympathetic gasps and exclamations. The express messenger, realizing that for once he was in no imminent danger of being bounced off his perch to fall ten feet under the coach wheels if he relaxed, abandoned himself to sleep, coming partly awake when Lucy Gans would shove his drooping head away from her shoulder.

Brandon was not surprised, when, after a late-morning stop "to stretch yer laigs"—the driver's delicate offer of the use of a gap-planked privy next to a sod-roofed trading post—he re-entered the coach to find Doyle and Lucy Gans side by side on the forward-facing seat and the messenger curled up on the seat next to his, his head pillowed on a mail sack, as happily relaxed as any of the Inskip prairie-dog merchant's charges.

"More restful for the poor fellow to ride backwards like that," Doyle said blandly, "so I felt I should offer to change."

As the coach jounced along in the midday heat, Doyle's Munchausening lost what little interest it had held for Brandon, particularly since he was now able to spin his skein of fancy in tones that had to carry only the few inches between his mouth and the half of Lucy Gans's ear visible under her coiled hair. Without making any overt gesture, he seemed to have spread out in the seat so that he was jammed against her as much as if there had been two others sharing the space with them. It seemed to Brandon that she was breathing faster than usual.

There still seemed to be no way Doyle could cash in on whatever influence he was gaining over Lucy Gans, as she and her brother would be on the way out of Boudin before nightfall and Doyle would remain there. Maybe he was just keeping his hand in, in the same way he might practice deceptive shuffling and cutting between games. Whatever Doyle was up to was, in any case, of no interest to Brandon, and he realized that the express messenger had probably hit on the best way to deal with a stagecoach journey. He tilted his hat over his face and sank back against the thinly padded backrest, letting the motion of the coach sway him to sleep.

He was jolted out of it by the impact of Lucy Gans's hat and head in his midriff, blasting air out of his lungs; the coach was shaking sickeningly on its springs—vibrating, he realized, from the shock of the sudden stop that had hurled the girl onto him.

Doyle pulled her back onto the seat; she quacked with alarm as she lifted her arms and reflexively dabbed at her crushed hat: "What? What? What?"

Strident but incomprehensible shouts, seemingly orders, came from outside; the coach rocked as if someone were climbing off it; the window next to Lucy Gans shattered as a hand holding a .44 revolver smashed through it.

"Passengers out! *Now!*" the man with the gun yelled. "No Frank Fearnot crap or them two git their guts blowed out!"

The gunman was masked with a dirty cloth, which suggested to Brandon that he probably did not mean to kill them outright unless a good reason for it turned up; he seemed to be standing on the coach's mounting step, grabbing the roof rack with his free hand. Beyond him, Brandon saw another masked man on a horse, with a double-barreled shotgun pointing down at the driver and Henry Gans, who lay prone on the ground.

Lucy Gans had kept up a single-tone keening, something like a steam whistle blowing for an improbably long time, since the window had exploded in her face. "We'll do as he says," Doyle said loudly, and reached past her for the door handle, to the bandit's presumed satisfaction, as little could be seen of his expression.

To Brandon's stupefaction, Doyle's hand changed direction and grabbed the bandit's gun-hand wrist, yanking it into the car and bringing the pistol alarmingly close; his other hand slapped his jacket open and snaked his own revolver out of its holster, brought it next to the bandit's staring-eyed head, and pulled the trigger.

The bandit fell backward off the coach step with an

agonized howl—his eardrum must have taken the full side blast from the muzzle of Doyle's weapon—dropping his revolver inside the coach. Through the thinning cloud of smoke Brandon saw the mounted man clap his hands to his face, flinging the shotgun away, and topple over to the other side of his horse. One booted foot caught in a stirrup, dragged it over the horse's back, then stopped, pointed in the air as the stirrup leather snapped taut. The horse screamed, danced in place for a moment, planting one hoof on Henry Gans's leg, and bolted away, his erstwhile rider bouncing headdown on the rocky trail. Even if he hadn't been killed outright by Doyle's shot, Brandon estimated, he would not have survived the first bounce.

His colleague, hand cupped over one ear, staggered frantically toward his horse, leaped aboard it, and spurred it in the direction the dead man was still taking, the trail now marked with irregular oblong dark streaks.

Doyle sighted along the barrel of his revolver at the fleeing bandit, lowered the gun, and gave Brandon the same thin grin that had accompanied his taking aim at the unsuspecting farmer in the Bull's Foot. He leaned out the window to hail the driver and Henry Gans, now bewilderedly rising from the ground. Brandon was certain that he was quite aware how much of him this brought in contact with how much of Lucy Gans; he had known divorces to be granted on evidence of less contact than that. Lucy Gans's eyes were wide and unfocused, and he supposed she might be unaware of the impromptu intimacy the situation had brought about. On the other hand, maybe not.

"You fellows okay?" Doyle called.

"Surest thing you know!" Henry Gans called. "My leg hurts some, though."

The driver's whiskers stood out as though he had grabbed both handles of an electrical generating machine at a fair, and he screeched at Doyle, "That 'air hoormungerin' morphodite had both bar'ls of that hoormungerin' shotgun trained on us whenas you popped off at 'im! Hennery an' me, he near as anything made stew meat out of us!"

"Man shot in the face with a .38, he'll be knocked backwards," Doyle said, "so even if he'd pulled the trigger, the shot would've gone over you."

The driver seemed unconvinced that Doyle's course had, in spite of its demonstrated effectiveness, been prudent, but the gambler, climbing down and producing a flat bottle from the side pocket of his jacket, soon quieted his agitation and complaints.

"Nerve tonic," he said, offering the bottle to Lucy Gans, who had recovered her wits and emerged from the coach to bend over her brother. Henry sat on the ground, wincing as he probed his bruised thigh. "Ease the pain."

Brandon thought he recognized the distinctive green color and brown label of a patent "swamp root" bitters running about forty percent alcohol, with a handsome dose of opium in each bottle. It ought to go a long way toward easing any pain and worries anyone might have. He wondered if Doyle kept it only for dispensing or eased his own pain with it, if he ever admitted to pain.

The express messenger, whose sleep seemed to have been deeper than Brandon's, came out of it only after the action was done, but he was soon enough apprised of what he had missed and insisted on resuming his seat next to the driver when the journey continued. Henry was back next to his sister, his battered leg extended to the seat now shared by Doyle and Brandon and supported by the mail sack that had served the messenger as pillow.

Henry, braced with a few swallows of the tonic, talked effusively about Doyle's daring, resolve, firmness, and courage in dealing with the robbery—in Brandon's view, more a matter of total unconcern about consequences—and expressed regret that he hadn't had the chance to draw his own weapon, an over-under derringer he displayed proudly. Lucy said little but looked often at Doyle with wide-eyed interest. Lucky for her they're going on from Boudin right away, Brandon thought. Or maybe unlucky, the way she sees it.

12

Whichever kind of luck it was, it seemed for a moment to have run out when, on the coach's arrival at Boudin in midafternoon, the driver announced that two wheels were on the edge of collapse and that the coach would lay over for repairs until morning. The jolting on the last miles of the journey had been severe but not, in Brandon's estimation, noticeably worse than the bone-shaking rest of the trip; and he had a strong suspicion that more of Doyle's money had gone to purchase the driver's decision.

However, it didn't seem to have bought all that Doyle might have expected. With only one facsimile of a hotel in Boudin, the North Star, travelers had no choice about where to stay; and, under the same roof with Lucy, it was a fair bet that Doyle could get the hoped-for return on his investments of self-advertisement and of cash. Henry Gans, however, was cheered by the news of the layover, as it would give him and Lucy a chance to visit longer, and enjoy the overnight hospitality of yet another uncle he had so far neglected to mention.

Doyle looked after them expressionlessly as they trudged down the dirt street, Henry listing strongly to the left as he limped along. He and Brandon entered the hotel. Brandon engaged a room for the night and left Doyle talking with the clerk, apparently exploring the chances of opening his gambling operations here.

In his second-floor room, Brandon threw his valise onto the bed and stood for a moment looking out of the window. The straggle of frame shacks across the road made Inskip seem metropolitan by contrast. Beyond them he saw a stretch of grassland hazed with bright flowers and, perhaps, a mile off, a dark-brown, moving mass stretching from north to south. He squinted, and made out several tiny figures on horseback flanking the mass, and a cloth-topped mule-drawn wagon near its northern end.

So that was what a trail herd on the move looked like. In a week or so it would be in Inskip or some other rail town, or maybe still on the way to a more distant destination, one of the reservations up in Montana. Perkins had told him pretty nearly everything about where cattle went and how much they fetched before and after fattening, and more of it than Brandon wanted stuck in his mind.

Boudin obviously existed to batten off the crews of the herds as they moved north, supply them with what they needed and, in the case of the few who would at this point in the drive have money, what they craved. The pickings would not be as rich as in Inskip, when every few days would see a paid-off crew getting rid of as much of their pay as they could, but what action there was would be intense.

Brandon lay on the bed, grateful for stillness and softness after the coach, though the hat was still oppressive, and began a comfortable slide into sleep. His last awareness was of footsteps and the creaking of a relaxed-upon bed in the room next door and, in a moment, the spicy pungency of Doyle's cigar smoke.

Brandon emerged from his sleep briefly after a long enough time for the patterns of light on his wall to have shifted substantially and heard sounds of activity: the metronomic creaking of the bedframe, gasps, a sort of soprano grunting, and an occasional piercing squeal. Evidently, Doyle had called upon local talent to make up for his lost sporting with Lucy Gans. He was grateful for the continued fatigue that drew him down into sleep again.

When Brandon came fully awake, the light on his wall was orange-red, and the sun's rays were at a shallow angle; he must have slept for a couple of hours at least. The entertainment next door seemed to have concluded, though a brief, faint sound of stirring through the wall indicated that at least one of the participants was still present.

He sat up, feeling unrested and aware of a tightness behind his eyes that could easily flower into a headache. It seemed to him that he had dreamed while he slept, but he could not recall the content; just a sense of an odd mixture of excitement, alarm, and grief. It seemed to him that a drink—or lots of drinks—of whatever the North Star's bar offered was just what was wanted to get the dry, brown taste out of his mouth, the tight band around his head loosened, and the dregs of dreams out of his mind.

The railed landing outside his room looked down into the bar. He surveyed it and saw Doyle, seated at a table in the center of the room, two decks of cards laid out on it like a store sign. The gambler, even seen at a distance, had an air of tension, like a runner poised at the starting line, and the atmosphere of the place echoed it. There were only about a dozen men at the bar or tables, dressed in rough, dusty clothes and high boots, some but not all still wearing their broad-brimmed, sweat-stained hats: the first group of trail hands riding in from the day's halting place for their first chance at letting off steam in weeks. Some were eyeing Doyle and the cards in front of him with enthusiastic anticipation; some were doing what they could to keep the bartender in perpetual motion; others gave their drink orders, compliments, and invitations to a bustling trio of waiter girls who seemed dressed for even hotter weather than they were experiencing, and to have experienced the depredations of a band of corset thieves.

Fumes of smoke, cheap perfume, and liquor, and the sounds of raucous talk and of a badly played piano rose from the arena below him, and Brandon went down the stairs with a stirring of excitement. This was the kind of place his search for the Kenneallys would be taking him to, and it was time he got accustomed to it.

He got a glass of whiskey and water from the bartender and went to Doyle's table; the gambler nodded at him to sit down. Doyle gestured at the piano player at the back of the room, flailing a Stephen Foster tune out of his instrument.

"Pretty, ain't it?" Doyle said genially, though his eyes remained empty. "'Beautiful dreamer, wake under me,' that how it goes?"

"Not quite," Brandon said.

"Near enough. I have to allow, this is shaping up to be a good day. Killed a man, bedded a woman, had a few drinks, and about to make a pile off these cowboys. Every sort of fun there is, all in one day."

Brandon looked at him with just a fraction more interest than revulsion. Not a Kenneally, but I'll bet this is the spit and image of the kind of man I'm hunting.

"Imagine a place like this is new to you," Doyle said.

"It is," Brandon said.

"Even towns like Inskip and Wichita, when the herds come in and the trail hands cut loose, they're nothing like this, Brooks." Brandon realized that Doyle had had more than a few drinks and was being, for him, sociable. "That marshal that ran me out of Inskip, there's nothing like that here. See, this here's the Neutral Zone; twenty-mile strip runs between the Kansas border and the Indian Nations, and there's no state, no territory, no country that's got the jurywhatsit—"

"Jurisdiction," Brandon said.

"Make laws, run things, nobody does that here. The businesspeople here, they got themselves a chief of police to see that property's reasonably safe and that any killings are fair unless they happen to people that don't matter. Aside from that, the rule is, do what you will. My kind of place." He gave Brandon the mirthless grin he remembered from the Bull's Foot.

A clatter of hoofbeats, a shrill *"Yee-heee!"* and a tattoo of shots sounded from the street. Brandon said, "Believe I'll go see what it looks like," and rose from the table. Outside the North Star, in the near dusk, he saw three horses a little down the street, sometimes rearing as their riders hauled back on the reins and fired revolvers into the air; the muzzle flashes were the brightest lights in the darkening air.

"Mr. Brooks?"

He turned and saw Henry Gans, leaning on a stick, standing next to him on the hotel porch. "Have you seen Lucy?"

"Not since we got here."

"She went out for a walk just after we got settled in at my uncle's. I took a nap, and when I woke up a while ago, she wasn't back. I wasn't worried at first, for I know she likes long walks, but with all these wild cowboys around . . ."

"I'm sure she'll be back soon," Brandon said. "Might be at your uncle's already; you may have missed her while you were looking. You go check that, hey?"

He left Henry Gans looking dubious and walked quickly inside the North Star and to Doyle's table. "Lucy Gans," he said. Doyle looked at him. "Came to see you. This afternoon," Brandon said.

Doyle lifted his eyebrows in a silent "So?"

"She's still there."

Doyle's expression remained unchanged.

"Well, you'd better—" Brandon stopped as two people came into his view at the same moment. On the railed landing, Lucy Gans emerged from the room next to his. Henry Gans, looking around as if for a familiar face, entered the barroom from the street end, directly beneath the landing.

Henry Gans saw Brandon and took a step toward him. A drinker at the bar looked up and saw Lucy Gans, now at the head of the stairs. "Hey, fellers, it's the screamer!" he crowed. "One we was hearin' half the afternoon, hootin' as she humped! Lady," he called up the stairs to her, "it's a fine thing to see someone as takes pleasure in her trade. Was me an' the boys t' take up a c'lection, you expect we c'd afford—"

He stopped abruptly as Henry Gans, who had heard his first comment, followed the direction of his gaze, walked up to him, and said, in a dazed voice, "That's my sister."

Looking at the boy's set, white face, the raucous drinker had the excellent sense to say nothing at all.

Henry Gans looked around the room and saw Brandon again—and Doyle, who had turned to inspect the action. Henry looked up at Lucy, who stood frozen at the head of the stairs, then back at Doyle and Brandon. Brandon saw with sick foreboding the tight, mocking grin on Doyle's face. Henry walked over to the table and said, "You . . . my sister . . ."

Doyle nodded. "And?"

Henry snarled inarticulately, dug his hand into his jacket pocket, and pulled out his derringer. "Get on your feet, damn you!" he said in a half-sob. "Draw!"

Brandon strongly regretted the impulse that had brought him back to warn Doyle. It seemed that associating with the man meant frequent appearances in the line of somebody's fire. He eyed the gambler's right hand, resting negligently on the table, waiting for the sleeve-holdout gun to appear.

Doyle slowly turned his head away from the enraged boy and faced Brandon. Got it all figured, Brandon thought. Decent kid, question of honor, no danger of getting backshot. Do what you will, that's the whole of Doyle's law, but other folks play by the rules. . . .

Doyle's face slackened and genuine surprise flashed in his eyes as a loud report sounded behind him. He leaned foward slowly, and a haze of brown smoke spread behind him, blurring Henry Gans's distorted face. Another gunshot drove Doyle facedown onto the table, tilting his hat off to stand upside down in front of Brandon. Smoke and the smell of charred wool rose from a black-rimmed hole in his jacket collar, and another wound at the base of his skull oozed redly. Blood trickling from his mouth pooled among the scattered cards.

Seems Henry—Lucy, too, come to think of it—picked up on this "do what you will" business fast enough. Kid's going to need a defense lawyer, and I can't see any way it isn't going to be me, none of my business though it is.

In the event, defending Henry Gans was not a demanding task. The chief of police appeared on the scene within a few moments and took charge. He was the most dissipated-appearing individual Brandon recalled to have seen, looking as though he moved through life with a perpetual hangover. He appeared barely strong enough to carry the massive shotgun, considerably larger than the one the would-be stage robber had used, that he clutched in one hand. The patrons of the bar became subdued in manner and low-voiced in conversation as he entered, apparently regarding him with more respect, even wariness, than Brandon would have expected.

Brandon had settled Henry Gans into a nearby chair and taken his pistol but left Doyle undisturbed. Blood had now covered most of the surface of the table and dripped slowly onto the floor. Brandon wished that the barroom's level of noise would get back to normal; in the comparative quiet, he could hear each drop hit the bare wood. Henry Gans had said nothing since the shooting; Lucy Gans had subsided to a sitting position on the top step of the staircase and was leaning against the banister post, either resting or in a faint.

"This one shot that one?" the chief said, pointing first at Henry Gans, then at Doyle's body. At Brandon's agreement with this summary, he asked, "Why?"

"There are extenuating—" Brandon began.

"He insulted my sister!" Henry Gans said furiously.

Brandon heard a mutter from a man at the bar and hoped Henry Gans had not: "Insulted 'er over an' over ag'in, till as she wore out or got a sore throat."

"The deceased treated the young lady shamefully," Brandon said carefully. "Her brother was naturally—"

"Deceased's name?" the chief asked.

"He was a Mr. Doyle, Daniel Doyle," Brandon said. "A professional gambler, as I understand. He—"

The chief lifted Doyle's head and looked at the slack face, now smeared at the nose, chin, and one cheek with blood.

The open eyes looked to Brandon pretty much as they had when Doyle was alive. "I know him, seen him here before," the chief said. "Due for this a long time now. Type of man like that, all you wonder is how he's going to get hisself killed, when it happens and who does it don't signify much."

"I assure you that my cl— that this gentleman had the most—" Brandon began.

The chief looked sharply at Henry Gans's derringer, which Brandon was still holding. "That the gun that did it?"

"Yes." Brandon felt it was something of an achievement to have made an uninterrupted statement to the chief, though a short one.

"Well, for God's sake don't give it back to him till he's on the way out of town," the chief said peevishly. "I don't want him making any more trouble. We got to get this fellow out of here and buried and deal with his effects, and that's more'n enough for tonight."

The chief glanced at Brandon's surprised face. "You don't know this town, I guess," he said. "We use common sense here, and when you got the kind of a man that's supposed to be killed, like I said, it ain't of much interest who gets to do it. We don't even have a jail here, so I ain't about to do things like arresting folks for shooting. If there's property damage or theft into it, I fine 'em and collect on the spot, and if all's they got is their clothes, then they go naked, as there's no law against that here. And when there's unacceptable disturbances and dangerous rioting, as might happen, I just turn up with old Susy here"—he gestured with the shotgun—"and loose off a barrel or so into the crowd. Sometimes it's rock salt, sometimes it ain't, so it keeps folks respectful and guessing."

Doyle had clearly found the right kind of place to live and die. Brandon remembered his comment about having a fine day. Well, it had in the end encompassed most of the possible significant experiences.

"Absolutely not," Brandon said. "Not a mention, not a hint. Ever."

Lucy Gans had come out of her faint, or reverie, and Henry Gans out of his near-catatonia, and both were seated in Brandon's room half an hour after the chief's departure, followed by two underlings carrying Doyle's corpse; one of these was now clearing Doyle's gear out of the room next door.

"But I will be living a lie if I don't confess to Edwin!" Lucy Gans said, having announced to Brandon and her brother her intention of making a clean breast to her Fort Smith fiancé.

"You won't be living anything with Edwin if you do," Brandon said. "People working in the law, they're not going to be understanding about anything irregular. And you, Henry, you keep mum about killing Doyle, same reason. Edwin's not going to want a killer for a brother-in-law, so it'd be unkind to let him know he's got one."

"We weren't brought up to lie," Henry said stiffly.

"You weren't brought up to do fornication and murder either," Brandon said, "and you took to it pretty quickly, I'd say. And in any case, you don't have to lie. I don't expect Edwin will ask you if you let your head get turned, so to speak, by someone in your travels, or ask you, Henry, if you had occasion to shoot anyone. If he doesn't ask, then you don't have to lie. And in fact, since fornication and murder are crimes, and you haven't been charged or arrested by a competent authority—or even the incompetent one that obtains here—you can't in law really be said to have done anything."

The Ganses turned this proposition over for a space. "My," Lucy Gans said faintly, "the way you put it makes it all seem like a dream, something that didn't really happen."

"You make it come out our way as good as if you was a lawyer, not a cattle buyer," Henry said.

"There's a lot that goes into cattle buying," Brandon said.

Brandon pulled the revolver from the holster belted to his side, aimed at a rock about six feet from the left side of his horse, and fired. The recoil jolted his arm, and the pungent smoke stung his eyes and blurred his vision as dust geysered a good six inches from the rock. The horse took no notice of the noise, smoke stench, or the small explosion of earth and plodded on. Brandon suspected that any animal that had done much duty in or near Boudin was hardened to gunfire at any place and time.

Like the trail gear—frying pan, pot, canned goods, coffee, blankets and ground cloth, saddle, tack, and so on—Brandon had bought the horse from a source the chief of police had recommended. He didn't consider the man particularly trustworthy, but he thought that the windfall of the considerable stake Doyle would have had to have with him to carry on his trade, and which certainly was not going to inure to any heirs or estate Doyle might have, might allow him to give an impartial opinion. He had certainly taken possession of Doyle's weapons, to the extent of offering them for sale to Brandon.

After a momentary hesitation, Brandon closed the deal. He knew almost nothing of handguns—he had done some target shooting, years before, with cap-and-ball pistols—but the arsenal of a practiced professional gambler ought to have been the result of informed choice, and should do as well as anything he could get, at a good deal higher price, from a gunsmith.

The revolver was a .38, lighter than the .44s or .45s that seemed favored out here, but Brandon found its heft comfortable, and the double action, which allowed him to fire merely by pulling the trigger instead of fanning the hammer back for each shot, convenient. Doyle or a gunsmith had evidently tinkered with it to reduce the stiffness and heavy trigger pull that undercut the advantages of most double actions, and it cocked and fired almost as easily as a single-action pistol at full cock.

The other piece of armament was Doyle's sleeve-holdout gun, a short-barreled single-shot .30-caliber pistol partnered with a spring clip attached to a sleeve garter; a flexing of the arm could deliver it into the hand, as Brandon had seen done at the Bull's Foot in Inskip. This was in the valise lashed behind the high saddle, as it hadn't seemed useful for the ride down to Texas. He had in fact bought it more on impulse than out of any felt need; it was there, and a bargain, and there might be a time when some such stratagem would be wanted.

The saddlemaker had called the huge saddle he'd sold him a "hull," and the name seemed apt. It was certainly nothing like the smart English-style saddles he'd used for the little riding he'd done in and around St. Louis, seeming more like the back of a child's hobbyhorse, nesting the rider between the high horn in front and the cantle in back, resting on a huge slab of leather curved like half a barrel, and dagged with thongs, cinches, protective tongues called fenders, and the stirrups and stirrup leathers. Gentleman jockeys and hunt-club members would sneer at it, but after a few hours and perhaps twenty miles' travel, Brandon was grateful for its firm capaciousness. He could make sudden movements, such as drawing and firing the revolver, without paying conscious attention to keeping his seat.

He drew and fired again, this time without taking conscious aim, just pointing the index finger of his gun hand at the target rock, and saw dust fly from it and a bright smear of lead appear near its top.

Brandon rode south, keeping to the edge of a wide stretch of bare earth that stretched across the grasslands like a giant's roadway. Where the gound was not totally churned up, it bore the overlaid imprints of hoofs, mostly the small ones of cattle, occasionally the larger, shod ones of horses, and here and there the snaking tracks of wagon wheels. Mudpies of cattle dung decorated the trail in a wide-spaced scatter; Brandon thought there should be more, then realized that the droppings of most of the trail herd would have been stirred into the earth by the hoofs of the animals behind. A not unpleasant barnyard smell drifted from the manured ground, reinforced by that of the sunbaked grass all around and a faint echo of the richness of cut hay.

It was past noon by the sun, and Brandon was sure he was well out of the Neutral Zone and into the Indian Territory, whatever difference that made. To either side of the deserted cattle trail, the grasslands stretched away, but the ground here was more irregular than the almost-level area just below Inskip; there were hills in the distance and rises nearby, some cut by winding creeks, and trees, singly and in small groves, broke the skyline, so that the bowl of the sky lost a touch of its encompassing immensity. The grass at the margin of the trail had been cropped short by the passing cattle, and Brandon could see purple and orange wildflowers that the longer grass away from the trail concealed.

He could see several miles in every direction, and though armies might have been just over the horizon, it seemed equally possible on the evidence that he was totally alone on the face of the earth. Brandon thought a moment and realized that he had probably not been out of the immediate vicinity of another human being in years; at the most he had been a mile or so from Ned Norland during that hallucinatory episode in the mountains. *I could turn this horse east or west, or take a seizure and die right here, and nobody'd ever know it, most likely. Nobody expecting me to do anything, nobody concerned, nobody meddling. No reason for doing anything except that it's what I mean to do.* Somebody called Charles Brooks, detective or cattle buyer, depending on how you looked at it, had left Inskip and then struck out from Boudin. It would be time soon to work out who it was, and what manner of man, who would end his southward ride at Bascom in a week or so. It seemed to him that the man named Cole Brandon hadn't made it very far out of St. Louis, that a new entity dedicated to the hunt and the kill had taken over the operation of his body.

He turned over Edmund Chambers's comments on acting and the mask becoming the self if you wore it long enough. He suspected that no one mask would be in place long enough to shape his face, if, by now, there was any longer a real face for it to conceal. And Chambers was probably right about observation giving you the key to the role: He was pretty sure he could do a convincing representation of Dan Doyle or the erratic chief of police in Boudin or the rock-steady marshal. The prairie-dog seller might be beyond his range, and Rush Dailey certainly was.

A gleam of sharp white on the trail ahead caught his eye. It grew as he approached, and took form: a long skull bearing wide, recurved horns, set on a man-high tree stump. One of the Texas longhorns that hadn't made it to the railroad and the slaughterhouses, now a trail marker, he supposed, or just some cowhand's idea of outdoor decoration.

Not planning it, he drew the .38 again, focused on his target, and pulled the trigger. Dust and wood fragments scattered out of the dark oval of one eye socket, and the skull jerked on its post. *You seem to be getting the hang of this, Counselor. Be sure of what you want to hit, and the gunhand will work out how to do it.*

The skull dwindled again to a point of white, then was lost as Brandon rode south through the scented grass and wildflowers.

13

Beyond the river—shallow and fordable, as the last northward-bound trail gang Brandon had encountered had told him it would be—a steep bluff reared up to the west, following the line of the river curving west and again south. It seemed to form an intermittently wooded plateau stretching several miles westward, sloping gradually toward the south. A few miles south of the river, still following the cattle trail, Brandon came to a rutted wagon road crossing it, and turned off to the right.

"First road you come to 'crost the river'll take you right inter Bascom," the trail boss had told him. "No place else fer it t'go."

The road, sometimes bordered with trees, followed the bottom of the south slope of the plateau. For the first time in a long while, Brandon saw cultivated fields and, occasionally, a farmhouse. The sun was not far above the top of the plateau, and the light lying on the fields and stretches of prairie had a golden quality.

He topped a rise and was looking ahead at what had to be Bascom. It had a solid, settled look, very unlike Inskip and Dysart, and had the clustered look of the towns he was used to, as if it had grown out from a center, not merely accreted along a line of track.

The rutted wagon road broadened to a packed-earth street as he entered the town. It was lined with trees tall enough to have been thirty or forty years old—practically antique out here—and some of the buildings looked to be about the same age, though they were well maintained. A little past what seemed to be the center of town, a few streets ahead, he saw a gleam of white, pointed like the horn of the skull he had passed his first day on the trail: a church steeple.

He passed the fenced yard and shed of a livery stable on his right; on his left, a roofed-over plankwalk fronted a line of stores—barber shop, grocer, haberdasher. There were some late-afternoon strollers and a neat-looking wagon and team hitched to a post in front of one of the stores. Brandon's clothes, coated with trail dust that combined with a week's sweat and a crossing of the Red River that morning, were covered by a thin layer of dried mud. He smelled accordingly and had the unaccustomed sense of being the most disreputable-appearing person in sight.

This did not seem to matter to the desk clerk at the Butler House Hotel, an imposing three-story building at one corner of the open square—plaza was what they called it out here, he recalled—that seemed to mark the heart of the town. He took a room, as Carter Bane, a name that had seemed to come to his tongue automatically as soon as he had realized that cattle buyer Charles Brooks would have to go back to the limbo whence he had come. He arranged for the stabling of his horse, and for a hot bath as soon as it could be managed, got his key, picked up his valise, and went up the stairs to the second floor.

Feeling lighter as well as cleaner—he had left a substantial layer of silt on the bottom of the tin tub in the bathroom down the hall—Brandon enjoyed the feeling of clean if wrinkled clothes as he lay on the bed. The yielding surface of the mattress and springs was an ultimate luxury after so many days of rocking in the saddle, punctuated by sleeping on the inflexible earth.

The sun was behind the rim of the wooded plateau that formed the horizon to the west, but the sky still glowed and lit his room, reflecting from the wallpaper and bedclothes to cast a faint glow on the intricate embossed patterns in the stamped-tin ceiling. Brandon superimposed on them a mental map of his ride from Boudin to Bascom, tracing his course down the open space between repeats of the basic pattern. Along about the fourth laurel wreath, that was where he'd come across the first trail herd, a long, weary way from Corpus Christi on the Gulf, and, in return for a bountiful meal and an evening's sociability, had helped the crew in the day-long job of getting cattle, horses, and cook wagon across the Canadian River. It was probably the hardest physical labor he had ever done, and it gave him a fierce and unexpected sense of accomplishment, as well as a feeling of having earned his place at the cookfire that night.

The jokes, songs, and yarns he absorbed but could not add to. The trail hands seemed to have created a kind of civilization of their own, with its rules, customs, and imperatives, as different from the rest of the world as that of Homer's Greeks. What they did, and why they did it for the meager pay it brought them, were things Brandon could not understand clearly; but their unquestioning belief in their life and work impressed him. He had watched and listened to the hands, the trail boss, and the hot-tempered cook, and marked their characteristics and mannerisms. Should it be called for, he could at least talk authoritatively with, if perhaps not pass himself off as, someone in that life.

One thing that would make that easier was the scrupulously observed custom of polite incuriosity about a stranger's origins, occupation, or motives for traveling. "Been on the trail long?" "Yes." "Goin' down into Texas?" "Yes." The two unembellished answers had been enough of a signal to forestall any further inquiry, without any loss of amiability.

Brandon smiled thinly as he imagined a trial interrogation conducted on that principle: "Anything you'd care to say about this business?" "Don't believe so." "I wouldn't want to pry, of course; step down."

Over by the bunch of tin grapes a chambermaid's feather duster had missed was where he'd met the Indians. Three of them, mounted, driving a longhorn. They were cheerful enough, though wary, and stopped to talk for a moment.

"Wohaw," one said, pointing at the steer. "Like you pay money use bridge or ferry, herd pay beef pass through Nations. So we eat meat sometimes, though buffalo most gone."

Brandon was fascinated by the man's voice, which had the curious quality of seeming to come from his general neighborhood, not directly from his mouth—possibly because he moved his lips very little as he spoke. He was reminded of a ventriloquist he had seen in a vaudeville show once, making a wooden manikin on his knee appear to speak. When the other two spoke rapidly to each other in their own language, their faces moved in unison with their speech; so he supposed that it was difficulty, or perhaps distaste, that immobilized their features when they spoke English.

With that element in mind, he might be able to do a convincing imitation of an Indian speaking English, for whatever good that might do him. Who—or what, in fact—would he be imitating here in Bascom? What line of work would Carter Bane turn out to be in?

He turned over this question in his mind for a moment, then decided that the choice didn't have to be made yet. Under the unwritten No Embarrassing Questions Statute, he could appear without explanation and set about his main business, finding Sam Canty's Lazy Y ranch and Sam Canty's foreman, Jack Kestrel. If the multihued reports of Kestrel from Inskip were even approximately truthful, contradictory though they were, he shouldn't be too hard to find—just walk toward any sound of gunshots and the yells of the maimed and wounded, or inquire of the undertaker where business was liveliest.

The bar downstairs would likely be a good place to start finding out what he needed to know. If that wasn't productive, he remembered having seen a saloon sign protruding into the street at the far side of the plaza; that could be his next stop.

He rose and reached for his jacket, draped over a chair back to allow some of the wrinkles from many days' journey folded in the valise to vanish, then moved past it to the open valise. Whoever Carter Bane was going to turn out to be, he was at the edge of the forest where the bears and panthers lived, and from this point on, he'd better be armed.

For a surprise, what the Butler House bartender poured and slid over to him was not some mislabeled local moonshine but actually bourbon, a not-bad sour mash, smooth on his tongue and warming as it went down. Back in St. Louis, his preference had been for rye, but, at the moment of ordering, it seemed to him that Carter Bane would be a bourbon man. In that case, maybe from Kentucky, if asked. No great speech differences from eastern Missouri, but maybe softer, a little less sharp in the tones.

Brandon turned and surveyed the barroom. It was about the same size as that in the hotel in Boudin but otherwise didn't much resemble it. It had something of the comfortable look of a good club such as he had known in St. Louis, with carved wall panels, a crystal chandelier, and solid, comfortable chairs and tables. The patrons were more diverse than would be expected in a metropolitan club: from soberly dressed men of a mercantile or business aspect to overalled and roughly dressed men, probably farmers and mechanics. In any case, the local solid citizens, vertebrae in the community backbone. Brandon considered that Carter Bane's attire fitted in well enough not to cause remark. As in a club, the patrons were all male, as was the staff; the hotel seemed to feel it could do without the attraction, and the trouble, of waiter girls and unescorted women.

Association in Bascom did not seem determined by class lines, if the clothes in fact reflected those lines: At some tables, farmers drank with merchants, mechanics with businessmen. They drank and talked in groups of from two to four, and the sound of talk was low and relaxed. The Butler House bar, Brandon estimated, was not Bascom's place for hard drinking but for social and business relaxation. Maybe not the place to get very far looking for Jack Kestrel.

The only other lone drinker in the room was a short, quietly dressed man at a table in the corner. A wide-brimmed hat on the table contrasted with the sober wool suit, suggesting that he might be a prosperous rancher, though he looked not forceful enough to administer what Brandon had come to learn was a disaster-prone, often dangerous business. Maybe a haberdasher in the habit of wearing new items around town as an advertisement; he had that diffident aspect that goes with making the customer feel that the expensive shirt he selected was actually his own choice, and a wise one.

The lobby door clattered open and what might have been two apparitions from Inskip, or even Boudin, lurched in. They wore range garb—crumpled wide-brimmed hats, canvas pants tucked into boots, loose jackets—and as they passed behind Brandon to find a place down the bar from him, he caught a powerful whiff of sweat, overused underclothes, and booze.

The one nearest Brandon had a long, ungroomed mustache with gray, straggling ends that suggested it had been used to dust a severely unclean surface, and glaring, reddened eyes that roamed with universal detestation around the room. He slapped his hand on the bar and called, "Hey, bar dick, slide a bottla yer best horse piss down yere!"

The barroom's patrons had stirred uneasily at the men's entrance. The shouted drink order seemed to remind them that they had finished their evening's recreation and had things to see to elsewhere, and, singly and in pairs, they began leaving the room.

The worried-looking bartender seemed to debate refusing to serve the men. He cast a glance at the vulnerable rows of bottles and large plate-glass mirror behind the bar and, with visible reluctance, put a square bottle and two glasses in front of the men.

"Thisyer's a better place 'n Varnum's," the drink orderer said, looking sardonically at the continuing exodus. "Better class o' people, knee-deep in refinements and elegancies."

His companion, facing him and therefore Brandon as well, reached down to scratch at his knee—from the men's look and smell, he could imagine that they were supporting a thriving population of "bed rabbits," as Ned Norland had called lice—and the loose jacket swung aside to reveal a gunbelt and holstered revolver. "They had no call t' throw us outta there," he complained. "A little fun's natcherl, a place like that."

The bartender looked dramatically regretful at having served the men, or perhaps at having ever come to Bascom; Brandon inferred that men who would incur ejection from Varnum's, whatever that was, were the worst of news.

"No women here, though," the mustached man said truthfully, though there were now almost no men, either. The last party was making its way to the lobby door, leaving of the original inhabitants of the barroom only Brandon, the unhappy bartender, and the unimpressive fellow at the corner table. "Cain't have a high old time without some women into it."

"You ain't no good to no woman," his companion scoffed. "Thatair prod o' yours cain't neither git high ner into nothin'."

Irritation mounted in Brandon. These men were offensive enough in themselves, but they were also making hash of his intention to gather information—or at least find out if there were any to be had here. They also seemed, from the stiffening of the mustached man's shoulders and the snarl that came from him, to be on the edge of a confrontation that could devastate the room and the few remaining bystanders.

"You leave my prod outta this, pissant!"

"Why not? Outta ever'thing else a'ready," the other man said.

The mustached man gobbled with rage and reached down, managing to articulate one word: "Draw!"

In a long glide and turn, like one of the fancier waltz steps, Brandon was down the bar and between them, one hand clamped like a steel cuff around each gun-holding hand and forcing them over against the bar. The two men flailed at him with their free hands, trying to reach their weapons and fan back the hammers to fire; their efforts faltered and stopped as he looked at each in turn.

He made his face go completely slack and focused his eyes at a point well beyond the faces in front of him; that was his best estimate of how to achieve Doyle's walking-death look. He hoped his calculation of the circumstances was more accurate than Doyle's final one had been. "No," he said in the toneless voice Doyle had used in the Bull's Foot. "Not here."

"Hey, you sonofabitch," one of the men protested, "you—"

"No." Brandon—or the identity he had drawn on like a mask—looked intently at one man, then at the other. This identity did not care if he killed one or both of the men or they killed him. It saw them as it saw all men, as dead to start with, with only the time and place needing confirmation.

Another note was added to the concerto of stenches emanating from the men, the sour reek of fear. Their grip on their weapons relaxed and they clattered onto the bar. Brandon shoved and they fell to the floor behind the bar.

The vanishing of their property seemed to rouse the men from their trance of surprise and fear, and one wrenched his hand free of Brandon's grasp. "You cain't—"

Brandon shoved his hand, palm up, into the man's shirt front, then flexed his arm. The holdout pistol appeared magically, its mouth nestled against the fourth button from the top. "This'll make a hole half an inch wide through your guts," he said in a near whisper, forcing the men to strain to hear. "Only one shot, but you'll wish there were two, one extra to put you out of your misery."

"But we ain't armed now, so you wouldn't . . ." the man whose wrist he still held began, then looked into Brandon's eyes and decided that it was not a point worth making.

"Out," Brandon said, finding that the dead tone he was working for was coming naturally to him. He gestured with the palm-held pistol, and the men turned and walked to the lobby door, Brandon close behind them, hand out as if to pat them on the back: Three friends, an observer might conclude, the palm gun being hidden from view, taking their leave of a place whose possibilities seemed to have expired.

The recent patrons of the bar, now gathered in the lobby, opened a path to the street door, looking at Brandon and his charges with interest and speculation. Brandon saw them outside, said, "Ask the hotel for your guns tomorrow. Maybe you'll get them," and watched them shamble dispiritedly down the street.

He stepped back inside the lobby, met the curious glances of the crowd with a bland smile, and went into the dining room. There was an excellent chance that he could have been dead or dying on the barroom floor by now, and the thought—or at least the awareness that he was not—seemed to have produced a considerable appetite.

He noted that Carter Bane's dinner was served with greater ceremony and respect than any of Cole Brandon's had ever been. It was the underlying touch of fear that sharpened it, he decided.

After most of the day on the trail, the confrontation in the bar, and a substantial meal followed by a cognac—the Butler House's cellar was well stocked—Brandon considered that he should be ready for sleep but found himself instead lying fully dressed on the bed, running his eyes over the ceiling patterns, deeply shadowed toward the edges of the room by the warm light of the coal-oil lamp on his table.

He had considered the idea of returning to the bar to pursue his inquiries about Sam Canty and Jack Kestrel, but saw that any conversation he would get into would turn on his handling of the two toughs, very likely raising speculation about Carter Bane that he didn't want. Whatever the regional *mores* of noninquiry might be, the respectable element anywhere had a keen interest in knowing just who they were dealing with. Anyhow, Varnum's might be a better place for information. Maybe he'd missed a bet with the two hardcases; might have done better to buy them a drink and pick their brains, if any.

He traced wreaths and grape clusters with his eyes as he

pondered another point about the confrontation in the barroom: Why bother? It hadn't been his business, there'd been a risk, it might wind up impeding his quest for information. He could just as well have moved off with the others when the uglying started, not stayed there alone, which amounted to looking for trouble. Not quite alone, though—the insignificant fellow in the corner hadn't left either; probably paralyzed with fear.

A knock at the door brought his gaze down from the ceiling. Hotels everywhere, it seemed, had the damnedest practice of needing to do something to the room at almost any hour of the day or night. If he ever saw Jess Marvell again, he would ask her the reason for that. "Come in," he called.

It was not a sheet-laden or broom-bearing chambermaid who stepped into the room but the corner-sitter whose conduct, or nonfeasance, he had just been ruminating on. Brandon sat up and swung his feet to the floor.

"Mr. Bane," the man said.

"Yes," Brandon said.

"I'd like a moment of your time, have a word with you," his visitor said. His voice, like his presence, was understated, but Brandon had a sense of latent power in it.

"All right," Brandon said. He gestured toward a wooden rocking chair next to the bureau. "Sit down."

The man sat, carefully hitching up his trouser legs to keep the knees from bagging. *Haberdasher for sure.* "Interesting time in the bar a while earlier."

"It was that," Brandon said.

"Facing down two armed men, quarrelsome men, drunk men," the man said, "now, that's a mighty risky proposition. Safer to just leave, the way the others did." *Or sit mouse-quiet and do nothing, for that matter.*

Brandon summoned up Bane, the bourbon-drinker, dead-eyed drunk terrorizer. "Not that much of a risk," he said flatly. "People in that state, you act sudden and sure; it's over before they work out what to do."

"And," said the man, "if you know that the way you mean to have it is the way it's going to be, whatever or whoever's in the way and whatever they're carrying—you *know* that, then that's likely how it turns out."

Brandon blinked. This haberdasher seemed to have a pretty good idea of how the minds of people like Carter Bane worked. Maybe Jack Kestrel bought his socks at his shop. "There's that, too," he said.

"Now, you saw what the barroom's usually like," the man said. "Quiet place for quiet folks, that's what the Butler House is. And it's Mr. Canty's firmest idea to keep it that way."

"Canty," Brandon said, with a successful but taxing effort to avoid showing surprise in his mien or voice.

"If you don't know the name, I'd know you weren't from around here even if I didn't know you weren't from around here, so to speak," the man said with a faint smile. "Mr. Sam Canty is one of the founding settlers of Bascom, came up here after he and the rest whipped Santa Anna. Laid out the town, brought in settlers—farmers, mostly—went into cattle himself some years back. Built the hotel soon's the town got sizable and owned it ever since, along with the rest of what he does. Plus which he is duly elected justice of the peace here in Bascom, so there isn't much that doesn't concern him."

"And disorder in the hotel certainly would," Brandon said. "I'd think that, as justice of the peace, he'd be able to handle that with fines, contempt of court citations, orders to keep the peace—and soon." *Watch it—Bane probably wouldn't know all that legal business.*

"Mr. Canty owns the hotel and his ranch, not the town," the man said. "And the taxpayers don't care to foot the bill for much of a police force, and they expect that what there is will go to keep farmers and storekeepers from being robbed first, and any disorders afterwards. So Mr. Canty has been considering whether to hire somebody to sort of keep the peace in his place, for this tonight wasn't the first such broil there's been. If the Butler House gets known as a rowdy place, it'll be a disgrace to Mr. Canty, and a hole cut in his pocket, and Mr. Canty is particular upon both those points."

"And," Brandon said thoughtfully, "you're sounding me out for the job."

"Just so," the man said. "A long shot, but you rode in from the north on your own, took a room until further notice, don't have the look of a man with pressing business, and you handled that trouble in the bar as neatly as I could imagine." *Imagine, indeed—imagining's as far as you'd get in that setup.* Haberdasher seemed less of a likely trade for the man; maybe he was Canty's bookkeeper. "If you're of a mind to consider it, you could talk with Mr. Canty tomorrow out at the Lazy Y."

A good job for Carter Bane, maybe, but how would it serve Cole Brandon's ends? Not too well. "I . . . well, it's an interesting proposition, Mr.—"

"Kestrel. Jack Kestrel."

"—and I think it'd be a fine idea to go see Mr. Canty," Brandon finished, switching tracks in midstatement. It looked as if Carter Bane was about to accept employment. Fast work, considering that he'd been born only a few hours before.

14

We was almost on 'em before they knowed we was coming. The grass was that tall and we was that quiet. And they was mostly asleep, tired from the march and it bein' the heat of the day. We was less 'n a furlong from their breastworks when our cannon cut loose and we commenced to run at 'em and the fifers commenced to playing and the drummers to drumming and we was all yelling like madmen, we was all screaming, 'Remember the Alamo!' 'Remember Goliad!' "

As Sam Canty had not been at the Alamo or Goliad massacres, Brandon was not treated to his reminiscences of them. On the other hand, if he had been at either, he would be unlikely to have survived, and Brandon would not now be getting a first-hand account of the Battle of San Jacinto that would have fascinated anyone a lot more interested in Texas history than he was. He expected that this narrative would eventually display some connection with the problem Sam Canty proposed to lay before Carter Bane and hoped it would be soon. Canty appeared to be of a type trial lawyers dread dealing with on the witness stand, unable to consider and answer an isolated question, but constrained to begin at the beginning of what they knew and go on in remorseless detail. Painful experience had taught Brandon that if he cut in with any suggestion of moving on to the relevant and competent parts—as he had done with reasonable success with Ned Norland's saga—the whole narrative line would be reeled in and played out all over again from the beginning.

Yet he found there was something compelling about the picture of Canty, forty years younger and a good bit leaner, in the transports of a killing rage, whooping and running through the grass to battle and death. A sturdily bulky man, sixty-some, balding, he sat in the parlor chair with the paradoxical mixture of relaxation and alertness Brandon supposed he would demonstrate in the saddle. His broad face was seamed by strong, determined-looking vertical lines beyond the corners of the mouth and, below the eyes, was the color and texture of light saddle leather; the upper part was paler, shaded from decades of prairie sun by his broad hat brim.

"Houston was yelling at us to stop and fire," Canty said, "but we was too far off still for it to do any good—we knowed better 'n Sam Houston, or thought we did!—and then Deef Smith come a-riding down our line and a-howling for us to fire, and it come to some of us that we needed to shoot to make the Mexicans keep their heads down, ne'mine about hitting 'em, so we done that, aimed, fired a volley, and ran on. And then we was amidst 'em, shooting and stabbing, and they broke and ran, and it was done in less 'n twenty minutes, Santa Anna broken and running too."

Canty exhaled, something just short of sighing, and looked in a direction some four decades past Brandon. "The battle was done, anyhow. Then we got to the killing. Chased 'em to the bayou, and when they clumped up there trying to wade across, we butchered 'em, shot into 'em till as we run out of powder and shot, then clubbed 'em with our gun butts like rabbits. Went at it till dusk."

Brandon said nothing. "It don't weigh on my conscience," Sam Canty said, "but sometimes it plays out like a magic-lantern show in my mind, only it's moving, not standing still like a photograph. After the Alamo, and them killing the prisoners at Goliad after giving 'em safe conduct—and, I guess, after we'd retreated halfway acrost Texas, scairt and mad—I don't expect we could've done anything else. Likely some of those fellows had been in on the killing at the Alamo and Goliad, but they was in the same uniform anyhow, and they paid the price for wearing it. I figure we killed about six hundred, most of 'em after the battle, and that's a little more 'n they murdered at the Alamo and Goliad. And I work it out that we had to do that, or the accounts wouldn't balance. And if it weren't all the same fellows that did the killing that *we* killed, well, you don't go for a soldier if you expect to get treated fair."

Oh, the accounts have to balance, but it's neater if you cancel out the ones who did it, precisely, like a surgeon cutting out a tumor. Is one of them working for you, old reminiscer? A good point about shooting to make them keep their heads down, even if you're not close enough to kill. I can see there'll be times that could come in handy.

Canty grinned. "You'll be asking, Bane, how all that lashes up to why you're here." Brandon let his face signify polite acceptance of the statement, not impatient agreement. "Not close, in fact," Canty admitted, "but it's San Jacinto that got me up here, and whenever I got to talk about San Jacinto at all, seems I can't do any less than tell the whole of it. See, them that fought at San Jacinto, we was all given land for it—the Donation Lands they called it, a section a mile on each side, wherever the land wasn't owned yet. And I knowed about this country up here, that had good farming land, and grassland north of the river, and a trail over to Santa Fe with an old stone trading post the Spanish put up long agone, and nobody living here. So I got together with a half-dozen of the fellows that was in the fight, and we took our sections up here and made ourselfs a town. Platted it, anyways, and commenced to getting settlers to move in and start a-building. Called it Bascom after Jim Bascom, one of the half-dozen of ours that died of wounds after San Jacinto."

Bascom had prospered from the start, Canty said, and he had gradually become the leading influence in the area, as his original partners had sold off their holdings at substantial profits and drifted away. The farmers had found good markets in the growing towns and cities to the south and had not suffered from the closing of the trail to Santa Fe, still the possession of a bitterly resentful Mexican regime. After that government's attempt to reverse the annexation of Texas by the United States had resulted in the transfer of California, Arizona, and New Mexico as well to its suddenly enlarged northern neighbor, the trail to Santa Fe had remained in disuse, the established Texas markets being ample and easy of access.

"I was the big cheese around here, for fair," Sam Canty said. "Built the Butler House Hotel and saw to it that it was first-class, staked a man in building the general store and went partners with him in it, lent money on easy terms to folks I figured would be good to have living here, and let 'em make me district judge."

"Not mayor," Brandon said.

Sam Canty shook his head. "A man that runs for office is like a dog in a dog and pony show—got to learn to walk in a way he ain't made for, do tricks, jump through hoops other folks is holding, bark as if he was speaking, and lick a lot of hands to get fed. I just had to tell some fellows down in Austin that they needed a court here, that I'd build a slap-up courthouse out of my own pocket, and that they could make me a judge if they wanted. So it was all arranged upright and dignified. All's I care about is that things go according to the rules hereabouts, so's everybody gets a fair shake. I'm not one of these fellows that has to run everything his own way, d'you see?"

"Sure," Brandon said.

After a time, Canty's eyes had wandered across the river to the grasslands beyond, a huge fan of prairie stretching to the north, rimmed by waves of hills to the east. These afforded considerable amounts of timber and were rich in streams and lakes and pasturage.

"In them days, somewheres around '50, wild cattle was kind of like game up thereaway," Sam Canty said. "Buffalo, antelope, wild horses, wild cows, all strolling around and eating the grass. The cows got away from the Mexican farmers and ranchers down near Old Mexico long time back and spread out and bred like horned rabbits, damn near, so there was a mort of 'em around. But there wasn't much use to 'em, see, for the market for meat wasn't all that big. Hide and tallow was what there was the most money in with them cattle, and I decided I'd see what I could make doing that, 'cause I was getting kind of tired of town living and doings."

Canty had built a ranch house—the core of the one they now sat in—toward the eastern margin of the fan of prairie, about ten miles north of the river—hired some hands, and commenced ranching in a small way. "Nobody didn't own it, so it was open for the using," Sam Canty said. "Early on, a couple Comanches got some disputatious about that, but we convinced some of 'em and the rest drifted off."

Word of rising prices for beef in the east had prompted him, as it had some other Texas ranchers, to drive a herd to the nearest point on the railroad, then in Missouri. "Got five times what it cost to raise 'em," Sam Canty said, "but it was an almighty long haul, and we lost a lot on the way, mainly through knowing treble naught about what we was doing. And then there was the War, and we wasn't studying how to get cows to the enemy just then."

But in the first couple of years after the War, the huge increase in the wild and ranch herds, the snaking of the railroad across Kansas to bring access hundreds of miles closer, and the steadily expanding eastern market for meat transformed Texas ranching into something that would have raised J. P. Morgan's bushy eyebrows in respect. Canty had the cattle, he had experience, he had a core of seasoned hands, and in a short time he had a substantial amount of money.

"So here I am, respected, a judge, well off from the cattle trade and getting weller, head down in clover, right?" Sam Canty said.

"No," Brandon said. "Or I wouldn't be here."

"You got the right of it," Sam Canty said. "I will now tell you about what the problem here is."

When Dorn Varnum had come to Bascom five years

before, he had struck Sam Canty as an asset to the town: apparently seasoned in a variety of businesses, with a fair amount of cash in hand and looking to invest it. Canty's partner in the general store was developing itchy feet, and Varnum seemed like a good replacement. It turned out that Varnum wanted sole, not shared, proprietorship, but he was willing to pay reasonably to buy Canty out of an enterprise he hadn't been much interested in for some time. This left him tied to Bascom only by the Butler House Hotel—mainly run by a capable manager—and his intermittent court duties, which suited him well, as the ranch was taking more and more of his time and concern.

"Made a go of it right off, too," Sam Canty said. "Got in a lot more stock of stuff folks wanted and got the business to humming. And a store like that, you know how it's a place that the men kind of hang around and talk and mebbe do some dealing. Well, Varnum set out a couple benches and tables, so as there was almost a kind of meeting place, like as a clubhouse."

"And next thing, he'd opened up or bought into a saloon, and he was hip-deep in politics," Brandon said.

"Well, yes," Canty said. "Kestrel tell you about that?"

"No," Brandon said. "Kind of thing that's known to happen." It was a progression he'd seen enough times in St. Louis, one of the recognized paths to an alderman's seat.

With no interest of his own in politics, Sam Canty had not minded Varnum's success in that line, which took the form not of running for office but of gaining influence over those who did. His expansion into the saloon trade was also unworrying at first; but the shabby bar that he took over, a kind of den for the broke and discouraged, soon blossomed into something else.

"Glass and oil lamps and paintings and fancy woodwork till hell wouldn't have it," Sam Canty said. "Drew off some of my trade from the Butler House bar, but not enough to vex. And waiter girls that was filling orders for a lot more than drinks. And then the gamblers come in, he let 'em set up tables there—give him credit, he seen to it that they ran square games, far's I hear—and there commenced to be heavy betting and heavy losing and heavy drinking after, and some fights and shootings, which there wasn't never none of in Bascom to speak of before."

Canty, getting set to use his office to clamp down on Varnum's disorder-promoting activities, was dismayed to find that a recent reformation of the town statutes had reformed out of existence the strictures against gambling. The town council, almost all the members of which were on the friendliest of terms with Dorn Varnum, had apparently decided that since the laws against prostitution had never been called into play in Bascom history, there was no problem about it and such laws were therefore superfluous. Thus when Varnum erected four one-room residences on property he owned on Bowie Street, around the corner from his saloon, and rented them to some ladies in the habit of renting themselves for brief periods of entertainment, there was no law for it to be against.

Judge Canty might have been able to instruct the police force to discover some ordinance the cribs were violating, but the council, noting Bascom's exemplary quietness and order, had reduced the force to a chief and one policeman, both council—in effect, Varnum—appointees.

"Well, it's a shame to see a good town turned into a reg'lar Sundown and Tomorrow or what," Sam Canty said, "but still, Varnum or no Varnum, the voters elect the council, and they get what they vote for. They want to rub cheeks and jowls with whores and tinhorns, that's their choice. I got the Butler House Hotel, I got the ranch, and I'm still judge hereabouts, that's enough for me."

But Varnum did not seem to share Sam Canty's live-and-let-live attitude. He was encouraging farmers to settle on grassland that Canty had used as part of his range for decades, and was talking of a Greater Bascom that would occupy all of that range.

"You see, land claims is some cloudy out here," Sam Canty said. "We worked it out okay with the land south of the river when we set the town up—there was old land grants, and our Donation Land grants give us pretty good title. But when I went over the river, I done what the other fellows getting into big ranching done, and that's to use what's there, and if the legalities come into it, get the hands to file a bunch of claims all over the range, like a ladies' polka-dot-pattern dress—not covering the whole of it, d'ye see, but enough so's can't nobody else use the same range. That works out fine in practice, but any egg-sucking hydrophobia skunk of a lawyer could likely tear it all up."

"They're good at that," Brandon said.

It had lately become clear that Dorn Varnum had close ties to some powerful people in the state house, though apparently not enough to push his plans through fully. It was uncertain what the scope of those plans were, but a main element seemed to be to obtain possession of the full extent of Sam Canty's range and immediately sell it off for building lots and town expansion.

"Ne'mine what friends in Austin he's got," Sam Canty said, "he won't be able to do that while I'm still up in the saddle. I got friends there, too, and I'm the by-God judge around here." Canty's immediate worry was that Dorn Varnum might be trying to outflank him. Some brawls—not of their making, Sam Canty claimed—had started to gain Canty's hands the reputation of being quarrelsome and disorderly; rowdies not directly traceable to Varnum were losing the Butler House its reputation; a barn of one of the farmers supporting Varnum had been burned and the fences of others destroyed. The discovery of the slaughter of some Canty cattle was considered by many to be a possible motive for these last acts.

"If we was to find a fellow that's been killing or stealing our cattle, it wouldn't be barn-burning or fence-smashing we'd do," Sam Canty said, "but something more permanent and thoughtful-making. Though I don't suppose it'd smooth things over much to say so. Anyhow, it ain't none of my men that done any of that, and there's no proof who it was nor why."

"Who benefits?" Brandon asked.

"Varnum, accourse—anything weakens me helps him."

"Not proof in law, but it makes sense to assume that he's behind it, then."

"I do," Sam Canty said, "and I am making my plans according. And that is the which of the why you're here."

"Jack Kestrel said that you needed a kind of bouncer at the Butler House, to keep order," Brandon said.

"That was in my mind when I asked him to keep a eye peeled for someone likely," Sam Canty said. "But I been feeling that there is more called for, and, just now going over it all with you, it come to me the more clearly." He grinned briefly at Brandon and said, "So you see there was some use to the old man yarning on till the cows come home, though they don't do that around here, just stay out on the range."

"More called for," Brandon said flatly.

Sam Canty looked at him appraisingly, nodded very slightly as if ratifying a decision he had tentatively made, and said, "I need to know what is going on in Bascom, know for sure if it's Varnum, and just what he's up to and how he's doing it. So what is called for is a man that can size up what is happening, can find out what's not out in the open, and can take care of himself while he's doing that. What Jack Kestrel tells me, Mr. Bane, that could be you."

That could be me being a lightning rod for whatever trouble's brewing in Bascom is what you're too tactful to say, Mr. Canty. And I don't read "take care of himself" any other way but shooting the ones throwing the lightning.

15

Brandon pondered for a moment. With the unrest Canty had described, and the association of the shaved-wood flower with someone belonging to the Canty ranch, it seemed close to certain that Bascom was where he should be looking right now, and the offered job was a fine way of looking for a Kenneally without seeming to do so. It was also about as far as you could get from something Cole Brandon should be doing, but it might just be Carter Bane's meat. On the other hand, there was a good deal more plausible candidate on the ground.

"Could be a job for Jack Kestrel, what I heard about him up in Kansas," Brandon said.

"Kestrel's got a lot of jobs," Canty said shortly. "He's needed at what he's doing." Brandon weighed the words and the manner and came up with the clear feeling that ranch foreman and general assistant to Sam Canty did not complete Kestrel's job description.

"What Kestrel tells you enough to go on?" Brandon said. Bane, he was finding, tended to barber his sentences fairly closely.

"He was impressed," Sam Canty said. "Plus which, talking with you here, I see for myself that you're quick at seeing into things, and you got an almighty amount of patience. A man that can hear me through San Jacinto and the rest withouten a yawn, that man can watch at a hole forsoever as long as he has to for whatever's going to come out. If you're interested, though, best to have Kestrel in and see if there's anything else about you that's needful to know."

Brandon having signified that the matter was to be pursued, Sam Canty went to the front door and opened it, calling, "Hey, Kestrel!"

Jack Kestrel, looking not quite as slight in his workmanlike riding outfit as he had in a suit the night before, snapped to his feet on the porch, leaving the chair he had been sitting in rocking frantically. In the porch rocker next to him Brandon saw a large, handsome young woman in a cotton print dress. Her broad-cheeked face and red-blond hair had enough of Canty to give her a nine parts certainty of being a daughter. She was looking at Kestrel with a kind of amused friendliness that briefly stabbed at Brandon, reminding him of when he had seen such a look on Elise's face. *She's made up her mind about him; now it's up to him to see it and figure what he's going to do. If, of course, he isn't the man I've come here to kill.*

Sam Canty called brusquely, "Get on in here, Kestrel. Little more talk with Mr. Bane."

Brandon had spent much of the mostly silent ride out from town with Kestrel in stitching together a past career that he could present to meet, or at least divert, close inquiries; but he found that Kestrel was not interested in the whole of his past, just a few patches of the fabric.

In answer to Kestrel's politely guarded questions about trouble with the law, Brandon allowed that he had more than a passing familiarity with the operations of criminal justice but was not actually wanted for any offenses.

"Now that holdout gun you showed those fellows last night," Kestrel said—to Brandon's surprise; he had thought that it had been well concealed from the corner-seated Kestrel, who must indeed have sharp eyes—"that's something you expect a professional gambler to have, can be rigged to put a card in the hand as well as a gun. That a line you follow sometimes, Mr. Bane?"

"No," Brandon said. "Got it from a gambler. Man name of Doyle."

"Dan Doyle? I've run across him. Surprised he'd let it go. He sell it to you, down on his luck?"

"Far down as it gets. Shot dead, place called Boudin, up in the Neutral Zone."

Kestrel nodded slowly, as if, like the police chief in Boudin, he found it suitable that a man like Doyle should be killed in a place like that. He looked at Brandon inquiringly. "And you . . . ?"

"I was there when he died," Brandon said. Whatever conclusions Kestrel and Canty drew from that statement, and from his possession of the dead man's weapon, they did not ask that it be elaborated on.

Kestrel studied Brandon for a moment; Brandon eased himself into a combination of Doyle's dead-eyed look and the impassive firmness of the town marshal in Inskip. Bane had to seem thoroughly in control but with a deep vein of deadly lunacy—at least that was what these fellows seemed to want.

"I'd say he's the man," Kestrel said to Sam Canty.

"Agreed," Canty said. The specifics of the offer were that Carter Bane would be carried on the books as assistant manager at the Butler House Hotel—at a wage only about twice that of a cowhand, Brandon realized, though the Butler House provided better quarters than the ranch bunkhouse—but would be expected to appear there only from time to time during the drinking hours of the night, to forestall or stop trouble. The rest of the time he would put in acquainting himself with Bascom in the guise of an interested newcomer and finding out what he found out.

"I'll send one of the hands back with you. In fact, he'll stay with you, be able to tell you what you might need to know about who's who and what's what, run errands, back you in a tight spot, and Pony Express it back here with any word you want to get to me quick."

Sam Canty once again opened the door to the porch and

called to the girl still sitting in the rocker, "Lorena, go get Curly and tell him he's going to town for a while, and to get over here for instructions. And go see that Mr. Bane's horse's been fed and's ready to go back."

"Yes, Pa," the girl said. She rose, turned, and stepped gracefully off the porch.

"I'll see to my horse, too," Jack Kestrel said and, without waiting for a reply from Sam Canty, slipped out the door and followed Lorena.

Sam Canty looked after them. "After my wife died, maybe I should've sent her east to school. But I didn't, and I raised her to take this ranch over after I'm out of it. Maybe, wasn't for that, I'd sell up and get away from Varnum and all his foolishness and go get fat in Californy, but it's Lorena's place as much as mine, and somehow it seems that we got to keep it. I need Jack Kestrel almighty bad, but I am right now studying out if I am going to have to take him into the family or shoot him to keep him out of it."

In any group of a dozen men, Brandon's companion would inevitably be the one called Curly, even if several others had hair as acutely waved. It was mainly, Brandon decided, that there was nothing much else to notice about him: a round, but not fat, face; sturdy build; capable, long-fingered hands, perpetually active; light-hearted manner, given to anecdotes, jokes, and songs. Shorty, Whitey, Bluetooth, Big Foot, Cockeye—none of the physical feature nicknames would do. And something denoting his personality wouldn't work either: The Pleasant Kid, say, didn't really have a ring, and he was something past Kid age anyhow—maybe mid-twenties.

"Now, this is some doings," Curly said, clattering along beside Brandon in the early afternoon heat. As on the ride out with Kestrel in the morning, they crossed the river at a plank bridge set on piles, ten miles straight south from the ranch house; the wide planks rested unfastened on the piles and shifted noisily as the horses trotted across on them. The river was narrower here, and the banks steeper, than at the ford some miles to the west, and Jack Kestrel had explained to him that, when flooding threatened, the planks could be pulled off or left to be carried downstream without destroying the base of the bridge.

"It renders my heart to think of all the fun and good times I am going to be missing," Curly went on. "The fellers will be chousing the cows in for branding, out on the range and throwing angry critters down and making 'em angrier and getting kicked, and eating sandy stew out of the chuck wagon, and coming in tired and sore in the nighttime to happy times in a bunkhouse with a dozen other fellers that has got so ripe the moskeeters don't land on 'em any more, and playing poker for matches, as our wages ain't due for some while yet. Bitter tears will start to my eyes as I think on that whiles as I am drinking of a Sazerac cocktail and eating turtle soup or sinking into a feather mattress at the Butler House Hotel. Or into one of them young ladies on Bowie Street, for that matter."

"Is that part of the job?" Brandon asked.

"Not strickly speaking, maybe, but I am willing to go the extry mile. Besides, them soiled doves get to know a lot of things, even outside improving theirselfs in their trade, from the customers. And it's the regular customers that's likely to be about what Mr. Canty wants us to keep open eyes for, so, come to think of it, it would be part of the job—maybe a real important part. Accourse, it'd look unchancy if a high-toned fellow like a hotel assistant manager was to resort to low dens of vice, but nobody wouldn't think nothing of a poor ornery cowboy resorting, so I guess it falls to me to waller in the sty. It ain't my way to complain, so I'll do the work in stony silence, except maybe some whoopin' now and then."

Brandon had the fleeting thought that maybe The Big Mouth Kid would have done as a nickname. But Curly's loquacity might come in useful for Cole Brandon's mission, if not necessarily for Carter Bane's.

The chance to test this came fairly soon. "Now Bascom is an okay place for a town that's growed up on farmers and is out at the back of beyond, but it ain't nowheres near as lively and gamesome as a Kansas cowtown, 'specially as when the herds is coming in. When we brung Mr. Canty's herd into Dysart end of last summer, us boys had us as high a old time as there is. Lost three fingers and a ear amongst us and drank enough to puke up every meal we had for near a week. When I went on back there with Jack Kestrel last month to see to selling the herd, since it'd had to winter over, Dysart was about done, though. They say that Inskip's the place now."

"So they do," Brandon said. "They also say that Jack Kestrel is all kinds of tough, but he seems a quiet enough fellow to me."

"Oh, he is quiet enough," Curly said, "but so's a rawhide whip until as it cuts through to your backbone, and then it's you that makes the noise more than it does. I ain't knowed him long, for I signed on at the Lazy Y only just afore the drive, but nor Injuns nor rustlers didn't bother us none on the way up, and I believe it's because they knowed who the trail boss of that herd was. Up in Dysart, he put on a suit that he'd had folded in his saddlebags and looked like any gent, soft-spoke and curried neat, but I seen hardcases walking backwards at a canter when they seen him coming, and fellows that picks the human flesh out of their teeth with railroad spikes speaking to him soft and humble. I never truthfully see him kill anybody, or even wound, but you *know* he'd do it and not even raise a sweat. I got to say, it's something to work for a man like that, whether he's a outlaw, like some say, or a lawman, or one and the other both, like Hickok and them."

He looked over to where Brandon rode beside him. "Seems that happens to me some often." Brandon was startled when, after a brief moment of incomprehension, he understood what Curly was saying. Bane, by reputation and demeanor, seemed to have classed himself with James Butler Hickok and Jack Kestrel—and it was all accident and bluff. And maybe it was with Kestrel and Hickok . . . not with Gren Kenneally and the others, though.

"Well," Brandon said lightly, "however that might be, it wouldn't do any harm to drop a word now and then while you're nosing around that this Bane fellow at the Butler House is pure poison. Make the hotel part of my job a little easier, maybe: Put a big skull and crossbones on the bottle, and people aren't much inclined to try what it tastes like."

Across the river, on the north bank that had until very recently been Sam Canty's exclusive domain, Brandon saw even rows of green cutting into the varicolored grasslands and a low house of unpainted boards. At the far edge of the field, something glinted in the light of the descending sun, as if it were fenced with tiny bits of metal.

16

Evening, Mr. Bane."

"Mr. Porter." Brandon nodded, and Bascom's barber seemed pleased with the acknowledgment of his greeting as he passed into the hotel barroom. For Porter, the presence of Carter Bane, rumored to have a checkered past and known by observation to be trouble for troublemakers, lounging comfortably near the bar entrance, was a little like that of a watch-lion, so to speak: dangerous but under control enough to guarantee the accustomed quiet and order of the Butler House bar.

Brandon had established in the last two days a routine of first sitting in the lobby to greet entering patrons, then a slow drift through the barroom itself, entering a conversation now and then if it seemed called for, ending up leaning on the bar and surveying the room with his best version of Bane's mocking imitation of amiability, and an air of constantly surveying the place to see who or what would be destroyed if gunfire erupted in different quarters of the room.

A couple of times already, men of the type he had ejected on his first night in Bascom had entered the lobby, met his flat look and wolfish smile, and decided to take their diversions elsewhere. Curly claimed to have talked up Bane's reputation enthusiastically, and it seemed to be having an effect.

Bane would like that, Brandon supposed, would feel a cold-blooded, reptilian amusement at the fear he inspired. It seemed to him that he was coming to understand Carter Bane pretty thoroughly as he played the role, and that he was not a likable man. If he ever saw Edmund Chambers again, he'd have to ask why there was something enjoyable about playing villains. He wasn't Bane by a country mile, of course, but acting the part felt pretty satisfactory.

"Mr. Bane!" Curly gestured at him from behind a pillar and called his name in the hoarse whisper of a stage conspirator, though the lobby was empty at the moment and there was in any case nothing clandestine in a meeting of one of Sam Canty's employees with another. The theatrical atmosphere seemed strong this evening.

Curly rolled his eyes and jerked his head toward the staircase, much like a horse abruptly and painfully reined up. Brandon rose and led the way up to his room. Curly closed the door and sank into a chair. "Good, they didn't see us together," he said.

Brandon felt like pointing out that it didn't matter half a buffalo chip, but that didn't seem to be a Bane response. He looked impassively at Curly, saying nothing.

"Well now," Curly said after a moment, "all's I got to report is about the same as yesterday. There ain't much said about whos and whats, but folks seems to feel that something's on the road to happening; the balloon's swole up and tugging at the ropes. The few farmer fellows that'd talk to me, they said that they'd heard that some of the Lazy Y boys was threatening the farmers out on the new places 'crost the river, which I know for a fact ain't so—Mr. Canty don't like 'em being there, but they're enough away from where the cows are so that it ain't a bother worth bothering about. And they said, kinda sneering, that they'd know what to do about it. And some of the merchants in town that's still friends with Mr. Canty, or anyhow on the outs with Dorn Varnum, they tolt me that there was said to be hardcases coming into town that didn't seem to have no lashings to anybody hereabouts. A couple is gamblers, but they all got the look of perfessers of gunmanship."

"Varnum," Brandon said.

"Well, likely," Curly said, "but he ain't been seen to share a dish of tea with 'em, nor hand out plans and instructions, nor do nothing beyond the genial host act, as most of 'em hangs around in his place, which don't say nothing much neither way, as it is about the only place in Bascom that that kind would go to. And they don't say nothing about working for Varnum nor why they's here."

"Been talking with 'em?" Brandon asked.

Curly grinned. "Well, no, they ain't sociable inclined, towards me, anyway. But I done some talking with some of the ladies over on Bowie Street, and they tolt me the hardcases didn't say nothing about whences and whithers and such. That type of fellow, when he's with a soiled dove, seems what he talks about is the soiling he's doing, the soiling he's just done, and the soiling he means to be at when he gets his facilities back."

"Nothing new, then," Brandon said.

Curly snapped his fingers. "One of the farmer fellows dropped something to another one that I don't guess he knew I heard. Something about a new kind of fence that'd show Sam Canty he didn't own everything in every direction no more. Amount he'd had to drink, I don't expect he'd know a fence from a fireplace."

Brandon recalled the glints of metal in sunlight at the far end of a field, seen on the ride back to town two days before. No reason to link that with what Curly had overheard, but, unreasonable or not, the link seemed to form itself clearly in his mind.

"Mr. Bane?"

Back at his post in the lobby, Brandon looked up. The man standing in front of him was the most elegant article he had seen in Bascom: well-cut city suit, polished shoes, cravat puffing out over the vest, curly-brimmed hat, a long, sardonic face punctuated by a neatly trimmed mustache. He hardly needed the man's self-introduction.

"Dorn Varnum, sir. May I invite you to join me for a drink in your excellent bar? Assuming I qualify for entry, of course."

Brandon gave him a Bane look—why be jokey with a man who wouldn't care one way or another if it turned out you needed killing?—and said, "Okay."

As they stood at the bar, Brandon realized that this was the first person he'd run across in some time who might have been part of Cole Brandon's sphere back in St. Louis. Varnum was polished, clearly sharp-witted, maybe even cultivated. Also enjoyable to listen to, at least for Brandon; Bane would not be actively impatient, as that wasn't his way, but the idea of taking pleasure in listening to someone talk was completely foreign to him.

"Progress!" Dorn Varnum said, raising his glass. "The nineteenth century's almost three-fourths run, the twentieth is looming over the horizon. You remember 1848, Bane?"

"Like it was twenty-six years ago," Brandon could not help saying, thinking too late that a grunt or nod would have done for Bane.

Varnum blinked and said, "Well, that's how far ahead of us 1900 is—the great age of railroads and traction engines, of machines and electricity, of cities rising in the wilderness, and fertile farms burgeoning to feed their citizens."

This time Brandon let Bane grunt. Varnum wasn't the kind that needed encouragement to speak, evidently. Cross-examining lawyers wept with delight to get specimens like this, who could usually be persuaded to spill any damaging information they might have just by being allowed to speak.

Brandon sipped at his whiskey. *Don't let that confuse you about this man. Everyone's a fool some way, but he may be as formidable as Sam Canty says he is, and don't ever forget that.*

"Every year new inventions promote progress, Mr.

Bane," Varnum said. "Cheap, strong fencing for safe fields—that'll revolutionize farming, especially out here; make possible the development of huge farms wherever the soil will sustain them. That's what the future holds for Bascom, farms and towns to the horizon and beyond."

Brandon looked at him, letting Bane's face register polite attention and the absence of any intention of commenting.

"Well, of course," Varnum said, as if there had actually been a reply, "that's going to be hard for Sam Canty to swallow. He's had things his way for a long time, but times are changing. Mr. Canty has been important to Bascom, but Bascom's growing beyond Mr. Canty, and I'm afraid that he's going to resist that. He is a hot-tempered man and may kick against the pricks if it comes to that." Bane's mouth muscles stifled Brandon's grin. *You try that quotation on Canty, he'll tell you just which one he'll kick against.*

Varnum set his glass on the bar and said, "It would be a pity for that to happen, Mr. Bane, for Mr. Canty to throw away the chance he has to be in on the growth of a newer, bigger, better Bascom."

A couple of reminiscent anecdotes, a comment on the weather, and a mildly salacious joke served as a thin disguise for the fact that the evening's business had been completed with the delivery of the last observation, and Varnum soon took his leave.

"Pleasure, Mr. Bane. Enjoyed talking to you."

Brandon applauded his choice of words: "to," not "with." A couple of grunts and nods had been his main contribution to the conversation, making him an ideal interlocutor for someone of Varnum's temperament. Brandon nodded and said, "Varnum." That was about as effusive a parting as Bane's temperament allowed. *Now I have been given a message for Sam Canty, and it's not that clear what it is. The message I get is that Dorn Varnum is a smooth proposition, and it may be Bane's job to ruffle him some.*

"Now here you are," Brandon said aloud to himself—he was finding that being the laconic Bane in public required some sort of redressing balance in private—"embarked on the grimmest kind of business there is, and caught up in some bucolic civil war *in posse*, and you've got to make it all wait while you go buy some socks!"

He held up one of the pairs he had brought from St. Louis. For someone who had done such little walking for the distance traveled, he had punished the socks badly. They were tissue-thin at the heel and frankly exploded at the toe. Probably beyond darning. . . . For the first time in quite a while, the sharp pang in the midsection and the following sense of vertigo reminded him of who had last darned his socks and that she wouldn't be doing that—or anything—ever again.

It passed, and he went downstairs and out into the sunny street, turning over in his mind the discovery that, once these stabbing shocks passed, he was not unhappy. Not happy, by any means, but . . .

"Appropriate" was the word that occurred to him—awkward, but "content" was misleading, and what he seemed to be feeling was that he was doing what he was supposed to be doing. And that he would feel more—whatever it was—if he kept on with that. *I think much more in that style, I doubt I'll ever be able to get my brain working clearly enough to do a brief or draft a plea again.* Brandon realized that he was not expecting to be called on to do those things in the future, either.

Varnum, he saw, did not act as a resident manager in his store. As he stepped into its cool, high-ceilinged interior, he experienced a variety of odors—spices, wool, leather, machine oil—and saw a woman of about thirty behind the long counter at the side of the store, the only occupant of the establishment at the moment.

"Can I help you?" she said in a deep voice that held a note of muted pleasure or amusement. She looked guardedly pleased with herself, and Brandon had to admit that she had reason. She was not candy-box pretty, but she had a generous mouth, yellow-brown eyes over high cheekbones, and molasses-colored hair in a coil at the back of her head.

She searched out the socks efficiently and was able to offer him a surprising selection of patterns; maybe Dorn Varnum made sure he'd be able to keep up his sartorial standards by calling on his own stock.

As she was wrapping his purchase, it occurred to him that a store manager could be a good source of information, and he introduced a note of Dan Doyle as ladies' man into the Bane portrayal. "I hadn't thought much of Bascom till now," he said, "but I believe it's got amenities I hadn't been aware of." Cole Brandon, had he made such an approach, would have looked into the lady's eyes, but Bane + Doyle gave an appreciative glance at the bosom that swelled the gingham shirtwaist worn by the manager. It was in character, and also she seemed to be of a type that would not resent the attention.

"Bascom's a nice enough place, Mr. . . ."

"Bane."

"I thought so—the new . . . assistant manager at the Butler House. You have been talked of. We almost rhyme, Mr. Bane—I'm Sally Dumayne. At any rate, it's a pleasant town, with much to recommend it."

"I would admire to learn about that, should you care to act as my guide," Brandon said. "Starting, perhaps, with dinner at the Butler House?"

Sally Dumayne smiled. "That is very kind of you, Mr. Bane. But, I will tell you frankly, I am not free to dine with gentlemen. I have a friend who would take highly unkindly to that, even if I were so inclined. Mr. Dorn Varnum."

Brandon studied her face and was prompted by what he saw there to say, "Such a situation would make the evening the more enjoyable, Miss Dumayne. Fruit that is not forbidden is in a way flat." That was a good bit beyond Bane, and probably stretching it for Doyle, but he was unlikely to have to play to Sally Dumayne and to his usual audience at the same time.

"I am more a meat-eater than fruit, Mr. Bane," Sally Dumayne said, smiling cheerfully, "so I will again decline your offer, though with thanks for making it."

Brandon left, thoughtfully dangling the string-wrapped

parcel from a middle finger. Sally Dumayne might be Varnum's girl, but she had been amused—appreciatively amused, he'd guess—at his advances, and that suggested that she might not be attached to Varnum and his interests with intractable firmness. An uncertain ally could be more dangerous to Varnum than a frank enemy.

17

As Brandon neared the piling bridge, he saw three riders approaching the river on the far side. By the time he was clattering across the loose planks he was able to identify them as Sam Canty, Jack Kestrel, and Lorena Canty. They halted and waited for him to come to them.

"What brings you this way, Bane?" Sam Canty asked. "Something happen in town?"

"Not really," Brandon said.

"Glad to hear it," Sam Canty said gloomily. "No news is good news. Out here, we got news. But you're here for a reason."

Brandon nodded. "Some things Dorn Varnum said I thought you ought to know. Anyhow, seemed he meant me to pass 'em on, so I am."

He turned with the other three and rode east with them, keeping to the top of the low bluff along the river. Sam Canty listened to Brandon's account of Dorn Varnum's remarks, thought for a moment, and said, "That about him wanting me to have a chance to be in on the bigger and better and bodaciouser Bascom, I estimate there's about as much to it as a cow fart in a blue norther."

Brandon glanced at Lorena Canty, who jogged along in

her divided skirt, registering neither ladylike reproach nor amusement at her father's comment; he supposed that the capacity for either reaction had been used up long before, growing up on a working ranch. "Would say you're right," he said.

"Wants to be able to say he's cooperative and agreeable, and you're the mossback that won't see reason," Jack Kestrel said.

"Did he say what kind of fencing he was talking about?" Lorena Canty asked.

"No," Brandon said, "just that it'd make a big difference."

"You ain't asked us why you find us riding away from the ranch and away from where there's any Lazy Y cattle these days," Sam Canty said.

Brandon said nothing. What Canty had said was clearly true, and not a direct question, so Bane would not feel it necessary to reply.

Sam Canty sighed. "The reason is, like I said, we got news this morning. One of the farmers along the river here, about five miles on, seems to have got his house or barn or such burned last night. One of my riders saw smoke that way this morning, and he came to the house and told me. Didn't go close, since I've told the hands to check anything unusual out with me before they go have a look these days, but he squinted and it seemed to him he could see a patch of black where some kind of building used to be. Like I told you, there's been a barn or so burned lately in some of the farms south of the river, but this'll be the first this close to me, if that's what it is."

"Nobody's dared say right out you had anything to do with the other barn burnings," Lorena said.

Sam Canty said glumly, "Likely they will with this one, being on what used to be my range. I mean, I let a fellow settle here and set to farming, since I got plenty of better grazing elsewheres, and I tell him to take a beef now and then if he's short of what to feed his family, and I give him a load of hay for his critters when he started in, and once fotched the doctor out from town when he sent word his woman was sick and he couldn't git away to go in himself. Do anyone a few favors, he'll blame you for anything bad that happens; how it goes from what I've seen. You help a man, he figures you owe him."

"I don't blame you, Mr. Canty," the farmer said.

Sam Canty looked surprised and pleased. He and the rest had dismounted as soon as they came up to what remained of the farmstead, since four people on horseback could not converse with one afoot without giving the appearance of intended intimidation. The crops did not appear to have been damaged, but a large rectangular area heaped with huge, middling, and small pieces of charcoal, still emitting tendrils of smoke and heat that carried almost a hundred feet to where they stood, testified to the destruction of what had been a fair-sized farmhouse. Off toward the barn—intact, but decorated with a fan-shaped scorch mark indicating that the arsonists had at least made an effort there—a woman and two big-eyed children peered at them from an opening in the improvised canvas top of a farm wagon, their temporary, and mobile, home. It was too far to read faces clearly, but Brandon thought their looks held fear and loathing, and no wonder.

"Glad to hear it, Wilkinson," Sam Canty said. "You know I—"

"Mr. Dorn Varnum was particular on that point," Wilkinson said. "Reminded me of what you done for me, said you was an honorable man, and not one to do this kind of thing."

"Varnum's been out here already?" Jack Kestrel said.

"Couple hours back," Wilkinson said. "Had heard of my fire from someone as saw it from acrost the river, told me, and come on out to see what help he could be of."

"Good of him," Sam Canty said. "And you say he gave me a clean bill of health?"

"Oh, yes," Wilkinson said. "Explained as how, what with you getting on into the years of ripeness, you couldn't be expected to know everything your hands was up to, and—"

Sam Canty made a wordless noise that was something between the gobble of a turkey and the squeal of an outraged pig. "Interesting, Mr. Wilkinson," Jack Kestrel said. "Mr. Varnum believes that Lazy Y men did this?"

"He didn't like to think so, but, he says, who else would it be? Cowhands, drifters like that, they don't value the work of folks' hands, and they got this crazy notion that some of us farmers been taking your cattle—without permission like what you give me—and so they go out and hooraw the farmers."

"One thing he says I agree with," Jack Kestrel said, "when he asks who else would do this. Now that's a question it's worth thinking on a while, Mr. Wilkinson. You keep at that, you look past the Lazy Y men, and you might come up with something interesting. As for the hands, I'm their boss and I'll tell you, they know about hard work. If they drift, it's because they go wherever they can make a living at what they do, and in these times that's harder than ever. They're not going to go out and do a low, sneaking thing like this over some unexplained missing cows."

"That may be so and it may not be so," Wilkinson said, looking mulishly at Jack Kestrel. "But cutting my fence seems almighty like saying this is still supposed to be Canty range, and who is it'd be interested in seeing as I receive that message?"

"Fence?" said Lorena Canty.

"Couple hundred dollars' worth," Wilkinson said sadly. "Mr. Dorn Varnum read of it being made back in Ohio and stocked some of it, told me as how it would bring farming into modrun times, and let me have a third of a mile of it at a special price, plus waiting a while for full payment. And now it's all cut down. Most of it I can tack up to posts again, but some's cut in such short snips I'll have to replace it. And at eighteen cents a foot, I don't see how I can do it, unless Mr. Varnum's accommodating again."

"I think you'll find he will be," Jack Kestrel said dryly. "What's so almighty wonderful about this fencing?"

"Easy to put up fast, don't take but some posts to tack it

to, and keeps beasts to their own side of it better 'n a palisade," Wilkinson said. "Show you." He walked to a heap of oddments near the scorched barn, bent to pick something up, and returned to where they stood. "Here."

He held up a twisted double strand of heavy wire about two feet long, into which at intervals were fitted short loops of the same wire, with outward-facing sharpened points. Brandon could see that any creature pushing against it would abandon the project quickly, so that two strands at the right height would keep out almost anything but rabbits and prairie dogs.

Sam Canty's eyes opened wider as he looked at it and his face stiffened. Brandon could trace his thoughts: This wire fencing could certainly bring farming into modern times and, given enough land greed and determination on the part of the expanding farmers, put an end to Sam Canty's kind of ranching.

Brandon could understand why Canty's reassurance of Lazy Y innocence in the matter of the burned house, and his offer of any assistance needed, was made with some stiffness. Wilkinson's declination of the offer and the statement that he had friends to see him through were made with an equal reserve, very likely born of unappeased suspicion.

Brandon, Sam Canty, Lorena Canty, and Jack Kestrel rode away from the farm in silence for a while; then Sam Canty spoke: "They'll parcel all the open country up with that damned wire. Cows'll rip themselves on the points and the screwworm'll get to 'em and they'll die bawling."

"Cows aren't the smartest animals there is," Jack Kestrel said, "but there is some things they can learn, and I would suppose that getting stung by a fence will educate them fast."

"Herefords," Lorena Canty said.

"What the thunder you talking about?" Sam Canty said.

"Remember, Pa, a year and some back, you were thinking about bringing in some Herefords to try crossbreeding them with the longhorns—get an animal that could stand up to the trail like the longhorns but would have the heft and the meat of the Herefords. But you couldn't work out how to keep the Herefords, the longhorns, and the crossbreeds away from each other so's you could control the breeding."

"And this horned wire's how to do that!" Jack Kestrel said. "Pick out a section of your range any size you like, fence it in, put the different bunches of cows where you want, and you got all the control you need of what they get up to."

A little to Brandon's surprise—he had Sam Canty pegged as stubborn on principle—the rancher seemed taken with the idea. "High damn," he said, "that might could do it, so it could. Couple years, could have a herd of critters that'd fetch two prices, top-grade meat and lots more of it. Heydee, maybe I'll see if Mr. Dorn Varnum can make me a good price on five, ten miles of it."

As Canty, Kestrel, and Lorena talked over aspects of the cattle-breeding scheme, Brandon was considering Dorn Varnum, though not as a possible source of fencing. His comment about Sam Canty's loosening grip on his men was outright mockery as well as damaging; and it was highly interesting that he had had word of Wilkinson's fire in time to be out there so early.

The low line of the bridge across the river came into sight. "We'll turn north," Sam Canty said. "No need for you to come back to the house with us, Bane, is there?"

"No," Brandon said. "Be best to get back to town, see what's being said about the fire there."

"Whatever it is'll be what Varnum's brought back and spread around," Jack Kestrel said.

Brandon nodded.

"Something's caught at the other side of the bridge," Lorena said. Brandon looked and saw something dark showing through the spaces between the pilings.

"A log," Jack Kestrel said.

"A log as big around as a hogshead," Sam Canty said dubiously. The four riders urged their horses to a faster walk, then halted as they came to the far side of the bridge and saw what the current was pushing against a piling.

"Not long dead," Sam Canty said after a moment.

The horse's body had not begun to swell, and its

unstiffened legs and head moved flaccidly in the current. A thin crescent of bone glinted at the edge of a bloodless, river-washed hole behind one staring eye.

Jack Kestrel leaned forward in the saddle and studied the dead animal. "That's the horse Harry Briggs was riding, and that's his saddle."

"Harry Briggs?" Sam Canty said.

"Hired on last month," Lorena said. "I signed him up while Jack was on his way back from Kansas; one of the bunch we needed to get started on the roundup. Dark-complected fellow, played the mouth organ sometimes."

"I recall him some," Sam Canty said somberly, with a slow swing of his glance from the horse to Kestrel to Lorena and to the open land beyond them. Once again Brandon believed he could follow his train of thought: If he had let management of his hands pass so far to his daughter and to his foreman that he had to be reminded of who one of them was, there might after all be something to Dorn Varnum's taunt the farmer had relayed. . . .

"Now," Jack Kestrel said slowly, "start with you figure someone shot Harry's horse from ambush. Then you got to figure what is Harry doing about that? I don't estimate he dragged the horse over to the river and dumped it in, with his saddle still on, to keep the range tidy."

"Joking doesn't help," Lorena said. "Harry's shot, too, and likely floating down the river. He could have gone between the pilings easily."

Sam Canty and Jack Kestrel nodded. "Barn-burnings, stolen stock, now this. Appears to me that the balloon has gone up for fair. Won't matter what I say, the boys'll have blood in their eyes when they hear about this."

Kestrel said, "And we'd worked it out for half a dozen to have some time in town tonight—not been off the ranch for close to a month. Be crazy to let 'em go with this in their craw, almost as crazy to keep 'em back without telling 'em why."

Brandon decided to allow Bane a moment of helpfulness. "If you cut loose the saddle and gear and cache it here in case your man ever does turn up, and you push the horse between the pilings and let it go downriver, I guess your men don't have to hear about this until you choose to tell them."

Lorena and Sam Canty looked at him with a mixture of distaste and respect that indicated that the suggestion was what they might have expected from Carter Bane: dishonest, callous—and what had to be done. Jack Kestrel said, "Let's get to it, then, Bane."

The Cantys searched for a hiding place for the gear while Brandon and Jack Kestrel waded into the river and began tugging at the dead horse. It was bulkier than Brandon had imagined, and its skin was slimy to the touch.

Kestrel slipped, sinking in the river up to his chest, and cursed, then righted himself by grabbing at the dead horse's mane. "Damn," he said. "Killing's got to be done sometimes, but no denying the bodies make trouble after. This damn horse is as big as a barn, but even men are a damn sight of trouble to get rid of if you can't plant 'em lawful in a cemetery. Coyotes dig 'em up, floods wash 'em out, even knew an earthquake to heave one up and put him on display like at the undertaker's. Corpses make trouble, and the fellow that finds a way to handle 'em safe will have the lawmen and the detectives beat four ways from the ace, no doubt about it."

Brandon freed an iron-shod hoof from the bridge piling; the bulky body dipped a little, then swung away and began moving downstream. Brandon looked after it, pondering what Kestrel had said. It struck him as the observation of a man used to corpses as a feature of his work. True, Kestrel was said to have been a tough town marshal, but professional involvement with cadaver disposal seemed more like what could be expected of an active criminal. The kind of man who would ride with Gren Kenneally, say.

As the horse's body vanished downriver, Brandon studied Jack Kestrel, but could come to no conclusion. That would have to wait.

Brandon's horse plodded down the street past the livery stable—another of Dorn Varnum's enterprises, as he now knew—and toward the Butler House Hotel. The sun was halfway down the western sky, but still putting out enough heat to maintain the warm-poultice effect in his trousers that had been steaming his lower body since he'd helped Jack Kestrel and Sam Canty carry out Bane's recommendation. It would have been better to wear the canvas trail trousers than the more formal wool ones, but he had been expected to have an undemanding ride and a conference with his employer, not wade waist-deep in a muddy river to manhandle a dead horse past a row of upright logs.

A sharp hiss, like a leaking boiler, drew his attention to the entrance of an alley next to the livery stable. Curly stood in it, working his face and nodding his head like someone giving a broad interpretation to the role of a lunatic in a melodrama, then disappeared rapidly. Brandon wondered briefly what he had meant to convey, then gave it up.

At the stables behind the hotel, he led his horse to the stall it had been assigned and found Curly crouched in the empty stall next to it. "Sharp of you to've caught on I was signing you to meet me here," he said.

"You made it plain as day," Brandon said, starting to rub the horse down.

"Any doings out at the ranch?" Curly asked.

"Nothing much." As with the rest of the Lazy Y hands, Curly was better off not knowing of the disappearance and presumed death of Harry Briggs. "Here?"

"Well, now," Curly said, dropping his voice to a hoarse whisper perhaps meant to keep his words from reaching the three other stalled horses and the stable cat, "there has been substantial business at the telegraph office today. Mr. Dorn Varnum has set the operator to burning the wires, practically. Now, in the ordinary way of things, everything about such is confidential, 'lessen you can look over the operator's shoulders and read what he's tappin' out off'n the forms, but it happens that the operator paid a noontide visit to a lady on Bowie Street that I have the familiarity of, and he chanced to let something drop that I was able to conduce her to pass on to me."

Brandon gave him a flat Bane look, and Curly decided not to wait to be asked admiringly what the transmitted information was. "Each and every wire was to Austin," he said portentously. "Half a dozen at least, and number of words no object, like sending a newspaper story, practically, the op said."

"About what?" Brandon asked.

Curly shook his head. "The lady is good at loosing tongues, but the op loosed up only so far. The tenor and contents and dispositions of the telegrams, them he would not forthcome, except that they was such as would astonish. If she'd knowed it was important, there is things she could've done that would've had him writin' out copies in a fair hand from recollection, but she didn't, so there it is."

Brandon considered the news. Dorn Varnum was evidently calling in whatever notes he held in the state house, and some kind of official moves would develop. What they were and when they would happen would have to be seen. "Some of the Lazy Y hands are coming to town tonight for some fun. You tell one of them what you told me and make sure he gets it back to Canty."

"Good to see the boys ag'in. Expect we'll wind up at Varnum's, even though he and Sam Canty is on the outs. A saloon is a saloon, whoever owns it, and none of the boys looks on the Butler House as a place to unwind. I recollect one of the fellows is a dab hand at the mouth organ—if he's in the bunch, we can have a fair old concert amongst the revelries."

"Maybe," Brandon said. Mention of the telegraph office brought to the surface something he had been putting off. A wire to Jess Marvell might be worthwhile. The wooden flower that had brought him to Bascom was the strongest lead he had, but it was admittedly tenuous, and it wasn't beyond possibility that she and Rush Dailey would turn up something worth following up after this venture had either paid off or come to nothing. They would mail anything of interest, of course, but it would take an almighty long time to get here and be picked up by someone acting for Colin Binn. SEND REPORTS TO ME AT BUTLER HOUSE HOTEL BASCOM STOP SIGNED CARTER BANE ought to do it, unless Jess Marvell was now supplying reports to other people with the same initials as Charles Brooks and Colin Binn. "What time's the telegraph office open to?"

"Half-past six, usually," Curly said. "But it's closed now."

"Till when?"

Curly shrugged. "Till they hire on a new operator. The one that was there, he told the lady in Bowie Street that he'd took a sudden dislike to Bascom and was leaving for his health. Got a ride with a freighter taking some farm stuff south, about as soon's he left her."

Brandon looked at Curly for a moment, speculating whether he might have some other overlooked nuggets of intelligence he had not thought worth volunteering, such as that Dorn Varnum had proclaimed himself supreme generalissimo of Bascom and seceded it from Texas and the Union. If the reaction of the telegrapher to sending Varnum's wires was to treat himself to a farewell fornication and escape from town by the quickest means possible, it was a good bet that some prime-grade catastrophe was poised to drop on Bascom.

Brandon stepped out of the barroom and into the Butler House lobby. The worn canvas trousers he had donned while the ones he had immersed in the river were being restored to respectability, though washed and pressed, drew some curious glances from the patrons but no questions. Bane was not a man whose sartorial choices the prudent commented on.

He sat in the armchair, relishing its comfort. Even after the long ride from Boudin he was not a seasoned horseman, and the ease of the chair was welcome after the nearly six hours he'd spent in the saddle this morning and afternoon.

From outside drifted the distant night sounds of Bascom, or of the only part of Bascom that produced much sound after sundown—Varnum's saloon: a jumble of voices punctuated by occasional barks of laughter or anger—at this distance it was hard to tell which—intermittent howls that were probably songs at their point of origin, and the tinkle of the saloon's piano. The volume was fuller this evening than usual, and Brandon supposed that the Lazy Y hands were in for their evening's diversion.

He snapped upright as the noise stopped suddenly and completely for about the space of three heartbeats. Then he heard enraged roaring peaked with shrill shouts, the crash of breaking glass, and shots: first by ones and twos, then a cascade of explosions, like a bundle of firecrackers tied together by their fuses and set alight all at once. He stepped to the front door and onto the porch. Down the street toward Varnum's, light flickered and flashed—somebody had set the hanging lamps that lit Varnum's swaying wildly, he guessed—fitfully illuminating a shifting group of figures in the street; miniature lightning flashes winked in unison with the sound of shots.

Footsteps pounded down the street toward the Butler House, and Brandon slipped Dan Doyle's .38 from the holster belted under his jacket, then returned it as Curly bounded onto the porch.

"They're sayin' as some sonofabitch kilt Harry Briggs and his horse!" Curly gasped. "He ain't been seen in a day or so, so the fellows believed him, and laid it to Varnum and commenced to take the place apart, and the farmers and the hardcases, they laid into the boys, and all hell is loose and stampedin'!"

A horse raced by, almost invisible in the night, seemingly propelled by muzzle flashes from the pistol its rider, twisted in the saddle, fired behind him. "Lazy Y?" Brandon asked.

Curly shrugged. "This dark, who the hell knows who the hell's who? The boys got sense, they'll be away from here soon's they can."

"You're out of it, anyhow," Brandon said.

"Hell, I just come to let you know what's up," Curly said. "When there's this much doin', I don't look to let it pass me by!" He broke his revolver, fished in his pocket for cartridges, slammed them into the cylinder, slapped the weapon back together, and ran down the street toward the shouting and the firing.

Brandon looked after him. It wasn't his fight, and it certainly wasn't Bane's. Bane had a job to do. He turned and entered the lobby, now filling with anxious patrons who had heard the tumult. "Nothing to worry about," he said. "A little trouble over to Varnum's. But let's shove some of the furniture here over against the street door and windows, in case it spills up this way. Best we sit it out here. Anybody armed is welcome to stand guard here with me, and drinks on the house when it's finished."

18

After about a quarter of an hour, it seemed that any shooting still going on was concentrated south of Bowie Street. Brandon peered out of the front door and looked down the street. Light still spilled out of the front of Varnum's saloon, but it was no longer agitated; it diffused through the layered cloud of gunsmoke that hung in the street like a luminous fog. He could see a couple of sprawled shapes in the street. At least one seemed to be crawling toward the plankwalk.

Brandon left the manager to take over the guarding of the Butler House and see to fulfilling his promise of drinks on the house for the volunteer sentries, and stepped into the darkened street. He could hear firing, frequent but sporadic —it seemed to him to lack the purposeful quality of a shootout or aimed volleys. It was shooting for the sake of shooting. He moved down the street, keeping in the shadows when a patch of building or walkway was lit up by the lamps at Varnum's. A flicker of yellow-red a couple of streets ahead caught his eye, feebly washing up the front of the church and outlining a group of men in front of it.

Brandon drew his gun and sprinted as silently as he could toward the church. Close to, he saw uneven lengths of lumber leaned against the door and four or five men creating brief flares as they struck matches to help along the uncertain flames growing in a piece of rag or paper at the base of the heap of wood.

They burn the church, whoever they are, and everybody's going to be lynching everybody else on general principles. Bane, Brandon, or anyone else I might be, none of us is going to have that. Brandon knelt, steadied his firing arm on a bent knee, and pulled the trigger three times as fast as he could, shifting his aim slightly between shots.

Dust fountained from under the face of a man bent over the burning paper or cloth, a piece of lumber sprang away from its place in the heap, and a man squealed and clapped at the side of his face—Brandon had been trying for his hat, but didn't mind an earlobe, which made the point at least as forcefully. The hours of marksmanship practice on the trail seemed to have paid off. In a low crouch, he dove toward a water barrel that offered concealment, eased his head and gun hand out from behind it, and triggered off his last three shots—good that the double action meant he didn't need to keep the hammer on an empty chamber—then ducked back to reload. When he looked out again, the would-be churchburners had gone and the fire was a harmless smolder. Brandon went over, kicked the lumber away, and stamped out the last embers.

Brandon walked back toward the Butler House. Outside Varnum's, he looked in through the opening that had held the large plate-glass window, now glittering fragments in the street. The place looked severely disordered but not destroyed, and there were already half a dozen drinkers back at the bar and tables, with one intrepid waiter girl circulating among them. None of them had the look of cowhands or of anyone inclined to be hospitable toward a man known to work for Sam Canty, and Brandon kept well in the shadows as he passed. There were no bodies in the street any longer; they had either removed themselves or been removed, and whether they would be patronizing Dorn Varnum's saloon or the undertaker was something the next day would reveal.

Among the large, straight-edged glints that came from the

glass shards he saw a thick dotting of metallic gleams, and at the same time he noticed that his boots were encountering something other than the normal complement of street pebbles. He bent over and picked up a brass cartridge casing. This was where the firing had been heaviest, all right—but it was surprising that it had been that heavy. Recalling the steadiness of the fire—which, in fact, was still sputtering in the distance—it seemed to him that some pitched battles in the War must have used less ammunition. Brandon walked past Bowie Street, which seemed to mark the northern border of the disturbance. The shops on Main Street were darkened and apparently intact. His hand tensed on the revolver as he saw a hulking figure in the dimness in front of the barber's.

"Who's that?" he called.

"Who wants t' know?" The reply came in a voice it would be unkind to describe as quavering; Brandon recognized it as that of a frequent, and unpaying, customer at the Butler House bar.

"It's Carter Bane, Chief Dedman," he said. "Trouble about died down?" It was clear that the police chief—also embodying a full half of the police force—assumed this to be so, or he would not be out in the open. The impression Brandon had formed was that the chief was probably honest, but so innocuous that it hardly mattered.

"Seems to of been mostly at Varnum's and the other side of there," the chief said. "Stores along here seem okay. Wonder if Varnum's has been tore up bad." He gave a visible twitch as more gunfire sounded, though at a considerable distance.

"Back in business," Brandon said. "Where's your constable?"

"Emmet is seeing to what's doing the other side of Bowie," the chief said.

Brandon walked north on Main Street with the chief, who was regaining composure as door after door proved properly locked and the sound of gunfire receded in distance as well as dwindled in frequency.

A change in the quality of the darkness resolved itself into a pale patch of light in front of Varnum's store as they approached it. "Lamp or so lit in there," Brandon muttered.

"Maybe Mr. Varnum or Miss Dumayne is in there guarding it against pilferers," the chief said hopefully. He stepped to the door and knocked on it twice with the barrel of his revolver.

The rapping this caused was fairly feeble but seemed instantly to produce a piercing scream that might have been "Help!" followed by some definitely wordless shrieks, mixed with male shouts, some thumps that shook the plankwalk, and the sound of breaking glass.

The chief stepped back from the door, as if appalled at what his knocking had produced. Brandon pushed past him and wrenched the door open. The single lamp burning on the countertop showed him a scene of shadowed disorder in the store and somewhat more clearly illuminated a group of men at the rear, next to the counter. As they began to turn toward him, Brandon triggered off four shots, not bothering to aim. *San Jacinto tactics—thing is not so much to shoot them as to make sure they don't shoot.*

The men leaped and scrambled over the counter, kicked open the rear door, and disappeared into the night. Brandon half expected to hear the sound of galloping horses, but the flight seemed to be on foot.

"Thank you, ohmygod, thank you!" Sally Dumayne pushed herself into a sitting position on the pile of dress goods on which she lay sprawled. Even in the feeble light, Brandon could see that her hair was disordered and the bodice of her dress torn away from one shoulder; there was a shadow on her cheek that could be a large bruise, and her lips looked puffed.

He stepped to her and said, "Are you all right, ma'am?"

"Them men, did they . . ." the police chief said.

"I am all right, and no, Chief, they didn't, not even try to, just handled me some roughly. I expect they were here to loot, but you and Mr. Bane drove them off before they could do anything anyhow."

Sally Dumayne took a packet of pins from a case on the counter and secured the tear in her dress.

"Who were they?" Chief Dedman asked. "Cowpunchers? I got a notion it was the Lazy Y fellows that had a lot to do with this trouble tonight."

Sally Dumayne said, "I couldn't say they were, and I couldn't say they weren't. Don't know who they were, and never got a good enough look at them to know them again anyhow."

Brandon looked at the bruise on her cheek and her puffed lip and considered that whoever had given them to her had to have been standing in front and close to—thus visible and presumably memorable. A good cross-examiner would have his description, and probably identity, out of her in no time, but that wasn't Bane's concern.

The chief poked his head out the front door, listened for a moment, heard no gunshots, and declared the hostilities officially over. "All the same, I will escort you home, ma'am, so as to offer protection in case of any dangerousness," he said, having in mind, Brandon was sure, that Sally Dumayne's lodging was directly away from the scene of the night's disturbance.

Sally Dumayne secured the store's outside doors and left with the chief. Brandon walked toward the Butler House in the darkness, considering the many interesting things about the Great Bascom Riot, including its impressiveness as a spectacle compared to the minor visible damage and injury; how it might tie in with the earlier events of the day across the river, at the piling bridge and in the telegraph office; and where the good old legal inquiry *cui bono*—who profits?—came in.

"One thing we have to consider, of course," Dorn Varnum said, "is who would do something like that. Since it's known that you and I have had our differences lately, Sam, it would make a certain kind of sense for your men to attack my store."

Sam Canty had appeared on the point of flashing into apoplexy at the "Sam," but then seemed to take into account that agreeing to Varnum's suggestion of a "talk to clear the air and settle things in a way that's best for the good folk of Bascom" had pretty well foreclosed any strong resentment at the familiarity.

Canty had appeared at Brandon's room at the Butler House not much after nine in the morning, pressing him for a report on the events of the night before. "Couldn't make much out of what the boys told me when they got back last night"—all of them, including Curly, who had concluded that Bascom was not a good place for a Lazy Y hand to see the sunrise in, and none seriously wounded, as it turned out—"so I set out early to get word on what's up here. Gather someone let drop about Harry Briggs being disappeared?"

"Not me," Brandon had said. Their conversation had been interrupted by the delivery of the note from Varnum, suggesting a meeting at the Butler House—"my own establishment being cumbered with the work of repair"—at "half after eleven in the forenoon," a touch of elegance that infuriated Canty.

Now Varnum, Sam Canty, and Brandon sat on the porch of the Butler House as Canty worked at overlooking Varnum's unwanted intimacy. Each had a drink at hand, more as props to indicate civilized sociability than for pleasure. Brandon said, "Unlikely it was Lazy Y or any other cowhands."

Varnum raised his eyebrows.

"Ran off afoot, no horses. They aimed to be away fast, so they'd have ridden if they could," Brandon said.

"You might not . . . have wished to hear horses, if I may say so," Varnum said with every evidence of politeness.

Brandon smiled thinly. "Chief Dedman didn't hear them either. Don't believe he has any . . . wishes not to hear anything."

"They could have left their horses someplace and come to the store on foot," Varnum said.

"They could've spread their coats out and jumped from a roof like flying squirrels," Sam Canty said. "About as likely as a cowhand sauntering around town afoot in a riot. My boys was mounted and out of here soon's they could get clear without getting shot. Had to fight their way to where their horses was hitched, but as soon's they done that they was on their way."

"They tell you," Varnum said.

"They tell me," Sam Canty said flintily.

The sun was almost overhead now, and Brandon could see Emmet, the constable, stooped over in the street down near Varnum's saloon, from which the sounds of hammering could be heard. He was carrying a bag into which he dropped objects retrieved from the dust of the street. Brandon squinted to try to see what they were, then guessed that they were the cartridge cases ejected during the gunplay. Now that his attention was focused, he could see brassy glints in plenty, and Emmet's bag was already distended. Half-a-dozen cowhands and even a score of hardcases and farmers, even with two guns and full gunbelts each, couldn't have come near creating that much martial litter, or have kept up the volume of gunfire.

Where had all the ammunition come from?

"Miss Dumayne might be able to give some particulars of the men who looted my store and outraged her," Varnum said.

"Didn't seem able to last night," Brandon said. "Said straight out she wouldn't know them again."

"Really," Varnum said flatly. It seemed to Brandon that Varnum had been expecting Sally Dumayne to have had good descriptions of her assailants—and that he hadn't talked with her since the incident.

"Well, whenever they left," Varnum said, "your men—or someone, let's be fair—found time to try to fire the church, and that's really over the line."

"As is well known," Canty said heavily, "your average cowhand is a confirmed church-hater and goes about torching same and hanging parsons to the nearest telegraph pole."

Varnum sipped his drink and looked solemn. "The church, my saloon, my store, the reckless gunfire . . . Sam, the important thing isn't if the Lazy Y men did all that, but that it happened. Law and order, Sam, law and order—that's what we don't have in Bascom now."

"There is plenty of law in my court," Sam Canty said. "If there was some outside of it, say in the streets, as it might be a real police force with a real police chief, why then the same could bring in any and all wrongdoers to the court and they would get nicely lawed up and dispatched to the pen or the hereafter, according to their deserts. You get enough law, the order takes care of itself."

Brandon looked closely at Varnum. He was saying the right words, but there was no force, no effort to persuade or convince. It was as if he were speaking for a court record, just to have it down that he had made the arguments. Somehow, it had the sound of justification for whatever it was he was going to do anyhow.

Varnum shook his head. "It's a little late for that, Sam. A town in terror, a church endangered, property destroyed . . . it can't go on. And, for whatever reason, the duly constituted authorities aren't up to stopping it."

"A court is not a goddamn company of Texas Rangers!" Sam Canty said. "We depend on the police—and the police are your handpicked pet prairie dogs!"

Varnum shook his head sadly. "Bluster won't solve anything, Sam. Impartial, stern justice is what Bascom needs. And I have made it my business to see that that is what Bascom gets."

Sam Canty's face flushed with the effort of suppressing his anger, and he seemed to be searching his mind for something constructive to say, possibly a Comanche medicine man's curse that would fry Varnum where he sat.

The comparative silence of near noon in Bascom was broken by a distant shout from the north end of town, taken up and repeated by many voices. Canty looked sharply in the direction of the hubbub; Brandon saw that Varnum continued to look calmly south, apparently ignoring it.

The shouts and yelps, still not heard as distinct words, drew closer. And they heard another sound building behind him: the sound of many hoofbeats shaking the ground and the jingling of metal.

Around the edge of Varnum's livery stable a pair of horsemen came into view, wearing wide-brimmed hats, blue coats, and yellow-striped trousers tucked into shiny boots. Brandon could not yet see the sabers dangling from their belts or the scabbarded rifles slung from the saddle, but he knew they were there.

The three men on the hotel porch watched silently as the troop of army cavalry emerged into full view and approached the plaza. Varnum was the only one of them smiling.

19

A bulky man at the rear of the troop slid from his horse and strode toward the Butler House porch, the twin gold bars sewn to his epaulets glinting in the sun. A lean, dusty trooper with fat sergeant's chevrons on his blouse sleeve followed at a few paces' distance.

"One of you Barnum?" the captain called. "What kind of circus you got here, Barnum?"

"It's Varnum, with a *V,* Captain. Dorn Varnum, at your service, sir."

"Oh, hell, the wire said Barnum, thought sure it was the circus man," the captain said morosely. "No damn circus, day's ride across the damn prairie and no damn circus at the end of it." He grasped the porch rail, and Brandon inhaled a portion of a cloud of whiskey, sweat, and saddle leather that surrounded the cavalry officer. If he worked at it a little more, Brandon thought, the captain would be able to see circus acts that weren't there. He was holding some folded papers, which Varnum, leaning forward, removed from his grasp and studied.

"This a damn hotel?" the captain asked, looking past them at the lobby.

"It is," Sam Canty said. "The Butler House Hotel, known for—"

"Got stabling?"

"Of course," Sam Canty said.

"Vacant rooms?"

"Some. They—"

"Two to a room, thass five, plus two for commander—sleeping quarters, office. Seven rooms vacant; if not that many, turn 'em out."

Sam Canty looked baffled. "Captain, what . . ."

"Plain English!" the captain said fiercely. "Commandeering quarters for troops, horses. Think Troop J, Twelfth Cavalry, going to billet in a damn boardinghouse, spear potatoes, chicken legs with sabers?" He saw the glass on the table next to Varnum, took it, and drank it down.

The trooper attending the captain stood a little away from the porch and managed to look as if nothing out of the ordinary—or, indeed, nothing at all—was happening.

Dorn Varnum looked up from the papers he was holding and said, "What Captain Meyner overlooked mentioning is that, in response to the deterioration of civil order in Bascom, he has been detailed to place the town under temporary military administration." He flourished the papers. "These are Captain Meyner's orders."

"Damn right," Meyner said. He took Brandon's glass and emptied it. "Meyner's orders here, Meyner's law there. Keep order, shoot looters on sight." He waved at the now dismounted troop of cavalry, a score of lean, seasoned soldiers, ready, Brandon knew, to use their sabers and guns to carry out any order from the raving drunk Dorn Varnum had brought down upon Bascom. It was a fair bet that they despised him, but the bars on his shoulders made that verdict irrelevant.

Brandon saw that among the pack horses at the end of the troop was one laden with a bulky, grooved cylinder, some wooden cases, and a pair of wheels sized for a small cart. Whatever control Meyner meant to exert would be backed by a rapid-fire Gatling gun, which would certainly discourage any rioting mobs Bascom might muster.

"Lemme see them orders!" Sam Canty said. Varnum handed the papers over and Canty scanned them rapidly, mumbling angrily as he took in their contents. Brandon looked over his shoulder and squinted thoughtfully. He was not familiar with the elements of establishing military control in a civilian setting, but these orders seemed, to say the least, slapdash.

"Huh!" Sam Canty said, returning to a passage that had just drawn Brandon's attention. "At least this don't meddle with my court. Them soldiers take over from the police, which a couple moderately smart porkypines could do anyhow, but when they catch the badmen, it's me they haul 'em before."

It was just that point that was sounding a warning, like the buzz of a diamondback, in Brandon's mind.

After setting the startled manager and Captain Meyner's adjutant to arranging the details of the troop's billeting at the Butler House, and with bitter politeness offering Meyner and Varnum the hospitality of the bar to discuss details of the establishment of martial law in Bascom, Sam Canty urged Brandon upstairs and into his room.

"Well, now," he said, once the door was closed, "that's a facer, but it ain't as bad as it looks."

No, worse, Brandon thought but did not say.

"With all them horse soldiers around, ne'mine what kind of cowpat with ears is commanding 'em, it's a fact that there won't be the kind of carryings-on there was last night. And if as somebody tries something and the troopers catch 'im, why, then court gets right into session and we show how justice operates hereabouts. And if it's a Lazy Y man, though I misdoubt it will be, or a farmer, or one of Varnum's hardcases, well, he gets treated without fear nor favors."

"It's not usual for civil courts to have any standing when the military are in charge," Brandon said.

"Thass crazy!" Sam Canty said. "What do you know about it anyways, Bane?"

Right, Brandon knowledge, not Bane. "Something I heard."

"Well, I am going to do more than hear," Sam Canty said.

"I am going to wire the fellows I know in Austin and see how this come about. If or not having the soldier boys here is a good notion, it come about underhanded and through the wrong underhand, and I aim to see that what kind of law enforcement we got in Bascom is by the advisement and consent of the duly constituted authorities here, not some conniving saloonkeeper."

Brandon broke the news to him that Bascom had been without a telegrapher for about a day now. "And if you rustle up someone who can tap a key to get your messages out, I'm pretty sure Meyner's going to look at the telegraph office as abandoned property and anybody going in there as a looter—"

"And shot on sight," Canty finished gloomily. "But anyhow, I'll find a way to work it out. It's a fact, the soldiers is here because the town got to running wild, and they'll go some ways toward taming it."

"The timing doesn't fit," Brandon said. "Varnum did his telegraphing yesterday, late morning, and the troop was on the march for a day, Meyner said. The riot wasn't till last night. Way it looks, Varnum sent word the town was out of control and troops were needed, *then* saw to it that it *went* out of control so the soldiers would have something to get their teeth into when they got here. And there was a lot more ammunition fired off than any bunch of men would likely be carrying around. Supply and demand, but this time the demand came before the supply, and Varnum providing both." This was more verbose and reasoned than standard Bane, but Brandon thought that Sam Canty had too much on his mind just now to notice any lapses in characterization.

The rancher looked at the far wall of the room, running his right thumb back and forth across the tips of his fingers as if he were mentally tallying items in an account. After a moment he pursed his lips in an unvoiced whistle, then spoke slowly: "Got to follow a crooked and narrow trail here, seems like. Don't get in a place where we have to face off against the soldiers, but don't let Varnum use 'em to wipe us out. One thing worth remembering about the Alamo is not to let yourself get boxed up that way. I will study out what to do, though it's a job for more than one head."

He looked calculatingly at Brandon, who searched rapidly for reasons why Carter Bane would not be a helpful strategist, gave an imperceptible shake of his head as if deciding against a briefly entertained idea, and said, "Jack Kestrel'll be good at that, though it carks me some to depend on him overmuch. Between us we might could figure out a way to handle that Meyner so as to do us some good and Varnum some hurt."

Brandon let Bane decline comment. He heard a faint bellow, muted by passage through a couple of the Butler House's floors and walls: Meyner, though whether in drunken laughter or drunken abuse, he could not tell. Sam Canty and Jack Kestrel would find it hard going, exerting any control over the captain—it would be hard enough, Brandon expected, just to get him to pay attention, let alone see reason.

"Now, that wire," Sam Canty said.

"Telegrapher should be in tomorrow, next day," Brandon said.

"Not that kind of wire, Bane—the stuff with the points Wilkinson showed us. A great use for it just come to me."

Brandon displayed Bane's version of excited inquiry by lifting an eyebrow.

"I b'lieve if you fed a length of it to Varnum till it come out his hind end and then kind of swabbed 'im out with it, why, it'd clean out all the trash and corruption and improve his disposition something wonderful," Canty said wistfully. "Do a lot for mine, anyways."

The only evidence of military presence in Bascom was the two-man mounted patrol that moved at a slow amble up Main Street, then laddered down, traversing the cross street, pausing for ten minutes to mount guard in the plaza, nicely compensating for the lack of statuary, before repeating their routine in the south part of town. A few small boys, and rather more dogs, who had formed an enthusiastic entourage for the cavalrymen during their first few patrols, had abandoned them by sundown, and they continued their slow rounds unaccompanied far into the night.

Captain Meyner had not ordered a curfew—either there was no excuse for it, or Varnum had seen no reason to promote a measure that would drastically cut into his saloon's revenues—but the meager night life of Bascom dwindled even more, the townspeople seeming to have decided that home was the best shelter until it was known which way the wind was blowing. The disturbances of the previous night had been alarming enough; if they erupted again and were met with professionally armed opposition, the center of Bascom would be no place for anybody but those bent on selflessly enriching the undertaker.

Varnum's saloon did a brisk business all the same, since the troopers, except for the pair on patrol, had made it their clubhouse, drawn by the raffish atmosphere and perhaps even more by Varnum's willingness to grant credit to the town's defenders. The Butler House bar, in contrast, held only Meyner and Varnum by about ten o'clock. Some of the usual patrons had tried to converse with Bascom's new administrator but were unable to get a handle on his style of discourse, which seemed to be a kind of hash of complaints about the pettifoggers who had hampered his military career and advancement and fragments of anecdotes which, had they been complete, probably would have demonstrated his remarkable bravery and capability. They had given up after a few attempts and left the Butler house far earlier than usual.

A little after ten, Varnum levered Meyner to his feet in easy stages, rotated him to face in the direction of the door, and, with one hand holding an elbow and the other pushing against the small of the back, urged him forward. Meyner's body faced the prospect of smashing facedown onto the floor if its feet followed their preferred policy of staying where they were; it made the prudent choice of rocking into an unsteady walk, guided by Varnum's hand.

Alone and doubting there would be any further custom, Brandon told the bartender to close up and left.

In his room, he lit the lamp and settled himself on the bed.

It was a little early to turn in, and he felt not nearly tired enough for sleep; but there wasn't much else to do but pay a call at Varnum's saloon, and he could think of at least four reasons against that. He had no books with him, and it would be highly un-Bane to pass the time in reading, anyhow. Carter Bane, Brandon supposed, would pass his leisure time thinking about men he had killed and how to kill the next ones he might have to.

Given the circumstances, that might be the best thing for Cole Brandon to be doing, too.

A single rap sounded at the room door. Not Canty's tattoo, not the chambermaid's muffled three knocks, not Curly's conspiratorial scratching. Brandon made a bet with himself about who it would be, said, "Come in," and won his bet.

"Evening, Bane," Dorn Varnum said.

Brandon sat up and swiveled, setting his feet on the floor. Varnum looked at him for an instant, then, seeing that the invitation to do so was not going to be made, sat unasked in the straight-backed chair.

"Hard getting the captain to bed," Varnum said. Brandon saw no reason for Bane to comment on this and kept him silent.

Varnum waited a moment, then went on: "He's a brute, no more brains than a bull, but I've got a ring through his nose, and he'll never get drunk enough so he won't feel it when it's tugged."

Got the ear of some people in the War Department who can protect Meyner from being disgraced and court-martialed for probably just about everything he does—and who can decide to withdraw that protection . . . that'll be what that ring is. And Varnum is telling this to Bane for a reason. . . .

"You're wondering why I'm talking to you this way, Bane," Varnum said. "I'll tell you frankly. It's because you're a wild card in this game, and I want you in my hand, not in Sam Canty's. I'm dealing, and I've made sure I know who gets what cards, and you throw things off."

"Wild card can be worth a lot if it gets you the pot," Brandon said. "If the pot's any kind of big."

"It's big enough, and your compensation would be highly worthwhile," Varnum said.

"Farms."

"There's plenty of money in farming," Varnum said, "and there'll be more, with the new barb-wire fencing that's coming in—you don't know about that"—*And* you *don't know it's Sam Canty's ambition to add it to your diet*—"but that and the new machines, steam combines, reapers, they'll make farming into big business. For someone."

"Not you," Brandon said.

"You're right. Plant, grow, harvest, sell—there's money to be made at that, sure, a dollar at a time. But you don't see farmers with yachts and private railroad cars, do you? Who *do* you see with those things?"

Brandon raised both eyebrows this time. "Well, no," Varnum said, "I guess you don't move in those kinds of circles. Drift around the frontier, sometimes gambling, sometimes hiring out your gun and your readiness to use it, that about your speed, Bane?"

"Close," Brandon said.

"The people who have those things are the men with vision, Bane," Varnum said. "They look at a piece of land or a map or a document and they see where the money is, waiting to be dug out or maybe gush out like a coal-oil well in Pennsylvania. They're like dowsers, that can tap the ground and tell you where to dig your well. Now, around here, there's farming and there's cattle, and some nice dollar-by-dollar money to be made at both, I'll agree. But real money, money by the bushel, that's different."

The difference, as Varnum explained it, seemed to be that a better use of the land than growing food or building a town was selling it to people who wanted to grow food or build a town—so long as they never got to do either and the land could be sold again to the next batch of hopefuls.

"On the map, even on a brief visit, the place looks as if it could support miles of farms, to the horizon and beyond in every direction. And there's good farms already in being, and a solid little town. But the thing is, that's about all there'll be here for a long time. More farms would mean too much produce for the small market the stuff they grow here reaches, and it'll be decades before there's a railroad through here. So if you set up a township—out in Sam Canty's grasslands, say—and lay out lots and streets and print a four-color prospectus showing the county seat and the university and the bustling waterfront where the steamboats come in, people will flock to buy town lots or farm acreage, according to their dream."

"And when the town doesn't get built and the farmland's prairie that can't be farmed without throwing more money at it than any of 'em'll have, then they'll sell up for what they can get or just give up and move on," Brandon said. "And then it all gets sold all over again, new four-color, new town name."

"You'd be good at this, Bane," Varnum said. "You grasp the essentials quite quickly—and, I see, can expound on them when you have to. Yes, with the base I have here, I can promote a huge amount of town development on Canty's land once he's off it, and the time's coming close when he will be. Easier if you're on my side, not his, but either way, soon."

Brandon considered what Varnum had said, and what he had not said. "You been planning this a while. I'm the only one of Canty's people you've tried to shift?"

Varnum shrugged. "Had a talk with Jack Kestrel last month up in Kansas, when he was up there again finally getting a buyer for Canty's last year's herd. Thought he might be fed up with working for somebody who didn't have the sense to get his herds up to the railroad early enough in the year to get a fair price. But Kestrel didn't see it my way, chose to stick with Canty, though I offered him—" Varnum stopped suddenly.

"More'n you're thinking of offering me," Brandon said. "Fair enough, for I'm no Jack Kestrel. This scheme of yours, it seems to call for considerable travel—up to Kansas and what."

"Farther than that," Varnum said. "Even getting ready for something this big, let alone putting it over, calls for plenty of cash, and last summer and last month I went and got some, talked to some people in Chicago and thereabouts. So I made a detour out to halfway across Kansas to meet Kestrel in complete privacy. Might as well not have bothered, though."

Brandon went through the fiction of considering Varnum's offer for his defection, conditionally haggled over terms, and promised a decision the next day. "Don't bother double-crossing me and telling Sam Canty, if that might be in your mind," Varnum said, taking his leave. "Not a damn bit of good will it do him, he's as good as plucked, drawn, and stuffed now, with you or without you. Knowing what's going on will do him about as much good as a chicken understanding what the axe is for."

When he was alone, Brandon lay back on the bed and breathed deeply several times, trying to bring his thoughts into some order. He was thankful that he had put in effort in creating Bane as a character, for it was Bane who had had to finish the interview with Varnum—once Brandon understood that Varnum had both been with Jack Kestrel in Dysart—almost certainly in Kestrel's room at the Bright Kentucky—and had been away from Bascom, "getting cash," at about the time of the train robbery in Missouri. Kestrel might be the whittler of the wooden flower found in his room, but so could a visitor. Either, then, could be the Kenneally gang member who had carved the flower at Mound Farm in the hours before the massacre of Elise and the others.

While Bane had dickered and procrastinated with Varnum, Brandon had been considering grabbing his revolver from the nightstand and firing it into Varnum's face until his head was a shattered ruin, with no more form than a burned-out house at Mound Farm. But the certainty wasn't there, and, while it would probably improve the world somewhat to remove Varnum, Brandon was not interested in general benefaction.

A thick coldness coiled inside him, a profound revulsion that seemed to reach to the ends of his fingers and toes. Think what he might, reflect on grief and vengeance, what it came down to was that the thought of the men who had murdered his family continuing to live was too disgusting to be borne.

20

This time the knock was a fast succession of half-a-dozen taps at the door. Brandon consulted his watch and found that almost an hour had passed since Varnum had left him. He had not been sleeping but lying on the bed in a kind of frozen torpor, not thinking, not feeling any more than a snake, or a rock, might. The tapper did not sound formidable, and he called, "Come in."

Sally Dumayne stepped into the room, and Brandon stood up. "Ma'am. Take a seat," he said, pointing to the single chair.

She sat down. In the light of the lamp, he could see the bruise on her face; it had not faded as much as he would have expected, but her mouth was no longer swollen. She wore the same dress as she had the night before, but the rip had been skillfully mended. "I wanted to thank you for helping me last night," she said.

"It wasn't anything," Brandon said—quite sure that that was the exact truth as she flinched involuntarily at the words.

"You could have been . . ."

Brandon shook his head. "Not likely. Those fellows were

primed to cut and run when anyone showed up. And no real damage done to the store or the stock, just things upset around and about. Probably the worst of it was my shots into the wall."

Sally Dumayne stared at him angrily and said, "What're you saying, Mr. Bane? Those men tried—they tore my dress, they hurt me!"

Brandon looked at her expressionlessly.

"I was so relieved when you—and Chief Dedman, of course—came in just in time and drove those men off. I don't know why you would think they would have run away without that. And . . . well, I felt safe when I saw you, d'you see? And I didn't mind so much being hurt or . . . exposed that way."

She touched the neat mend at the shoulder of her dress. Brandon considered that a severely Presbyterian banker's unmarried aunt might have been embarrassed at having revealed as much of her person as the ripped dress had displayed, but not many other women. Sally Dumayne's intimation that he had seen her practically naked was intended, he suspected, not as an accurate account but as an element of an atmosphere she was trying to create. In the closed room, he was now aware of a scent that overrode the acrid undertone of the coal-oil lamp: spicy, floral, musky, a combination of some *eau de cologne* and Sally Dumayne.

"At the store the other day, when you bought those socks," she said, "you . . . well, you didn't make any secret of it that you liked me, and . . . well, it made me feel good that it was you that came when I needed helping. And . . . well, I know I said I couldn't have dinner with you, but seeing what you did for me, it doesn't seem fair that I don't . . . well, find a way to show you I'm grateful." She fingered the mended tear again, which appeared to require resting her hand on the upper slope of her breast and sliding it back and forth slowly.

Counsel putting you on the stand as a friendly witness would be advised to train you out of those "wells," Miss Dumayne. Any half-competent cross-examiner will cut you up and drop the pieces down each well. And you don't have to remind me that it would be enjoyable to rub you where you're rubbing, but that's not what's going to happen.

"Varnum," Brandon said.

"Well, I know I told you that he . . . that we . . . but that's truly got nothing to do with . . . I mean, there's no reason—"

Brandon leaned forward and touched the tip of his forefinger to the bruise on her cheek, then let it drift down toward the mouth that had been puffed last night. "Varnum."

Sally Dumayne pulled her face back from his touch, but only after a full three seconds. "You're truly talking nonsense, Mr. Bane," she said huskily. "What matters is that you like me, as a woman. I know that, you showed it plain enough in the store that first time. Well, now I'm here, we're alone in your room, Mr. Bane, and I believe I am having to do altogether too much talking just now." At the end of her statement a touch of vinegar mingled with the honeyed tone. She reached and drew to her the hand that had touched her face, laying it gently to touch her throat and rest at the neckline of her dress.

Her flesh was cool, and the hollow at the base of her throat formed a fragile nest for his forefinger. He flattened and spread his hand, feeling the ledge of her collarbone under his fingers, and pulled the hand away. "And that's Varnum, too."

Sally Dumayne sprang to her feet and glared at him, her face in a contortion of scorn. "Mr. Bane! That is a vile suggestion, an atrocious insult! How dare you . . ." She stopped, her face twisting, and sank back in the chair. Her mouth was clenched to stifle involuntary sounds that seemed to be forcing themselves from her, but finally relaxed to allow something between a sob and a laugh to emerge.

"Oh, dear, I shouldn't have tried 'How dare you!' Every time I hear it it sounds silly, like a hen clucking but trying to sound important. Whoever's doing whatever, it's plain as pitch he dares to do it or he wouldn't be doing it. Oh, dear." She blew out her breath in a final rueful gust and stared at Brandon.

He grinned at her. Bane was too limited, certainly too humorless, to handle this, and Cole Brandon would have to step into the part for a space. "Looks like you didn't dare keep on what you were trying," he said. "So Dorn Varnum sent you here, to act as a kind of cat's-paw."

"Not a paw, exactly—that is . . . oh, dear, forget I said *that!* But he did . . . he thought it would make you more interested in throwing in with him if you . . ."

"Had a close association with someone on his side," Brandon said. "So he persuaded you to come here and . . . persuade me."

"Yes," Sally Dumayne said, so quietly he could almost not hear her. Then she looked up at him and said with a bitter humor, "Different methods, though." She fingered her face. "You were right, he hit me last night to make the business in his store look convincing. And when I didn't want to come here tonight, he hit me again. Persuasive, yes."

Brandon looked at her thoughtfully. The stain of the bruise became less prominent as her face reddened. "I don't mean that . . . being nice to you was so awful to think about that I had to be beaten into it . . . for that's not so. But to be traded to you like a . . . a pair of socks, that's cheapening, or maybe it isn't for me, considering, but it makes me see how cheap I've become, and that's worse."

"If you can't keep from laughing when you say something foolish," Brandon said, "and you can't keep from being honest when you're put to it, I can't see how you're cheap in any way that matters." The logic of that was a good bit weaker than he'd care to try in court, but it seemed to cheer Sally Dumayne a little.

"Oh, God," she said with a short laugh. "Well, anyhow, you're not buying, so I guess I'm not cheap enough. That's something. You're *not* buying, are you?"

"No," Brandon said. "It's not you, but everything else—wrong time, wrong place, wrong way, wrong reason."

Sally Dumayne looked at the floor. "Now," she said, "I've

been humiliated and I've failed at what I was supposed to do. Surprising that I feel pretty good all the same. Maybe best I go away and think about why that's so. Good night, Mr. Bane. Thanks for . . . thanks."

"Good night," Brandon said. After the door had closed behind her, he looked at it for a space, then got up quickly from his bed, grabbed his jacket from the wardrobe, slipped into it, and stepped out into the corridor. He heard, drifting up the wide staircase, the light tapping of Sally Dumayne's shoes as she crossed the deserted lobby and went out the front door. When the door closed behind her, he moved quickly down the stairs and to the door and pushed it partly open.

If Sally Dumayne were heading north, toward her lodgings—to sort out, as she had indicated she would, her thoughts—it might be a good idea to follow her at a distance and see her home safely, perhaps come to her aid if the cavalry patrol got offensively inquisitive about the presence of a lone woman on the streets of Bascom toward midnight, when females should be securely ensconced at home in bed, at work in Varnum's saloon, or in bed and at work in the cribs, according to their degrees of respectability. And if she headed in any other direction, it would be highly interesting to know where and with what purpose.

He eased his head out and peered to his left, up Main Street. The dim outlines of the buildings were undisturbed by any motion. He turned and looked in the other direction, where the light from Varnum's saloon's front window cast a patch of brightness on the plankwalk and rutted roadway and turned a drift of thin night mist into a faintly luminous transparent cloud. Against this he saw the hurrying silhouette of Sally Dumayne and heard the faint tap of her shoes on the plankwalk.

Brandon followed, stepping as quietly as he could, and had narrowed the distance between them substantially when she turned—not, as he had expected, into the saloon, but into the alley just short of it. He sprinted to the alley opening and looked down it to see her moving behind the saloon building. He followed and found himself in a cluttered yard facing the building's back porch and a flight of outside stairs leading to a landing and doorway on the second floor. One lit window, the top sash down, shone next to the back door. Brandon moved to stand against the wall alongside it. The murmur and rumble of talk and the tinkle of the piano drifted back from the front part of the building.

His eyebrows lifted as he heard Varnum say, "Don't need you here. Go up and turn in," but he relaxed as he heard a muttered protest from another male voice and Varnum's clearer reply: "Have a drink in your room—you've got a bottle—but you know damn well you're not going out to the bar. Nobody's going to see you till I say so."

Brandon ducked around the corner to the alley as the door opened and the slap of boot soles sounded on the staircase. He risked a glance around the corner and saw the brief flash, as in a magic lantern show, of a face, lit up, then swallowed by darkness. The only impression he formed was of a long nose, sharp-pointed as if kept to the proverbial grindstone. He heard the opening and shutting of a door from a higher level and stepped back onto the porch and to where he had stood before. The light flooding from the window was so bright that even a cautious look around the edge of the window frame would illuminate his face with the vividness of stage limelight.

"Didn't bite, eh?" he heard Varnum say. Evidently he had missed the opening sentence of Sally Dumayne's report, though it was hard to infer what it had been.

"No," Sally Dumayne said.

"A man of more delicate tastes, of more discrimination, than we had thought?" Varnum said silkily.

Sally Dumayne's voice roughened. "He was interested—I don't make mistakes about that kind of thing. But he's a cold fish, that Bane, and he doesn't move fast."

Brandon's eyebrows went up again. Sally Dumayne was distorting the scene in his room out of all recognition. Why?

He strained to hear Varnum's response as the whining strains of a harmonica, like a train whistle with a bad cold, descended from the upper room. Varnum's underling seemed to be testing whether solitary music making would compensate for his exile from the delights of the saloon. He grimaced as he identified the noise as a fair effort at "Beautiful Dreamer," the last tune Dan Doyle had heard in life—it was a fair bet the late Mr. Doyle had not had any subsequent serenades from the heavenly choir.

"—move at all, and which way?" The first part of Varnum's reply had been obscured by a harmonical wail of the bars whose lyric had to do, if Brandon recalled aright, with sounds of the rude world.

"Oh, he's leaning toward you," Sally Dumayne said. "Had a couple things to say about Sam Canty that showed he doesn't think much of him or his chances, with or without Bane's help. Made it clear that he goes where the profit is, and he doesn't see that that's with Canty. Didn't go further than that; just let me know how he saw things in general."

That's a good reading of how Carter Bane operates, Miss Sally. But it's getting further and further away from what happened. Cui *goddamn* bono, *for sure, not to say* quo vadis *and* quid elevat *to boot.*

"And no . . . ah, palpable expression of this interest you claim to have seen?"

"Not a toucher, Mr. Bane isn't," Sally Dumayne said. "But he looked me over, eyes as cold as pickled onions, careful but no way excited. Made me feel like some pair of socks he was thinking to buy. But he's buying, I'm nine parts sure, and he'll be ready to wear 'em when the time comes, if you take my meaning."

"Quite clearly," Dorn Varnum said. "Why do you think he's hesitating, then?"

"Because it's your offer that's on the table, and the longer it stays there, the more you'll sweeten it, that's what he thinks."

"And he's right, up to a point," Varnum said. "But if he's not with me when the ball opens, the market for Mr. Carter Bane's stock will be bearish indeed. I can use him as a gun, but if he times it wrong, all he is is a target." He was silent for a moment, perhaps reflecting on this conclusion, then said, "You're staying."

"I want to get on home," Sally Dumayne said. "Tired, and I'd just rather—"

"You're staying," Varnum said with a flat implacability that Carter Bane would have envied.

Brandon could see, almost as clearly as if he had risked a look through the window, Sally Dumayne's face sag and her eyes close, then open as she said quietly, "Yes, I'm staying."

It seemed that what bore on his business had finished being talked of, and he was strongly disinclined to hear what would be happening next, so he stepped off the side of the porch and into the alley leading to the street. The musical accompaniment to his thoughts changed character as the upstairs serenader abandoned his beautiful dreamer in favor of the bouncier "Derby Ram" as Brandon walked down the alley.

Sally Dumayne's false report would have the effect of keeping Dorn Varnum from pressuring him or treating him as an enemy for as long as possible. Why had she gone so far for Carter Bane? And what, indeed, did that say about how far Dorn Varnum could rely on her? When the ball Varnum mentioned opened, to whose tune would Sally Dumayne be dancing?

The plaintive sound of the harmonica chased him with the old song's refrain:

Didn't he ramble, didn't he ramble—
He rambled till the butcher cut him down.

21

Something circled in the high sky, a black shallow V, sliding like a fragment of ash against the harsh blue. Hawk or some kind of buzzard, surveying the distant ground to see what it might provide for lunch, Brandon supposed. Here at the top of the plateau to the north and west of Bascom, the sky seemed even vaster than it had on the prairie. The edges of the stony, sparsely treed stretch that had humped itself up above the ground level at the south side of the river fell away in every direction from where Brandon had briefly pulled up his horse, so that the sky seemed to continue down below it and might indeed contain it entirely, forming the inner surface of a huge sphere containing only this arid piece of ground and this man—and the patient predator that circled above him.

He had realized that morning that Bascom was stifling him. Even the low buildings and wide streets were confining in a way that the far more built-up and congested St. Louis had not been. Or it might be the tangled and knotted threads of the fabric of the plots and intrigues that wrapped Bascom that were troubling him: Varnum, Meyner, Sally Dumayne, and whatever self-serving games they were playing. And were Sam Canty and Jack Kestrel as straightforward as they appeared? Certainly Kestrel was not yet free of the suspicion of being the Kenneally whittler he was hunting. A ride to no place in particular that would take him away from Bascom for several hours had seemed like the best remedy for the miasma of inertia and uncertainty that had enveloped him when he awoke that morning. So Brandon had retrieved his horse from the Butler House stables and climbed the high slope to the west of town.

He urged the horse into motion again, and it picked its way across the rock-strewn waste. Far more than on the long prairie ride down from Boudin, he had the sense that something important could be waiting for him at any bend in the trail he was following almost unconsciously across the plateau. Probably the old abandoned track to Santa Fe, he thought. A sense of anticipation rose in him, and he was strongly reminded of the trip in the St. François mountains with Ned Norland. A totally different landscape, dramatically jagged, heavily forested, a spectacularly varied sky: but similar in suggesting that it was a stage for significant events.

The light struck at him from nearly white slabs of rock that lay by the trail, and he realized that he was nearly ready to turn around and return to Bascom. At the end of a slight downslope ahead was a high scatter of rocks; he decided to ride far enough to see what lay beyond, then end the outward leg of his journey.

Once past the rocks, Brandon found himself at the top of a long stretch of barren open land that sloped shallowly downward to an intermittent line of trees curving around to the north and east. These followed the line of a long-dry branch of the river he could see glinting in the sun some miles away. The descent of the land was interrupted by the bulge of a low hill or knob about halfway to the line of trees. It was topped by a large white stone structure, glaring in the nooning sun almost as if it were radiating light rather than reflecting it.

The poorly marked and eroded trail his horse had been following went down the slope, presumably to a notch he could see in the bluff above the dry river bed, though he was unable to follow it visually on the rocky ground for more than about a hundred feet from where the horse now stood. If it followed a straight line to the notch, it would hit the base of the hill on which the stone building stood.

Brandon squinted and made out a principal block, looking to be fifteen or so feet high, and walls enclosing a yard and linking some outbuildings to the main one. The wall appeared to be broken for the space of a few feet at one point, and irregularities in the lines of the outbuildings suggested that they had fallen into some disrepair. The old trading post Sam Canty had mentioned, he supposed, sited to be convenient to the users of the trail and to river voyagers, yet, perched on its slight hill, with that vast stretch of open ground around it, highly defensible against whatever predators might covet its contents.

A swift movement behind him caught his eye and he turned in time to see the hawk—or whatever—that had been circling far above now in a fast glide not more than fifty feet up. It rocked gently as it sped through the air, adjusting its speed and trim; Brandon could see the feathers at the end of the wings spreading like fingers.

They folded like a door clapping shut and the bird dropped behind some rocks about fifty feet from where Brandon's horse stood. He heard a thump and a noise something between a squeal and a snarl; then the bird reappeared, flapping its wings hard, seeming to stagger through the air as it gained height slowly. Its erratic path brought it within twenty feet of Brandon, and he saw that it held a lean, writhing form in its scaly talons. A weasel, he supposed. As the bird and its prey passed him, he was astonished to see that the weasel's head seemed to be buried in the bird's throat—no wonder it was flying unsteadily.

The hawk gained height and flew more strongly toward the west, and in a few moments passed beyond Brandon's range of vision, presumably still clenching the weasel in the terrible vise of its talons, still with the weasel's terrible fangs locked in its throat—even after the last of life was gone from the weasel, Brandon thought, its jaws would remain clenched, inexorably killing its killer. The mutual destruction reminded him for the first time since the night of

Casmire's death the coin he had found in the ancient Indian mound, with its depiction of the snake swallowing itself, the killer and the killed in one. It was in his stuff somewhere, he thought, and wondered why he had put it so firmly out of his mind. Maybe because the clue of the carved flower had been clear enough to follow without the "guidance" Ned Norland had weirdly claimed the old medallion might give him.

The incident seemed almost as unreal as the hallucinations that had assailed him in the mountains with Norland, and profoundly disturbing in a way he could not pin down. It was time to be getting back to Bascom, and to whatever Carter Bane was to be called on to do.

As the horse jogged along the stony track, Brandon frowned. The Bane identity, the mask, was becoming natural to him now, which was probably a good thing as far as his mission was concerned. But the thought that it might become more than natural—become nature—that his face, so to speak, might alter to fit the contours of the mask, evoked a feeling of dread. Yet again, Bane and Brandon both seemed to be pulled aside from their paths by irrelevant events and concerns. The fates of Sam Canty and Sally Dumayne, for example, had no bearing on what Cole Brandon, presently d.b.a. Carter Bane, was up to; yet Brandon was letting himself take a hand in these matters, and Brandon knew that when whatever catastrophe Dorn Varnum had prepared was exploded, he would be fully involved.

Whatever was going to happen to the eagle and the weasel, at least they were clear and life-and-death firm in their purposes. Riding down Bowie Street, Brandon saw figures darting from the small boxlike buildings that housed the ladies of the night—also morning, afternoon, and evening, if Curly's reports were correct. Their dress ranged from elaborately exhibitionistic gowns to flannel wrappers, but these differences were overlooked as they mingled with the townsfolk making for the plaza.

As Brandon guided his horse carefully amid the pedestrians, he wondered what had brought them out. Turning the corner of Bowie and Main gave him a view of the plaza, and his first impression was that the circus Meyner's drunken fancy had led him to expect had in fact materialized. Half-a-dozen mounted soldiers ringed a group of four riders in range gear; behind them were several riderless horses, then a buggy and four more riders. The driver of the buggy, even at a distance, had the look of Sam Canty and proved to be him when Brandon rode along the edge of the plaza and past the main assembly of horses and men.

"Hey, Bane," Sam Canty hailed him. "You're just in time."

"For what?"

"Edifying parade of captured horse thieves, imprisonment of same in the *juzgado,* preparation for trial. Trial itself tomorrow, verdict and sentencing also. Full speed ahead for justice!" Sam Canty said happily.

As he explained it to Brandon, a few hours before four of his hands had found the four men now in military custody on the Lazy Y range, leading a string of horses with clear efforts at concealment. Challenged, they had produced a dirty scrap of paper they claimed was a bill of sale, but the hands were not convinced. Neither was Sam Canty, when they brought it—and the men and horses—back to the ranch house at gunpoint.

"Seen right off it was fake," Sam Canty said, holding up a crumpled paper. Brandon looked at it and, with an effort, deciphered the childish scrawl:

> The undersinged hearby sells to the byer the 4 hroses discribed hearwith

followed by ramblingly detailed but probably accurate listings of the animals' attributes, and ending

> Attestted to by my hand and singature this dayt,
> Gendro Nichik
> Coopers Bend

"Those fellows had a high old time with that, all right," Sam Canty said. "Give theirselfs some fun making up a name—I expect it means something dirty in one of the Injun tongues—never figuring it'd get looked at close. Any road, it's a plain fake, and it'll just be evidence against 'em, not for."

Canty had sent a fast rider to Bascom to alert Captain Meyner and to request that a patrol come to take charge of the prisoners, whom Canty's men would be herding toward town, along with the horses they had stolen. "Chance to show we c'n cooperate neat as pie," Sam Canty said, "and it went fine, we turned 'em over just about at the river and followed 'em on in. I'm setting the trial for tomorrow, and me and the boys'll stay over—they're the ones as collared the thieves, so they'll be wanted as witnesses—plus Curly, who'll kind of ride herd on 'em, being more familiar with the metropolitan ways of Bascom." Sam Canty looked past Brandon and raised his voice as he went on: "He also says he knows the faces of a couple of 'em from Varnum's saloon."

"Entirely possible," Dorn Varnum said, approaching from behind Brandon. "My place isn't as exclusive as the Butler House bar, so it's not surprising that some of the less savory element put in an appearance there. If they don't steal horses while on the premises, there isn't much I can do about them. I need hardly say that there is no connection between these malefactors, if such they are proven to be, and myself."

"As I will have the proving of it, proven it will be," Sam Canty said.

"Success to you." Dorn Varnum turned to look at Brandon and said, "Miss Dumayne sends her regards, and asks me to tell you that your purchases may be picked up when ready. If necessary, the price can be adjusted." He inclined his head to Brandon and to Sam Canty, turned, and walked toward where Captain Meyner seemed to be trying to understand what this new crowd of horses and men signified and what he should be doing about it.

"Purchases?" Sam Canty asked.

Brandon looked thoughtfully after Varnum. A not very well coded reminder that Sally Dumayne was part of the deal Varnum was offering Carter Bane, and that other terms were still open to negotiation. Was the offer genuine, he wondered, or was it Varnum's way of keeping Bane passive until the start of the "ball" he had talked of to Sally Dumayne? "Socks," he said. "Might get something off if I buy a dozen pair."

"Hey, Captain," Sam Canty said. Meyner had lurched his way to the buggy, and now steadied himself with one hand on the front wheel and looked glassily up at Canty. "Some doings," Canty said. "I got to say that I wasn't dancing the fandango with joy when you fellows showed up, but I am persuaded that you can do a better job of holding onto these horse thieves and keeping 'em fresh and sweet for the trial than that Dedman and his Emmet would."

"Civilians haven't got the stomach keep order," Meyner said. "Lemme see bill sale."

"That fake one the horse thieves tried to pass off? That's evidence for the trial, so I'm—"

"Lemme *see!*" Meyner said, reaching up and making grabbing motions with his fingers. Sam Canty shrugged and handed it down.

Meyner managed to focus on it and take in what it said. He looked up at Canty and said, "This Nichik's signature, that's forgery, you say?"

"There *ain't* no Nichik, Captain! Those fellows just made up a name to stick at the bottom of their numbskull fake! Godamighty, you ever see a bill of sale look that stupid?"

Meyner did not appear to resent—or perhaps did not notice—Sam Canty's indignant glare but said stolidly, "You dunno everybody Cooper's Bend."

"Well, *no,* but—"

"Somebody you dunno could be a Nichik. This could be his signature."

"Oh, now, *that's* . . . that's . . . hum." Sam Canty's face resembled that of a man chewing a whole lemon as he reluctantly absorbed the thought that this drunken cavalryman standing, with some difficulty, before him was speaking with enough sense to have destroyed his contention that the bill of sale was an unquestionable fraud.

"Cooper's Bend five or some hours from here," Meyner

said. "Send sergeant, fast rider, he'll check, back tomorrow. Find if Nichik or no Nichik, sold horses or didn't, this his bill of sale or isn't, gonna be trial or not." Meyner turned and strode away, clutching the disputed bill of sale. He walked briskly, with only a slight rocking motion to betray his state; maybe, Brandon supposed, he figured that speed might keep him upright, the way it did a bicycle.

"I swear and allow," Sam Canty said, "it's some shaking up to find myself out-logicked by a rum-sponge like that. All the same, it's just logicking, not sense. That bill's a fake, got to be, but Meyner has the right of it, got to have it checked and proven so as to get the whole case hammered together and nailed down. Smarter'n I give him credit for, to've seen it right off like that."

Meyner was more capable than he appeared, Brandon was also sure. In his experience, dedicated drunks often exaggerated their condition somewhat, partly to establish a level of behavior bad enough so that an unexpected worsening of the actual state would be less noticed. But he wondered if Meyner's instant grasp of the problem with the bill of sale and his proposal for solving it were entirely spontaneous. He found that he wanted to discuss this point, and some other things, with Jack Kestrel. Any suspicions aside, Kestrel did seem to be operating in Sam Canty's interests, and it made sense to behave, with appropriate precautions, as if he would go on doing that. He looked for but did not see Kestrel among the Lazy Y riders behind them, and he asked Canty where he was.

"Back at the ranch," Sam Canty said. "Lot to be done, and someone had to be giving orders and deciding things pretty steady. Couldn't turn the job over to somebody with no readying for it. But he and Lorena'll come in for the trial tomorrow. By then he'll be able to parcel out the work to them that can do it right, and we got a fair chance the place won't fall to ruin before we get back."

Ahead of them, at the far end of the plaza, the captives had dismounted and were being led to the jail, which formed one side of the courthouse, and two cavalrymen were leading the horses, both their own mounts and the ones they had claimed to have bought, up Main Street.

"Stable 'em at Varnum's livery, I expect," Sam Canty said. "No place else for 'em. Varnum'll prob'ly put in an almighty great bill to the court for feed, but I won't allow anything that's beyond reason."

22

At eleven the next morning, Brandon, Curly, and Sam Canty were sitting on porch rockers at the Butler House, looking down the plaza toward Bowie Street. For close to an hour, beginning around ten, Sam Canty had complained steadily, speculating whether prairie dog holes, Indians, bandits, rattlers, sunstroke, or sudden loss of memory provided the most plausible explanation for the delay in Meyner's courier's return from Cooper's Bend. But he had finally worn himself out and, to Brandon's relief, sat silently, staring gloomily down the street and chewing on an unlit cigar. A sulking Canty was not an inspiring companion, but a good deal more restful one than a Canty in a constant state of fulmination.

"Another goddamn farmer," Canty said, watching a horse emerge from the side street. Then he leaned forward as he saw the blue cloth underlying the dust that coated the rider. "No, by thunder, that's him, and why he's dragging along as if he had all the time in the world I won't pretend to understand."

The horse was in fact moving at a moderately fast walk, though by no means a pace or a trot, and was almost opposite them, approaching the jail. "Three, four hours' ride," Brandon said.

"Well, hell, yeah," Sam Canty said. "Don't suppose you can keep a horse at speed that long without close to killing it. But you'd think he could come in with a big finish, make it look good, like the Pony Express. Anyhow, he's back with the word that there ain't no Nichik to write fake bills of sale to horse thieves, so that's all settled and regular."

He stood up. "I best get my good suit jacket on, for the judging. All's I need else is over to the courthouse, so we c'n get the trial going soon's the soldier boys bring the accused there. And heydee, there's Lorena and Jack Kestrel, turning up just in time for it all." He waved vigorously, and Brandon could see two riders approaching them down Main Street.

When Kestrel and Lorena had stabled their horses behind the hotel, they joined Canty, Brandon, and Curly on the porch. "Any time now they'll haul those fellows next door to the courthouse, and we can get the trial going," Sam Canty said.

Brandon noted that no provision seemed to have been made for either a prosecuting or a defending attorney, and wondered what sort of trial would be conducted without them. It did not seem a Bane question, so he did not raise it. He suspected that Canty, whatever the statutes read, operated under his own version of the Napoleonic Code, serving as judge, prosecutor, and jury, and acting on the assumption that the accused were guilty or they wouldn't be there. Vestiges of the Code still present in Louisiana's legal system had gained New Orleans the reputation of a place never to have trouble in, and it looked as though this part of Texas might be the same.

The sun was straight overhead, and Canty was checking his watch for the fifth time in seven minutes when the door to the jail opened and Dorn Varnum emerged. He walked across the plaza, raising little puffs of dust that shone like steam as they emerged from the dark irregular circle of shadow at his feet. His pale brown hat and suit seemed to glow of themselves in the harsh sunlight, then to shut off abruptly as he passed under the edge of the porch roof.

"When they going to hand them fellows over for trial, Varnum?" Sam Canty called.

"Trial for what?" Dorn Varnum said.

"Horse thieving, damn it!" Sam Canty said. "As you damn well know."

Brandon saw Jack Kestrel stiffen, and was sure the foreman, like himself, had made a rapid leap to a highly unpleasant conclusion, one which Sam Canty would apparently have to have thrust on him.

"When there's a legitimate bill of sale, there's no theft, is there?" Varnum said lightly.

It was beginning to hit Sam Canty now, and he kept silent, only staring at Varnum with a ferocious intensity.

"Sergeant Dulany was fortunate in finding the livery establishment of Gendro Nichik, a recent arrival in Cooper's Bend from the icy realms of the Tsar, without much trouble. Mr. Nichik not only confirmed the transaction and identified his bill of sale, but wrote out a more detailed statement, fully as wretched in spelling and penmanship as the original document, though I am sure a great deal more creditable than any essays you or I, Canty, might make in the Russian language."

"What. The. Hell. Do. You. *Mean?*" Sam Canty pushed the words out in individual packages, opening his teeth just enough to allow each one to escape before snapping them shut again.

"They have a different alphabet, you see," Varnum said. "Makes it difficult—"

Sam Canty's howl cut short Varnum's explanation of Cyrillic characters, and he said, "Well, since the bill of sale's been proved genuine, there's no case to answer, and the gentlemen are to be turned loose, that's the long and the short of it. Appears you and your men, surely out of a praiseworthy desire to see that crime did not go unpunished, acted too hastily."

Varnum was right, Brandon reflected. And it was also true

that Sam Canty had acted just as anyone knowing him would assume he would. An uneasy vision flickered in his mind of chess pieces on a board, both black and white being moved by the same hand.

"Your men treated them fair and square, they say, and they appreciate that. Also they understand how the mistake could have been made. Next time they buy some horses, they'll try to deal with a seller who has a clerk to copy things in a fair hand, and maybe a notary to put a seal on it." Varnum was relishing Canty's humiliation. Neither Cole Brandon nor Carter Bane had any stake in this quarrel, so Brandon wondered about the source of the strong feeling that Dorn Varnum would look a lot better leaking a lot of blood from a large hole in his chest, face, or belly.

"So Meyner's turning 'em loose," Sam Canty said. "I want to talk to him about that."

"Nothing to talk about," Dorn Varnum said. "In any case, the captain was up all night, not wanting to relax his vigilance until this matter was settled, and he's retired for some rest."

"Taking a nap in one of the cells?" Sam Canty asked scornfully. "Sure-God hasn't come out of the jail since we been here."

"After he had heard the sergeant's report and made his decision, the captain's work was done," Varnum said. "And, as he felt that it might be unseemly to presume upon your hospitality at the Butler House so soon after having been forced to disoblige you, he accepted my offer of the use of my quarters at the rear of the saloon for his immediate recuperation."

Translation: Meyner's done what you want him to do, so you sneaked him out the back way to your place, where he can dive into an unlimited supply of booze and make whatever use of the waiter girls the booze lets him. Brandon exchanged glances with Jack Kestrel, who seemed as dubious as he was about the situation. It smelled of Dorn Varnum's contrivance as strongly as a blown-out lamp reeks of coal oil, but all it seemed to have accomplished was Sam

Canty's humiliation. If Varnum hoped that this would result in Canty retiring from his part in the affairs of Bascom, it seemed likely to prove a serious miscalculation.

The door to the jail opened, and four men emerged. They held bedrolls and in some cases saddlebags in their arms; evidently the bureaucratics of the return of their effects was what had caused the delay between the decision to release them and their actual departure.

They stood at the edge of the plaza, looking around as if to get their bearings, then started north toward the entrance to Main Street and the distantly visible livery stable, where their horses had been put up overnight. The troopers lounging around the jail area ignored them.

Lorena Canty leaned forward, suddenly tense. "That second man," she said.

"In the buckskin jacket?" Sam Canty said. "Damn hot for this weather."

"Wasn't wearing it yesterday," Jack Kestrel said slowly, "but it looks—"

"I'll swear it's Harry Briggs's!" Lorena said. "That big circle of pale leather on the back—that's not a common thing, I remember noting it—had a fancy design, a flower, burned onto it with a running iron."

Sam Canty was in motion, Kestrel and Brandon following him off the porch, before Lorena finished speaking. She jumped down the steps and caught up with them. Dorn Varnum waited a moment, then trailed them as they strode quickly toward the trudging ex-jailbirds.

As they approached, Brandon could see that the circle of leather on the buckskin jacket bore a pattern of interlaced leaves executed in heavy brown lines.

"Harry Briggs's, all right," Jack Kestrel said softly. "And the sonofabitch is toting Harry's saddlebag, for certain: big stain on the corner, shaped like a buffalo head—no two like that."

"Hold it, you men!" Sam Canty called out. Brandon had not seen him draw, but a massive revolver with a barrel at least eight inches long filled his hand and pointed at the four men.

Brandon and Kestrel slid their own guns out and aimed them in the same direction. Brandon wondered what to do if Canty's order to halt were not obeyed. It seemed extreme, even for Bane, to shoot people in the back simply for keeping on walking with their arms full of their belongings. Fortunately, the four were more certain about what the situation required, and stopped, turned, and raised their hands in front of them about level with their shoulders, dropping what they held onto the dusty, hard-packed surface of the plaza.

Brandon could see Dorn Varnum coming up behind them, stopping back a few feet. Lorena Canty was some distance to his left, clutching a handbag in her left hand, her right concealed in it. She wouldn't want to goad the men by adding a woman's weapon to the guns trained on them, but if it came to gunplay, Brandon was sure, she'd be adding her fire to it and sharing the risks. He chanced a glance around and saw that down the street, three troopers outside the jail were standing, looking at them. At the other side of the plaza, Curly had emerged from the alley leading to the hotel stables, and was looking at the scene in astonishment.

"We been cleared fair and proper, old man," one of the four said. "Now just stow yer guns and let's us fergit about this whole thing."

Sam Canty ignored him, and said to the man in the buckskin jacket, "You. Kick your saddlebags over this way." The man looked at Canty's gun and the flinty hardness of his face, then skidded the bag over to near Jack Kestrel. Kestrel knelt and reached inside the bag, keeping his eyes and gun barrel trained on the four men. He pawed out a blue shirt and held it up. "Briggs's?"

"Can't tell," Lorena Canty said. A few pairs of socks proved equally anonymous; then Kestrel held up something that glittered in the sunlight. "Yes," Lorena Canty said.

"Harry's spare harmonica," Kestrel said flatly. "Hole punched here in the top where that snaggle tooth of his wore it. I remember seeing it in both of 'em."

"You got any explanation of where you come on a jacket and a mouth-organ and a saddlebag belongin' to a man nobody ain't seen in days 'cause he's most likely shot dead?" Sam Canty asked.

"We don't have to account to you, old man," the one who had spoken earlier said. "Any questions, the law can ask 'em—that captain."

"I am the law, not him," Sam Canty said, "and the law is going to ask you a right smart heap of questions right and goddamn away! Turn around and get on back there. Not the jail; we're going straight to the courthouse this time!"

Two of the cavalrymen who had hurried up from the jail stopped on one side of Sam Canty, avoiding his line of fire. "You can't do this!" one of them said. "The captain turned these men loose!"

"And it wasn't because he was . . . that is, it was all lawful and proper, for the bill of sale for the horses checked out, so there wasn't no horse-thieving," the other trooper said, apparently unused to not having to apologize for his commander's actions. "So you can't hold 'em, Mr. Canty, judge or no judge. We got our orders about that."

"About the horse-stealing," Sam Canty said. "You ain't had orders about holding 'em on suspicion of murder and theft of property, which new evidence of has just come to light. You can't have any orders about something that hadn't happened when the orders was give, now can you?"

"Ah, no," the first trooper said. The second trooper grinned.

"If Captain Meyner comes to a point whereas he feels like giving more orders," Sam Canty said, "you can tell him where to find me. Conducting a judicial inquiry into a primer fussy case of crime at the courthouse, to determine is there proper and sufficient cause to hold the ones that done it for trial. Then in about half an hour, holding the trial. He waits much after that, I might could be calling on him for the lend of you fellows for a burial detail." He turned toward the alley next to the hotel and called, "You, Curly! Get the boys and head 'em for the courthouse. It's witnessin' time!"

Dorn Varnum looked blankly at Sam Canty. It appeared that his plan of facing Canty with a *fait accompli* in the release of the prisoners and removing Meyner from the scene to avoid any chance of argument had misfired badly. Herding the men toward the courthouse, Brandon strongly hoped so—and wished he felt more certain that Varnum had really made that bad a mistake.

"Tolt me he'd drawed it hisself with a runnin' arn, Harry did, copied it offen a label to a bottle of medicine the cook gave him for a gripin' gut once."

Curly's identification of the decoration on the buckskin jacket complete, he stepped from the witness stand and joined Jack Kestrel, Lorena, and Brandon in the front bench. "Think he believed me?" he asked Kestrel.

"'Course he believed you," Kestrel said sourly. "He knew what you were going to say already, and you said it." Brandon could tell that Kestrel was as unhappy as he was with the proceedings. It was not just that they were a travesty of legality—that was not uncommon out here—but that Sam Canty was rushing ahead with an almost manic certainty. The last time he had done that, arresting the four men for horse-stealing, the results had not been good, and apparently Kestrel shared his suspicion that this was not going to turn out any better.

"Well, I ain't never been a witness before," Curly said. "Courthouses ain't places I care to familiarize with." He went over to stand with the other Canty hands.

Sam Canty, acting as court clerk, prosecuting attorney, and chief prosecution witness at once, with the other witnesses, his hired hands, serving as bailiffs to guard the prisoners—more Genghis-Khanic Code than Napoleonic, Brandon decided—was doing an excellent job of presenting the case against the four as waylayers and murderers of Harry Briggs, at least to his own satisfaction. The prisoners, carefully trussed by the cowhands, stood mulishly mute, and the few attending townsfolk looked interested but open-minded, or perhaps vacant.

Brandon could hear a steady murmur from the courthouse porch, where there was a larger crowd getting its sense of the events in the courtroom from peering in the windows and listening to what was relayed to them by an observer standing in the doorway. After the random but persistent shooting of two nights before, Bascomites seemed to feel nervous about gathering in places they could not get away from instantly.

"Let the record show that one and all has agreed that the buckskin shirt in evidence is the property of Harry Briggs, missing and for damn near sure dead." Sam Canty, elevated above the seat level of the room, dipped his pen in the inkwell on the bench and wrote briskly in a large ledger.

"Now, as to the next evidence, this mouth-organ," Sam Canty said, taking it from a pile of objects at the side of the bench. He raised his voice as the murmur from the crowd on the porch grew suddenly louder and continued to increase in volume, as if its members were calling each other's attention to something startling on its way to happen. "This very mouth-organ, as me and my hands has many a time seen being mouthed and fingered by the prob'ly deceased, when-as he would cheer us with 'The Derby Ram' or move us with 'Beautiful Dreamer' or . . ."

Brandon stiffened, then leaned toward Kestrel and muttered, "Where's that door along the wall lead to?"

"Back of the jail. Why?"

"I think you'd better be ready to grab Miss Lorena, get the both of you through there, and on away from here as fast as you can. We have been well and truly dropped in the privy."

Kestrel's astonished reply was overborne by the sudden final swell of noise from the porch, the slamming back of the door, and the sound of cavalry boots on the floorboards: the heavy but unsteady tramp of Captain Meyner's and the crisp slap of those of three of his troopers.

"The *hell's* going *on* here, Canty?" Meyner bawled from the back of the room. His face was the color and texture of a slice of rare roast beef, though more contorted, and Brandon wondered which of the pleasures offered by Varnum he had been summoned so hastily from.

"The District Court of Bascom is in session, Captain," Canty said, "and I will thank you to observe order."

"Freed these men, bill of sale valid. What're you playing

at, you old fool? Gonna turn to looting next, we'll know how to deal with *that.*" He gestured at the soldiers standing next to him.

The troopers looked embarrassed but determined. If you drew the line at obeying the orders of a demented drunk, what would happen to the Army?

"There is no question about the matter of theft of horses, Captain," Sam Canty said. "That is a done gone thing, and does me no credit, I'll admit. But this here is a different case, a case of disappearance without no cause, a case of evidence of violence, a case of wrongful having of property, and all tied together most wonderful and circumstantial. There ain't no mistakes about bills of sale into this one, Captain."

"You're a better shot than I am," Brandon muttered to Jack Kestrel. "You wouldn't care to shoot Canty somewhere startling but not serious to put a stop to this, I suppose?"

"What the hell for?" Kestrel stared hard at Brandon.

"Better than what I think's about to happen," Brandon said. "Be ready to break for that door."

"The hell you talking about?" Meyner said. "Disa-damn-pearance of who?"

"One Harry Briggs, lamented cowhand of the Lazy Y," Sam Canty said solemnly. "Foully waylaid and lost to the sight of man—"

"Again you're speaking too soon, Sam," Dorn Varnum said from the doorway.

Without surprise, Brandon saw standing next to him an otherwise nondescript but needle-nosed figure. He might as well have been playing 'Beautiful Dreamer' on the harmonica, as he had the night before last in the room above Varnum's, but Varnum seemed content to observe some restraint in his effects.

Sam Canty goggled at what was clearly not the ghost of his vanished hand. Clearly, he could not take in every aspect of the intricate web Dorn Varnum had spun around him, but he could take in the chief element. As Brandon had told Kestrel, Varnum and Briggs between them had Sam Canty looking up at the underside of the privy seat, and no toeholds to find.

At Sam Canty's wordless roar of outrage, Brandon shoved Jack Kestrel hard into Lorena Canty.

Canty reached under the bench, produced not one but two revolvers, and fired both in the direction of the doorway. Briggs and Varnum dove to either side of the door, and the bystanders who had been in it scattered, shouting.

Kestrel grabbed Lorena around the waist and pushed her ahead of him toward the door to the jail; Brandon followed.

Meyner shouted, drew his saber and gestured wildly, nearly maiming the trooper nearest him. The troopers drew their revolvers and fired toward where Sam Canty continued to shoot, now surrounded and masked by an expanding cloud of smoke.

Kestrel and Lorena were through the door, then Brandon. As he turned to pull the door closed behind them, he saw Sam Canty, still roaring, bound from behind the bench and shatter the wide window behind it as he leaped to the ground outside. The room was fogged with gunsmoke, steadily added to as the troopers and the Lazy Y hands—and, for all Brandon could tell in the haze, some of the spectators who might be joining in without any notion of what the sides were—kept up a steady fire.

23

Brandon eased his head out of the jail's side door and peered down the alley to the plaza. Running figures appeared briefly at its entrance, moving in different directions, and two mounted troopers dashed by, waving their sabers, but no one turned, nor appeared to look, into the alleyway. Shouts and gunshots sounded in the courthouse, in the plaza, and, it seemed to Brandon, were spreading away from the immediate area.

He turned to Jack Kestrel and Lorena Canty, pressed against the wall behind him, and said, "Safe to rush for it now, I'd say."

Jack Kestrel nodded. Brandon turned and sprang across the alley, coming to a crouch among a jumble of empty barrels and crates at the back of a building. Jack Kestrel and Lorena Canty followed him an instant later. They looked around and saw that their shelter would be effective only against casual inspection from the side. Toward the rear was an open expanse of grass, then the backs of a row of houses. Someone looking out a rear window might not notice them, but just as well might. A small open shed some yards to the rear of the building they were behind, containing a flatbed wagon and an incurious mule, offered no worthwhile hiding place.

"Where's this?" Brandon asked.

"Varnum's store," Jack Kestrel said.

"Great," Brandon said glumly, remembering the interior of the store: wide open, except for the area behind the counter, and the stacks of merchandise forming temporary aisles. "We'd be spotted in there as easily as out here, anybody comes along."

"Why are we running away? What are we hiding from?" Lorena Canty asked.

"Your pa's a fugitive right now, as I see it," Jack Kestrel said. "And we're part of his crowd, so we're in for whatever treatment they have in mind for him. Also, if he gets away back to the ranch and you're taken, they've got a ring through his nose they won't be shy about pulling. You know darn well he'd throw his head back and bare his throat to the knife if he had to do it to get you free."

"So he would," said Lorena Canty. "Well, as we've got to stay hid, there's a little room at the back of the store; the ladies use it when they're trying on dresses. It's out of the way, and somebody just looking into the store might not think to look there."

Brandon looked beyond where they were, along the backs of the stores along Main Street, a dismayingly open space stretching to Varnum's livery stable at the north end. At any moment someone might come out and see them among the crates. A women's dressing room might not be the ideal place to hide, but it was not absolutely suicidal. Another burst of shouting and an imperative bugle call came from the general area of the plaza, followed by a few more gunshots. Brandon tested the handle on the store's back door; it turned, and he opened it and stepped inside.

It was cool and dim in the store, and dark cloth shades hung over the streetside windows. Evidently Sally Dumayne had decided to close up when it became clear that Bascom was in for a more interesting day than usual.

"Over here," Lorena Canty said. She led the way to a corner of the room behind the counter and pulled aside a length of fabric hanging on the wall to reveal a door. She opened it and stepped inside, motioning Brandon and Jack Kestrel to follow her.

It was large for a closet but small for a room, about six feet square, with a bench along the wall facing the door. A full-length mirror was fastened to the back of the door, and light was provided by a window high enough, Brandon was relieved to notice, so that nobody could see them—a necessity, of course, for a dressing room.

Only ten minutes, maybe less, had passed since the eruption of gunplay in the courtroom, but they were as fatigued as if they had been running for a mile or more. They subsided gratefully onto the bench and for a moment savored their apparent safety.

Kestrel's, Lorena's, and his own face stared at Brandon from the mirror. As at the tailor's in St. Louis, the full view, more distant and complete than the daily close-to image shaving entailed, made him look like a stranger—but, then, the mirrored alien had had an undefined, Everyman or No-man quality; now it was definitely somebody, just somebody he did not know. Alert eyes, but the face stiff, something brutal in the set of the unsmiling mouth: Carter Bane's face.

Jack Kestrel and Lorena Canty had an unnerving look of being not quite themselves; twins, maybe, but something not entirely right about them. Probably it was only the mirror's reversal of their images, left for right; but perhaps, like himself, Jack Kestrel or Lorena were assuming masks. Somehow, even if that were so, he was less and less able to believe that Kestrel was concealing an identity as a thief and murderer. Clearly, if Varnum were the man he was after, Kestrel could not be—could not even be an accomplice, unless he were going through an extremely elaborate and pointless charade.

All three of them were looking with increasing discomfort in every direction, but they seemed unable to refrain from locking glances—seated as they were, they almost had to study their own faces or the others'. Brandon rose and leaned against the window wall, grateful to have the opposite one to look at, containing four hooks for hanging garments, one of them occupied by a voluminous blue linen coat, and a pasted-up catalog page depicting a remarkable variety of corsets and corset covers. Not a gripping vista, but an improvement over three pairs of mirrored eyes.

Jack Kestrel gave a sudden slap at his vest pocket, then rummaged rapidly in the opposite pocket, his jacket, and trousers. "Damn," he muttered.

Brandon asked, "Lose something important?"

"Yeah. It's—probably fell out in the jail or when we were sprinting over here." Kestrel looked worried and irritated.

The three of them stiffened at the sound of footsteps in the store. Kestrel and Brandon exchanged glances and eased their revolvers into position for rapid aiming and firing; Lorena Canty took a deep breath and clutched her handbag.

"I'll just get my coat, I think I—" Sally Dumayne blinked once as she opened the door of the dressing room, took in its occupants with a rapid glance, and continued without pause. "—left it in here—yes, here it is."

She took the coat from its hook, draped it over her arm, held up one hand with the fingers spread wide, closed it, then held up the other beside it and spread both sets of fingers, nodded her head emphatically, and left, closing the door behind her.

They heard her voice and a man's in a brief exchange, though the words did not carry, then footsteps and a door closing.

"Back in five to ten minutes?" Lorena Canty said.

"Expect that's what she meant," Brandon said.

"So we wait here while she rounds up Varnum and Meyner and Dedman and anybody else around and fetches them right to us?" Jack Kestrel said. "I mean, after all, she's Varnum's . . ."

"So she is, but I get the feeling that that doesn't carry much weight any more," Brandon said. "Choice is, we trust her and wait, or we go out back, where anybody's likely to see us and raise the alarm."

"We can trust her," Lorena Canty said slowly. "I saw how she looked at us. A woman who's going to betray another woman, she'll look sorry about it, or cat-satisfied. She didn't, just looked like she'd decided what she was going to do, and then she did it. She'll be back, and she'll be working out a way to help us."

Jack Kestrel looked dubious, but accepted Brandon's opinion that trusting Sally Dumayne might be unwise but that going outside just now would be disastrous.

At the sound of footsteps in the store, Brandon fished out his watch and checked it: six minutes. They tensed as the door opened, then relaxed as they saw that Sally Dumayne was alone.

She spoke to Lorena Canty first: "Far as I know, your father's all right. He and three or four of his men got to their horses and out of town in the confusion. Captain Meyner and about half his troop are following them, but it took them a while to get started, and I doubt they'll catch them up before the river."

"Meyner's authority would be dubious the other side of the river," Brandon said, not much caring that it was in no way a Bane comment. "His orders referred to Bascom, not the whole area. He can probably justify anything he does this side of the river, but not more."

Jack Kestrel gave him a curious look and said, "Any case, once across, Sam and the boys can lose themselves, set up an ambush, or fort up in the ranch house. I'd say you're right, they'd have to give up if they don't overhaul 'em before the river."

"Mr. Varnum stayed around for a bit, trying to find out where you three had gotten to," Sally Dumayne told them. "Said you were involved in the usurpation of authority, that's what he called it, as much as Mr. Canty, and you'd all have to be held for trial. He seemed to be just about raving mad at you, Mr. Kestrel—said he knew you'd gone through the jail because you'd dropped something there, but thought you'd probably tried to escape across the fields. Told the troopers Meyner left in town that you were armed and dangerous and they shouldn't take any chances with you."

That is, shoot him on sight, Brandon translated silently. What the hell did Kestrel drop, to have that effect?

"Where's Varnum now?" Jack Kestrel asked.

"Rode after Meyner," Sally Dumayne said. "Either wants to be in on capturing Mr. Canty and the rest, if it comes to that, or tell Meyner what to do next."

"You're helping us," Lorena Canty said. "And that means you're going against Mr. Varnum. Why?"

Sally Dumayne shrugged. "A man like Mr. Varnum, he has a way of making you do what he wants, even making you *want* to do what he wants. And sometimes what you do makes you hate yourself, and you still can't help doing it. And then it may happen that it comes to you that it doesn't have to be that way"—she threw a quick glance at Brandon—"and if there's a chance to do something decent, then you can do that."

She studied Lorena Canty and looked briefly at Jack Kestrel. "If you're really, *really* lucky, Miss Canty, you may never find that out for yourself. Now let's get you out of here."

Brandon breathed shallowly, trying not to cough or sneeze; the dust from the sack of feed resting on top of him was urgently promoting one or both. He and Jack Kestrel were jammed against the sides of the wagon from the store shed, with Lorena Canty sandwiched between them, concealed under a load of feed sacks. Sally Dumayne directed the mule down the open space behind the stores in the direction of Varnum's livery stable.

Brandon heard the grinding of the wheels' iron tires become muffled—riding on hay or something like that now, not the hard ground—and the wagon slowed and stopped.

"We're inside," Sally Dumayne said. "It's all right to get out now."

They heaved aside the sacks of grain, clambered down from the wagon, and stood up with relief. They were at one end of a long line of stalls, empty except for four horses.

"Mr. Varnum took those four men out with him to go after Meyner," Sally Dumayne said, "so the horses the trouble was about, they're still here."

"Not for long," Kestrel said cheerfully. "Three of 'em, anyhow. If they weren't stolen before, they will be now."

"Four."

All of them, Kestrel a little bit the least, jumped at the sound of a disembodied voice seeming to come from nowhere.

Curly stepped from behind a partition, grinning. "Been biding my time here since I busted out of the courthouse, until as I figured out where to git to and when. But now you're here, Jack, why, I c'n turn her all over to you and say yessir and go do what you tells me to go git done. Ridin' away from here, far and fast, that sounds like a prime idee."

When Sally Dumayne reported that the cavalrymen remaining in Bascom had moved off to the southern part of town, Brandon, Kestrel, Lorena, and Curly made their way out of town through alleys and little-traveled streets and were soon out in the scrub woods at the base of the slope leading to the plateau. They would have to come into view as their ascent took them through some bare spots, but they were at enough distance so that they might remain entirely unnoticed; and there would be no reason yet to assume that the fugitives had found any horses.

On the stony plateau, they kept up a moderate pace, following the trail that Brandon had used—only the day before? It already seemed like a week ago. Yet the afternoon heat shimmering from the rocks was intimately familiar; he scanned the sky and wondered where the hawk and weasel were now—dead and drying in the sun, locked in mutual destruction?

"There's the ruins of the old trading post along here," Jack Kestrel said. "Maybe we could run across that, see if we can get some rest there, study out where to go next."

"More than ruins," Brandon said. "Rode out there yesterday. Main building looks pretty whole, though some of the outbuildings and walls are starting to fall apart."

"You do get around, Bane," Jack Kestrel said.

* * *

The stone buildings of the trading post glared in the sunlight and grew larger than Brandon had expected as the four riders drew closer.

"That is in damn good repair for an abandoned building," Jack Kestrel said.

They passed the side of the building, which Brandon estimated as about twenty feet high, and came around the front, facing the slope down to the river. A wide door about fifteen feet tall, made of heavy timbers, was centered in the wall, hinged with broad straps of thick leather spiked to the stone. Patches of plaster had fallen away from the stones of the walls, but the place was less ruinous than Brandon would have expected—the preserving effect of the dry air, he supposed.

"Fee fi fo fum," Curly said. At the others' surprised looks, he added, "Old-timey story my granser used to tell. Was a giant that had a lot of treasure, and whenas folks came to take it off him, he would say that fee fo business and then he'd eat them. I expect it was like a giant way of saying grace. That door, it looks big enough for a giant to walk through an' not stoop neither."

The door was flanked on each side by a row of narrow, high windows. They held no glass, but brackets at top and bottom suggested that they could be shuttered against cold or rain.

Keeping wary eyes on the windows, at which no sign of movement could be seen, they rode along the front of the building and came to the first evidence of disrepair, a wide gap in what had been a five-foot-high stone wall linking the building with a roofless, partitioned stone structure that had evidently once been a stable.

They put their horses through the gap and found themselves in a yard formed by the remnant of the wall, the stables, the massive main building, and a crude shed constructed of logs attached to its side.

"Nobody's hailed us, no horses around, so nobody's here," Jack Kestrel said. "Let's look around. Could be a good place for us to lie low till dark, then we can work our way back to the Lazy Y and see what's up with Sam and the boys."

"Shouldn't we keep going?" Brandon asked.

Kestrel shrugged. "Indian might trail us across that plateau, but horse soldiers aren't that good at tracking. Far's they know, we could've gone in any direction."

They left their horses in the roofless stalls and entered the shed. It contained piles of debris—broken crates, rags, and crumbling bits of paper—and a decrepit-looking wagon, one wheel of which canted outward.

There was a door—a normal-sized one—in the side of the main building. Kestrel pulled it open, with a slight grating sound as its bottom dragged on the ground, and Brandon felt an immediate rush of unease that he could not understand. Then he realized that a door in an abandoned trading post, a door that had not been opened for years, *should* have set its rusted hinges to squealing—and this one had not. The frown on Jack Kestrel's face showed him that he was not alone in his concern.

They stepped quickly into the massive stone building and stopped. The windows cut into the front and side walls admitted ample light, including, through the west-facing front windows, the rays of the sun, now beginning its descent, which laid bright oblongs on the irregular flagstones of the floor.

Even before his eyes could make a sketchy inventory of the room's contents, Brandon's nose registered a medley of odors: the mustiness of cloth and canvas, the taint of coal oil, the tang of gunpowder, the faint smell of metal, and others he could not identify. The bales, barrels, and crates ranged along the walls and stacked in the center of the floor bore out what his nose had told him: This was no deserted trading post but a storage depot very much in use.

Kestrel said, "Oh, my lord!" with an alarm in his voice that Brandon had never before heard. He walked quickly to a row of crates along the back wall and pulled up a covering slat on the top of one with a screech of pulled nails. "Damn!" Brandon, behind him, looked into the crate and saw it filled with pasteboard boxes; the printing on them was too small to read even at two feet or so, except for the word CARTRIDGES in bold type.

"Damn!" again, as Kestrel opened another crate, and the smell of oiled metal wafted out. "Sharps fifties, enough to kill all the buffalo that's left. Though I doubt they're meant for buffalo. They're just as good on men, for sure."

"Jack!" Lorena Canty called from a corner of the room. "There's war bonnets here, spears—Indian stuff! I don't—this can't be left from the Santa Fe Trail days!"

"No, it's not, it's from the Dorn goddamn Varnum days, and that's right now!" Kestrel said harshly. "Last time I was out this way, last summer, place was empty except for the trash outside. All this came in since, and it's plain enough what it's for!"

"Ain't to me," Curly said plaintively. "Heydee," he added more cheerfully, "now here's a case of best-grade knives—razor-edge Sheffield steel by the look of 'em. Never can have too good a knife, my thinking." He held up a knife admiringly and slid it into his jacket pocket. "I will leave the price for it, or maybe not. If it's cash or credit, either one, I got to tell you, whole damn store out here amongst the rocks, it don't make sense."

"Out-of-town branch of Varnum's emporium," Brandon said slowly. "Where the ammunition came from for all the shooting the other night. And what's here is what he'll use to make sure nobody settles his new towns for too long. . . ."

"You know about that?" Kestrel asked.

Brandon nodded. "Tried to sign me up."

Without Brandon seeing it happen, Kestrel's gun was out and ready to rise to cover him. "From here on, I've got to be damn sure I can trust you, or I'd be better dropping you right now."

Brandon said, "He tried to get you with him, too, and you're here, not with him. So am I. Even if I was playing a deep game, I wouldn't gain anything by coming this far. You and Miss Canty wouldn't have made it out of the jail."

Kestrel muttered, "But you didn't know—hell, yes,

you're right. For whatever reasons you've got behind that poker face, Bane, I guess you're with us for now. And now is when we have to get out of here. Curly, let's get the horses ready." He holstered his gun and moved toward the door to the shed.

"Jack, we were going to stay here till dark!" Lorena Canty protested.

Jack Kestrel motioned urgently to Curly, who nodded and went out the door. "We were going to stay in a deserted trading post," Jack Kestrel said, "not a storehouse of weapons, ammunition, and God knows what else, that belongs to a man who means to see us locked away or dead! The cavalry may not be able to track us, but Varnum can't overlook the chance that we'd come here. Remember, Sally Dumayne said he'd picked up my notebook, and he's certain to think I know more than I do, and if I did, this is where I'd have come on purpose, not by accident!"

The shock on Lorena Canty's face indicated that she understood the details of what Jack Kestrel was saying more clearly than Brandon did, but it seemed to add up to the need to get away from the trading post rapidly.

He heard the sound of a sharp impact on stone and a rapidly receding whine, and a startled shout, and the faint, far-off pop of a gunshot. Curly burst through the door, wide-eyed. "Sumbitch shot at me!" he gasped.

"Where from? Who?" Jack Kestrel asked.

"No, he didn't hit me, thanks," Curly said heavily. "The sumbitching horse soldiers, thass who, excuse the language, Miss Lorena—"

"Expect I'd say worse if somebody shot at *me,"* Lorena Canty said.

"—down the slope in the arroyo, looks like half the troop, behind the bank to it, like a trench. Passed by where the wall ain't and chanced to glance down thataway, and I seen heads and blue coats and guns sticking up, and I stopped fer a look, and next as I knowed, one of 'em shot a chunk out of a rock next to me, and I come on back in here where the climate's healthier."

Jack Kestrel said to Brandon, "Let's have a look." They looked carefully out of two of the window slits, staying as far as possible out of the revealing direct sunlight. Brandon saw, at the bottom of the rocky slope, the hard line marking the near edge of the dry river bed, broken by the notch marking the way of the old trail, and the matching line of the far edge. He could see, as Curly had said, a few buff-colored hats and a flash of uniform blue amid the rocks along the near edge. It seemed to him that there were more rocks than there had been when he had surveyed the scene a few days ago, and he supposed they represented a sketchy attempt at constructing a parapet for safer firing. Beyond the far bank was a clump of trees, and a dozen or so horses were there, head down; it was too far to see clearly, but he assumed they were stake-tethered.

"Must've got here not much after we did," Kestrel said gloomily. "Saw the horses, circled around, and settled themselves into that natural trench. If they'd waited five minutes and stayed hid down there, they could have shot us off our horses in the open."

"Comforting to know we've got their stupidity working for us," Brandon said. "Maybe Meyner is as dumb as he looks, though it's hard to credit." He didn't care about the curious look Kestrel threw him; the Bane personality was pretty threadbare and ill-fitting by now, and he would have to be doing what the situation called for, not what the character he was portraying would be expected to do. The mask could be resumed, or exchanged for another, when this was done with—assuming there was a living face to put it on. And it was now abundantly clear that Jack Kestrel was performing his own masquerade, whatever that might be. Brandon was about ready to abandon any hope—or fear—that he might be the Kenneally flower-whittler.

Kestrel turned away from the window and strode back to where Curly and Lorena Canty waited in the center of the room. "They're settling in as if they mean business, but it's a kind of standoff. They can keep us from getting away, but there's three hundred yards of uphill open ground between us, and the hill, and all of 'em charging in a bunch wouldn't get a third of the way."

"I'm not suggesting this," Brandon said slowly, "but is there a good reason not to parley with them, maybe negotiate a surrender, then see what we can do with whatever judicial system they turn us over to? We haven't done anything criminal."

Curly looked at him with frank amazement. The Carter Bane he had been siding might have denied unlawful activity as a tactical matter in dealing with the authorities, but not among friends.

"We haven't, Varnum has," Jack Kestrel said, gesturing around the room at the goods piled in it, "or he's about to. He's got enough arms and stuff here to run a small war, and it looks as if he's planning to use Indian trappings as uniforms once in a while. Now he knows we're here, and he's bound to think we came here because we knew what was here. Surrender or not, we're not going to get as far as any authorities or anybody we can tell about this. If we don't get shot here and they take us, Varnum has that rum-soaked Meyner under his thumb enough to make sure we get shot trying to escape or steal his whiskey, maybe. Curly, you get over to a window and keep an eye on them."

Curly went to a front window, peered, then ran to one in the side wall. "Dust and something, way off," he called.

Brandon and Kestrel joined him and saw a trail of dust about half a mile distant to the south, coming from something hidden behind a cleft in the rocks. Brandon squinted and thought he saw a horse and rider, then another horse, riderless but heavily laden, pass between a gap in the line of rocks.

From the front window they could see, as before, scraps of buff and blue indicating the presence of the dismounted cavalry. Brandon caught a flicker of light brown as someone moved down the trench and guessed it to be Varnum.

"Nothing yet," Kestrel said. "Don't see they'll try a charge, but they'll probably open fire soon, see if they can scare us into running or giving up."

Brandon stiffened as a shudder of chill ran through him. Almost everything about it was different, but one essential element was the same: a siege, with attackers and defenders for the moment at a stalemate. When the firing started, he would experience some hint of what Elise and the others had gone through at Mound Farm—not the actuality of the horror, not the fear of being held hostage, but the simple situation of being under fire.

"Damn," Curly said. "I hate this kinder thing. It comes to shooting, out in the open, in the saddle for druthers, that's for me."

"You were out in the open a couple minutes ago," Jack Kestrel said dryly. "Care to try it again?"

"I hate being shot at indoors, like a turkey in a box," Curly said, "but I hate worse being shot at outdoors by a dozen fellers behind nice thick rocks so's I can't shoot back and do any good."

Brandon had been going over several things Jack Kestrel had said since their arrival and started to come to some conclusions. "You're more than Canty's foreman, that's something everybody knows—hardcase, been on both sides of the law, the legendary Jack Kestrel. Any of that reputation true?"

Kestrel studied him. "Reputations can pop up like mushrooms—things get blown up as they get talked about. Sometimes useful in the job. Sometimes all you have to do is let folks tell what they say happened and turn it into a better story."

Brandon nodded, feeling wryly amused. "The job—state, federal, or private?"

"Private," Kestrel said. "Nationwide Agency, head office Chicago, near as good as the Pinks."

"Heard of them," Brandon said, insanely tempted to ask if Kestrel knew one Warner, of the St. Louis office.

"Now wait a sheep-dipped minute!" Curly broke in. "Jack, are you saying you ain't what folks say you are? Saying you're a *detective?*"

"He is," Lorena Canty said. "Pa hired him almost a year

ago, 'cause he was getting almighty worried about Mr. Varnum and thought he might be behind some of the things that were happening around here. Best way for him to do the job was to be our foreman. Could get around a lot more than a regular hand could—and it turned out he was a mighty good foreman, too." She threw Jack Kestrel a proud glance, as if she were somehow responsible for his capability as foreman.

"High damn," Curly said dispiritedly. "All the time, I been feeling a nice, warm glow that I was riding with one of the great owlhoots, fellow that could bull his way through anything, and tear up a town or tame it, as the fancy come to him. I tell you, a detective is quite a comedown from that. It is like getting cozy with a dance-hall lady and then finding out that she is a missionary, sorry, Miss Lorena—there ain't nothing outright disgusting about it, but it is some feeble."

"Oh, I did a lot of that," Kestrel said. "Got around some before I went with the agency. Things get blown up, like I say, but there's some solid fact in with the gas."

"And now Varnum knows who you are," Brandon said.

Jack Kestrel grimaced. "Sally Dumayne said he picked up something in the jail and went crazy—had to be my notebook, with some observations and conclusions about him. Nothing to identify me or the agency, but he wouldn't have to be much brighter than a possum to figure what it was about. And it's plain he's figured it out, and also that he's figured he can't have us walking away from here. Let's see what we can do about that. Curly, you keep lookout while we check the guns."

The case he had opened held twenty of the octagonal-barreled heavy rifles, the metal oily to the touch but not coated with protective grease. The .50-caliber cartridges were packed in pasteboard boxes stacked in crates; Brandon estimated that there were a couple of thousand.

"More than we're likely to get a chance to fire off," Jack Kestrel said, "but it's nice to know we don't have to be stingy." Under his direction, they loaded all the rifles and stood them against the front wall.

"Something moving down there," Curly reported.

Brandon and Jack Kestrel moved to separate windows and looked out and downhill. Brandon could see movement among the rocks; then something appeared in the notch in the near bank of the dry creek and was manhandled into place behind some rocks. It was supported by two wheels and had the look of a small cannon.

24

The Gatling," Jack Kestrel said. "Must've been what we saw joining up with 'em a while back."

"Bad news," Brandon said.

"Not a good weapon for this kind of thing," Jack Kestrel said. "It—"

A rapidly flickering pinpoint of light appeared at the front of the Gatling, and Brandon, Curly, and Kestrel sprang away from the windows. A wailing snarl of displaced air and the ripping sound of the impact of dozens of metal slugs on rock in the space of little more than a second assaulted their ears. A cloud of rock dust from the walls drifted through the windows, joining the one that had been chewed from the rear wall by the shots passing through the window; spent slugs ricocheted wildly through the room, a few of them bouncing off its four inhabitants but not with enough momentum left to do any damage. The angle at which the Gatling had to fire up the slope confined its effect to the upper third of the rear wall.

"It can put out a lot of fire," Jack Kestrel continued calmly, "but it has to be in the open to do that, and it's more a machine than a gun. You'll see what I mean."

He dropped a box of .50-caliber cartridges into his jacket

pocket, grabbed five of the loaded rifles by their barrels, and walked rapidly from the room, trailing the stocks on the floor. "Give me a minute to get set, then get off one shot from the furthest window on the far side, and for God's sake duck right away. Get it as close to the Gatling as you can."

Brandon took up his position, keeping in shadow as much as possible. At the end of a slow count of sixty, he aimed the rifle at the distant and momentarily silent gun—manned, he could see, by two troopers crouching as if they were unhappy about being out of the trench—and pulled the trigger.

The heavy recoil drove him back without the need of Kestrel's injunction, but not before he had seen dust spurting a few yards to the left of the gun position.

Another burst of slugs raved through the window Brandon had just left and etched more random designs on the back wall. As the noise echoed in the room, they heard a series of heavy booms from outside, almost as rapidly as a revolver could fire. Brandon risked a look through the window farthest from the one he had fired from, and saw the two gunners leaping for the shelter of the trench out of a smear of rock dust suspended in the air, mixed with the cloud of smoke from the two bursts the Gatling had fired.

As the air around it cleared, Brandon could see that the gun was skewed in its mount and pointing upward. At that distance, he could not see details of any damage, but it had a subtly distorted look.

Five more heavy shots sounded from Jack Kestrel's position, and the Gatling seemed to flinch sideways before a new fog of powdered rock hid it. When this cleared, the gun was on its side.

Kestrel came back into the room, dragging the rifles. "Load these up again, Lorena. We'll want to keep 'em feeling discouraged and unventuresome."

"Two fellows gettin' set to jump out and haul the Gatling back, looks like," Curly reported from his window. "Want me to drop 'em?"

"No," Jack Kestrel said. "I am pretty sure I knocked it out bad enough so's they can't fix it out here, so no harm in letting 'em take it back. And if we can get through this without shooting any soldiers, we're in a lot better spot later on. We shoot close enough to make 'em keep their heads down and stay where they are, we're all better off."

"It is new to me to shoot at fellows to do 'em a kindness," Curly said, "but I will get the hang of it. Gatling's gone. . . . There's one now, raising his leetle head like any prairie dog. . . ."

The room reverberated with the blast of the shot, and the acrid smell of burned gunpowder drifted among them. "Down, like a hole opened under him," Curly said cheerfully, "and not a hair on his head hurt. It is kind of fun, even if it ain't as definite as the reg'lar way."

"One of 'em's skoochin' out front," Curly said, "a couple hairs to the left of the cottonwood."

Brandon took a deep breath, closed his eyes, steadied the rifle in his grip and then in a single fluid motion swung the rifle onto the broad sill of the narrow window opening, flicked his eyes open to get the full view of what lay downslope before the glare blinded him, shifted to bring the rifle's front sight to bear just to the left of a blue-coated figure hunched over next to the twisted tree, squeezed the trigger, and let the recoil swing him around and out of the opening. Two brief whining whispers ending in a whip-crack, and a metallic thud signaled the passage of a pair of slugs through the window to their impact on the stone of the room's back wall and their fall to the flagged floor.

"Near miss, but it druv him back," Curly said, peering through the far window. It had not been used as a fire port and so had not drawn any return fire, and whoever looked through it had been careful to move slowly.

For half an hour now, there had been a desultory swapping of shots, usually provoked by the cavalrymen testing whether they could make a move safely. One had worked his way through the rocks about a hundred feet ahead of their position before being spotted and driven back with a series of shots carefully aimed a safe couple of yards behind him.

"Setup like this," Curly said, "the thing is, keep cool

whiles as you can, don't get yer head shot off, an' wait fer opportunity to knock—er maybe lift up the latchstring quiet-like, so's you'd best be a-listenin' and a-lookin' and alertin' for it."

Brandon was sourly amused at the cowhand's assumption of an experienced view of mortal-danger sieges. But if a touch of the blowhards helped him to deal with what was going on, why not?

Lorena Canty came up behind him, took the rifle from him, and handed him another one, loaded. He leaned it against the wall under the window and moved to the observation window as Curly stepped back. A drift of smoke hung above the escarpment at the bottom of the slope.

Brandon squinted against the sun, lower in the sky and inching to the west. In not too long a time it would be directly in their faces, blinding them and also targeting any face looking through any of the windows. As it was, the sunlight was glaring off the pale rocks and earth of the slope, making it almost as bright as a snowbank, distorting vision. In a little while, if the troopers had the sense for it, they could roll in the dust till they were as white as the rocks and then charge uphill with a good chance of not being seen until they were most of the way up. Or they could wait a few hours and stroll uphill in the dark. Without an ounce of fellow-feeling for Gren Kenneally, Brandon had to admit that he was facing the same problem: getting away before the place could be stormed. Without hostages to massacre or buildings to burn for distraction, it was going to be a chancy matter.

Lorena edged beside him to look down the sun-battered slope. He thought of warning her to keep back, but did not. She had been through more today than a good many troops had experienced during the War, and had taken it as coolly as any veteran might be expected to. She didn't need to be warned not to take chances. Also he liked the scent that emanated from her: mostly sweat, and no wonder, after the hard ride in the sun and the scramble for temporary safety, but a touch of something floral and feminine that was a reminder that there was more to life than glaring sun, dust, and gunfire.

"Hey," Jack Kestrel called from the back of the room. "Bane, Lorena, come on over here. Curly, you keep the cavalry meek and biddable for a while."

Brandon and Lorena Canty found him hefting a bundle of what looked like sticks of clay. "Varnum's ready for about anything," he said, "including moving mountains, like it says in the Bible, only without any faith needed for the job. Dynamite."

The term was a new one to Brandon, and he looked questioningly at Jack Kestrel. "New stuff. Kind of a clay sponge soaked with nitroglycerine. Doesn't go off if you shake it, though," Kestrel said, doing so, and giving Brandon an instant of stabbing chill. "Needs fuses and detonators. Great for mining."

"No mines around here," Brandon said.

"Not particular about what it blows up. My guess, he gets some paper township sold off to the suckers, lets a few of 'em start up homesteading and building, then he lets all hell loose—Indian raids with the genuine trappings straight from the theater supply house, stock shot at night with those long-range Sharps, maybe farmers the same way, and to cap it off, houses and barns blown up mysterious. Lots of barrels of coal oil here, too, which I misdoubt is all meant for lanterns, so figure barn-burning and prairie fires thrown in." Jack Kestrel looked around the room with a grimace. "If they'd keep, I expect he'd have a couple crates full of grasshoppers, just to make sure there's no disaster overlooked."

"Then change the name, do another gilt-edged prospectus with engravings of all the amenities, and sell the same land all over again to the next bunch," Brandon said.

"Crazy a scheme as any hophead could come up with, but out here crazy happens as often as not. Ten years ago, anybody said he aimed to get rich making cows walk to Kansas and then take the train east would've been fitted for a straitjacket and no questions asked. What I was figuring him for was something else completely, something the agency already had an interest in—one reason they were ready to take the case when Sam Canty brought it in. Up in the Neutral Zone, over toward the west end of it, there is a whole boiling of outlaws of every kind. No law in charge, so it's a refuge for anybody who makes it there. We'd been getting hints that some folks were getting set to organize things up there, marshal all the hardcases into a kind of army that could go out and raid all over, then dodge on back. Be a help for a bunch like that if they had a friend not far off that could be a spy, helper, fixer, and supplier. When Sam Canty told the agency what this Varnum was up to, it seemed like he might be a good bet for that. But it's just some damn craziness of his own, nothing—"

Curly's rifle fired; its stock rattled on the floor as he set it down and grabbed its neighbor, swung it to the window, and shot again, reminding them that Dorn Varnum's craziness had an immediate and lethal aspect.

"Nothing to do with the Kenneallys," Jack Kestrel finished. "They're a sizable gang of professional criminals, the ones we'd heard might be setting themselves up to organize the outlaws in the Neutral Zone," he added, seeing Brandon's expression of astonishment. "But it seems that—"

"I hear you say that Varnum is hooked up with the Kenneallys?" Curly called from his post at the window.

"No, other way around," Jack Kestrel said. "Thought he might be, but nothing to show he is."

"A load off'n our minds," Curly said. "Was Varnum to be in with them fellows, our hides'd be stretched on the fence by sundown, I shouldn't wonder. Where the Kenneallys step, a weed dies, I always heard. Dorn Varnums I laughs at, cavalry boys I treats with pity an' scorn, but when it comes to Kenneallys, why, there's where I knuckle down an' sob like a squirrel."

"Nice you can find something to joke about," Jack Kestrel said. "Kenneallys or not, Varnum's got what it takes to—" He glanced at Lorena Canty.

"Kill us all," she said calmly. "I can see that as clear as

you can, Jack. And you know that we aren't just going to sit here waiting for it, so let's start working out what we're going to do."

In the moment's silence that this suggestion produced, Brandon found that in fact his mind had been studying out what course of action to follow without his being consciously aware of doing so. He looked at the dynamite sticks Jack Kestrel had set down and said, "Did you find the detonators and fuses for those? They easy enough to put together?"

"Yes to both," Jack Kestrel said. "But it is a losing proposition to run down there and throw them like baseballs."

"So it would be," Brandon said. "That's why that's not what we'll be doing."

"Bickford fuse burns two feet in a minute," Jack Kestrel said.

"We'll figure on that," Brandon said. "Allow ten seconds or so to get the door open and the wagon moving, a minute to roll downhill—twenty-eight inches looks about right."

Kestrel nodded and clipped the fuses protruding from the four bundles of dynamite, measuring them against the six-inch barrel of his revolver. He wedged the dynamite carefully in the oil-soaked rags that were packed around the barrels and cases lashed to the wagon bed. Brandon checked the ropes fastened to each end of the pivoted front axle, which terminated in giant loose coils on the floor, each of which consisted of lengths of rope tied together to make a line something over three hundred yards long.

The four of them pushed the rickety wagon—Curly had hammered a cotter pin into the hub of the loose wheel, giving it a semblance of stability—so that its rear faced the massive front door.

Brandon took a last look out the observation window. The slope looked rocky, but the remnant of the old trail seemed to lead straight enough toward the notch in the escarpment, with no major boulders blocking it.

He turned to where Curly stood by the door. "Latch."

Curly slid the heavy iron strip out of its bracket and set it on the floor; the door seemed to shudder and slide outward an inch or so.

"Fuse." Kestrel struck a match and darted its flare around the wagon; sparks spat from the long cords protruding from the bundles of dynamite.

"Door!" Curly jumped at the door, hit it hard, ran with it as it shuddered open, then dove for the shelter of the doorway as the first shot from an alert rifleman whickered past him.

"Wagon!" Brandon, Curly, Jack Kestrel, and Lorena Canty, bunched at the rearward-facing front of the wagon, shoved hard, then sprang aside as it lumbered through the doorway and started down the hill. Brandon and Kestrel crouched, one at each side of the doorway, watching as the coiled rope attached to the wagon's axle whipped by them. Brandon reached down and took a palm burn as he exerted a gentle pressure on the speeding rope; the wagon had been veering to the left, off the trail, but, as he had hoped, the light tug guided it back on track.

The wagon was at the bottom of the hill and on the gentler downslope, moving faster now, going in and out of clouds of rock dust thrown up by the increasing volume of fire directed at it. Brandon saw a small case fly into the air and smash onto the slope behind the careering wagon; its spilled contents winked metallically in the sun. The wagon shuddered under several hits at once and lurched to the right; Kestrel's pull on his rope—marked by a yelp of surprise and pain as it sandpapered his palm—corrected its course.

The slope flattened somewhat, and the wagon slowed. Brandon cursed as an upslope he had not seen cost it even more speed, and he had a horrible instant of thinking it might be coming to a stop; then it dipped and accelerated once more.

Brandon could see rapid movement along the rim of the trench, buff hats moving to the left and the right, away from the notch the wagon was aimed for.

He had no idea how long the wagon had been on its way—or, more to the point, how long since the fuses had been lit. Then he was aware of Lorena Canty's voice: ". . . Sixty-eight one thousand, sixty-nine one thousand . . ."

He looked to where she stood and saw that she was holding up two fingers. About ten seconds to go, if Jack Kestrel had cut the fuses the right length and the troopers didn't shoot them out or the detonators didn't fall off or—

The wagon was ten yards short of the notch in the escarpment when it blossomed in flashes of blinding light, followed in a second by a thunderclap. Smoke and fragments of various sizes exploded outward, and one wheel spun madly sideways across the hard ground, struck a rock, and bounded gracefully into the dry river bed. The disintegrating wagon and its contents moved ahead even as they were falling apart, and as they slammed into the notch, the heat of the explosion ignited the breached barrels of coal oil in rapid sequence. A red sun glowed briefly, then became a massive tree of flame veined with smoke; a mushroom of black spread above it. Brandon saw with astonishment what looked like a child's toy cannon fly lazily through the air, turning twice before it hit the ground and became a shapeless jumble—the Gatling must have been left just about where the exploding oil barrels had hit.

In an instant the fiery tree became a curtain as the flaming oil spread away from it on both sides in the river bed; the troopers were more plainly visible now as they traded concealment for speed and raced from the oncoming rivers of flame.

The burning oil roared like a waterfall; then above the noise they heard what sounded like a continual volley of musketry, and the browner color of gunsmoke joined the black smoke of burning coal oil. The cases of ammunition were at last being set off by the flames and, from what could be seen, spurring the troopers to more determined flight.

The smoke hid the sun from them, darkening the scene as if by an eclipse, and then deepening the shadow as a firm breeze pushed it toward them, creating a murky fog bank that crept up the slope. A trick of the wind thinned the cloud toward the left, and they could see to the grove of trees where the troop's horses had been staked out. There were only three there now, and the others were streaking across the open land beyond, freed from their tethers by the panic strength the wagon of destruction had lent them.

Though there did not seem to be any further need for it, caution had become a habit during the afternoon of siege, and Brandon, Jack Kestrel, Lorena Canty, and Curly observed the spectacle from the edges of the doorway. The drifting, oily cloud crept up the slope like a rising tide.

"Considerable turnabout," Jack Kestrel said thoughtfully. "How'd the idea come to you, Bane?"

Brandon had not considered that question, but suddenly realized that there had been a precedent for breaking a siege with the dramatic use of fire: Gren Kenneally at Mound Farm. It was maddening that he still had no indication if this incident were connected to what he was here for, though Kestrel's investigations seemed to have removed Varnum from the Kenneally orbit. Assuming that Kestrel was in fact a detective and not the Kenneally gang member who had left the carved flower in his room at the Bright Kentucky. No, Lorena knew him as a detective—but how did she know? Was Jack Kestrel of Bascom any more a detective than Charles Brooks of Inskip?

With an effort, Brandon recalled himself to the present moment and said, "Just thought it'd be nice to roll something down on 'em and set my mind to figuring out what'd—"

Out of the near edge of the cloud of smoke an agitated figure appeared, tigerishly streaked with black and pale brown, screeching and gasping in wordless rage. It leaped toward them, covering ground at an astonishing rate, and Brandon saw that it gripped pistols in both hands. Still running, it raised them and fired rapidly, outrunning the puffs of gunsmoke. The shots were badly aimed, and Brandon heard only the whisper of one bullet at a distance.

He grabbed for his own revolver, but before it was out, Curly had reached down for one of the loaded Sharps, brought it up waist-high, and fired.

At the thunderclap of the shot, an invisible fist seemed to

strike the running man in the chest, slamming the upper part of his body back, while the frantic legs made another step, climbing into the air, then churning once before he hit the ground. His weapons were airborne for an instant, sped by the last involuntary fling of his arms, then clattered on the stony ground as his heels gave a final scrabble and fell still. Brandon could believe now that one of the half-inch slugs, placed right, would drop a buffalo.

Curly took another loaded rifle and kept a wary eye on the smoke cloud as he followed Jack Kestrel and Brandon to where the fallen man lay. Lorena Canty stayed in the doorway.

The streaks of darkness they had seen when the figure appeared were soot from the burning coal oil, which smudged the face like war paint, and the lighter areas were the fashionable fawn of expensive suiting fabric, and the slack face was Dorn Varnum's. *If he's the one I came here to kill, he's dead and I didn't do it. And how the hell will I ever find out?*

"Saw it was all up and it drove him crazy," Jack Kestrel said.

Brandon looked at Curly. "Crazy or not, him coming at us like that, you didn't have any choice about shooting him. No need to feel bad."

"Why would I feel bad?" Curly said.

With almost shocking suddenness, the fire, having exhausted the oil and finding only scraps and leftovers to feed on, collapsed inward on itself and was visible only as erratic tongues of yellow-red darting up from behind the escarpment; the last billows of smoke, detached from their source, drifted away like a soiled thunderhead.

Kestrel squinted off to the left, seeing movement through the thinning smoke there. "Troopers in a bunch there; don't seem to be minded to do anything. Expect they're working out what comes next." He thought for a moment, then called, "Lorena! Any white cloth in amongst the stuff there?"

Lorena Canty reported the presence of some pale canvas, out of which Curly, under Jack Kestrel's direction, cut a large rectangle with the knife he had appropriated fron Varnum's stock, nailing it to a long pole found lying in th shed. The knife proved its quality by shortening the pole t the five feet Kestrel specified with a minimum of effort fron Curly.

"Truce, not surrender," Kestrel explained. "We've got t get them and us on the move out of here, and we'll have t talk to do that. Don't fancy above half having to make i clear to Meyner that he's got no cards left in his hand."

As it turned out, that was not necessary. The dusty smoke-smeared sergeant who, followed by a trooper trudged up the slope to meet the flag-carrying Kestrel an Brandon halfway between their positions reported that hi commander was suffering from burns and battering.

"Was taking a drink, bottle up to his mouth, when yo fellows set off the fireworks," the sergeant said. "Spilled i all down his front, then a chunk of something burning hi him and set the booze alight. Charred his uniform some thing fierce and burnt off his mustache. About took a fit then he, ah, fell and hit his head and he ain't come to yet."

Or that's what they'll tell him when he comes out of it Brandon thought sardonically. A gun butt behind the ear i a good way of making sure a lunatic won't be around t make a disaster even worse.

"I dunno what we're s'posed to do," the sergeant sai wearily. "Most of the horses gone, the Gatling wrecked, an that civilian that was running things . . . ?" He looked pas Kestrel to where a sprawled shape lay some distance fron the trading post.

"That's him," Kestrel said. "Came at us shooting; we ha to drop him."

The sergeant nodded. "Heard him cussing you folks swearing to kill you fast, slow, and sideways. We was al hightailing it away from that burning oil, but he just wen through it, screeching and just not giving a damn. Bu without him, and without the captain, we just don't hav any orders for this. *I* don't know what this was all about why we was shooting at you and what we was s'posed to d with you if we captured you, and it's a puzzle to me what t do next. 'Course," he said slowly, "it makes it easier that you fellows are such bad shots—never hit none of us, except the Gatling magazine took Turner in the shin when you shot it off the gun."

"I did that?" Jack Kestrel said, pleased. "Hoped, but I wasn't sure, that distance."

"So you *ain't* bad shots then." The sergeant nodded. "Obliged to you for not boring us a extra nostril or so."

"No quarrel with you boys," Jack Kestrel said. "So you've got no casualties to make up for—bar Meyner, if you care about that—and no orders to go on with the fight, and a lot of other work to do. Like getting Meyner and the recent Varnum back to town, getting your horses back or replacing them, and explaining to the quartermaster what happened to your fancy pepperbox gun. You get on with that, we'll get on our way, and we'll call it a day, okay?"

"We got to take the civilian back with us?"

"Bury him here if you like," Jack Kestrel said, "but I think there'll be enough questions to answer without that. Better everybody back in Bascom knows he's dead for sure."

"We got three horses left only," the sergeant said sadly. "One for carrying the captain, now one for this fellow, that leaves only one amongst the rest of us, and it's a mighty long way back, walking most of the way and trading off riding once in a while. I wonder could we wrap the civilian in something and drag him behind? Not as if he would feel it."

Jack Kestrel shook his head. "You know how rough the ground is from here to Bascom. Varnum'd get there more sort of used up than you'd want to explain. Load him on the same horse with Meyner; then there'd be two for you fellows to trade off rides on."

"Captain wouldn't like that, not no way, was he to wake up in the course of it," the sergeant said.

"Does he have to?" Jack Kestrel's fingers stroked the butt of his holstered revolver.

"I guess there ain't no rule about tidying up a place after you've forted up in it and killed the feller that it's his place," Curly said. "At least I ain't never heard of it." He lounged comfortably on a packing case at the rear of the storeroom, contemplating its disorder.

Brandon looked around the room. The descending sun painted the back walls with vivid, almost blood-red oblongs, the bottom edges of which inexorably retreated along the floor to the walls. In some places the geometrical shapes were broken by the piles of goods Varnum had stored to further his plans. Many of these had been knocked askew by their search of the contents, and others lay wrenched open in the middle of the floor, their contents scattered around. Near the windows most used for firing, and in the doorway, ejected cartridge cases lay in drifts, and deformed slugs from the shots that had been fired into the building lay everywhere, like droppings from giant lead-eating rodents. The place had clearly been inhabited by careless visitors, but, as Curly implied, who was going to complain? And who, Brandon wondered, was now the owner of this stuff and what would he do with it?

"Don't worry, Curly, I won't draft you for housekeeping," Lorena Canty said. She was inspecting the opened crates and peering into some of the unopened ones, checking to see if there might be some items both portable and useful at the ranch—as a kind of payment, she said, for the trouble Varnum had put them to, something he wouldn't miss after all.

Through a south-facing side window, Brandon could see the cavalry troop's remaining three horses, one carrying two equally inert bundles draped across its back, two carrying two temporarily lucky troopers, pick their way up the hillside. They and the half-dozen dismounted soldiers kicked up clouds of rock dust that glowed in the reddening light of the descending sun. They skirted the rise on which the trading post lay and after a while were lost to sight behind the scraggly trees and standing rocks.

"They's safe off, headin' south and east," Curly said when Brandon reported his observation. "Now, should we head off north and east, we'll be on the trail for the Lazy Y and there not much after dark, ready for trading of experiences and brags and doubtless a good feed." He stuck his new knife into the planking of a packing case in the manner of someone spearing a succulent piece of beef.

Through the open doorway Brandon could see the large irregular dark patch on the ground where Dorn Varnum's blood had drained from the fist-sized hole in his back. Curly's anticipation of a meal didn't seem affected by his recent killing of a man. Brandon tried to recall if killing Casmire had diminished his own appetite, but couldn't summon up a clear memory.

"Yeah," Jack Kestrel said. "Bascom's nearer, but we'd better see how things are with Sam and get a sense of what's going on in town. Let the cavalry boys decide what the story is, and make sure we know it before we hit town again. Curly, you were going to see to the horses a couple hours ago before we got interrupted. Give it another try?"

"Sure thing, boss." Curly plucked his knife out of the planking and walked from the room. Lorena Canty held up a steel-headed tomahawk from an opened crate and said, "Just the thing for the chickens."

Kestrel stretched his arms and began strolling around the room. "Interesting afternoon we spent here. Learned a lot about each other."

Brandon paced slowly beside him. "You being a detective and all."

"And you, Bane," Jack Kestrel said. They reached a corner of the room and turned. "I made a mistake, reading you as a plain roving hardcase. Could be you're as tough as you show, but there's a sight more to you than that. It's your business what it is, of course. Out here, seems like 'most everybody's not only what he looks like but at least one person else. I would have said Harry Briggs was a dirt-plain waddy, but there he is playing the disappearing corpse in Varnum's melodrama—near as anything did for Sam when he was resurrected, too. One big thing I value about Sam and Lorena, they're what they are and that's it, only one each of 'em. For the rest, you never know who else you're talking to when you're talking to them, if you take my meaning."

"True enough," Brandon said in a voice that stopped Jack

Kestrel in midstride and snapped his head around for a direct look at Brandon's face.

Brandon watched his hand moving down, dream-slow, to close its fingers around something amid the debris next to the crate where Curly had been lounging. As at Mound Farm and the Bright Kentucky, for the third time he picked from the floor of an abandoned room a stick deftly sliced and shaped into an opening flower.

25

It's a piece of whittling, a *flower,* man," Kestrel said, "not a scorpion. God, you look like one of those devil masks the Indians carve. What the hell's wrong?"

Brandon gestured with the wooden flower. "This . . . Curly, he's . . . Curly's a Kenneally."

"You lost your mind, Bane? Curly a Kenneally—he can't be!"

"Nor I ain't," Curly said, stepping into the room. "Not a blood Kenneally, but Bane's got the right of it. I rode with Gren Kenneally—*yahay!"*

He gave a sharp yelp as his hand dipped, sending his knife flashing through the dim room and into Jack Kestrel's right arm as it lifted his revolver. The gun boomed but the shot went wild; Curly triggered off a shot that took Kestrel in the upper chest and slammed him to the floor, eyes staring. As Brandon was lifting his revolver, Lorena Canty screamed, "Jack!" and ran from the back of the room toward Kestrel's body; Curly snatched her to him and pivoted her to face Brandon's weapon, with his own jammed into her ear.

"Drop the damn gun er her brains go out the other ear like a blowed egg!" he yelled. Brandon let the revolver fall to the stone floor.

Lorena Canty raised one knee high and drove her boot heel down and back onto Curly's foot. He howled and slammed the revolver against the side of her head three times. She went limp in his arms, her head lolling forward. Blood snaked down her blouse; Brandon could not see if it came from her nose or mouth.

"You sumbitch, Bane, how'd you know me for one of Gren's boys?" Curly's voice was high and taut-stretched. "No matter, and no good it's done you nohow. You stay like you are while I work out what I do next. Don't move, or I corpse Miss Lorena, then you. You don't credit I'd do that, you can go dig up a fambly, name of Brandon, back east in Missouri, they will give you a testimonial."

"I believe you," Brandon said.

"Damn, I got to move on outta here," Curly muttered. "I let any of you live, you post me as wanted for riding with Gren. But I corpse you, and the soldier boys know I was here with you, and the want's out on me for murders, and that ain't no improvement."

Did he hold Elise like that before he killed her? Was he the one? No matter, he was there and involved. Why is he talking? He's a dead man, only he doesn't know it yet. Brandon, at last knowing he faced one of the killers of his family, was surprised that he did not feel rage or hatred, only a sense of certainty.

"Tie 'em up, gives me maybe a day till they get loose. Corpse 'em, prob'ly longer," Curly muttered to himself. "But corpse 'em, they'll want me worse. Damn Gren, if he'd shared out in Dysart like he said he would, I'd've been out in Arizony last fall, not back down here to punch cows for a livin'."

The blocks of sunlight on the back wall were deep red by now, and the chattered monologue in the darkening room spun on as Curly debated whether murder or trussing would serve him best. Brandon realized that the easygoing cowhand was as raving mad as Varnum had ever been, and he wondered how a man was to know sanity from madness—or if there was any real difference.

"Take *her,*" Curly mused, "then t'other two wouldn't dast put out the word on me whiles I had her, but then iffen I let her go, she'd tell where I was when I did that, so that won't—"

Glancing at the floor, he saw Jack Kestrel's hand reaching for Brandon's dropped revolver, and swung his own away from Lorena Canty's head.

Without conscious thought, Brandon launched himself through the air at Curly. An outstretched hand clamped on Curly's wrist with the force of a giant pliers, and the revolver fell away. The momentum of Brandon's rush knocked the unconscious Lorena and Curly to the floor, Brandon atop both. He reached past Lorena's head and grabbed Curly's as if it were an impaled melon he was trying to pull off a fence post. Curly squealed with pain and horror; his hands scrabbled at the floor, and one found the knife that had been dislodged from Kestrel's arm and jabbed it at Brandon's shoulder, twisting his body so that Lorena Canty was pushed away to one side, no longer sandwiched between them.

The sting of the blade seemed to add to Brandon's strength, and he felt flesh and bone yield under his twisting, squeezing hands. Curly gave a bubbling howl that stopped abruptly as something made a snapping sound and his head suddenly lolled limply in Brandon's hands.

"No . . . no more, Bane." Hands tugged at his shoulders. He shook his head, clearing it of the haze that had filled it since he had jumped at Curly, and saw that Jack Kestrel was kneeling beside him and tugging him away from the body he lay on. Slowly, with great effort, like an old man, he got to his feet and looked down on Curly. The cowhand lay with his head at an odd angle, his face discolored and distorted. Jack Kestrel sat awkwardly next to him, holding his chest and breathing raspily. On his other side, Lorena Canty stirred and moaned, then raised herself on one elbow to look across Curly's body at Jack Kestrel.

Guess they're not hurt badly, Brandon thought. And

however they're hurt, they'll come through it. Those two, they sustain each other, and that'll see them through.

He looked back at Curly, who now seemed no more real than a dummy in a clothing-store window. *Two of them done. More to do, wherever they are. What was that he said about Arizona?*

26

Brandon paused before stepping into the post office, a boxy structure about the size of one of the Bowie Street cribs, and looked at the work going on at the livery stable, the next building down after the freight office. A man on an improvised scaffold had some time before applied a layer of brown paint over the portion of the stable's sign that had read DORN VARNUM, PROP. and was now carefully lettering in S. DUMAYNE, PROP. Judge Canty, restored to the bench, had dealt with Dorn Varnum's estate as one of his first judicial functions, and, relying on the facts of the case, common sense, and the disinclination of the feeble remnants of the pro-Varnum element to argue with him, had declared Sally Dumayne Varnum's legal heir.

With Varnum under ground and the cavalry troop hastily recalled to its post after some telegraphic conversations between Sam Canty and his Austin connections, Bascom was settling back to normality, or at least a new kind of balance of power. Sally Dumayne, as new owner of the town's three most thriving businesses, would have an influence on a level with Sam Canty's, but it appeared that they would be cooperating, not competing, and they seemed to have an interesting future in mind for Bascom.

And for Carter Bane, and that was giving Brandon some uncomfortable thoughts. . . .

It was cool and musty inside the post office, and something in the smell tugged at Brandon's memory, calling up an image of the law office back in St. Louis. Paper, that was it: piles and bundles of paper, clean paper diligently dirtied with information people felt somebody else urgently needed to know. Unlikely that there would be anything here for him anyhow, given the elaborately indirect mail route between here and Kansas, but he felt he should give it a try before dealing with what Sam Canty and Sally Dumayne had brought up.

"Any mail for Colin Binn?"

The clerk looked at him with a sharp frown. "You joking, mister?"

Brandon wondered if the man was a touch addled and said, enunciating clearly, as to a child, *"Coal*-in *Binn."* Then he snapped his teeth shut in irritation as Jess Marvell's joke, if it was that, had its weeks-delayed impact. She had pronounced it "Collin," so maybe it had been inadvertent. Maybe.

"Naw, it's a real name, Harv," the postmaster called from the rear of the room. "'Cause there is a letter here with that wrote on it. Didn't come through the mails but was dropped off by someone riding through from Boudin, that's why you didn't have the handlin' of it. You picking up for this Binn, Mr. Bane?"

"Yes. He . . . couldn't get to town."

"However much he might be *burnin'* to, hey?"

The postmaster's and clerk's chuckles at the shaft of wit followed Brandon into the street. He hefted the letter and inspected the address. Firm strokes with a clean penpoint, slanting a bit to the right, letters clear without being effortfully printed. Jess Marvell, whatever her taste in humor, had a handwriting that radiated capability and firmness of purpose.

As he walked toward the Butler House, he surveyed the post-Varnum Bascom. Chief Dedman, sitting outside the jail, at least sat alertly. Down past the plaza, tables, chairs and boxes sat in the street in front of the saloon; Sally Dumayne was giving the place a long-overdue cleanout, and was contemplating going further.

"Doesn't have to be a cheap, rowdy place," she had told Brandon a few days before. "Could be anything you want to make it. You've got the knowledge and the nerve to make it run right and keep it in order. You'd be a big man in Bascom, more so than Mr. Varnum, and you wouldn't have to go crooked to do it." She had also made it clear, though not enough to embarrass either of them in case of a misfire, that he could expect to be a big man in Sally Dumayne's life. She had not gone into who would deal with the tenants of the Bowie Street establishments and on what basis.

The neat paintwork and sparkling windows of the Butler House looked trim and inviting as he approached. There was an important role for him there, too, if he cared to undertake it.

"Once you got good land and good location, only thing that makes a town worth spit is its people," Sam Canty had said. "Last years, with Varnum in the saddle, it ain't drawed prime-grade folks, and every one such we can get here and get to stay is valuable."

Carter Bane's value would be best realized, Canty had said, as manager of the Butler House Hotel, with full responsibility for all its operations. "Grow with the town," Canty had urged. "Man in that position, in the public eye, hospitable to one and all in the bar, he could be bigger'n Varnum in no time."

Brandon tapped the letter thoughtfully on the palm of one hand as he stepped up onto the Butler House's porch and sought a chair. In the days since Curly's death, he had been considering his next moves. He had killed Curly—no exultation, just a necessity fulfilled. The others remained, but was the necessity as strong? And what, in any case, could he do about it? Curly had said something about Arizona before he died, and a letter Jack Kestrel had found among his effects in the bunkhouse had connected to that, though not helpfully:

Arizona Ttry.

Curly,

If you will get on out here where we talked about, up to K., we will thrive. Get shut of them cows and you and me will mine the miners. Looking to get my shareout soon.

O.K.

Was the "K." some Kenneally somewhere in Arizona Territory? Was "O.K." another Kenneally, or just an anonymous writer's way of saying that everything was fine? There was not enough there to go on, no matter what his resolve for retribution might be. And there was no denying that there was something gratifying in having the identity he had created, Carter Bane, being accepted, being valued, by people, having a place ready set for him at the bountiful table here. And in the comfortable bed of Sally Dumayne, if he wanted it.

Cole Brandon's concerns seemed somehow less real, just as St. Louis seemed a distant recollection, something from a past life. He slit the envelope with his thumbnail and withdrew the folded papers. They, at least, bore on Cole Brandon's interests—or Charles Brooks's or Colin Binn's. It was dated a week after he had left Inskip and written, he was glad to see, in the same highly legible hand as the address:

Dear Mr. Brooks,

I will not write you everything that Mr. Dailey and I have gathered, as it does not seem useful, though we have kept complete notes and will ship them to you or hold them for your perusal as you direct.

Re: Robberies, train, in Missouri. 1. On 14th inst., Jno. Burton or Barton said in Bull's Foot that his pocket was picked on train to Sedalia & that he was beaten and thrown from train. 2. On 17th inst., R.D. overheard lunch wagon patron at train station mention

"Missouri train job" to companion, adding that he was on way to California (terminus of line is San Francisco) to see one Connolly about this. Could refer to RR construction or promotion work, but thought would add for completeness. 3. On 19th inst. entertainer reported client told her of robbing train from St. Louis of jewels and gold and burying them in secret location. Offered her map of said location in return for services.

I do not see how any of these will help your investigations, but I know that in the detective business it is best to be thorough, just as it is in all businesses. I am doing that with the Bright Kentucky, and Mr. Dailey and I are also making a go of the lunch wagon, as it seems to be something train passengers want badly. We are working on an idea we have that would use what we are learning about lunch wagons and what I know about hotels that we think might be highly profitable, but please be assured that we will not scant your interests.

As I do not know how long you propose to stay at Bascom, I will hold further reports until I hear from you about that or have a new address (for Mr. Binn, or another name of your choice) from you.

Please be assured of my respects and appreciation for your confidence.

Brandon smiled briefly as he folded the letter and replaced it in the envelope. So solemn, earnest, and businesslike—you wouldn't know, reading it, the sparkle and energy that Jess Marvell radiated. Was that "another name of your choice" a sly admission of malice in the christening of Colin Binn? He would probably never know—would probably never see her again to ask. Just as well. They would be in touch only through her reports, if he let her know where to send them.

And where would that be? Would Carter Bane become a Bascom fixture? There was nothing in the reports, any more than in Curly's letter, to draw him any place else. The chance that Rush Dailey had misheard Connolly for

Kenneally and that the "Missouri job" was a criminal one was real, of course, but not large, and it presented nothing to follow up.

As he read Jess Marvell's report, he was aware of a growing noise coming from the south end of Main Street: yells and whip-cracks and, in a while, the rumbling of wheels. When he had finished, the sound was closer, and he looked up. A team of six mules was drawing a high, canvas-topped wagon through the plaza, encouraged by the shouts and lashes of the teamster. Brandon could see three more wagons following: a freight train on its way north, doubtless with some supplies to deliver to a consignee they wouldn't be expecting, Sally Dumayne.

"Be less lively, cheaper, when the train line gets built." Brandon looked up and saw Jack Kestrel standing next to him on the porch. He was bulkier than usual around the chest from the padded dressing over his bullet wound.

"Probably the next thing to hit Bascom, railroad fever," Jack Kestrel said. "Sam Canty, Sally Dumayne, they'll be out promoting and figuring ways to get the railroad to build through here, for once the line goes up this way, whatever isn't on it's going to dry up and blow away. Kind of thing you'll be in on, if you stay."

Brandon had a brief vision of Sally Dumayne, Sam Canty, and other Bascom notables bringing the railway in triumph to the town. Carter Bane was not among those present, nor would he be. Evidently, while he was wondering what to do, his inward self had made the decision: move on. To what was something that could be dealt with later.

"I won't be," he said.

Jack Kestrel nodded. "I didn't think you would, no matter what there is in favor of it. Been going over how I saw you when you came here, what I've seen since. You're on your way to something, and it isn't here. Not any more, anyway. What Curly had to do with it, and the Kenneallys, I can't pretend to say, and it's your business until you choose to make it someone else's. Thought you might give it over after

Curly got killed, but it seems you aren't. When are you going?"

"Tomorrow, I guess." Brandon stood up. "Just decided. Might as well get on and tell Sally Dumayne I won't be going into the saloon business."

"And so on," Jack Kestrel said.

"Well, yes."

Brandon walked to the store—still Varnum's, according to the sign; the sign painter, if decorative, was slow. Sally Dumayne was at the counter, dealing with a customer who looked, from behind, like a bundle of hides that had been rolled in the dust. One of the freighters, Brandon surmised.

"Now, a gamesome lady like you," the customer said in a voice something like the screeching of a rusty gate, "would be a agreeable companion fer a weary traveler, which same traveler ain't above bein' agreeable in any manners whatsoever as might be required, if you take my meanin.' It would be a pleasure to git you outside o' th' delicatest meal the town affords, by way of commencement of the proceedin's. Tonight is what I'm perposin' fer the enterprise, fer I am but a ship as passes in the night, though the wagon train don't go till first light, so the night's free fer more thanpassin'."

A double shock—who this was and what he was doing, or trying to do—immobilized Brandon for a moment. Then he stepped forward and laid a hand on the leather-covered shoulder.

"Ned Norland! What're you doing here?"

"Exercisin' the powers of my pers'nality on a lady as can appreciate 'em," Ned Norland said, turning to face Brandon. "Also travelin' with the freighters to give 'em the benefit of my wisdom about gettin' through the country hereabouts. Some time since we see each other, ain't it? I disremember yer name, which is a shame to me, seein' as you got mine so handy upon yer tongue."

"Quite a while," Brandon said, regretting the lapse of frontier etiquette and grateful that Norland was observing it. "Carter Bane, remember?"

"Comes back to me like a freshet in the springtime," Ne Norland said. "I will go over and see what play-pretties an foofaraws I might collect as will gladden the hearts of th sentimental Indian maidens or so, then we will go and drink and swap news."

Norland wandered over to inspect Sally Dumayne's inherited supply of frivolities. "I came to tell you I've decide to move on," Brandon said to her. "What you're offer ing, running the saloon and . . . well, that's great, a mar velous chance, something a man could do a lot with But—"

"But not you."

"No."

Sally Dumayne nodded slowly. "I didn't really think so. don't think this town, the people, were ever real to you, no the way a place is you live in. I think when you got here, you were already leaving."

Brandon thought about this. "I guess you're right. I can' talk about it, but I am on the move and it looks like I will b for a long time. So . . ."

"So."

Brandon looked over his shoulder at Ned Norland an leaned toward Sally Dumayne. "I know that old coot," h said, "and since he's troubling you I can get him away fron here easily enough."

"I can handle it well enough, thanks, Mr. Bane," Sall Dumayne said, then smiled as Norland came up to th counter with an armful of goods.

"Appreciate if you'd tot these up, ma'am, upon which will pay in gold, dust, greenbacks, er honeyed compliments as you prefers. Bane, let's us get on down t' that fancy hote at the plaza there and surround some drinks, leavin' n survivors. You, ma'am," Norland said, turning to Sall Dumayne, "six o'clock fer dinner all right?"

"Six o'clock would be fine, Mr. Norland," Sally Dumayn said.

"It is true that I am past my prime," Ned Norland said "but in that prime I kept four Injun ladies all at one and th same time entertained, happy, and tired. Even while coastin' downhill, if you wanter look at it that way, I sh'd be able to leave Miss Sally with some warmin' reckerlections." Ned Norland beamed into his glass before taking a swallow of the whiskey.

"But she—" Brandon began.

Ned Norland set the glass down and said, "She ain't goin' t' git nothin' out of it but a good feed and bein' carnally knowed till her knees don't work by a chewed-up old piece o' whang leather, that what it's in yer mind t' say?"

"Ah . . . well, yes."

Ned Norland grinned. "Think *she* don't know that?"

Brandon had to admit that she surely did—and, obviously, that that, at the moment, was what she wanted. What it came down to, he realized, was that it galled him that the first stranger who came by—let alone an odorous antique—was an acceptable substitute for what he had regretfully declined to offer. Evidently he didn't understand women, not that he had ever studied many. Had he, he wondered, understood Elise?

"You said news," he said.

"Yah." Ned Norland stretched and leaned back in the comfortable Butler House chair, took another swallow of his drink, and said, "The fambly re-onion business, back there in Crockett County, now that didn't hold a head of steam above half a week. Onliest thing we agreed on by then was that it was a disgrace and shame that we was kin. And when a ambrotype of one o' th' leetle pride and joys chanced t' remind me of a carnival attraction I useter know, Jo-Jo the Dog-Faced Boy, and I let 'em know of the uncanny resemblance, why, the civilities was out o' stock fer fair."

It was not clear to Brandon whether Norland's departure on riverboat for New Orleans had been voluntary or compulsory; but the relevant thing was that among the passengers had been one of the substantial men who had given Casmire an alibi at his trial.

"Got him alone and put 'im a few questions about who financed his test'mony and guv him the script, and what else he might know as could shed any lightnin' on the matter."

"And he gave you answers," Brandon said thoughtfully.

Ned Norland grinned. "You keep yer ears and mind open in forty-what years on the prairies and mountains, and you will learn lots of stuff that comes in useful. Through bein' willin' t' listen t' what the enterprisin' red man has t' say and observin' of his activities, I have become a dab hand at puttin' questions. I have had a Chiricahua 'Pache turn so forthcomin' after only five minutes of attention that he not only tolt me whereat the stolen horses was but guv me his secret name and confessed it was him stole the corn as was left fer the rain god. So this merchant weren't no problem."

Brandon decided he would not ask about Ned Norland's interrogation techniques, why the merchant had not reported him for employing them, and when and in what condition he had left the boat, as he felt he strongly wanted not to know these things. What he did want to know was what information the man had disgorged, by whatever means.

"Somethin', don't know how useful," Ned Norland said. "Paid by a lawyer he didn't know, but the instructions and the money come from old Quint Kenneally, Gren's pa. After the trial went their way, seems to've been some loose talk goin', and this feller picked up some of it. Was to've been a rendezvous fer the shareout, like we useter have in the trappin' days, some place in Kansas, but it didn't come off. Some of the fellers in the robbery got paid off, but some didn't and is kinder angry and hopeful both. Gren Kenneally was said t' be in er goin' to 'Frisco back about the end o' winter, but with er without how much of the proceeds ain't knowed."

"Told you quite a lot," Brandon said.

"They gits remarkable confidin', finally," Ned Norland said.

"Well, California, eh?" Brandon said briskly. "I had another indication that Gren Kenneally might be out that

way. But there was something else that suggested that Arizona could be worth looking into."

"Git to Arizony as easy from Californy as from here, or near enough," Ned Norland said. "Do 'Frisco first, then go on if called fer. Ride up t' Kansas, ketch a train, and yer snufflin' up the Pacific air in no time."

"On balance, that looks best. I'm grateful for the information," Brandon said. "But how in hell did you track me down here?"

"No trackin' into it," Ned Norland said. "No more notion where you was than where's last Thursday's piss. The wagon train come through here, and there you was. Happens all the time, out here—lots o' space, not lots o' people yit, so trails cross. What yer up to, that's somethin' you'd best count on. I had that feller share what he knowed on gin'ral principles—you come on a lode o' top-grade infermation, you don't toss it aside. Waste not, want not.

"New Orleans weren't no fun no more, so I come on over this way, hooked up with the freighters, and so here I am. Termorrer, a affectin' farewell to Miss Sally Dumayne, and we go on north. Where I come in useful is that I been where we're goin', a old tradin' post a few days from here that they're aimin' to fix up ag'in, serve buffler hunters and freighters. Was there in '38, I rec'lect—Adobe Walls, they calls it."

Brandon left his packing until just before his departure next morning. As he stuffed clothing and effects into his valise, he found a folded square of paper with something inside it—the medallion from the Mound Farm. He unwrapped it and looked at it briefly. Guidance, Norland had said. Well, his course was set for now—save it for when it was needed. He looked again at the self-devouring snake and the wolf, then rewrapped the medallion and put it in the valise.

When Brandon stepped out on the porch of the Butler House, carrying his valise, it was not much after sunrise, and the white façade of the courthouse seemed sprayed with a transparent, luminescent overlay. It and the flanking buildings running north and south on Main seemed flattened by the early light, as if on the same plane as the hard blue sky. The effect, Brandon realized, was of a painted canvas backdrop for a stage set.

Round the back, at the stables, he slung his gear on his horse and prepared to mount.

"Ride a ways with you? I'm going back to the Lazy Y." Jack Kestrel was leading his horse out from a stall down the line.

"Sure."

On the way out of Bascom, angling north for the river, Kestrel talked of his future. "I'll give it a shot, but I doubt I'm cut out for ranching. I do the foreman stuff well because I have to, otherwise folks'll wonder what I am and figure me for a detective. But that is what I am good at, and I am going to have to find a way to do it. Maybe get the agency to open an office down here, and run it for 'em."

"From what I've seen, there'd be enough business," Brandon said. They were almost to the river now, and Brandon could see the plank bridge.

"Less, with you leaving, I'd say," Jack Kestrel said. "Not saying anything about your business, Bane, but you're one of the ones that trouble moves toward." *Same as the marshal in Inskip said about Dan Doyle* . . . Their horses set up a brisk clatter on the bridge.

"So best I'm moving toward it, I guess. Listen, you know of any better route up to the KP railroad than here to Boudin to Inskip?"

Jack Kestrel thought a moment. "The trail to Dysart's about the same. Tell you, the old trail they stopped using three years ago when the quarantine stuff started, that'll take you in a good bit east of Dysart, but only a couple hours by train, and the trail's easier and shorter. At Boudin, 'stead of heading northwest, you go north by east, about, and you'll be to the rails in no time. So long."

He waved and turned his horse toward where the Lazy Y lay.

Brandon started up the trail, then turned and called to Kestrel, "That trail—if it hasn't been used in a couple of years, will I be able to follow it?"

"Any trail, cattle die along it, and the bones stay." Jack Kestrel's voice was only a little muted by distance as his last advice drifted to Brandon:

"Just follow the skulls."